THE OTHERLINGS

TIME

In outer space far from home
Time slows moments grow
The others life continues
Eons fly past in those same moments
Our lives end so quickly
Yet far away I last, my life stretched thickly
I awaken from a lasting cold
A new life I must be bold
My home so far from when I knew
Lost asleep my spirit caught
A glimpse to the side of which I sought
If only there for a second
Other lives had lived so long
I meet them there the bond so strong
All I knew and all I loved
The ones I loved were there for they were waiting
I came only moments later
Together again for just a second
Ripped away eons later
Thrust alive; awakened
The core of my life extremely shaken
New life, new friends, new way of thinking
The life I had gone for good
I now explore as I know I should
My life anew continues
I'll grow and live and love again
For I know they'll be waiting
My life will continue
This new life is mine and long
For living through this will make me strong
I smile for I know
Life is to live however drawn
After a life of searching
They knew it was a life worth giving
I know it's a life worth living

THE OTHERLINGS

And the Crystal Amulet

S. V. Hurn

DEDICATION

I am dedicating this book to my departed husband. He bravely fought two stage four cancers and had been nicknamed Miracle Mike by his doctors. He refused to surrender to the terrible side effects of numerous treatments over countless years. He swore he was not going to allow cancer to get him. Mike considered every day to be a good day if he woke up without a toe tag. He told his doctors countless times, "Your job is to keep me alive and not tell me how to live." That is exactly what he did for as long as he could. His pain and illness were only noticeable to the ones closest to him. He never complained and never gave in. Walking the beach and going for a coffee and a smoke was his daily medicine. When he became too ill for that one simple pleasure, he still tried to make the best of things.

In the end cancer did not take his life. Two tiny holes in his colon did that. He bravely decided to go to hospice and had a peaceful night sleep and passed the next morning within only minutes of Wicky and I arriving to his bedside. He waited for us and when he knew we were both there he traveled to the Other Side.

He never got around to reading my book, I suppose he thought it best to stay out of it. Towards the end I would sit beside him and read to him and he decided I was a good writer after all.

I hope I can make him proud.

Mike Woolford lived an incredible life from July 7th, 1946 to September 29th, 2019.

I will see you again soon, my love.

INTRODUCTION

I would like to start by saying, "I'm not a physicist." In fact, I am not a scientist, not even close. My passion has always been science of any kind. I once had a physicist say, "that I knew as much about physics as his cat and his grasp on physics was tenuous at best." I laughed so hard I almost fell over. My response was, "Well maybe he and I should discuss it over a can of tuna fish." That's fine, you can't blame a gal for trying."

With that being said, I asked many credible scientists for help with getting the science at the very least to plausible. I was told if it is reasonably consistent all practicing in the field should find it so. If it is laughably ridiculous, again, all physicist will find it so. My thought on that, is when dealing with anything that might fall beyond 'The Standard Model' of physics, all bets are off! I have never seen a grumpier bunch that didn't agree on anything. Don't even get me started on Quantum Field Theory!

When I started to write this tall tale, I had no idea where it was going to take me. Stephen King said, "If you're going to write about something, write about something you know." Very true indeed but I like challenges, and this book had many. But getting the science right was my biggest challenge. If not anything else I learned a lot.

Within this story you will find tidbits of genetics, astronomy, archeology, and of course physics. This is a work of FICTION. But I suspect back in the day when Leonardo DaVinci sat and created his flying machines and submarines there were probably some folk that may have thought him to be half-baked. Now, centuries later, we will soon find ourselves on Mars. For me nothing should be laughable, and everything should be considered plausible. Because if not for our imagination where would we be?

So, for those of you reading this book a little insight on The Large Hadron Collider at CERN and why it exists and why the human race has always tilted our heads to the stars or picked up a fist full of dirt and wondered about the furthest points of light or the tiniest bits of matter.

Break a rock in half, and you get two stones. Take one of these stones and throw it at the other and it will break again producing gravel. Throw gravel again against one another and this time it does not break. Does this mean you didn't throw it hard enough or does it mean it cannot be broken down any further? Is gravel the smallest particle that constitutes rock, or is there anything smaller? This question has been following us for millennia. Breaking down smaller and smaller rocks we ended up discovering molecules, then atoms, then we discovered the structure of the atom—a dense nucleus made of protons and neutrons surrounded by a cloud of electrons. But we kept going, throwing protons against one another in the hope of breaking it. This is no easy task, even the strongest microscope is not powerful enough to probe a proton. We built particle accelerators; large machines fueled by large magnets and pumps. We were able to extract a proton out of its atom and send it up to nearly the speed of light before colliding it with another proton. Then we broke down the proton to even smaller bits which we named quarks. For one question answered we were left with a hundred unanswered questions. When we probed further and further down, we found nature to be ever stranger. We saw anti-matter, a mirror partner of the matter we know which all has seemingly vanished from the universe. We discovered thousands of particles which should be building blocks of the universe yet even if we combine them all we cannot describe the structure as we see in the cosmos. We saw that gravity's interaction is fundamental to our daily life but absent in the microscopic world. We saw particles that could fly through the earth as if it were the vacuum of space and could spontaneously transform in one another. We discovered what we thought to be the fundamental symmetries governing matter only to later observe particles breaking said symmetries. We kept searching and designing more and more powerful experiments. The first particle accelerators were the size of a room and they are now the size of a city. In Europe, at the border between Switzerland and France lies deep underground a 27-kilometer-long ring; the Large Hadron Collider. CERN is the European organization for nuclear research. The LHC is the biggest machine ever built by mankind; a masterpiece carefully crafted by thousands of scientist and engineers over decades. It uses large magnets and enough energy to power a city. It accelerates and collides protons at incredible energies then probing their remains and trying to answer many of these questions that have confounded us from the beginning of time.

For now, the LHC is allowing scientist to find what makes up our mysterious Universe. In the future there will be many upgrades made and eventually newer and more powerful colliders. So, who really knows what is science fiction and what is science fact?

The year is 2063 and I died . . .
But my journey has just begun.

PROLOGUE

John Rosen stood on the conning tower of a Russian submarine. His narrowed green eyes shone bright against his bronzed, weathered skin. The day was still as death, the sky a hollow grey in endless twilight. The cold was a bitter thing that felt as if it were cutting right through him. Eerie, strangely shaped icebergs in brilliant shades of blue and aqua floated past. They had been molded by the strong winds that blew across the otherworldly landscape. Beneath him, the water was a deep purple so clear that the ice of the bergs could be seen fading away into the depths. This place was a most hostile environment, its secrets buried under a mile of ice formed over thousands of years. Whatever mysteries remained were slowly being exposed with the polar melt, but nonetheless the place still boasted to be the coldest and the most unforgiving environment on the face of the planet.

John stood quiet, filling his lungs with icy air...better than the small confines of the last long days that seemed to pass so very slowly with anticipation of what he was sure to find. The stress of being trapped in a metal tomb with tons of water looming overhead threatening to crush him at any given moment had caused an uneasy feeling in his gut, a paranoia that nagged at him. Perhaps it was simply a deep tiredness rising to the surface from deep within.

Simon Bedford lumbered over, pulling a woolen cap onto his bald head and hugging thick winter gear around his shivering body. Simon had been John's loyal friend and business partner for many years; bond of brotherhood defined their relationship.

"Damn, Johnny, tell me again why we didn't make this trip in the summer months? I think my face is going to freeze right off!"

John ignored his friend's comments on the weather and looked off into the distance as they slowly approached the ice shelf looming ahead. John said, a slight smile on his face, "Because we don't want all those tons of ice to come crashing down on us…that sort of thing can bring this mission to an untimely halt, messing up a perfectly good sub."

"Oh, right," Simon said halfheartedly, as he pulled the hood of his parka tight around his face, "I forgot that minor detail."

From behind, they heard the Russian sub commander approaching, footsteps resonating against the steel hull. His coat unzipped, he breathed in deeply, weathered bare hands gripping the rail for stability. Frost was already forming on his white beard. His grey eyes matched the colorless sky and his deep voice echoed across the vast emptiness. "Ah, just like beautiful Russian morning, this climate makes man strong. Not like your California sunshine where everyone drives convertible cars with designer sunglasses. That climate makes men weak and puny."

Simon shot back in his jovial way, "Yeah, but our women are better looking."

Their captain roared with laughter, slapping Simon hard on the back and almost sending him over the rail into the frozen depths below. "You go to Moscow, you find long-leg beauties there," he bellowed, rubbing his fingers together to indicate cash for love, and he started to sing the Russian anthem in a gravelly baritone. The robust man stopped at the hatch, still singing, sweeping his arm around to encompass the sub. "Everything has its price." John stared back at the salty old captain, holding his feelings close in hidden pain knowing only too well that someday the ultimate price would have to be paid.

The captain pondered this mission and said, "Ah! We go now…but maybe you want to swim? This water is good for the brain, it cleanses away bad ideas!" John and Simon ignored their captain's views about their mission and turned away from the railing. They took a few quick breaths of chilled air before going below. Climbing down into the musty confines of the sub, they secured the hatch behind them.

The sub began a slow descent into the frigid darkness. Patiently waiting on the command deck was the small team of scientists John had hired for the mission. A multi-billionaire could procure any type of expert and secure access to any means of transportation. This day was no different from any other day. When John Rosen wanted to get to the bottom of things he sure as hell did, without wasting a breath.

One of his team members scrutinized the data as it came in and said, "We are approaching the opening to the cavern at a depth of 478 meters. We will be clearing the ice shelf shortly."

John nodded his approval and asked to verify, "All satellite images confirm the entry is large enough, correct?"

"Yes, the imagery confirms the cavern and its water entrance are both adequate to accommodate our size." Simon was about to comment about the melting ice which was beginning to expose the structure within its cavern and underground lake, but he knew the importance of secrecy. Approaching from the top would, no doubt, be detected by anyone watching. John owned most of the satellites focused on Earth, but not all of them.

Suddenly, a loud crashing and scraping sound coming from above echoed through the sub's interior. The jolt sent everyone not seated tumbling to the deck. The captain shot a look of disapproval at the helmsman and shouted something in Russian that made young seaman squirm in his seat. He responded nervously, "Yes, Captain, I will avoid the ice best I can." Sweat formed on his brow. We are entering the tunnel now with approximately ten meters to spare on all sides."

The Captain stroked his beard. "Ah, very tight fit, but no problem. How you say? If the shoe fits."

Moments passed slowly and the crew cringed with every little creaking sound the sub made as it slid through the sunken tunnel. The guidance system indicated their path with a sharp pinging sound piercing the dull red glow of the cramped command deck. The sub crept through the pitch blackness, slowly approaching the opening above. The helmsman announced they were clear for ascent into the lake and cavern covered by hundreds of meters of ice.

John let loose a sigh of relief as he anxiously waited for the sub to break the surface of the lake. Outside there was just enough light filtering in from above to illuminate the vast cavern with a ghostly haze. The water appeared black and flat as an oil pit. The conning tower broke the surface with a hiss, like some kind of mythical beast emerging from the depths of the ocean.

John was the first out after the captain, climbing up the steps and exiting through the hatch, the cold still air hitting him squarely in the face. Slowly the structure came into focus as his eyes adjusted to the dim light. High tilted walls arose with their apex a mere shadow under the hazy, fading light from above. John smiled broadly as Simon came up behind him, wrapping a scarf around his face that muffled his shouts. "Holy shit, I'll be goddamned, now that is one hell of an ancient power plant."

The sub's crew was already busy prepping a Zodiac inflatable boat at the water line. In no time they were making their way across the frozen blackness. The hard rubber sponson crunching against the icy shore ground the Zodiac to a halt. Looming before them was the most perfectly preserved pyramid in the world standing just over sixty-one meters tall.

One of the Russian crew jumped over the gunnel onto the ice, slipping and almost falling into the freezing water. John tossed him a line and the crewman managed to drag the bow of the boat up onto the shore and tie off the end of the rope to a huge boulder of ice. John, Simon and their team of scientists leapt ashore, and with joints frozen and aching, their heavy boots dug into the ice as they made their way up to the edifice rising in front of them, the stone steps nearly buried by a sheet of hardened slush.

John had always known the significance to such a find and would now, finally, be able to prove his theory of the origins of mankind on Earth. But, for the time being, he would keep this information to himself.

With daylight hours dwindling, the team scoured the area, taking preliminary readings around the pyramid and trying to find the opening to the mysteries hidden within, while John kept a watchful eye over everyone involved. He knew that if information were to leak out about what he had discovered under the Antarctic ice everything he had worked on for so many years would be jeopardized.

John Rosen, with all his wealth and expertise, had been granted access to many top-secret operations globally, but this journey was very different from so many others that had led to dead ends. This was the hard evidence that was needed to blow the current theory of evolution out of the water. Over the years he had systematically taken over government-controlled data gathering as he carefully paved the way for his kind: an elite group that was slowly molding civilization to conform to his precious hierarchy, his New World Order.

Soon, he would have in his possession the truth to man's existence and prove the theory that he and a select few held the key to the future and the mysteries of our past. Discovering the answer to this enigma would be his ultimate achievement. He would substantiate his belief that written in our DNA is a code; a code left for us to decipher, a code that only a select few humans have retained in its purest form. Once the pieces were in place, his kind could find the path back to where we came from, where we belong amongst the stars.

"First things first," John said to himself as he took in his surroundings.

The light was fading fast and his crew began to pack up their gear. Tomorrow they would get out heavier equipment and start peering through the layers of ice and rock surrounding the structure.

Simon headed for the Zodiac. John watched him, intent on figuring out what was different about his friend of so many years, and called out, "I'm staying behind." A second Zodiac was speeding toward him across the black depths. As it approached, he could see all his gear was on board as requested.

Simon seemed stunned and annoyed by John's decision to stay behind and hesitated before saying, "Sorry, man, but I'm freezing, and a hot shower and a hot cup of black coffee sounds real good right about now, don't you think?"

John smiled back at him. "Hey, we did it, and I'm exactly where I want to be."

Simon laughed a nervous laugh. "Yeah, we did. Try not to burn the place down while we're gone and see you in the morning." John threw the line as Simon climbed aboard the Zodiac.

In minutes everyone had vacated the area just as he had hoped. John's trust in his associates had been waning over the past few months and the truth that he was about to uncover was meant for his eyes only. The theory of an ancient power plant, possibly alien in nature, had been the best cover story for this mission. In consideration of Simon's recent strange behavior, that would be the approach to the investigation for the time being.

The light was fully gone now. He turned his lantern on and waited patiently for his crew to disappear into the confines of the awaiting sub.

John was no stranger to exotic expeditions to parts of the world that only a few could access. Always in search of the same thing, the thing that had been left in his own DNA. The same code that was present in his only child, his daughter Dorathy.

As he pitched the tent, he noticed it still showed signs of its last adventure high in the Himalayas. He smiled as he looked around the darkened cavern, the pyramid reaching high over his head as it had for the last 40,000 years, untouched by man. Man had not built this structure; man had become a mere byproduct of what had been originally intended.

Flashlight in hand, its dull glow only slightly illuminating his path, he cautiously climbed the frozen staircase and found the depression in the stonework he had been hoping to find. Removing his glove, he pressed his hand firmly against the freezing stone and, as expected, heard a rumble from the depths of this ominous structure.

Passing through the now-open gateway to the interior, John carefully ascended the narrow passage into a resonating chamber, its high walls baffled. He could hear the humming of the planet, its frequency in perfect tone. Continuing, he came to a chamber in the same precise dimension as he had seen countless times before, in so many pyramids across the globe. Some were hidden by jungle, ice, water or earth, majestically standing through the millennia, dominating the scenery and all lining up toward a single constellation. Centuries had passed, leaving behind the remains of a forgotten religion, but here lay the one true structure that all others had only imitated, hoping to capture our imagination and create wonder. It was the reason to question the origins of humanity from the beginning of ancient times.

He calmly entered the chamber dimly lit by his flashlight. Inside lay an open coffer where he found what he was looking for—an entity of illumination, asleep, waiting for its release from earthly confines; its work done, its mission accomplished.

Around the being's neck was the key to the gates of Heaven. John shone his light over the near-transparent body and reached for the crystal amulet. As he held it in his hand, the vibrations of the crystal began to sync with his personal frequency and the amulet began to pulse.

The creature slowly awakened, large arctic blue eyes flickering, and John stepped back, releasing the amulet—the first form of human adornment. He could sense the being accepting his presence. The entity slowly rose from its long sleep and locked eyes with John. Instantly, John was flooded with information absorbed and understood the story of our existence and the action he must take.

The being bowed its head, removing the heavy chain from around its neck, and offered the amulet to John. John slowly extended his hand and reached out to take the glowing crystal. As he grasped it tightly removing it from the being's hand, the creature departed in a flare of light. The being had set forth on its journey home through the southern passage that John recognized was perfectly aligned to the nebulous light, the middle point of the sword of the constellation Orion.

John's flashlight flickered on the ground; its power nearly drained. He looked at his watch and was shocked to see the time. Time had passed differently in those few moments; hours had gone by unchecked.

He placed the amulet safely in his inside coat pocket and bent to retrieve his faltering flashlight. He made his way back to the tent with a warmth deep in his soul that would carry him through the rest of his life. John sat zipped in his sleeping bag and wrote in his journal:

October 1st, 2033

The Monks I encountered on my last journey proved to be right. What I sought was here, waiting for its release, and the truth of man's place in the Universe is now crystal clear. My fears are justified, as I don't believe our civilization is ready for the truth. Maybe in time we will evolve past our differences, but our differences are what will ultimately divide us.

Evolution was not intended to degrade, but time took its toll and it is apparent in our current environment that we have a great chasm that cannot be bridged. On that note we must do everything in our power to contain what we know the truth to be, and plan for our future elsewhere. Our natural resources are growing scarce; therefore, we must move forward with our thinking. Where there is an end, there is also a beginning.

In two weeks, I will address my brothers at Bilderberg, as it's time to pool our resources and move forward with our goals.

Dorathy must be protected and I fear that my life is endangered by this discovery. There are those who would want me out of the way and in time I hope to expose them who oppose me.

My friend, my brother, Simon...I feel there is something very troublesome there. I can't quite put my finger on it, but he seems to be defiant and fights me on every advance. Perhaps time will tell.

His room dark, John Rosen was sitting in an oversized Georgian chair, upholstered in the finest silk cloth. He was nursing his now warm martini and gazing at the sun as it set over the mountain peaks. It cast beautiful shades of amber, pink, and purple which reflected off the lake.

His hotel room door lock clicked and creaked as it was slowly opened. Without looking up, John now knew who had wanted him out of the way and he was saddened by the betrayal.

"Have you come to finish the job?" he asked, still looking out his picture window.

Although the voice was familiar, the sinister laugh was foreign. "Tragically, you still don't know who I am."

John slowly turned, his last sunset etched in his mind's eye, "What have you done, Simon?"

"Oh no . . . I'm not your precious lap dog anymore . . . now I'm in charge. Even your Illuminati brothers can't protect you now."

John could just make out the familiar face in the fading light, but the eyes were different somehow: hollow and without a soul. Not many had been able to outsmart the mighty Doctor Rosen, but this . . . he didn't see coming. He accepted his fate as he turned back to the window, the lovely colors fading to black of night. The last thing John saw was the face of his trusted friend reflected in the glass of the window.

The still glowing crystal amulet, hung on its chain made of a foreign metal, dangled to the floor as John's body went limp, his bloodied face pressed against the glass. His assassin bent over to pry the crystal from his lifeless hand.

Simon studied the amulet, pondering what powers it might possess, as the light faded from its core.

John always had the last laugh.

CHAPTER 1

From the time Dorathy Rosen was a child, she had looked to the stars as her escape. She gazed upon them and wondered about a life away from her turmoil, an escape from a life of constant torment. Her mother had died when she was four years old, and her father had raised her the only way he knew. It may not have been the best way, but it had been the only way he could keep her with him. Dorathy became accustomed to a life of being uprooted, moving from one country to the next, from one school to the next. The trials of fitting in had taken a toll and she began to respond to the constant ridicule of her classmates with hostility. Occasionally, she answered their taunts with physical aggression.

Her father was her rock, but to rely on him was somehow foreign to her. She knew even at that young age, that the only person she could rely on was herself. Dorathy wished every day that somehow today would be different, that perhaps someone would have a kind word for her. But she was always merely another new target.

Her father grew weary of the calls informing him that Dorathy was being sent home from her most recent school —although her private driver always offered a warm and understanding smile, shaking his head in amusement as she jumped into the front seat slamming the door behind her. John would come home late at night and would hear his daughter crying in frustration. He would rap on her bedroom door and calmly ask why so many tears, what had the other kids said to her today that left her so upset? She would wipe her eyes and softly say, "Kids called me ugly and told me I was stupid." Stupid was the one thing she knew she was not, but she felt she was the only person who knew it. Her father would sigh and wipe her tears away while examining her wounds.

"Dora, listen honey, you can't just go around slugging people in the face when they call you a bad name. You have to be stronger and wiser than that."

Dorathy struggled to understand what her father meant. She pleaded her case. "School is boring, and I just plain hate all of the other kids, and the teachers are mean to me, and I just don't want to go any more."

Her father would just sigh and look into her sad, big brown eyes and tell her that the kids picked on her because they were jealous of her smarts and her beauty. This gave her little comfort and she wished the kids could just accept her and not torture her as relentlessly as they did. John tried to give her other words of comfort, but the reality was that Dorathy excelled academically and was not being challenged. It became quite clear that something needed to change, and it was obvious she needed help.

John believed that the only way to get through to Dorathy was to enroll her into a program for academically gifted children. The next stop was the Far East, where he felt she would find her way, to learn, to study, and to find patience and awareness with meditation and discipline. The martial arts would give her the tools and the education would allow her to grow into a woman of substance. It was the right balance, and the formula worked. Dorathy grew to understand the world around her and became wiser than her years.

A love of science and engineering took hold and the past was never going to interfere with her ever again. After all, it would not be logical for one's past to dictate one's future.

As the years pressed on, John Rosen continued to make a vast fortune, at a time when modern civilization had come together to neutralize the ever- growing threats of hostile terrorist and corrupt governments. And then in one fell swoop, a mass military strike comprised of militaries from dozens of countries was coordinated. During this strike, Weapons of Mass Destruction were found and destroyed. It was to be the war that ended all wars.

The strike was to eliminate the world of corruption, radicalism, fanaticisms, and genocide, but in order to rid the world of these evils once and for all, the attacks had to be planned as if a cancer needed to be surgically excised without compromising the healthy tissue that surrounded it. The chaos that followed this day of reckoning obliged the free world to step away from what remained of that part of the planet. Whoever was still standing and fighting against the rest were left to their own devices. That part of the world was simply called the "derogated section." Humanity that was left within that realm of corruption was slowly becoming extinct, their DNA rapidly degrading. It appeared as if there was something buried deep within their very existence that prevented them from evolving past the hate and the barbaric behavior. They were slowly de-evolving.

Keeping the area isolated had been the most complex issue, but over time it became easier. Eventually all mankind would come together and work in unison to better itself. The planet could begin the healing process. Once all the turmoil had vanished from the globe, the world's resources were finally put to good use and technologies advanced in leaps and bounds. The planet and its population of nearly 9.5 billion souls were symbiotic; planet Earth and its inhabitants had come together at last. For a time, humankind searched for an everlasting peace that would bind all humans together for eternity. But as things go, there is always an end that leads to a new beginning; nothing is forever.

During this time the consumption of fossil fuel had become obsolete. John had designed and manufactured Green Energy, the first commercially utilized hydrogen-on-demand combustion engine. All it required was water, and through the process of electrolysis would produce hydrogen as a clean-burning, highly efficient means of energy.

After his success with hydrogen engines, John invested heavily in Deep Space Industries. This company had been formed decades before to develop the means of capturing asteroids to mine the rare minerals that lay within. Scientists began to develop new uses for these rare-to-Earth deposits of minerals, and technologies became even more sophisticated.

As different types of technologies were developed, John would invest in those that showed promise and put in place a team to accelerate their progress. While his fortune grew, he continued to invest in a variety of companies, one of which was exploring methods to use 3-D Bioprinting in the development of human body parts. This new technology engendered miraculous medical advances and people were living much longer. With greater longevity, people were able to expand their intellect to achieve other great discoveries. A momentous milestone was reached with the development of synthetic DNA; humans now had the ability to create life.

All these changes had impacted the world. John and Dorathy traveled together to remote places of the globe to determine how they could make things better for humanity. When her father was murdered, Dorathy was devastated by his death but she was certain that one day she would see her parents again on the other side. Though bound to science, her faith in a Creator was unshakeable. The only proof she needed was to look at the universe that surrounds us all. Her simple response to the naysayers was always 'absence of proof is not proof of absence.'

Dorathy had gone on to college to continue her education and earned a dual doctoral degree from MIT. It was no surprise to anyone that her chosen fields would be aerospace engineering and astrophysics. After graduating, she met her first love and faced an untimely pregnancy. Although it was truly not part of her plan, she went on to have her baby girl. It had been the best decision she ever made. The decision to marry, however, had been against her better judgment and she found herself raising her daughter alone when her marriage came to a tragic, but not unexpected, end. Her husband wasn't so much a bad person, as he was merely a man whom she could no longer tolerate. He thought her desire for mutual respect was obstinate He no longer found himself attracted to her, just as she found the relationship tiresome and uneventful. All, if any, passion that had been there once had vaporized long ago. It was not long before her husband had become detached and found himself with another woman. He wasted no time remarrying.

Dorathy thought of his new wife Tiffany as a short, skinny bag of bones, lacking natural womanly curves. She lacked any ambition to do something meaningful with her life and adopted an attitude of 'what can you do for me' instead of asking herself what she might be able to do for others. Dorathy was mystified by her ex-husband's attraction to his new wife, but as much as she wanted to deny that she had been untouched by his choice, she couldn't help but think that somehow, she had let him down.

Nevertheless, she had a beautiful daughter and had given her the name Athena, the goddess of wisdom and war. Her name stood for wisdom; to know a life worth living, and war-to make a life worth fighting for. Athena had also grown to be wise beyond her years; to look into her eyes was to believe she carried with her an old soul. Dorathy loved her as fiercely as any mother could. Athena was her best friend, confidant, and a reflection of herself. She treasured her connection with her daughter as it was the relationship she wished she could have had with her own mother.

CHAPTER 2

D orathy stood in front of the full-length mirror, critical of her figure, turning to grimace at her backside. With an annoyed sigh, she muttered her dissatisfaction under her breath. Athena turned the corner of the hall coming from her bedroom in the home they shared. "God, Mom, why are you always putting yourself down? You look awesome for fifty-one."

Dorathy snapped back, "I'm forty-nine I'm going backwards!"

Athena just rolled her eyes and said, "I love you, Mom, no matter how old you are today. Just make sure to be home from work early so we can celebrate with Kevin and his parents. I made reservations at your favorite Mexican restaurant."

Dorathy raised her eyebrows and with a half-cocked smile said, "Oh, they have my favorite tequila."

Athena added, "Okay, Mom, but do try and behave. You almost gave Kevin's dad a coronary last time and his mom is really trying . . ."

Dorathy snapped back, "Trying what . . . to like me? That woman has a stick shoved up her ass and I'm just trying to remove it for her."

"Jeez, Mom. Really?" Athena loved her mom, but she could be so overbearing at times. She shook her head and said, "I have to go now if I'm going to make my class on time. Just don't have too many shots—although I know Kevin would love another opportunity to drive your car home."

Athena smiled while giving her a kiss on the cheek, "Happy Birthday, Mom." With that she was out the door on her way to UCLA. With only one more year until graduation she would have her MBA and the plan was to get married and start her career running her grandfather's foundation. It appeared to be a good enough plan and Kevin was a good guy. It was very apparent he loved and respected her, although Dorathy couldn't help but think there should be more to life, something a bit more exciting.

With that thought, Dorathy stepped into her black stilettos, straightened her black pencil skirt and pink blouse, and was out the door. She loved driving the winding side roads to the Jet Propulsion Laboratory, where she had been working for the last few years.

Dorathy was not the type of woman who would be caught dead driving a slug of a car. No common automobile would suffice; for her it meant a finely tuned robust V-12 Aston Martin. Her black car matched the color of her long wavy hair and the curves of her figure, and the pure power of it was only matched by her spirit. Dorathy would turn the music up loud and place her sunglasses on her strikingly beautiful face, her tan complexion and sultry eyes inherited through her Mediterranean ancestry.

Slowly pulling out of the garage, she put the car in gear and raced down the street just to hear the roar of the engine. Speeding through the hills of Pasadena had become her daily adrenaline rush.

Today was to be no different from any other workday, but sometimes things don't always go as expected. Parking the car in her usual space, she entered the main building. Although JPL was always on the cutting edge of design engineering and was respected around the world, her building lacked that certain futuristic look one might expect to see. Instead it was a throwback to the earlier years of space exploration—but to change its esthetics simply to impress would be as nonsensical as straightening the leaning tower of Pisa.

After swinging open the heavy glass door, Dorathy walked across the large brightly lit vaulted atrium. The sound of her stilettos clicked against the marble floors as she strode across to the massive reception desk. The receptionist, Lisa, heard Dorathy's approach, peered over the top, and said in a whispered tone, "There's a big surprise for you in your office."

Lisa couldn't keep a secret if she tried. She was grinning from ear to ear, as if it were her own birthday surprise. She spoke softly. She thought no one else must know her secret, as she told Dorathy that a huge bouquet of red roses had been delivered labeled only, 'From a secret admirer.'

Dorathy curled the corner of her upper lip and furrowed her arched brows, whispering back, "How unimaginative." She pushed open the door to the inner offices, leaving Lisa wearing a sad frown. Lisa could only wish someone would secretly admire her and shower her with roses.

Striding down the hall with her head held high, Dorathy walked with purpose towards her office, passing the opened doors of offices of upper management and design engineering staff, most of which were empty. Only then did she realize why most everyone was loitering around. A small group stood in her way gushing birthday greetings.

Dorathy was well-liked. A hard worker, she always took the time to help in any way she could. She donated her time and money to good causes, whether work related or personal. As she drew near, smiling and gracious, she was directed to the break room. A coworker was lighting a single huge candle in the center of a scrumptious looking chocolate cake, since no one would dare ask her age. In unison, the group started to sing 'Happy Birthday'. As the song reached its end, one baritone chimed in with his Texas drawl. Today was her day and she enjoyed her coworkers and absolutely loved her job, especially since the commercialization of space and space travel had been so successful in the past few years.

She had previously worked during the past two decades both with The Elon Musk Trust's Space Exploration Technologies Corp., or SpaceX, and before that with the immensely popular Virgin Galactic and Launcher One programs that had commenced fifty years earlier. Richard Branson's concepts, partnered with the ingenuity of Burt Rutan, had fueled space travel for those mere mortals with the appropriate bank accounts. They believed that space travel should no longer only be aspired to by the chosen few, but that it should become a free enterprise allowing everyone with a sense of adventure to venture far enough to break the bonds of our earthy pull; to experience moments of weightlessness and to catch a glimpse of our small home from space.

After she had accomplished what she could with space commercialization, Dorathy went on to work on federally funded projects for NASA.

She felt comfortable in her position there and worked on the Human Mars Landing until it failed in its goal to send ordinary humans into space. At that point the determination was made to do the next best thing—to send synthetically enhanced humans. That part of the mission was a bit of a secret to the common folk.

Since space travel involves a set of constants that cannot be changed, the method of how to journey through it needed to be changed. By introducing synthetic DNA to human biology, the body's structure was altered, which would allow people to travel into deep space without suffering adverse effects. This new technology facilitated travel to the stars. However, the body of knowledge that would make it possible to construct a craft powerful enough to travel at the speeds required to complete a trip of the grandest of scale was lacking. This was yet another constant that could not be changed. Perhaps one day the knowledge to overcome that barrier would be acquired.

The Mars project, with many of the technologies her father had helped to develop, was a success and came at a time when Athena was young, and she needed to work on a project far less taxing. The day came though when NASA, hurting for federal funds, was forced to start the 'Private Sector.' It was only logical that she try her hand at private projects that worked hand in hand with NASA and JPL. New companies were being formed to address all aspects of space travel and the commercialization of space. JPL was hired to design whatever cargo was required, and the means to deliver it into orbit.

One of Dorathy's first projects with JPL for this new frontier was to design a Space Hotel for the Bigelow Corporation. Bigelow designed it, JPL built it and then leased a ride into space inside the belly of the new, as she liked to call it, *shuttle carrier service*. The New Shuttle Program had literally turned into a makeshift FedEx truck, but equally reliable and with a sturdy design that made it as safe as a trip to the supermarket.

There was so much wealth to be made by companies offering space-related services that the industry was growing exponentially. Advances in space travel made it as common as booking a trip on any airline. It had grown in leaps and bounds since the old pioneering days at Virgin Galactic and SpaceX. So many companies were commencing space flights that it became quite a competitive business, making the price affordable to just about anyone who wanted to go to the outer limits. Dorathy had always thought it was just a matter of time before we would leave our planet in search of answers to the questions that had always eluded mankind from the beginning of time.

After she enjoyed a piece of cake and thanked everyone for their kindness, the group disbanded and went off to their daily routine. After grabbing a drink out of the fridge to wash down her cake, Dorathy walked across the hall to her office. Prominently displayed on her desk was the biggest bouquet of roses she had ever seen. Tucked among the blossoms was a card that read "Happy Birthday from: your secret admirer." She stood over them wondering who in God's name did this and pondering what the hell she was going to do with them. They were lovely and very fragrant, but she couldn't help that a part of her wanted to throw them in the trash. On the other hand, it wasn't the roses' fault that some poor misguided fool was trying to impress her or seduce her, or both. So, she simply ignored them for the time being and dove into her piles of work.

Just then Hugo the director of JPL stuck his head around the corner of her open door, knocked on the wall and said in his loud, good-natured voice, "Looks like your human popsicle project is a go!"

God, how she cringed when she heard her attempts at being funny coming back to haunt her. She had coined the phrase in the early stages of the project and it unfortunately stuck. Although impolitic, it was an essentially accurate description. She had remained confident that her pet project would pass approval for company funding, and now the only thing left for her to do was to meet with the owner of Lifecor out in Scottsdale, Arizona.

For years Lifecor had been in the forefront of Cryogenic Freezing. They called it *long term Critical Care*. Terminally ill patients, death imminent due to cancer or other types of disease or defect, as death approached, would pay up front, sign over life insurance policies, or pay over time through annual membership fees, in order to be cryogenically frozen just before the moment of legally being declared dead. The expectation was that they would be revived when technology had produced a cure for their condition and had the answers to obtaining everlasting life.

Since this had become a popular way to handle the end of one's life, Lifecor had developed a plan to offer clients the option of a space send-off. Clients choosing this option did not necessarily expect to be revived, but to be preserved for a journey into the vastness of space. Most clients wanted to purchase, in a sense, immortality, to be revived no matter how long it would take, while others simply wanted the ultimate final farewell into the great unknown. Sending specially designed capsules into space seem to be a great solution for those who wanted a sense of one last adventure. Since the bodies frozen inside were kept at negative three-hundred and twenty degrees Fahrenheit and most of space was colder yet, it seemed like an easy transition to design a cryotube capsule to keep the bodies inside preserved for all eternity.

In the past, cryogenics had been used to transport harvested organs from the newly deceased, then brought back to life when defrosted for surgery. Logic dictated that if the procedures were to be performed on a newly clinically dead person, it would work the same, if what had killed the person in the first place was to be reversed. Therein lay the problem. Given the popularity of cryogenics and the dearth of the medical advancements to successfully bring back the individual and repair the fatal event, the cryogenically frozen patients were starting to stack up. Offering a new concept for cryogenic space flights seemed to be the next best step in offering clients a choice.

Dorathy contemplated the future of this technology and could foresee the popularity of space funerals. If there was a buck to be made, someone would think of it, label it, and sell it.

However, as medical technology caught up, only a handful of patients would ever be revived. And there were side effects . . .

Having put in a full day at her desk, Dorathy was ready to call it quits. She had a nice evening planned, dinner with her daughter and her soon-to-be in-laws, and then a weekend free to do a little relaxing by the pool with a good book. She glanced at her watch, finished up a few loose ends, grabbed her bag, and was walking down the hall when she remembered her leftover cake in the fridge. She would want to enjoy that later with some good red wine. Dorathy turned back to the break room. She opened the fridge door and, given her statuesque figure and the heels of her stilettos, found that she needed to bend way down to reach the lower shelf where her cake had been placed. Just then, she sensed someone coming in behind her. She straightened up quickly, cake in one hand while closing the fridge door with the other.

It was the engineer they had hired from Italy. He approached and gently pried the cake from her, sliding it on the top of the fridge. In doing so, he pressed himself very close to her and put his left hand around her hips, pulling her to him. Dorathy remained calm, as he whispered in her ear something seductive, using his smooth native Italian.

Shaking her head, Dorathy rolled her eyes and gently took his hand while she spoke calmly "Look . . . Guido?"

He softly spoke. "Carlo, my name is Carlo."

"Okay, Carlo." Fuming at this point, she almost spat his name. She suddenly twisted his wrist with precision and force, contorting it in such a way that it brought him to his knees. She could have easily broken it, but she just wanted to put a shot across his bow. She now spoke slowly and clearly, for him to understand. "Listen up, my young Italian friend. You might be able to get away with that with other women but NOT with me! *Capisce?*"

Carlo was stuttering something in Italian that may have resembled, "Uncle." Dorathy released him, looked down at him and raised her eyebrows as if to say, "Subject closed." She turned slightly, pulled the cake box from the top of the fridge and, as she walked out the door without turning, she tossed over her shoulder, "Thanks for the roses."

Carlo remained on his knees and rubbed his wrist. "Ciao Bella." Now he thought he was officially in love with Dorathy. He stood up to his height of nearly two meters and thought to himself how badly he felt for what he had done under duress. Even though he felt a piercing sense of guilt, he knew that his mission was of great importance.

Dorathy pulled into the driveway of her modest home, not the custom-built mansion one might assume. She was quite content with her older, remodeled home with its small yard and pool, tucked away in a quiet neighborhood in the Pasadena hills. For her, home was a comfortable space in which she stored her things and cooked amazing meals for friends, a place where she felt loved and safe.

Dorathy removed her shoes and stepped into the large kitchen, redolent with the scent of herbs and spices. Her special place, this is where she had spared no expense. After opening the massive door of her refrigerator, she grabbed a wedge of cheddar from the drawer and pushed the cake box onto one of the shelves. She looked at the clock and thought that Athena would be home shortly. There was just enough time for a quick dip in the pool and a drink before getting ready for dinner. She needed a cocktail if she were going to have to endure an evening with Kevin's parents. They were nice enough people, but a bit too uptight for her laid back, live and let live attitude.

After enjoying a couple hours of down time, she pulled her hair up into a messy, knotted bun and dressed for comfort in a pair of cropped dress pants and a blouse tied at the waist. The restaurant was, after all, a family-owned little hole in the wall, just a quiet little place. While she was putting on a dab of make-up Athena breezed in, calling towards her mother's bedroom, "I'm home. Going to freshen up, then we can go. Okay, Mom?"

Dorathy answered back, "Yup, almost ready."

A few moments later, they were seated in the Aston and off they went. Athena asked how her mom's day had gone, and Dorathy suddenly began to laugh so hard she snorted. She proceeded to tell Athena how everyone gathered for a little party and about the roses; that's when Dorathy was laughing so hard she could barely catch enough breath to tell her the story about Carlo.

"Oh God, Mom, you didn't." Athena was now laughing as Dorathy described Carlo's face when she brought him to his knees while almost breaking his wrist in the process.

Athena, half laughing and part serious, started in by saying, "Why the aggression, Mom?"

Dorathy shrugged her shoulders. "He's about your age and needed a little disciplining. Hopefully, he has learned his lesson with those Rico Suave moves. God, you know how I hate that. Men like that have no clue about women, so I took it upon myself to give him his first lesson on how NOT to approach a woman."

Athena giggled and said, "Mom, you're such a cougar." With that they were pulling into the parking lot and saw Kevin, Betty, and Ron getting out of Kevin's car.

The only obvious resemblance between Kevin and his mother, Betty, was the shape of their eyes. She didn't color her hair that was heavily streaked with grey and was wearing a flowery skirted dress that did nothing to flatter her figure. Kevin's father looked as if he had been attractive in his younger years, but lack of exercise and bad diet had taken their toll. He was happy to be in comfortable pants with his shirt all tucked in, making his belly more pronounced. Both were in their mid-fifties but acted and looked much older.

Kevin was a good-looking guy, tall, with a great tan and toned from years of beach volleyball. His brown hair was streaked from the sun, and he had piercing blue eyes. He and Athena made a great looking couple, as Athena had inherited her mother's Mediterranean exotic good looks paired with her grandfather's big green eyes.

Dorathy got out of the car and took a deep breath, letting it out slowly. Hearing her, Athena turned to her mom with a warning look that conveyed, *Be Good.* Dorathy muttered under her breath, "Yeah, yeah." They both waved and strode across the parking lot all smiles. There were hugs and kisses and Happy Birthday pleasantries as they entered the restaurant.

The restaurant decor had an authenticity about it; it felt as if they had been immediately transported to the Mexican Riviera.

Seated only a few moments later, they were handed menus and water glasses were filled. Their waiter proceeded to take drink orders. Although everyone else ordered the house frozen margaritas, as it was a celebration, Dorathy ordered her favorite tequila, a double and on the rocks. Betty shot her a sideways glance and said, "You really are celebrating tonight."

Dorathy retorted, "Well, it's better than curling up in a ball." Ron could sense a bit of irritation building in his wife, and asked what interesting projects had Dorathy been working on lately. Sipping her water, she said enthusiastically and without hesitation, "Cryogenics!"

Betty replied almost immediately, "Why?"

Dorathy didn't quite know where she was going with this, but what the hell. "Why?" Dorathy quickly responded. "Why not?" She knew by the look on Betty's face where this was going to go and thought, *Oh, well, she wants to go down that road, then let's go.*

"Well, Betty," she began calmly, trying not to sound condescending but failing miserably, "there are people who believe that although medical technology can't correct certain health problems now, the technology will be available at some time in the not-so-distant future. Say that someone has a terminal condition, whether it's cancer or some other fatal illness, and currently the technology does not exist to cure that illness, it does not mean in a few years scientists won't develop a cure. Therefore, at the time one is pronounced clinically dead, their body is prepared and frozen in hopes that they can be cured and revived or as they like to call it, 'reanimated,' at a later date. Pretty simple, really."

Betty had a frown on her face that spoke volumes. She shook her head and said, "The spirit has gone on to heaven, so it's impossible to be brought back from the dead."

Dorathy put her chin in her hand and looked back at her in astonishment. She sighed and bit her tongue, not wanting to offend her daughter's future in-laws. She said in a way not to sound superior, "Well, maybe your spirit finds its way back into your body when they wake you up." She continued, "What I'm saying is, that if a person dies and their spirit has gone to the other side, why shouldn't the same spirit come back to the person when revived? I just have a hard time believing a spirit carries a one-way ticket."

Betty argued earnestly, "If a person dies, it was God's will. Our Lord has called you home and it's unethical to try and change His will. Besides, why would anyone want to come back if they are living an everlasting life with our God in heaven?"

There were a lot of things Dorathy could say, but she wanted to add one more little irritant just to lighten her mood. With a huge grin, Dorathy offered a more esoteric argument. "Well you know, Betty, I understand that there are some people that have chosen to have just their heads frozen. These people believe everything that makes us who we are is all stored in the brain. So those individuals' brains are put in *suspended animation*. Then when they are revived their consciousness can be uploaded into whatever type of creature they want. Perhaps even a cyborg!"

Betty gasped, throwing her hand in front of her mouth, but before she could get on her soap box their waiter arrived to deliver drinks and take dinner orders. Dorathy slammed back her tequila and politely asked for another. Athena quickly changed the subject. Kevin and Ron were thankful for that, as the conversation was surely heading to hell in a handbasket.

After dinner they all said their goodbyes and Kevin settled his mother into the back seat of his car while his dad rode shotgun. Before Kevin could get the car started, Betty began to preach about Christian doctrine and that Dorathy needed to be saved. As she leaned forward into the front seat to be heard, she asked about Athena's religious beliefs, because she was emphatic that she did not relish the idea of her son marrying a heathen.

Kevin was annoyed. "Mom, you really need to get a grip. Athena is brilliant and she's a great person and so is her mom. I love Athena and we are getting married. You need to deal with it. Besides, you really need to open your mind and not hang out with those old ladies from church so much, I really think they're brainwashing you." Ron remained silent in the passenger seat and thought, *I'm not getting in the middle of this, I've had a long day and I just want some peace and quiet.*

Betty replied, "Okay, my darling. I just want you to be happy."

"I am, Mom."

After spending a nice, quiet weekend doing exactly what she wanted, Dorathy was excited on Monday to be moving forward with her cryogenics project. She was always enthusiastic about new projects, but she was passionate about this one. The thought of being frozen and sent into space for eternity gave her the feeling that somehow if the world were to implode, careening through space would give her a sense of immortality—that somehow, she would be the last survivor, the last evidence of the human existence.

CHAPTER 3

D orathy was looking forward to flying to Arizona to meet with the owner and CEO of Lifecor. Alex Mason was a brilliant scientist and a research doctor. Although the process of cryogenics preservation had been available for over a century, he wanted to utilize modern technology to perfect it. During his years of research, he had developed an accurate formula for the process of freezing and storing humans. Death had haunted him for far too long, while the ability to live his life had eluded him. He felt as if he were left in purgatory. Lifecor was his whole existence, and the means of perhaps giving others a life from death somehow made him feel whole.

After an exhilarating drive to her office Dorathy entered the building while the rising sun cast beams of light through the high, vaulted windows. As she approached, Lisa inquired about what she had done with her roses. Dorathy stopped and squinted for a moment as if deep in thought and, with a sigh, she said, "I totally forgot about them, guess I'll have to water them."

The suspense was killing Lisa, and she couldn't help asking in the whisper she always used when secret office romances were the subject of conversation, "Do you know who sent them to you?"

Dorathy couldn't help herself, always keeping her private life under wraps, and simply said, "Yes. Yes, I do," as she continued through the lobby, leaving Lisa to ponder whom it might be.

First thing on Dorathy's agenda was the meeting with Hugo the director of JPL and Jack, JPL's lead particle physicist, to sort through the details of her cryo project. When she reached her office, she gathered her files and stopped a second, leaning over to smell the roses, which had bloomed over the weekend and filled her office with their fragrant scent. She smiled and shook her head and murmured under her breath, "Silly boy."

Dorathy walked down the hall with a spring in her step that surprised even her. Getting out of town for a few days was going to be a welcome change. Entering the conference room, she noticed Hugo and Jack deep in conversation. Both men were in their early seventies although much younger in appearance; Jack with white spiked hair and bright blue eyes glowing against his perpetually tanned skin, and Hugo, standing a good foot taller, getting help from his worn-in cowboy boots and hat, always wearing a big Texas grin. Hugo was boisterous, while Jack was easy going and had a carefree attitude.

She approached and they suddenly halted their conversation, both looking at her with raised brows and pursed lips. She stopped and put one of her files down on the wood laminated table. "What's up? You both look like a couple of cats that got the bird."

Hugo smiled and said, "Ain't nothin'." Jack could hardly keep a straight face, his hands fidgeting in the pockets of his khakis.

Dorathy was beyond agitated by their behavior. She said with asperity, slapping her last file on the table, "What gives?"

Jack attempted to hold back laughter with little success and said, "We heard what you did to Carlo, that poor bastard."

Dorathy looked down at her bright blue suede heels against the wood parquets floors. It brought back a striking resemblance, but with the stark contrast, to the days gone by in the pioneering years where women in the office sported long pencil skirts and beehive hairdos and smoked while taking dictation.

She looked up, annoyed, and exclaimed somewhat more loudly than she anticipated, "Oh for fuck sake, are you kidding me? How does this shit get spread around so damn fast? He's too damned young, and should know better. He had it coming, and I doubt he'll pull that macho shit with me again. And that's all I'm going to say about it. Subject closed!"

With that, Jack and Hugo shut their gaping mouths and sat down, still giggling. Dorathy had always been treated like one of the guys as far as everyone was concerned. Bad language seemed to be part of her make up in a field that had traditionally been dominated by men. And, as far as everyone was concerned, bad language also seemed to fit her temperament.

Hugo said, "All righty, then," and pulled out his work and set it on the table. "So, let's discuss your human popsicles."

Dorathy, accustomed to the office bullshit, decided to ignore the jab that would defuse any lingering awkwardness from the exchange. She knew that she was well respected by every member of the management staff and had a great working relationship with both Jack and Hugo. Her outbursts were simply accepted as a personality trait that everyone was comfortable with because it always seemed to be comical when it occurred.

Smiling, she took out her files and went over the logistics of the project, such as design aspects, staffing, projected cost, etc. By the end of the meeting they had agreed that it would be best for her to fly out to the Lifecor facility to get a better understanding of what their management envisioned for the project. Perhaps then they would have the owner or one of their engineers fly back to spend some time at JPL for production of a prototype.

When the meeting ended Jack got up, gathered his things and said he was off to another appointment. He was going out the door when he chuckled to himself and shook his head. Dorathy was left guessing what was going through his mind. Meanwhile Hugo quietly asked Dorathy if he should have a sit down with Carlo about his behavior. Dorathy replied, "Absolutely not. I'll handle it. He has probably never been away from home or his momma for very long, so I'll talk to him and get him straightened out."

Hugo said with a smirk, "I'm sure you will . . . remind me never to get on your bad side."

She retorted with a smile as she walked out the door, "I'm sure you could handle it."

He thought to himself, *Yeah, maybe. If I were twenty years younger, I would have liked to have given it a shot. What a woman!*

Dorathy was walking back to her office when she glanced at her watch and realized it was lunch time. Dropping an armful of files on her desk, she walked across the hall to the break room where Carlo sat alone eating a cheese and bologna sandwich. She stopped to look at him, a bit closer this time and thought, *God he looks like a lost puppy.* She pulled out a chair and sat next to him. "How long have you been here?"

He said with his thick accent, "Abouta year," and then he started in on how beautiful she looked today, how her . . .

She cut him off sharply, saying with asperity, "How old are you?"

He stuttered slightly and said with a bit of hesitation, "Twenty-six."

"Okay, this is what we're going to do. You obviously have never been away from your home, except for your education, and you don't really know anyone your own age to socialize with. So this Saturday you are going to come to my home, and I am going to cook you a fabulous Italian dinner. You are going to meet my daughter and a few of her friends and they are going to take you out to a night club and perhaps you will find a nice young lady to mingle with, okay? Oh, and furthermore," she went on to say, "you need to drop this whole machismo thing, because it is not going to work on the type of woman you should eventually meet. Got it? I will see you Saturday at my house at 6:00 sharp, you can bring the wine."

With that she got up, straightened her skirt and strode over to the fridge, pulled out her salad and decided to eat at her desk while Carlo sat alone to digest her plan. Now the only thing to do was to try to get Athena to agree with it. She would, Dorathy was sure, once she presented her case to her.

Seated at her desk she called Lucy, their executive assistant. Lucy said she'd be right down to review travel details, so she could book Dorathy's trip to Arizona. A few minutes later, she showed up at the door wearing one of her customary brightly printed dresses accessorized with metallic gold heels.

Lucy was the same age as Dorathy, with bright blonde hair that just touched her shoulders, and a petite, toned physique. When she wasn't at work she was working hard at the gym. Her husband had a great job and made a good living, so she didn't really need to work, but she loved her job at JPL and was quite good at it. She was usually the first one there and the last one out. In fact, she was happy anywhere, if she wasn't home with her husband.

Dorathy loved hanging out with Lucy; they would go out for cock-tails after work most Friday nights. Lucy was one of those gals who was always the life of the party, with a bubbly personality and the tendency to stop and talk to anyone and everyone. When they walked into a room together most people would turn to look.

Lucy started by saying all in one breath, "Oh. My. God. I heard what you did to poor little Carlo, that is so hysterical! Did you see what Lisa wore to work today? Her boobs were totally hanging out. So, when do you want to go to Arizona? I looked at their website, pretty interesting stuff, I wonder what they do with all your blood when they take it out, be-cause you might need it after they wake you up. The owner, Alex Mason, he's sort of hot looking."

Dorathy, as usual, was struggling hard to keep up with Lucy's pinball train of thought and said, to focus her attention, "I think all I need for this trip is air from Burbank to Phoenix Sky Harbor, Sunday to Sunday, at a hotel within close proximity, and a car."

Lucy wrote that all down on her pad, got up and said, "Okay, good. I'll get it booked. Are we on for this Friday?"

Dorathy smiled. "Absolutely!"

Lucy bounced out of her office and down the hall, chatting to every-one on her way to the elevator. Everyone loved Lucy. If you were having a bad day, she had a magical way of lifting your spirits and she would do anything for you.

Dorathy sat at her desk pondering making a call to Alex Mason per-sonally. Now that the project was officially hers, she needed to get com-fortable with the fact that they would be working closely together to get it off the ground, so to speak. Closing her office door, she sat down and dialed his direct line.

After two rings he answered simply, "Alex, here." She couldn't place the accent right away, but guessed it was Australian. She spoke with a bit of hesitation at first, working to shrug off a case of nerves.

"Hi, Dr. Mason, this is Dorathy Rosen from JPL. I am the project manager and design engineer assigned to your project. I am due to come out to meet with you next Monday, if that works for you, and plan to stay the week to start out."

He replied, with a bit of excitement in his voice, "Yes, absolutely, I look forward to meeting you." And then after a slight pause, "Yes, the infamous Dr. Dorathy Rosen, your reputation precedes you."

Dorathy was unsure how she should respond to this statement. She stuttered a moment and felt herself tripping over her words as she spoke. "Ah, well, ah . . . what do you . . . mean?"

He knew he had made her feel uncomfortable, but figured she could handle it, so on he went. "Heir to the multibillion-dollar Rosen foundation, holds dual doctorates from MIT, and works at one of the most prestigious, scientifically advanced companies in the world. I am truly honored to be working with you on my project."

"Well, Dr. Mason," she caught her breath and exhaled slowly. I hope that you are going to be able to get past your illusions of my grandeur."

He let out a bellow of a laugh and responded, "And you have a sense of humor on top of all the rest. I think we'll get on just fine and call me Alex." He continued, "So Monday it is, say ten in the morning?"

She responded with a quick, "Okay, sounds good . . . then I'll see you next Monday."

She could almost hear the huge smile on his face as he replied, "Indeed, you will, Dora." And with that he disconnected.

She pulled the phone away from her ear and stared at it for a moment before putting it down and mused, to no one in particular, "Well that was . . . unusual." Alex had confounded her, and not too many people were capable of doing that. Still shaking her head, she went on with her work on some of her smaller projects in order to finish them up before the end of the week.

By the time Friday rolled around, with her work done, she was looking forward to a few cocktails with Lucy. She was putting some files away when Lucy popped her head around the corner of her office door. "Are you ready for some karaoke? I got some of the guys from *Lunar Dig* to meet us there." Lucy then pleaded, "Can we take your car? I love going in your car, makes me feel like a rock star."

Dorathy said, "Yeah, sure," with a smile. Lucy was bursting with happiness. She then broke out in song: "Sky dive naked from an airplane . . . ," holding her hand up and shaking her blonde head like a heavy metal groupie from the old days. Dorathy laughed and said, "You're nuts, girlfriend."

As usual, when they pulled up into the parking lot all eyes were on them as they got out of the car. Dorathy didn't need the attention but she certainly liked it. Her take on life was simple really: "Life is too short to drive a boring car . . . or really to just live a boring life." As wonderful and grateful as she felt for being born into this life of hers, something deep within her remained empty, a void that she couldn't fill. A true love had always been missing, but it was something more than that, something on a grander scale was surely missing from her life.

As soon as they walked in, they ran into the crew from JPL sitting at the bar. It was an Irish pub, complete with pool tables and darts off to one side, a small stage for karaoke with a smattering of little tables, and a large old classic style mahogany bar that curved around one entire side of the space. Being that the pub was so close in proximity to JPL, one could always expect to come across other coworkers mingling in a sea of khakis and blue shirts with sleeves rolled up. Of course, Dorathy and Lucy were the exceptions.

A couple of the guys had been there awhile and were a few drinks ahead. One of them approached Dorathy as they walked in. "Hi," clearly trying not to slur his words, "you work with Hugo and Jack."

Dorathy cocked her head to the side. "Yup, sure do." Encouraged by her response, he leaned against the wall to regain his balance. He continued, "You're one of the project managers over there, man those projects are fringe, really way out there," and he threw back his arm to represent distance.

Dorathy nodded her head in agreement and said, "Yeah, maybe, but it makes my job more interesting." At that moment Lucy ran up and grabbed Dorathy by the arm. Before Lucy could drag her away, the audacious drunk asked if he could buy her a drink; she simply said, "Nope," and off they went to sing a few duets.

After a couple of hours, they were ready to call it a night. As she always did, Dorathy tipped the doorman for keeping a watchful eye over her car, and he asked if she was ever going to let him drive it. She laughed. "Yeah, maybe, if you're good."

He responded, "Baby, I'm really good."

She burst out laughing, "Yeah, I don't doubt it, Scotty. Don't forget I know your mom!"

His buddy, who was loitering around outside with him, punched him in the arm while calling him a jackass. Both boys were laughing, and God knows what they were going to discuss after the two women departed, but surely whatever it was, it would only be in their dreams.

It was a beautiful Saturday morning. Dorathy woke up refreshed and energetic, so she decided to go for a nice jog through the hills surrounding her neighborhood. She strode out her front door and noticed Kevin's car was parked in the driveway. She sighed, thought about it a moment, and was forced to remind herself that her daughter was a young woman, engaged to be married. Although they were two consenting adults, after all, it still was hard to swallow that her little girl was all grown up. So off she went; she put her music on and turned up the volume of her favorite old tunes. Listening about island getaways always made her miss her beach house on her very own piece of paradise. She thought . . . one day.

When she returned, Kevin's car was gone, and Athena was putting breakfast away. "Hi, Mom," Athena said in a cheerful voice, "you want me to make you anything before I clean this all up?"

"Nah, thanks though." Dorathy went on to say, "So, tonight you're bringing Kevin and your friends Matt, Stacy, and Kim for dinner, and after dinner you're all going to take Carlo out to a club, right?"

Athena replied, without any enthusiasm in her voice, "Yes, Mother."

Dorathy raised her eyebrows, and asked, "What's with the melancholy?"

With a heavy sigh, Athena asked, "Why are you always bringing home strays?"

"Jeez . . . really Athena," Dorathy said with a disappointed note in her voice. She began to plead her case. "Look, Carlo is far from home, most likely the first time in his life, so all I'm trying to do is get him out with some people his own age. And maybe find him a girlfriend, so he won't be so pathetically lonely."

Athena retorted with a smile, "You mean get him laid?"

Dorathy smirked and rolled her eyes, saying, "Sure . . . why the hell not?"

"Speaking of getting laid, Mom," Athena rolled it right back at her, "when, if ever, are you going to find a boyfriend?"

Dorathy half expected this line of questioning as she had taught her daughter never to hold back in the art of communication. "Jesus Christ, Athena, I just have a truckload of men trying to break down the door to get in here for a good ol' roll in the hay, don't I?"

"No, you don't, Mom," Athena continued to shoot back at her, "and the reason why is because you chase all potentially suitable men away. In fact, they go running and screaming in fear!"

"Wow, really!" Dorathy snapped back, feeling vulnerable and went on to say, "Who peed in your damn Cheerios?"

"Okay, Mom, calm down," Athena said, trying to ease this sore spot with her mother and continued on in a calmer, more understanding voice, "all I'm saying is you haven't had a serious relationship since you and Dad split eons ago and I'm just trying to figure out why not?"

Dorathy, a bit of sadness mingled with a dash of regret, leaned up against the kitchen counter and simply said, "I guess I just haven't met the right person yet." She went on to say now with tears welling up, "I cared a lot about your dad, but ultimately he didn't want me, he needed someone else, someone I could never be, and I can accept that. I also can accept that I'm an independent woman and I have evolved to a point where I refuse to allow a man to control my life."

Athena hugged her mom now because she finally grasped what she was trying to say—she was looking for a partner . . . her soul mate.

Athena cradled her mom's face with both hands and kissed her

mother square on the lips. "I love you, Mom, and I know there is someone out there for you—it's just not the time yet, but he will pop into your
life when you least expect it."

Dorathy smiled and said, "My darling daughter, always a hopeless
romantic."

Athena replied, "I think I got that from you."

Dorathy, who was feeling a little bit brighter about her future and
possible romance with her soul mate, who was presently hidden away at
some far off place, decided it was a good time to take a shower and go to
the grocery store for tonight's meal of her famous fifteen-pound lasagna
and garlic bread. Dorathy loved to cook for guests and was a gracious
host. Tonight, would be fun and hopefully Carlo would hook up with one
of Athena's girlfriends, if not for any other reason but to turn his affec-
tions away from herself. She laughed under her breath, and reiterated,
"That silly boy."

Carlo showed up a bit earlier than expected. Dorathy was still layering
the lasagna when the doorbell rang. She wiped her hands on a tea towel
and answered the door. She saw Carlo standing there with one of those
free bags you get from the local liquor store filled with a variety of wine.
He was dressed in a closely fitted black shirt that outlined a toned muscular build and had paired his dark blue jeans with stylish black boots. His
thick black hair was cut short with just the right amount of length on top.
Dark eyes glowing against his olive skin, he stared back at her with a big
perfect smile. She thought to herself if she was younger, she would have
loved a little roll in the hay, but immediately dismissed that thought as
she directed him through the front door.

In a thick Italian accent, he said, "Thank you fora having me fora
dinner. I noa havea gooda food since I leavea my home ina Italy. My
momma, shea cooks for me every Sunday after Mass."

Dorathy smiled and directed him through the foyer and into the
kitchen. "Make yourself at home. My daughter Athena should be here
shortly with a group of her friends." She offered Carlo a glass of wine
as she could sense he was a bit nervous about the evening ahead. Carlo
accepted with enthusiasm and he picked one of the bottles of Chianti out
of the bag. He said, "Thisa one isa gooda bottle." Dorathy, too busy with

her tasks, handed a bottle opener to Carlo, who took it from her and sat at the opposite side of the bar facing the kitchen. As he was uncorking the wine, Dorathy asked, "So Carlo tell me about your family."

A big grin broke out across his perfectly sculpted face and he said with fondness, "Well my momma, she livea outsidea Romea, my Pappa hea die long time ago with the heart attack. Mya little sister, Maria, shea marry anda havea three bambinos. Shea no work, hera husband havea good job for the museum ina Romea. Ia go to University and me geta this job, I knowa I so lucky, but I was the topa my class. I love mya joba in the Robotics. I'ma so excited we gonna be sending to the moon soona. I tella my momma, shea thinks I goa into space, I tella her, "No Momma, we senda the robots toa space, but shea tella everyone I goa into the space.""

Dorathy giggled and said, "So you're working on the Lunar Dig Project. That's funny." She went on to tell him about the inside joke with that project; either we were there digging to find a huge deposit of sub-lunar water, or *The Mother Ship*.

He laughed and said he had heard that joke, that he hoped it was the latter of the two. He went on to tell her, "I wasa going toa try anda have my momma movea here to the USA, but shea no want to goa, she saya she too old now."

Dorathy asked in a concerned motherly way, "So what will you do, being so far away from your home and family?"

"I thinka I stay for a while, then mya uncle, hea worka for CERN for nuclear research in Switzerland maybe hea geta me a job there."

Dorathy perked up when she heard that, as she had visited CERN not too long ago. That trip was one of her favorite business trips. She had been one of the six people from her division that flew to Switzerland to meet with their engineers to go over new concepts in propulsion. It was not like Dorathy to grand-stand and she never used the corporate jet inherited from her father, but she hated to fly commercial for such a long journey and she had been dreading the flight. Although air travel had improved over time with the new faster jet engines that had taken the place of the older, much slower models, travel on commercial flights was still tiresome.

She had called Lucy and told her not to book the airline tickets just yet, that she wanted to check into something first. She then called her pilot and scheduled the flight. When she called Lucy back, she told her she had handled the air, but wanted Lucy to book a limo for all of them to the airport. Dorathy thought, "What the hell, may as well make it real special." Her colleagues were happy when they discovered Lucy had booked a limo, but were gob struck when they realized they were going over in a private jet. Most of them brought her lunches for weeks afterwards.

Dorathy asked Carlo, "Who is your uncle over there? I might have met him." He told her, and his name sounded vaguely familiar but something at the back of her mind nagged at her, that somehow, she knew him from her past.

Carlo was leaning in over the counter, "You working ona the cryogenics? You think thata is something you want to do whena you die?"

Dorathy popped the lasagna into the oven and started prepping the garlic bread. Spreading the roasted garlic over the baguettes, she stopped to think about what her choice would be. "Yes, I think I would do that, most definitely."

He wore a smile, but his eyes were saddened by the thought. Lowering his head, no longer being able to look her in the eye, he asked, "Ifa someone gonna wakea you up, I guess dying not so bad after all."

Dorathy pondered the thought for a moment, "Yeah, I guess . . . we all have to die, but if there is a chance of life after death, I suppose it's not so bad. She chuckled, "Doesn't mean I want to die tomorrow though."

Carlo sighed as he sat back against his bar stool, knowing that her future had already been set in motion, "Yes, everyone gonna die sometime. Maybe itsa okay if you die and youra life had meaning. Maybe whena you wake up, you have a better life and do important thingsa that maybe you coulda not even imagine."

Dorathy smiled, "Well, hopefully in this life I do what's important and meaningful and when I die and if, or when, I get revived in the future, I continue my life doing something even more extraordinary."

Carlo was feeling better about her project. "I hope you livea forever."

"Well Carlo forever is a very long time, why don't we just live in the moment for now?"

As that thought settled in with them both, the rest of the crew walked through the front door. When Athena stopped short, Kim and Stacy rear-ended her in the kitchen doorway. All three gals stood there with mouths hanging open, while they gazed upon Carlo. Athena smiled and introduced herself to Carlo, then quickly introduced Kevin as her fiancé and went on to introduce her suddenly very single friends. Before this very moment they were all in make-believe relationships, not wanting to be set up with a loser.

The wine was flowing, and everyone was laughing and joking while enjoying their dinner, the aroma of an authentic Italian meal lingering in the air. The girls were cleaning up, so they could talk in private. The discussion centered on how they were going to *share* Carlo tonight as if he didn't have a say in the matter.

Dorothy said, "Good, I'm glad you all like him. He's a good boy." With that she excused herself, said her goodnights, and commented on how her work was done.

The next morning, she woke with a bit of a headache she figured was from overindulging in the wine. She had been getting a lot of headaches lately and racked it up to not enough sleep. Still tired, she sat on the edge of the bed yawning, then dragged herself into her bathroom and rummaged through a drawer to find a pain reliever. She peered into the mirror above the sink and thought how old she was starting to look. She pulled at the side of her face. Her reflection stared back, telling her it was something much more than skin deep that haunted her. The years had passed by so quickly and only now showing in the lines of her face. A true happiness lingered in the background, shadowed by the stunning reflection that peered back at her.

Dorothy was not a vain woman, but she did take care of her physical appearance. She was comfortable going out in ragged gardening clothes without a stitch of makeup on—in fact during her time away from work she preferred to dress down, as she always dressed very well for her job. She was the kind of person that was very adaptable no matter if she was spending an evening at the Ritz or some smoke-filled dive bar out in the middle of nowhere. There were plenty of times long ago when she had been with her father so far off the beaten track that a tent and a campfire were all the comforts they had.

She was feeling very spent this morning and decided to go for a leisurely walk through her neighborhood rather than her normal jog, then she would pack for the week in Arizona. Before Dorathy knew it, it was time for Athena to take her to the airport. Dorathy grabbed her bag and wheeled it down the hall. She had dressed in a pair of linen pants and a light-weight cotton shirt for the trip, as Phoenix was going to be scorching hot this time of year.

Athena saw her mom approaching and grabbed her purse. "Okay, Mom, you ready to go?"

"Yeah, I think so," Dorathy replied, taking a mental inventory of all the work-related items that she needed to bring with her.

Athena tossed her mom's bags into the back of the car, "I think Kevin and I are going to go up to the wine country next weekend, so we'll pick you up on our way home."

Dorathy responded as she was getting into the passenger side, "Sounds like fun. Can you pick up some of my favorite wines for me, I'm running low on my *liquid gold*," as Dorathy liked to call her favorite beverage.

Athena agreed, "Sure, Mom, anything you say."

CHAPTER 4

As Dorathy's plane came in for a landing, she thought about the two years she had spent living there as a kid—boy how it had grown over the years. The city lights seemed to blaze all the way to the horizon and beyond. Grabbing her bag, she stepped outside to get the rental car shuttle and was nearly thrown back from the blast of heat as the automatic doors opened. Even at almost eight o'clock at night it was still well over a hundred degrees. She thought of the old reply locals had for someone who would comment on the temperature: "Yes, but it's a dry heat." No, it's just too damn hot!

Happy to finally reach her hotel and her room, she thought a little something to eat would be great before heading to bed. For a moment she contemplated just getting comfortable and ordering room service, but she wanted to make this trip feel like a bit of a vacation, so she washed her face, fluffed her long hair and decided to go down to the restaurant bar for a bite and a cocktail.

As she entered the restaurant she asked if they were still serving and was pleased to find that they were. The place was an elegant Japanese restaurant with a half a dozen hibachi tables to the right of a large bar and a sushi bar towards the back. With it being late, the dinner crowd had thinned, so she decided to go back and see about getting a little sushi instead of a big meal. She sat down and ordered a Hawaiian and California roll and that was more than enough. She was enjoying her dinner and having a little small talk with the sushi chief while sipping some warm sake, when a tall, nice looking man politely asked if the seat next to her was taken.

Taken aback, she looked around her at all the empty seats and politely replied, as not to offend, "No, it's not, but . . . ," with a pause, continued gesturing at the vacant tables in the restaurant, "I don't believe any of those chairs are taken."

The man spat out, "Bitch!" and stalked off. Dorathy was infuriated, threw her napkin down on the counter and thought, how could a stranger make such a quick judgment call? "How dare he!" She found herself on her feet, scrambling to beat him to the door. She caught up to him and said firmly, "Listen to me, that was rude and uncalled for! You come up to woman who is on her own, late at night, who is obviously single," and with that she waved her left hand in front of his face wiggling her bare ring finger, "and what? You might get lucky on your trip away from home? Maybe, perhaps away from a wife and kids? Therefore, as I'm not stupid then you assume I'm a bitch! Really?"

"Now if you had just taken a seat a couple chairs down and joined in conversation with the chef and me, perhaps then you might have gotten somewhere, but not likely. Don't you know that intelligent conversation is more an aphrodisiac than some stupid pickup line?" With that she sauntered back to her dinner.

The man, a bit stunned, walked out of the restaurant and took the elevator up to his room, wondering how she knew he was married.

The old sushi chef had a huge grin on his face. "You like my wife, you one spicy girl . . . we marry long time." They shared a good laugh.

The following morning, she woke with excitement brewing in her gut. She thought, are these butterflies? She hadn't felt this excited about a project since working with the Elon Musk Foundation and those first days after graduation at Virgin Galactic. She decided to get an early start by ordering room service and jumping in the shower. Gathering her work pad and files that were already packed and ready to go, she was out of her room and in her rental car headed for Lifecor.

As expected, it was another scorcher of a day. She drove past

Camelback Mountain and recalled a hike with her dad up the winding trail through the desert. They had stayed up there to watch the sunset and came down in the dark, armed only with a single flashlight that had a faulty wire, so it flickered as they walked, throwing fantastic shadows that she and her father identified as mythical beasts. They shared stories about the beasts as they made their way home. Dorathy had fond memories of this place and had wanted very much to return over the years, but life just sort of happens sometimes.

She found Lifecor to be a non-descript southwestern style stucco building, but with a modern edge. From the outside being painted a dark grey, lacking any flash or flare, one would not be able to tell if it had been used for manufacturing purposes, storage units, or for what it was: cutting edge technology. She was left guessing if any or all the number of buildings that surrounded it were also part of Lifecor.

She found what seemed to be a front entrance and parked nearby under a shade tree. Grabbing her cardigan, assuming it would be much cooler inside, Dorathy smiled, after all they were storing human popsicles. She approached the front door and noticed the butterflies were back and felt giddy. When she opened the door there stood Alex Mason talking to a young woman who sat in front of several monitors. He straightened to his full height and broke out with a huge smile. Dr. Mason wore a close beard and had twinkling hazel eyes with medium brown hair cut into a short carefree casual look. He was dressed in a pair of lightweight, faded jeans and a simple white long-sleeved shirt, with the top buttons undone and his sleeves rolled up. He wasn't overly handsome, but certainly easy on the eyes. He had a rugged look and carried himself with a confidence that made him even more attractive. In his mid-fifties, his age was revealed by the lines around his eyes, but by his tanned skin and toned, muscular body one could tell that he was a man that looked after himself and enjoyed the out of doors.

Dorathy stepped in from the near blinding sun and took a moment for her eyes to adjust to the dim office lighting. In that moment, she caught her first glimpse of Alex Mason and thought, *oh my, this is going to be tricky*.

Alex came around from behind the desk and she was able to see him, all of him. Dorathy swiftly concluded that she needed to tread softly and keep things professional. She knew he was single from his personal file, but she had to wonder why. Why indeed, had this handsome, intelligent and well-to-do man not been snatched up already left her mystified.

With that thought tucked neatly away, Dorathy extended her hand as Alex came up and held out his. He looked deeply into her eyes as they touched and Dorathy felt in that split second that he knew her deepest thoughts—that there was nothing she could keep secret from him, no part of her was hers and hers alone. He was going to know her every emotion without her ever saying a word. She gazed down at his hand holding hers and then looked up and held her breath, afraid that if she were to speak a single word, she would express her longing for a one true love. Dorathy said, "It's a pleasure to finally meet you."

Alex replied, in a quiet voice that conveyed much more than the spoken words, "The pleasure truly is mine." For a moment that seemed to last a millennium, they stood frozen in time. Alex then took a step back and got down to business to ensure his own emotional self-preservation. "Would you like a tour of what we do around here?"

Dorathy blinked and with a whispered tone said, "Absolutely."

Alex turned towards the desk and gestured, "First let me introduce you to our IT guru, Lori. There is nothing she can't answer or fix concerning our growing presence on the web."

Dorathy held out her hand and Lori graciously took it, but Lori knew what she had just witnessed moments before and had to try to hide a big smile. That hidden smile communicated approval, for she knew Alex quite well and had always felt the poor man was lonely and spent far too much time with the dead or dying, and that he deserved a life filled with love.

"It's great to meet you Dorathy, I've heard a lot about you. So, you're going to get our patients up into space. I think that's an awesome approach to offering people a secondary option." Lori went on to say, "Most people are trying to cheat death when others are really only looking for a sense of immortality. You know what I mean?"

"Yes, I do." Dorathy went on to say, "There is such finality when we die and are either buried or cremated. If one is preserved and frozen . . . metaphorically, frozen for all time, it gives one a sense of absolution."

Lori nodded her head in agreement. "Space, truly is the final frontier."

"Yes, it is, and it seems that the frontier is coming closer all the time."

Alex appeared spellbound by Dorathy. *She got it*, he thought. *She gets it. Finally, a woman that gets what I'm trying to do.*

Alex was over the moon. "If you like, we can get your things over to my office and I'll take you for the grand tour."

"Sure, that sounds great!" Dorathy was truly excited about this project and even more so now, for so many reasons. Lori, with a twinkle in her eye, looked at Alex and Dorathy and said with heartfelt warmth, "Enjoy the tour, and should I have lunch brought in today for you both?"

Alex said, "You know what, let's do that, but maybe order pizza for the whole staff. I really would like everyone involved with what we are trying to do here." He asked Dorathy if that sounded good to her and thought that he wanted to show the world how happy he was to have this beautiful creature next to him working together on his dream. He felt together they could conquer anything.

They stepped around Lori's desk and accessed the research offices of the building through the door behind it. Alex held the door open for Dorathy and said, "Ladies first." She looked up at him and smiled, for to be this close to him gave her goose bumps. Try as she might, she wasn't sure she could mask how utterly undone she felt in his presence.

As Dorathy turned her back to pass through the doorway, Lori gave Alex a knowing gaze and winked to signal her approval. Lori, in her early thirties, was the daughter of one of Alex's close friends, so Lori was very protective of him She was always giving him thumbs up or down when he started to see someone new. Knowing Dorathy's background and finally meeting her, it was an overwhelming thumbs up. Somewhere in the back of her mind she was already planning a wedding. Another hopeless romantic.

They entered the brightly lit room, a viewing area, and Dorathy felt a chill. Not due as much to the temperature, but to the rows of stainless steel, cylindrical coffin-like canisters that lined the walls and were stacked in round groupings that filled the entire space beyond.

Alex approached an electronic keypad and punched in a security code. "This facility has been built with reinforced concrete and lined with Kevlar, with the viewing glass being bulletproof."

Dorathy looked stunned and asked in disbelief "Why the stringent measures?"

Alex nodded his head in acknowledgment of her question. "There are many people in this world that consider what we are doing unethical from a religious standpoint and would like to stop us by any means."

Dorathy raised her brow and thought a moment about the implications. "Why would anyone really care--these people are gone . . . dead, for the time being and their souls have transcended to a place far beyond or perhaps very close? One could say the verdict is still out."

Alex agreed and offered an explanation. "Some believe that when a person has been pronounced dead the brain lives on. We immediately intervene by rapidly chilling the body and putting the person in a *suspended animation*. Depending on what you choose to believe, the brain houses everything that makes us who we are, therefore some patients have chosen only to have their heads frozen. Keeping the brain from damage and thus putting the person in this suspended animation until we are able to reanimate at a later date and have the means of creating a new body for them."

Dorathy already knew about this alternative, but thought it to be somewhat of a gruesome procedure and said, "Oh I think I'll just hold on to my body for the time being, unless, of course, I die at a hundred and twenty. Then I might reconsider." Dorathy pressed, "What of the spiritual side of things? Some believe that upon death the soul leaves the body for another type of reality that some would call heaven."

Alex opened the heavy door, allowing Dorathy to enter while saying, "Yes, the spiritual side of things. That is precisely why we have to take these measures to secure their safety."

Scanning this cavernous space, she found herself thinking of all the souls that lay frozen in time in this form of stasis; their lives cut short and loved ones waiting to see if technology had a chance to catch up while their own lives moved forward. She thought for a moment, *how can there be closure for the ones left behind*? Just then Alex put his hand on her back and said, "I know exactly what you're thinking Dora. May I call you Dora?"

There were too many emotions running through her to single any one of them out. She turned and looked up at him and said, "Yes, Dora is fine. My friends call me that."

Alex smiled and said, "This whole thing is wild, isn't it? Death can be so final, yet here we are amongst the dead searching for a chance at immortality, while everyone outside these walls scurries about their daily routines. And for the families wondering if there will ever be a time when a new discovery has been made and they will pick up the phone to hear, "Yes, I think we have it, we can proceed to reviving." The hope . . . hope being the one emotion in all of us that is even stronger than fear, hope can be a paralyzing emotion.

Dorathy whispered, "Yes, that is so true. They wait in here. And out there, is hope. I think sending them into deep space is the better option, I would want that for myself. Tell me Alex, how many people are here, frozen?"

He said somberly, "Nine hundred seventeen souls and counting." Dorathy looked around. The space was big but not that big.

Alex added, "We have three other buildings, plus the underground unit, for the *older models*."

Dorathy was slightly bewildered in the tone Alex had used. "Older models." she asked. "How old and how many?"

"Well," he said, "in the *basement*, and I use that term rather loosely, we have a hundred and thirty-seven, older model capsules and a dozen rather . . . ," he hesitated for a second, "much older, less advanced models where the individuals have been frozen using a far less reliable method of freezing."

Dorathy was now pressin. "How old?"

Alex replied with a heavy sigh, "For the most part, of the hundred thirty-seven there are quite a few that are at least a couple of decades old, and the others are well over a half a century old. We ended up with the old cryocapsules as other companies failed due to poor fiscal management, or obviously ran out of time. Because of that, we receive financial assistance from the federal government. The fact is that no one knew what to do with the old models when companies folded for one reason or another. So, they end up here and every now and again someone uncovers another storage unit somewhere, which had been left unattended for God knows how long, and we get the call. Most of that technology is now obsolete and the persons within are most likely never going to be revived."

Dorathy was stunned by this information. "What you're telling me is that many of these people had been forgotten over the generations. Families simply forgot they ever existed or were unable to pay for their continuing care. So, they have no hope of ever being revived due to old technology and the fact that you know almost nothing of what happened to the person frozen within?"

Alex nodded. "Yes, but never is a long time coming. Maybe, God only knows, just maybe. Who's to say what humanity can do in the future? I guess you can say nothing is impossible and nothing is absolute. So, they wait . . . and we hope."

Dorathy felt sad, but she had to know the truth. "Tell me, I know you have been fine-tuning your technology. Have you been able to revive any of your patients, and if so, how was that accomplished?"

"Let us walk, because that question requires much discussion. But first, let me take you to the basement so you might get a better grasp."

As they walked past dozens upon dozens of cylinders, every now and again a release of cold gas would puff a delicate waft of icy fog from the side of a cylinder. It was an eerie feeling knowing someone was inside frozen to a solid mass. Dorathy could almost sense the presence of spirits lingering, waiting through the years, passing from this reality to the next, back and forth . . . waiting.

At the end of the building they reached the door to an industrial size elevator. Alex gazed at Dorathy and thought, "How beautiful she is." He wanted so much to put his arm around her, to hold her close, to say, "I'm here for you and I will comfort you if you want that of me."

Dorathy caught his glance and said, "I'm fine, really. After all, it is fascinating what you have done here."

Alex smiled, "Dora, always a true scientist."

"Well yes, I guess I am. Curious minds need to know."

The elevator arrived, the door slid open and they entered together. With a bit of a grind, the doors shut and with a clunk they began a slow descent. Bouncing to a stop, the doors opened into a pitch-dark room with only the interior light of the elevator to guide them out. A motion detector sensed when they stepped out and the lights flickered on. The room was approximately 140 square meters with concrete walls and an open ceiling that had exposed air ducts and pipes with visible electrical wires. A cold haze lent the space a sense of eeriness. A shiver ran up Dorathy's spine with the reality of death, a long time waiting, staring her in the face.

Here lay a room of people frozen using old technology, with the dozen or so frozen bodies from decades past. Dorathy scanned the room, noting the technology was very different from the capsules they had walked by moments before. These looked forgotten and antiquated, as if they were props from an old science fiction television show. "Tell me Alex, what are the major differences between these and the others upstairs?"

"Actually, Dora, there's not a lot of difference in the hardware. It's the way they were frozen, not so much the way they are kept frozen. The medical technology we use to prepare our patients is far more advanced now."

Alex surveyed the room with a confident stance, his hands clasped behind his back. He went on to say, with not much emotion, as he was a doctor of medicine and the human body was his field of expertise, "When a person signs up for this procedure, the time comes for us to intervene depending on current laws within each state. Say here in Arizona the procedure can be scheduled ahead of time. Just as a cesarean can be scheduled for a birth, this procedure can be set for one's planned date of death. Other states are different, where our team must wait on standby for one to be declared clinically dead for us to intervene.

"Dorathy said, "You mean to tell me that if a person knows they are dying and decides they no longer want to suffer from what is killing them, they can schedule a date and what? You . . . kill them?"

"Well, Dora, you know it is a tough decision for families to make. But if their loved ones are in a lot of pain and there is no quality of life left, sometimes it's far easier to make that decision. Besides, doing it that way makes the person more viable for retrieval and the success rate goes up exponentially."

"What is the procedure, exactly?" Dorathy asked, scientist to scientist.

"In a nutshell, at the time of clinical death our team anesthetizes the individual and begins by manually pumping the heart and lungs, while starting to cool the body down rapidly to stop the body's metabolism and rate of decomposition. We then remove as much of the fluid from the body as we can; this includes all the intra- and extra- cellular fluids as well as blood, urine and other bodily fluids. We then inject into the body a cryoprotective fluid--a type of medical grade anti-freeze and with it a vitrification agent." At that, Dorathy's eyes grew wide. Alex saw her expression. "Yes, because if we don't, when the body reaches its maximum low temperature of negative 320 degrees, it is at that point a solid mass and therefore may fracture. Also, the formation of ice that otherwise would have formed is damaging to the cells." Dorathy understood but didn't like the thought of it. Alex went on to say, "We inject sixteen types of preservation fluids into the body to protect it from further damage to the cells and to prevent any effects from decomposition."

Dorathy was amazed at this technology and would be further impressed if someone had survived the freezing process, as she was familiar with the studies of his initial research. "Okay, so tell me, does it work? Have you restored someone's life by reviving and medically treating a patient?"

Alex bluntly said, "Yes, seven people are walking, breathing proof it works."

Dorathy was a bit skeptical of the way he just answered her question. She said, "There is more to this story that you're not telling me."

Alex nodded. "Yes, there is, Dora, but that is a far lengthier conversation to be had, as it addresses the spiritual side of life and death."

Dorathy knew when to leave certain subjects alone, and this was one of those times, so she nodded and said, "I understand, and I have to admit I am very curious. I am also open-minded and whatever it is that needs to be said, it will not sway me one way or another with this project."

"I'm very happy to hear that," Alex said.

Dorathy walked up to one of the old relics and wiped the dust from what appeared to be an engraved plaque, its surface cold to the touch. She read it out loud, "John Smith, born 11/23/1959, died of colon cancer 02/04/1999 . . . this person died sixty-three years ago."

Dorathy looked up, her eyes sad. "Overall that isn't that long ago, but when one looks at the incredible advances in technology that with each passing year seem to leap forward exponentially . . . if this person were to be revived, he would be so out of place, so far removed from this reality, our world would be foreign to him."

"Exactly, Dora," Alex exclaimed. "This explains why some people are turned off to cryogenics while others embrace it. Some people are hopeful that they would not stay dead for too long, while others fear that when they are revived the lives of their loved ones have moved forward without them, or so much time has passed everyone they ever knew will have long been dead and gone."

Dorathy turned to face him. "I think, at least for myself, I would prefer to feel somewhat immortal by simply being frozen in time and sent off into space as a gesture of one last adventure into the unknown, a journey that would last forever. I have to say that is exactly what I would want for myself." With a smile on her face to lighten the mood, she said with enthusiasm, "Where do I sign?"

Alex said, "My first customer," and they both laughed. He smiled, "Let's finish the tour."

Dorathy brushed her hands together to get the dust off and studied John Smith's capsule. She thought, "What kind of world will he be a part of, if technology ever were to catch up to him?"

They entered the elevator and Dorathy's eyes remained fixed on John Smith's capsule as the door shut. Time, she thought, makes our daily routine and the lives we lead seem so insignificant, for time is relentless and marches forward no matter how we strive to slow it down. How incredibly small we all are when compared to time.

Alex noted the somber expression on her face and knew what she must be thinking. "Time sometimes stretches into a long wait." As the elevator clanked into motion, Dorathy sighed in agreement.

They exited the elevator and Alex looked down at his watch. "How about some pizza with the staff before I take you to our prep room?"

"Prep room?" Dorathy thought about the grizzly procedures inflicted on a newly dead person and then said, "I think we should definitely eat first." Being an engineer, Dorathy did not have much of a stomach for medical applications. She said, "I hate needles." Alex laughed the hearty laugh she had heard once before over the phone. As they walked back past the way they had come, Dorathy asked, "Is there a lot of maintenance to be done to keep the canisters in top operating condition?"

Alex shook his head, "Not really. We have a few people that do regular inspections just to make sure there isn't a major leak in any of them. We use liquid nitrogen in a vacuum to keep an accurate temperature within the canisters. The wisps of cold fog escaping from the gaskets means the pressure is normalizing."

They continued to walk past the door they originally entered and accessed the offices via a door toward the back of the facility. Alex held the door for Dorathy, and she moved past him a bit closer this time. She was walking in front of him and he dared a glance at her figure. He thought she was exquisite and thought to himself, *I don't want to make any mistakes with her, she is a dream come true.*

He caught up to her as she turned and said, "Hope Lori ordered enough pizza, because I'm starving."

"Ah, a woman with a healthy appetite, I like that, none of that picking."

"Oh, yes," she said, "I can eat most people under the table, and I love to cook."

"Good," he said, "because I love to eat as well, and I'm not a bad cook either."

They said, almost in unison, "You can clean up." They both laughed.

At the end of the hall was a large break room with a full kitchen and one large round table that appeared to double as a meeting table as well. As they entered, Dorathy noticed Lori, several men that looked to be part of the maintenance staff and a couple of guys who could be part of the medical staff. Everyone had already served themselves from the pizza boxes set in the middle of the table, but there was still plenty left. Alex offered Dorathy a chair and introduced her to his staff. After introductions had been made and everyone engaged in small talk, one of the men, whose name was Dennis, felt comfortable enough with Dorathy to broach a certain subject.

Dennis, with a bit of gusto, said, "So Dorathy, how do you like all our human popsicles?"

Dorathy almost snorted her soda out of her nose. "Oh, my God," she said, "you obviously have been talking to either Jack or Hugo! I never thought when I used that phrase ever so loosely a year ago, and keep in mind it was taken completely out of context, it was going to come back and bite me in the ass, as it seems it has."

Everyone laughed and Dennis said, "It is, after all, a very common approach to what we do here."

"Well," she went on to say in her defense, "it was never said out of disrespect."

Alex loved the way she interacted with everyone; she was personable and genuine. She possessed everything he ever wanted in a woman. He thought how lucky he would be if she returned his affection. He vowed to not rush it, to let things unfold. Over the years he had become so lonely and wanted so much to feel love; that one special love that only happens once in a lifetime. He prayed that she was the one.

After lunch, as promised, they went with Stuart and Mark, the doctors on staff, to the prep room. The room could have been any surgical suite at any modern hospital. The equipment was of the highest caliber. Dorathy was impressed with both the area and the staff, who would work together to perform the procedure of freezing an individual. "Well done," she said. "I'm overwhelmed by the care taken to ensure that your patients and their families have the best you can offer."

The remainder of the week went well. She learned all she could of the operational needs of the canisters so she could design a suitable means of transporting them into deep space. She and Alex worked well together; they could almost read each other's mind and came to a point where they started to finish each other's sentences. They laughed about it. Dorathy, being the jokester, kept Alex in stitches and so often his gut hurt from laughing. He felt he was falling in love with her and, as determined as she might be to keep her feelings under wraps, he sensed she had the same feelings for him.

At the end of the day on Friday Alex inquired if she had plans for dinner. He wanted to take her downtown to the revolving restaurant at the top of one of the old buildings. Alex said he was ready to discuss the seven people who had been revived. Dorathy had known not to press him for that information and that he would get around to telling her at some point during the week. So, she agreed. "Dinner would be great. Sounds like a nice place, let me go back to the hotel to freshen up. Will you pick me up?"

"Of course," he said. "Say, seven o'clock?"

"That's perfect. Gives me time to unwind, maybe take a bubble bath." He loved her smiles.

On her way out of the building she said her goodbyes to all her new friends at Lifecor. Everyone knew she would return. Their attraction to eachother was obvious.

Alex walked Dorathy out to the car and opened her car door for her. I'll see you in the lobby at seven, then."

Dorothy smiled. "I can't wait," and waved as she drove away. Her heart was pounding because she wanted so badly to grab his face to give him a long passionate kiss. But she had to refrain from doing such a thing. She must maintain some professionalism, but said under her breath, "Screw professionalism! God, he's amazing."

When she got back to her hotel room, she decided to raid the courtesy fridge for a couple of little bottles of red wine to lend her a little help relaxing. Dorothy was thinking about the incredible week she just had while she ran the water, filling the tub with froth. As she sank down into the tub the fragrance of the steaming water soothed her nerves. She had to hand it to Lucy, this place was grand. It had great amenities and the room was spacious and luxurious. The bathroom was huge with Italian marble tiles surrounding a huge Jacuzzi tub. She poured her wine and lifted her glass to toast herself. "Thank you, Lucy, you are the best." She sank into the water and let her mind wander. Thoughts about Alex of course, and whether they would become an item in time. She thought about taking him to her private island beach house in the South Pacific. She attempted to stop this train of thought, but she was fighting a losing battle. "God, he's gorgeous," she said as she sank her head under the bubbles.

After a nice, somewhat relaxing bath, she got ready for her date, the first for quite some time. As usual, she came prepared and had packed a very simple but elegant little black dress and a pair of black high-heeled

sandals. She was a bundle of nerves and could hardly contain her gid-
diness. It had been years since she had been out with a man, and even
longer since she'd been with a man. With that thought she felt as if she
might just explode from anticipation.

Alex was perfect in every way: successful, intelligent, kind, gentle,
great sense of humor . . . Oh my God, the accent! Great dresser, tall,
ruggedly handsome . . . She said to herself, "I guess good things come to
those who wait, and I have waited a long damn time for a man like him.

Preparing to leave the room, she checked her watch and looked
through her little black satin bag to make sure she had everything she
needed: lipstick, powder, room key, phone, credit card, ID, pain reliever . . . "Damn," she said, "where the hell did I put that bottle? Shit!
I feel another headache coming on." She searched her large case and
found it, quickly popped two in her mouth and swallowed, putting the
small bottle in her evening bag. She did a quick scan of the room, left a
light on, and headed down to the lobby. She exited the elevator, stopping
to check herself in the mirror on the opposite wall and thought *not bad
for an old gal.*

Dorathy was entering the lobby as Alex came through the glass doors
of the main entrance. They caught each other's eye at the same moment.
He had on a pair of black slacks with stylish shoes and a nicely fitted
long-sleeved, steel grey shirt, left untucked with the top buttons undone.
The mere sight of him left her breathless. They had just spent the whole
week in grubby clothes and coveralls and now here they were looking
their best.

Alex tried not stare at Dorathy but couldn't help himself; she was simply stunning, and he noticed every head in the room turn as she walked
by. She was of course oblivious to the attention being paid.

Alex leaned in for a kiss on the cheek and offered his arm. "Shall we?
Madame's chariot awaits." He felt the envy of every man in the lobby and
was walking proudly with this beautiful creature on his arm. He opened
the heavy glass door for her and once again offered his arm to lead her
through the parking lot. Alex had made sure to park his car close to the
entrance as he knew women with high heels could only walk so far on
uneven surfaces.

They approached his black sport coupe. He couldn't look away from her. "You look absolutely gorgeous this evening and I am a very lucky man."

She graciously replied, "Well thank you, kind sir. You don't look half bad yourself and, I might add, you smell scrumptious."

Alex laughed, and said, "Yes, I clean up pretty good."

Dorathy said, "I guess we both do . . . just a bit of a contrast to the way we have been looking while working on the concrete floor this past week."

Alex opened the passenger side door and handed her into the seat, noticing long toned legs as her dress fell open to her thigh. He shut the door and couldn't help himself thinking how much he would love to run his hand up her leg, but he respected Dorathy more than any other woman he had met in his life. He thought, *there will be time for that, hopefully, in time." And then, optimistically, "Hopefully, sooner than later.*

They drove past Camelback Mountain and Dorathy told him about her days spent here as a kid and how much she enjoyed living there. She refrained from telling him about the struggles in her childhood. As they came into downtown Phoenix, she admired all the lights that decorated the trees and cactus, and told him how her dad used to take her to the baseball games when he was not working--but her voice trailed off as she recalled that her father was only really around during holidays and sometimes not even then.

Alex could hear her sadness in her voice and said, "You miss him."

With a heavy sigh, she said, "Yes I do, every day." He reached over and squeezed her hand. He glanced over with a sympathetic smile and said, "I know, I miss my family too. It's hard to be an orphan, at any age."

For the next few moments they drove in silence, and Dorathy took in the sights that were somewhat familiar to her. So many things had changed, but for the most part it had remained the same.

Alex said, pointing out the window, "Look at the architecture of the new addition to the Arizona Science Museum. It's amazing how it looks as if it's going to fall over in a stiff breeze."

Pulling into their destination, Alex drove up to valet parking. While he was getting his ticket from the attendant, Dorathy was stepping out of the car with the help of another attendant. The young man was eager to be of assistance, offering his hand. Alex took over immediately and offered his arm. Stepping through the doors he commented on how he loved the wine selection here and hoped she would do the honors of selecting a bottle, as he knew she was quite familiar with good California wines.

They reached the top floor and the elevator doors slid open directly into the restaurant. The hostesses checked their reservation and, as requested, they were seated at a small, private table by the window. The restaurant was quiet tonight as all the tourists had left for cooler climates for the summer. Alex, always the gentleman, pulled the chair out for Dorathy as she sat.

It was a lovely evening, the lights of the city sprawling out to the horizon. During dinner Alex talked about his childhood growing up near Sydney, Australia. His parents owned a boat and they would go out almost every New Year's Eve to watch the fireworks over Sydney Harbor. He talked about his little sister always trying to push him overboard and how when she succeeded one night his father had to jump in after him. They laughed and cried as they shared their life stories. Such fond memories and such tragedies in both their lives. Alex's sister died at a young age, killed by a drunk driver, his mother died of cancer and his father had passed away only two years ago of old age. Alex had never been married. He said, "I guess I'm just waiting for the right woman to come along, but I do regret never having kids. All the same though, sometimes I just feel I'm very happy I didn't."

Dorathy told him all about Athena and her ex-husband and how it had been a mistake to have married him. "But," she said, "I had this notion that Athena needed a full-time father around. I suppose that came from mine not being around much while I was growing up. Well, you can't change the past and you certainly can't allow it to dictate your future."

During a lull in their conversation, Alex took Dorathy's hand across the table, looked into her beautiful dark eyes and asked, "Do you believe in God?"

Dorathy blinked and pondered the question for a moment. She wasn't turned off by the subject in the least but was curious where this topic might lead. She hesitated for a moment, so she might choose her words accurately. She said in a gentle voice, "I believe in an afterlife. I believe in a Creator of all things. Do I believe in the Pearly Gates with angels and an old white bearded man—not so much. I think," she went on to say, "when you look out into the universe and down upon our Earth from space you see clearly the proof of a higher power. My wish is that everyone would get the opportunity to witness and sit in awe at the beauty and the power of such a sight."

Alex smiled and said, "So what if I said I had my own proof?"

Dorathy was intrigued. "I would say I would be very open to you sharing it with me."

Alex straightened in his seat. He looked around the room and said, "I know you have been waiting to hear about the seven people we have been able to revive."

"Yes," Dorathy said, "I figured this was where the conversation was going. Please continue."

He took a quick breath and exhaled. "Okay, where do I start? The first person, a man of sixty-two died of heart disease and he lay frozen for seventeen years. As you know, with the advancements in bioprinting, a new heart could be formed. After the long process of defrosting, and I say that instead of the word we more commonly use, 'reviving,' we kept him on life support while we used his stem cells to form a new heart. He now suffers from some of the obvious side effects like memory loss, depression, lack of certain motor skills, and so forth-- all of which will become better over time. But the thing that seems to have the greatest impact on him is the ability to recall his time away, as if he had spent his time in another place or dimension. It's amazing really; to remember every detail of his time spent on the other side. It seems that this alternate reality is just as real as this world, and when I say world, I mean as if the other side was an actual place, not a state of being."

Dorathy was truly astonished by the information Alex had just shared and was left almost speechless. It took a while to sink in and she finally asked, "What about the other six people, have they also suffered the same effects? If so, is there a part of the brain that has suffered damage? But

I'm sure every type of test and scan must have been made to ensure the patient's life was never in jeopardy."

Alex replied, "Yes of course, absolutely. Every one of the patients had undergone a thorough exam, and all seven suffered the same aftereffects . . . I don't want to use the word delusion, but it's amazing that every one of them report the exact same thing. And no one has been able to explain it away. It is only reasonable that we assume that what they are reporting is factual."

Dorathy leaned her head into her hand. "That is astounding information, it simply cannot be ignored. All through history we have heard of near-death experiences, but this sounds completely different. What you are telling me sounds much more detailed than a tunnel of light and floating over your body. This sounds more like some type of transcendence."

Alex nodded excitedly and said, "Yes, and there is more to it. What they are describing sounds like they can travel through space-time, as if they are operating at a different level."

Dorathy slammed her hand against the tabletop in a moment of excitement and laughter. "Yes," she exclaimed. "Physicists, the grumpy bunch that we are, have been arguing over dark matter, wormholes and theorizing about bending space-time for two centuries!" Dorathy went on, "All matter operates at different frequencies or vibrations. When thinking in terms of Quantum Field Theory, the fundamental particles making up matter are treated as wave-like excitations of a quantum field. So perhaps the medium that they are traveling through is the quantum field. I would say that somehow they have acquired the frequency to travel through dimensions."

Alex said, "But one would have to assume that they had traveled from our reality to a different reality. Their bodies lay frozen for decades, but the spirit had traveled on to the next level, another dimension--heaven, the spirit world, whatever you want to call it; they seem to have gone there. So, you're saying, Dora, they have picked up and maintained a frequency that gives them the ability to travel back and forth, but only by the mind or spirit."

Alex thought more about his newly revived patients and continued, "I think this may be the reason three of the seven have committed suicide, stating in notes or messages that they prefer not to be bound by the limitations of this state of being. Furthermore, what they describe as the other state of being is not *spiritual* in nature but solid, an actual place, another planet, perhaps in another dimension."

Dorathy said, tilting her head to the side, "But you can't prove it, can you?"

"No, we can't."

Dorathy leaned back in her chair and shook her head. "Well I, for one, believe what you're telling me." Then she said, "You sure know how to show a girl a good time."

Alex looked around the restaurant and then down at his watch. "I think we closed the place down."

"I'd say so." Dorathy looked around. "It's usually a good indication it's time to go when they start vacuuming the floors." Alex laughed in agreement and called for the check.

On the drive back to the hotel Alex asked Dorathy if she had made any firm plans for the weekend since she was scheduled to stay until Sunday. "Well," she said, "I thought about going up to Sedona for a little hiking, would you like to join me?" She couldn't bear the thought of not seeing him again tomorrow.

Alex replied with a very enthusiastic, "Yes." If she hadn't asked him to join her, he would have been deeply wounded.

They drove into the parking lot. Alex turned the ignition off and came around the car to open her door. Unsure where this was going to lead, she felt that she dare not ask him up, nor should she linger in the parking lot. Extending his arm to her, Alex said, "I'll walk you to the lobby, have to make sure I deliver you safe and sound."

Due to the lateness of the hour, the lobby was deserted. Dorathy said, "Thank you for a great and very enlightening evening. I thoroughly enjoyed our conversation."

"So did I. Dora, you are an incredible woman."

Dorathy wanted so much to tell him that she was falling for him, but said instead, "Would you like to leave tomorrow, say 8:00 a.m.?"

"Sure, sounds great, I can drive if you'd like." She was happy about that as Phoenix traffic was even worse than LA traffic.

Alex leaned in and hesitated for a moment but could not resist and stole a soft tender kiss, which she returned. They both wanted more but were compelled to refrain from taking it too far too quickly. Alex then caught her hand and kissed it, as well, before departing. Dorathy entered the elevator and as the door slid shut, she danced a little jig of happiness.

Dorathy had a restless night filled with thoughts of Alex: that he seemed to be the perfect man for her and where their relationship would lead. Dorathy had been alone for so long she became worried that somehow, she would not allow him into her world, that she would resist change to her lifestyle. On the other hand, she was desperately lonely and longed for true intimacy with that special person who would be her life partner. She suddenly felt sorrow that all her life had been spent with emptiness in her heart that only a man could fill. She hated to admit to herself that she needed a man, but there was no denying her longing to be loved, to be truly loved for all the good, and the bad.

Tossing and turning she thought about the people that had been revived, how they must adjust to this new world they had returned to and how horribly alone they must feel. And what Alex had said about their ability to somehow travel from this reality to the next. She was trying desperately to wrap her head around it. Just then a theory dawned on her. She switched on the night-stand light and wrote a few notes to share with him. She said, "Could it really be that simple?" She reached over and tuned out the light. "I have got to get some sleep."

CHAPTER 5

She woke after just a few hours, a bit groggy. A quick shower, then she dressed, packed the things she needed for the day, and went downstairs for a bite to eat. Alex would arrive shortly, and she began to get excite; the mere thought of him started her blood pumping. She thought about their kiss last night, so soft, so sweet, and became weak in the knees. Dorathy wanted that passion in her life and wanted it to last the rest of her life. Her thoughts were clouded by excitement, but she had to ask herself, could Alex be that man, that one person that she longed for?

It was just about eight o'clock as she paid her bill and headed into the lobby, where she caught sight of Alex sitting on one of the sofas. He saw her right away and stood. He was wearing khaki cargo shorts and a simple fitted blue T-shirt with hiking shoes. She felt as if she was walking on a cloud and ran towards him. He grabbed her and hugged her close, looked down into eyes while brushing her bangs to the side. "Are you ready my love?"

She smiled widely and said, "I am ready for whatever you have in store for us."

Alex kept his arm around her waist and said, "Okay, let's go on an adventure."

They left the building arm in arm. Alex said, "I went to the liberty of packing everything we need for a sunset dinner. I thought we might stop at this little place on the creek for a light lunch before we head out for our hike."

Dorathy was familiar with Sedona and knew the place well. "Oh, I love that restaurant, they have the best roasted salmon in a puff pastry."

Alex laughed. "I love your appetite."

For the next two hours in the car they talked about their hopes and dreams for the future, as the past was irrelevant. They spoke about life on this planet and how everything was changing so rapidly. Dorathy said, "I sometimes have a hard time keeping up with technology. Seems as if as soon as I have grown accustomed to a new engineering idea, something else comes along and I must learn it all over again. It can be very frustrating at times."

Alex agreed with what she was saying and added, "Medical technology is ever changing and is moving forward in leaps and bounds, but the brain I have to say, although many discoveries have been made, is still one of those things where cracking its mysteries is still a long way away. Brain injuries are still usually very hard to reverse and difficult to treat."

Dorathy just remembered what she had written down on that note pad in the middle of the night. "Oh, Alex," she exclaimed, almost jumping out of her seat, "I have a theory for you. It came to me last night while I was desperately trying to sleep. Okay, you said that these individuals can go back and forth between this reality and the other—perhaps it's like looking through a veil. Say, for a moment, that because they had spent so much time on the other side, they were able to adapt and somehow maintain a frequency from that side.

Alex asked, "Tell me again about frequencies."

Dorathy continued, "All matter vibrates at a specific frequency. As an example, you know the door that separates the storage area and the offices at the back of your building?"

Alex followed along. "Yes, go on."

"Say it's a locked screen door, you can see through it, but you can't walk through it.

Alex shook his head and said, "You lost me."

Dorathy went on, "There is quantum teleportation, which is like transmitting the state of an atom or proton from point A to point B. What if the screen is all that separates the realities, like a thin veil or a 'Brane' and our spirits can travel through It, like we use the internet to send information? It's limited to information, not matter, but suppose that somehow there were a way.

Alex thought for a moment about what she was saying. "What about ghosts? People have been seeing spirits all through history."

Dorathy answered, "Maybe for that same reason some of us have the ability to see through the screen. I suppose that's why psychics can make a good living at connecting with the dead. Now for a real mind bender," she said, "try this on for size. You said that these people were describing the other side as an actual place. I think that could be quite possible. It could be another dimension, maybe a planet in another dimension or a whole other universe." Now Dorathy was becoming really animated. "Say you were standing in the storage area and I'm in the office, and in order to get to me without dying you merely have to go out the door leading to the main entrance, go out to the parking lot, go around the back of the building and enter the office from the back parking lot, walk down the hall and there you are, standing beside me. Like a back door to heaven," she said enthusiastically.

Alex was contemplating her theory. "So, you think there is a way to go to this place without having to die first? Interesting concept, I like it! I must wonder if humans can evolve to where we can leave the planet in search of the answers to where this alternate reality might exist. I suppose all we would need is the technology to travel there once we were able to figure out the coordinates." Alex looked over at her. "I really do love the way your mind works."

Dorathy loved how easy it was to talk to Alex. How she longed to have someone to communicate her every thought to, her every emotion, to have someone who listened and was genuinely interested in what she had to say. And for that to also be someone she was equally interested in. Alex seemed too good to be true, or was that just self- doubt creeping in to steal away her joy, to gnaw at her right to happiness?

They approached the restaurant and Alex reached over and held her hand as they walked through the parking lot. Dorathy felt like a teenage girl with a new boyfriend. It was a beautiful day with a light, warm breeze, birds chirping and the sound of a calm babbling creek just beyond the trees. A light fragrance of pine wafted toward them on the breeze. Memories of this place came rushing back to her. She and her ex-husband had come here for the day before Athena was born. She wondered for a moment where they had gone wrong, but quickly dismissed those thoughts. She was making new memories for herself with the incredible man standing beside her.

She noticed Alex looking at her and he said, "For a second there you looked a thousand miles away."

She shook her head. "I'm just so happy to be here with you and I want to hold on to this moment for a lifetime."

Alex smiled and kissed her on the forehead. "If you want, we can make a lifetime of memories together."

Although Dorathy was not quite sure how to respond to his offer, she knew in her heart that he was the one, even after their short time together. He had to be the one, but she had to be logical and time would tell of course. Time was something she had, so she thought. She had to take it slow to make sure it was right. She looked up at Alex. "Yes, I would like that very much."

Alex clutched her hand firmly, as he felt the same way. Just then the hostess came up and showed them to their table. It was the slow season in Arizona so there was hardly a soul around. They were seated at a wonderful spot right next to the creek. They enjoyed the scenery and each other while they ate a magnificent lunch and shared a great bottle of wine.

Out of the blue, Alex asked, "Have you ever been to a psychic?"

"Yes, I have a couple of times. One time in the middle of nowhere I saw a shaman at a little place outside of Calgary."

"You know Sedona is known for its mystical powers and its vortices. So, if you wanted to go for a quick reading before we head out I would be open to that. I know a little place right across the street."

Dorathy said, "You know what, that actually sounds real fun. A little guidance might come in handy right about now." She smiled at Alex.

He said with a bit of sudden panic, "Hopefully she doesn't tell you to dump me on the spot."

Dorathy laughed. "It would take a hell of a lot for me to do that to you—you would have to be very naughty for that to happen."

Alex retorted, with a bit of a twinkle in his eye, "I will try to behave and refrain from being naughty . . . at least for the time being."

Dorathy caught what he had just proposed and laughed loudly. "Baby, you can be naughty all you want . . . oh, oops, did I just say that out loud?" She was giggling. "I think the wine has gotten a hold of my inner voice!"

Alex let out a roar of laughter and said, "God, I love you, girl!"

Dorathy heard the words and they didn't frighten her. She felt relieved that he was obviously feeling the same way as she was feeling about him. The thought of letting go and letting it happen was taunting her; love is right here in front of you, so take it. She knew if she were to feel it for the first time in her life, it would be for eternity. For it was a love she had never known, and she was tasting it now. As the words floated across the breeze, they echoed in her soul and landed in her heart. She was hanging by her fingertips and below waited the endless love ready for her to fall into. Closing her eyes for a moment she took a leap of faith and let herself go.

After lunch they walked across the street hand in hand; she was floating on a cloud. They walked through the door of the building that had a huge sign hanging outside, *Psychic Readings and Reiki Healing*. The storefront was filled with healing crystals and rocks, incense and oils, and books about the vortex, ancient alien theory and abductions. The walls were covered with old science fiction movie posters and the wall shelves were filled with props. The young woman behind the counter had multiple body and facial piercings, several colorful tattoos and wore her hair in hot pink and purple dreadlocks. She looked up and asked if she could be of any help.

Alex cleared his throat. "We were wondering if we could book a reading, right now if possible."

She asked, "Do you want a separate reading or a couples reading?"

Alex and Dorathy both shrugged their shoulders and Dorathy said, "It might be best if we went separately so we could compare notes."

The young gal smiled, piercings pulling at her skin. "Let me go upstairs and see if Victor and Caroline are around."

While she went up to check on their availability, Alex and Dorathy looked around the store at all the memorabilia and books. Dorathy picked up a book on numerology, "Oh, Athena would love this, I think I'll get it for her."

While she was going through other books, Alex was sniffing the oil samples and said, "I think I found something I can use." Dorathy turned to see what he had found, only to see the label on the bottle read, *Male Pheromone 100% guaranteed to attract the opposite sex.*

Dorathy laughed so hard she nearly snorted and exclaimed, "What, you want me to rip your clothes off and jump your bones right here in the aisle?"

Alex slumped in dejection, and said in a pathetic voice, "Maybe," as he returned the bottle to the rack.

Dorathy gave him a sideways glance and a little smile that spoke volumes. "Silly man." They heard the clatter of the colorful woman coming down the stairs to collect their money for the readings. "Please follow me upstairs and I'll introduce you to Victor and Caroline."

Once upstairs they decided that Dorathy would see Victor and Alex would have his reading with Caroline. They entered through separate doors into small offices, noting the décor was much the same as the storefront, but with the addition of burning candles and lava lamps. There were also black lights that enhanced the glowing effects of the life-sized creatures and space mobiles that were distributed amongst science fiction memorabilia. Alex had brought his sister here once before her tragic accident and had had a fascinating reading with someone who had worked here, but that was a long time ago.

Dorathy sat facing Victor. It was difficult to determine his age; he looked like he could have been anywhere between forty and sixty years old. He had the mannerism, quietness, and intellect of a much older person, but without outward signs of age—only a few strands of grey intermingled with his long dark curly hair and beard. Behind the round lenses of the glasses he wore were the eyes of wisdom that came with age, but without the wrinkles associated with it.

Victor spoke calmly and quietly as he took Dorathy's hands in his. After a few moments with his eyes closed, he drew a breath and slowly let it out. "You have an adventurous spirit with a lust for life and any-thing life can throw at you. You are always up to challenges but will be up against a challenge that will seem incomprehensible. You will have no choice and will have to adapt." After a few moments of silence, he said, "You have a daughter and she is the light of your life. She is older now and has her own life to live." He stopped and with a sigh that reflected her sadness, he said, "You lack your one true love, but I see him, he's out there waiting. He's from far away. He will help you regain what you have lost. He will love you like no other man could possibly love you. Reluctantly at first, you will return his feelings." Another moment passed and Victor said, "Your job is very fulfilling, and it will take you out to the stars." He shook his head and said, "There will be a choice that you have already made, this choice will make your life difficult for you, but with-out it you will have no life."

Victor sat back, trying to make sense of what he could see in her fu-ture. He looked into Dorathy's eyes; he could see her pain and sensed a tragedy but could not comprehend the nature of it. "You have a great happiness coming to you, this happiness will last the rest of your life." He asked if she had any questions.

Dorathy had to ask and would kick herself if she didn't. "Do I have a soul mate, and have I met him?"

Victor would not hide the facts as he saw them and said, "Yes, he is what will drive you to your future." It was a lot for Dorathy to take in and to make sense of. She couldn't think of anything else to ask. Victor told her it was nice to meet her and said she could wait downstairs. She said her thanks and goodbye. Victor following her out, watched her make her way down the stairs, and tried desperately to connect what he had seen to the world as he knew it, as it was sure to haunt him for quite some time. These were visions he would be unable to shake, nor could he make sense of them. He thought that there must be a greater meaning to his visions, but they were beyond comprehension.

Meanwhile, Alex had his reading with Caroline. She had bright red hair and looked a bit worn around the edges with a very matter-of-fact air about her. She sat in her room with a variety of whimsical figurines laid out to be admired, and shelves of stuffed animals from her travels.

"Have a seat." Alex grabbed a chair and did what he was told. Caroline asked for Alex's right hand and gazed at his palm for a few moments. She looked up and said, "You are a very lonely man, always looking for perfection. You're always trying to fix things that are out of your control. Don't do that, because it will control your life. You have met someone, but I see tragedy with this person and there is a choice you will have to make."

Caroline sat in silence for a moment to reflect on what the universe was showing her, but what she saw was not coherent, and she struggled to make sense of it. She saw death and life, but it wasn't linear, and it was a disturbing vision. She shifted in her seat and struggled with her train of thought. "Your work takes a lot of your time lately, but now is the time to start planning other things. You are going to start a new life with this person—enjoy it now and make the best of it as long as you can. You suffered a great loss in the past. Your sister, she is showing me that she died in a car accident. She's here now, standing behind you."

Alex wanted badly to turn in his seat to see if he could look through the veil that separated them. Caroline paused. "She is telling me you need to be happy, that she wants you to marry this woman." Caroline shook her head and paused for another moment. "This woman, she will be gone for a while, but you'll see her again . . . her love for you transcends time." She then said brusquely, as if what she saw was disturbing, "Make the most of it." Caroline spoke a little more gently now: "Look, it's okay for you to be happy. Your sister's death was not your fault and all this time you have been burdened with the guilt of her death. You can't do that anymore; you've got to let it go."

Alex was trying very hard not to show any emotion, but he was falling apart on the inside. He was desperately holding back the tears he'd pushed aside for far too long. The guilt he had felt was somehow slowly being lifted away as his sister gave him permission to live again. Caroline could see his pain clearly written all over his handsome face. She asked if he had any questions for her and all he could do was shake his head. "No."

Standing, he shook Caroline's hand and with a squeeze as if to say more than he could articulate, he softly said, "Thank you."

He wandered out into the hall and could barely walk down the stairs.

For the first time since he could remember he was walking without the weight of an immense burden bearing down on his shoulders. When he reached the bottom of the stairs, he saw Dorathy sitting in a chair staring off into the distance. She sensed his approach and looked up at him. She saw such pain and such joy combined with a dash of fear, that she came to her feet and took his arm. "Are you okay?"

He looked at her and said, "Yes, I think I'm going to be fine. With you I will be fine." Dorathy kissed him on the cheek. Alex looked down into her eyes and saw her confusion and conflicts of her own and said, "Hey, let's get out of here and go for our much-needed hike." She nodded in agreement, and they crossed the street and got into the car without another word spoken.

They sat in the car in silence while going over their respective readings in their heads. Finally, Alex broke into their musings by reaching over and holding Dorathy's hand. She spoke first and said, "I think we are going to have a spectacular sunset tonight."

He glanced over. "Yes, and I brought us jackets and flashlights. I know this place pretty well; I come here a lot to get away from it all."

A few miles down the road Alex parked the car in a dirt lot where the trail began. He popped the trunk of the car open and pulled out a camping backpack rigged with everything they needed for a romantic sunset picnic, while Dorathy shoved the jackets into her bag. Alex slung the pack over one shoulder, locked the car and shoved the keys into his pocket. Then he pulled Dorathy to him and gazed into her eyes and said, "I'm falling for you, Dorathy Rosen, I hope that's okay with you."

Dorathy put her hands on his face and stepped in for a kiss, a long passionate kiss, the kind she always had only dreamed about. Alex let the pack slowly drop to the ground and put both arms around her and kissed her back as if he wanted this moment to last forever.

No one could stop this relationship from growing into a lifelong commitment. It was done and sealed with a kiss—this was to last an eternity.

They began to walk slowly at first, but it soon became a brisk walk as they raced the sun. They talked about their readings and tried to make sense of it all. Dorathy told Alex as much as she felt comfortable telling him, which was pretty much everything. And Alex did the same. He said, "The guilt I have been hauling around about my sister's accident has been crippling me all through my life. You see, I have felt responsible for her death since that terrible night. She was dating my best friend Chris, and we were all at a pub together. I was trying to hook up with this girl from one of my college classes and we all had a bit of drink down us. My sister was living with me at the time, so we went down to the pub together where she hooked up with Chris. I left in hopes of getting laid of course and left her at the pub. Chris was responsible for taking her home.

Alex teared up and stopped in his tracks. Dorathy halted and held his arm and tried to comfort him. Alex continued, "If I had been there, I would have taken her and Chris home . . . I should have stayed . . . I should have taken her home." Alex paused and could barely hold on to his composure. "They were struck hard on the passenger side by a drunk truck driver. My sister was killed instantly; Chris suffered severe head trauma and has been left in a vegetative state ever since." The tears were flowing freely now. "You see, Dorathy, I have spent my whole life looking for something perfect, when really I was just using that as an excuse not to live. I have always felt I didn't deserve to live or find happiness with someone, that it was my fault their lives were cut short. So, there you go. This woman today connected me to my sister and, somehow, I feel now I can finally put all that guilt aside, I can finally be free of it."

"It's never too late to start your life." She hugged him close and whispered, "I just hope you want me in it."

Alex kissed her and said, "I do, absolutely I do."

Somehow Dorathy and Alex could finally put their tragic pasts behind them; they could move forward together and carve out a bit of happiness for however long it may last. How was it that events that happened so long ago always seem to smudge the future? They made a vow that from this moment on they would not let the events that had left them so wounded be allowed out from the shadows where they had lurked.

They hiked for a couple of hours up through the high desert and came to rest atop a rocky plateau overlooking the red rock valley below. "What a spectacular view," Dorathy said. "It's amazing to see the beautiful colors of the red desert against the contrasting green of the trees. The desert truly has its own beauty and I can see why it is such a mystical place. I would love to sleep with you here in the desert tonight underneath these billions of stars."

Alex had a wide smile and said softly, "I can arrange that," as he unpacked the gear he had brought in his massive camping pack. Dorathy started to help and said, "You really do come prepared, don't you?"

"Well you never know what you are going to need, so I tend to bring everything."

She laughed as she pulled out a roll of toilet paper. "I guess so."

Alex rolled a plush sleeping pad out onto a flat rocky outcropping that fell steeply down below and asked Dorathy if she was a restless sleeper or tended to sleepwalk. She laughed. "Well that would be one way to end a very nice day with a splat," she said as she peered over the edge.

Alex had even packed a couple of pillows and a huge down sleeping bag for extra padding against the rock floor. As he continued to unpack the food and wine, he located the small music speaker he had thrown into his pack. He had downloaded calm relaxing Native American flute and drum music onto it. He looked up at Dorathy and said, "I hope your flight tomorrow is not very early in the morning."

"No, it's not," she answered. "I don't leave until four-thirty in the afternoon."

"Good, because we have all night to enjoy each other's company. It's entirely up to you."

Dorathy contemplated staying here on this rocky ledge all night with a man she had met a little less than a week ago. She thought about how it had been years since she had been with a man; and an amusing recollection flickered across her mind. How Lucy laughed at her once ages ago and said if she were to advertise her vagina, as one might put out an ad to sell a used car, Dorathy's would read: *gently used, like new, low miles*. And with that funny thought, she said holding back a bit of laughter, "I wouldn't have it any other way."

Alex was wondering why the laughter and asked, "Did I say something funny?"

Dorathy could only shake her head and, with a bit of a stutter, "It's nothing . . . really just something funny a coworker said to me once, sort of embarrassing really and I promise to tell you someday . . . but really, it's not important."

"Okay." Alex was hesitant to press her and decided to leave it alone for the time being. He motioned for her to sit down. "Hey, good looking, take a load off and have a seat next to me on top of the world." They both felt as if they were on top of the world for the first time in a very long time.

As she was sitting down, she said, "Hope you brought enough food and wine, because you must know by now, I love to eat."

"Yes, you do, and I must ask how it is you don't weigh . . . ," he was going to be kind, " . . . much more than you do."

She laughed, "Don't you know my Indian name is *Runs for Food*." It took him a second to figure it out and he burst into laughter. "Oh, that's me," she said. "I run so I can eat, otherwise I would be a bit . . . hmmm portly."

"Well, no running tonight. Guess you're going to have to figure out another way to burn off some calories."

"Oh, I think I can come up with a couple of other ways of doing that."

He responded, not looking over at her, but feeling a bit bold, "Yeah, me too."

They were drinking and eating and deep into one another as sunset approached. They stopped for the moment of silence to witness this beautiful spectacle of nature. How could something that happened every day of the year, all across the globe, hold our undivided attention no matter where we were in our lives—no matter where we might live, we sit in awe of something so routine yet somehow inspiring; perhaps it is a sign every day, that the next day would bring forth a new beginning.

As the sun cleared the horizon Alex put his arms around Dorathy and kissed her deeply, as he had never kissed a woman before. He ran his hands through her long black hair and looked into her soul. He finally spoke the words because he truly felt that he loved this woman with all his heart.

"I love you Dorathy, I truly do; you have given me my life back."

Dorathy looked back into his eyes and said, "Alex I love you with all my heart—I have been trying to resist you since the day I walked through your door, but I can't, and I won't. I feel you are my one true love that I have been desperately waiting for all of my life."

With that they fell back into the pillows and covered themselves up as the temperature was dropping rapidly. They made love under a star-filled night as if it was the first time. Both had waited for far too long.

At first light they woke, still entwined in each other's arms. Dorathy said, "I wish we could stay like this forever."

Alex kissed the top of her head. "Yes, I wish that too, but life tends to move ahead at light speed sometimes. So maybe we should just look towards the future with happiness and plan our life together."

Dorathy shifted to look him in the eye and said, "I do look forward to the future, our future."

They drove back into town and ended back at the hotel where Dorathy had been residing. They showered and snuggled, completely insepara-ble, while making plans for visits either work- related or otherwise. The dreaded time had come for Dorathy to pack and leave for the airport.

After she checked out and they put her bags in the car, they kissed re-peatedly. Never wanting to be apart, they made vows to make this wonder-ful newfound love work over distance and time. Whatever changes needed to be made they were going to make them, come hell or high water.

Alex stood in the parking lot blowing kisses as she pulled away. He went home with hope, with excitement in his steps. He had a lot to do, and the quicker he could make his arrangements, the faster he could change his life for the better.

While Dorathy sat on the plane, she looked through the photos she had taken over the week. She thought how incredibly handsome Alex was. *How lucky am I to have met such a wonderful man?* She smiled to her-self and fell instantly asleep, head propped up against the bulkhead. She dreamt of going on a long overdue vacation to her beach house. Thoughts danced through her head of a white sundress and flowers in her hair, and Alex with a white shirt and pants. Vows of everlasting love. Countless sunsets, and nude morning swims. Lounging the afternoons away in a hammock slung between two palm trees, the warm trade winds lulling them to sleep. She thought she could do that forever. By God, she could afford it and want for nothing more the rest of her life.

CHAPTER 6

Jarred awake as the plane touched down, Dorathy was still blurry-eyed when she started to gather her things. Athena would be there with Kevin to pick her up. Dorathy had called her before boarding to let her know the flight was on time. They had spoken briefly, but Athena could hear a kind of happiness that she had never heard in her mother's voice. A woman's intuition could read volumes from just a single word spoken. She couldn't wait to get her mom alone and hopefully Kevin wouldn't hang around too long. Athena decided to suddenly become tired from their weekend away in the wine country--maybe that would give him the little needed push to continue home.

As soon as they entered the house and Kevin was well on his way, Athena cornered her mom in the kitchen. "Okay, Mom, tell me about your trip."

Dorathy started in by telling Athena about the technology and how well the staff all worked together. "You should see this place."

"No, Mom, I want details and I'm not talking about the décor!"

Dorathy was flabbergasted. "What are you talking about?"

Athena bit back, "Don't even try to pull that routine with me, Mom, I'm smarter than that!" Indeed, she was.

Dorathy pulled a stool from the bar and sat down with a thump. "What does my love life have to do with you?"

"Mom . . . the fact that you just said *love life* pertains to the fact that you might actually have one. So, do you?" she asked with a Cheshire cat smile.

Dorathy sighed deeply, something she had done frequently over the years when dealing with her daughter. "God, Athena, can't I have any secrets?"

Athena was hurt and Dorathy saw it written all over her daughter's face. "Okay . . . okay. If you must know, and you would have found out soon enough, you will meet Alex most likely in two weeks anyway. So yes, I have had, I mean we started to . . . shit," she said under her breath. A long pause followed so she could come up with an explanation to account for the pieces of her lonely life made whole in just under a week. "Alex and I are in love and he will most likely move in with us and we will probably get married, and there I said it, there it is in a nutshell."

Athena was floored. She took a step back and leaned against the stove. "Wow . . . I wasn't expecting that, I just thought you were going to say you went out on a date. Holy shit, Mom! That's . . . wow . . . sudden, like maybe a little . . . I don't know . . . like too fast? You're always telling me not to rush into things, now you tell me this."

"Look darling, you know better than anyone how lonely I have been. I'm fifty-one years old and it's about time I get my time in the sun. I'm not getting any younger."

"Mom, does he make you happy? I think I already know the answer to that since I can feel your joy beaming from across the room. Okay, I just don't want you to get hurt. I need to meet him. So, you say he's coming in two weeks. I'm going to make sure I'm around so I can get a better handle on this."

Dorathy assured her she need not worry. "You're not going to be around that much, are you?"

Athena got her drift and said, "Oh, geez, Mom! No. I'll spend the nights at Kevin's."

It seemed the conversation was over, so Dorathy said, "I'm going to take a bath and call Alex."

Athena had to go there by saying, "You're not going to have phone sex, are you?"

"Jesus Christ, Athena!"

With her big green eyes twinkling, she said, "Just saying, Mom . . ."

The next morning Dorathy was humming no particular song while she got ready for work. She jumped into her car and sped off with squealing tires. The neighbors had grown accustomed to that sound over the years while slapping their husbands for looking and wishing for their younger years. Dorathy was never going to be that little old lady from Pasadena.

For the first time, it seemed, Dorathy saw the flowers blooming on the trees and the small wildlife scampering about the grassy knolls. She smelled the air and thought how fragrant it was. Over the years she had become inured to her surroundings, and senses finally awakened, she felt alive.

Entering her building she called out, "Good morning," to Lisa, with a joy that had always seemed to be absent from her greeting in the past, somehow making them less than sincere. This morning was different. Lisa looked over her glasses at Dorathy and responded, "Hi. You're back," while thinking how different she appeared. That thought progressed immediately to considering whether Dorathy could have possibly met a man and, if so, Lisa needed to find out who it could be.

Dorathy walked down the hall to her office, and, as she always had, greeted everyone as she passed. Lucy was lingering outside of Jack's office when she saw Dorathy approaching. Whatever she glimpsed in Dorathy's expression resulted in her attention to conversation with Jack fading rapidly. Lucy bounced towards Dorathy and said with her big bright smile, "Yay! You're back! How was your trip, the hotel was awesome wasn't it, did you eat at that Mexican restaurant I told you about . . . ?" And, with an abrupt ceasefire from questions, she followed Dorathy into her office and sat down on the opposite side of the desk. She scrutinized Dorathy for a few seconds to confirm her suspicions. Lucy gazed at Dorathy, eyes squinted, slowly got up, shut the office door and leaned back against it. "OH MY GOD! You got laid!"

Waving her hands Dorathy shushed her, giving her the stare down. "What the hell are you talking about?"

Lucy, still standing against the door, reached over and lowered the blinds to the window adjacent to the office door. She turned and crossed her arms. "Tell me everything," and then she gasped, as her hands went to her mouth to cover up the words coming out, "Oh . . . you slept with Alex Mason, didn't you?"

Dorathy was shocked. Did her best friend suddenly possess the ability to read minds? Lucy gasped again, "Oh you did!" Now Lucy was jumping up and down clapping her hands. "Tell me, tell me! He is such a hot looking cupcake; I want all the details!"

Lucy, now fired up, was shooting questions at Dorathy at an astounding rate. Dorathy couldn't take the bombardment and sat down, legs sprawled and said, "Lucy! Look, it all sort of just happened, I tried to fight the attraction—we tried really, but it is what it is . . . we love each other!"

Lucy was beaming with delight for her friend and said quickly, "I want to be in the wedding; oh, please . . . you should get married on the beach!" Lucy was off to the races again and had Dorathy's whole wedding and life planned out in mere seconds. Lucy loved weddings, loved new relationships and loved being married, at least for a little while, which explained the fact she was on husband number four and by the sounds of it these days, was still counting.

Dorathy calmed her down. "Yes, you will meet him. He's coming here in two weeks, but for Christ sake don't say a word, because I don't have to tell you how things get spread around this joint and him being here is work related, get my drift?"

Lucy got it. "Okay, so you guys are going to just act 'normal,'" she said sarcastically and laughed, "Well, good luck with that!"

Dorathy knew she was right and felt slightly panicked—how could she possibly hide her relationship with Alex? Then she became irritated. "You know, I shouldn't have to hide anything! I have worked here for how many years, donated countless dollars to research grants over the years and have always given the utmost respect to my colleagues. Why should I hide anything? It's not like it's anything new around here, the whole damn place can be downright incestuous at times."

Lucy understood how Dorathy fell. "So, what do you think you should do?"

"I know what I feel like doing, and that is walk right into Jack's or

Hugo's office and just tell them . . . point blank." She paused. "Yup, that's what I should do, just say, 'Hey Hugo I slept with one of our accounts.'" Dorathy dropped her head onto her desk in agony; she felt as if she was in purgatory.

Lucy laughed and said, "NICE! Yup, that is what you should do . . . NOT! "Have you lost your mind and your virginity?" Lucy thought any more than two weeks without sex meant you had reverted to virgin status.

Dorathy was being tormented by her past—remembering her younger years being chased by the paparazzi, with horrible photos of her splashed on the covers of magazines. She suddenly had a hard time breathing as the past crept up to remind her of her torturous childhood. Her need for privacy had dominated her adult life. She knew at times she was being unreasonable and tried to convince herself that no one really cared who she was or what she did. But she just couldn't shake that part of her life. It was, in fact, who she was, that was never going to change. She was a Rosen and along with that came the fanfare she tried to ignore, with little success. "Shit, just let me think about it awhile."

Hugging her friend close, Lucy told her how happy she was for her. "Dorathy, if anyone deserves a little happiness in their life, you do." With a reassuring pat on Dorathy's cheek, Lucy stepped out of the office, gave a small wave, a wink and said, "Let's do lunch, SOON."

Dorathy now felt like she really needed to put her guard up. She had a meeting with Jack in ten minutes. Right on schedule, she knocked on Jack's door and asked, "Are you ready to discuss the project with Alex . . . Mason . . . Dr. Mason." She thought, *God I suck at this.*

"Yeah, sure, have a seat." Jack was a quiet man and despite his white, spiked hair, no one could ever judge his age by his appearance. He leaned back in his chair and asked, "Did you have a good trip?"

Dorathy kept her replies short and concise, to not trigger any suspicions. "Yeah, it was fine. Got a lot accomplished. I have all the design specs for the canisters and I feel I can fully incorporate the existing design into a space-worthy vehicle with a small, long-life propulsion pack."

Jack interrupted her train of thought. "Speaking of propulsion, sounds like our friends at CERN have discovered something very intriguing with their studies from the particle accelerator." He gestured down at the file lying open on his desk. Dorathy was all ears and Jack went on, "Seems they have possibly cracked the mystery that has been confounding us for decades. Well you remember a while back they had discovered some interesting deviations from the Standard Model predictions in flavor physics. They had several measurements that all show a deviation in the same direction; none of these measurements were highly significant on their own but it was a curious trend. LHCb collected a dataset that had led to far more precise measurements. In a short time, me thinks this indeed would have led to finally, without a doubt, breaking the Standard Model, but something even more spectacular happened!"

Dorathy gasped, wide eyed, "Oh, Jack, please tell me, because that would be amazing news. My God, that could change everything we know about physics and to finally, after centuries, have the answers we've been looking for! Perhaps to find a way of using this information to travel through space! Tell me, so how did they finally do it?!"

"Well it seems that the power station that feeds CERN was struck by a couple of well-timed lightning strikes during an LHC experiment, which induced an ultra-high frequency time rate of change in the power systems and produced multiple time derivatives in the rotating beam packets. Apparently, this stimulated the quantum vacuum, carving a perfect spherical void in the LHC beam tunnel."

Dorathy's mouth hung open as she contemplated the significance of such a discovery. "Jack, do you know what this could mean? What the implications are? We might be able to recreate such an event and use it for higher dimensional travel!"

"They've requested that we send our best to check out their findings and, well, you are the best. I know you have a lot of work to do on Mason's project, but I think this takes precedence. At least check it out and see if there is any validity to it. Just might be a whole new way of thinking about how we get around the stars. Pretty spectacular, if you ask me. Imagine manipulating that type of science This could be the start of a bold new world for us out there."

Dorathy's mind was racing and was overwhelmed contemplating the reality of such a discovery, but of course she wanted to be a part of this. "When do you want me to go?" The thought of going to check out this technology was irresistible. Jack was right, this could change life as we knew it. The entire time she was thinking about the exhilaration of working with colleagues at CERN, she was hoping that Alex would want to go along for the ride. She loved Geneva and would love to share this with him.

Jack looked up from the file open in front of him. "They're still trying to organize a time when the international science community can all come together in a huge disclosure arena. Everyone is going nuts trying to align themselves for technology rights. So really, I think they need to get that all sorted out first, and they will."

"You're right. Something this big, they won't waste too much time getting their ducks in a row if they plan on presenting this to the rest of the world. It is fascinating though. Last time we were there they thought they had it figured out and maybe they finally did it this time. Imagine the possibilities if we could bend space-time at will and bring the destination to us, rather than trying to travel through it. It is truly amazing."

Jack had always been hopeful about the new ways this technology could be used and had been closely following advances in the field. I'll keep you posted on how things progress over there. When the Higgs was discovered, what, fifty or so years ago, it gave us a clue on how it might lead us to something more and slowly, over the years, other discoveries were made that told us there was, absolutely, more to it . . . shit, sort of like when electricity was discovered—now look at us. This truly is the beginning of a new world."

Dorathy left Jack's office, trying to wrap her head around what they had discussed. She was looking forward to this trip for many reasons, but the only one she could really focus on was, *going with Alex.*

She spent the remainder of the week pulling together her design for Alex's project, all the while contemplating the reality of what she was working on. Eventually, as Voyager had a century ago, the capsules containing a cryogenically frozen person would leave our solar system for intergalactic space. She laughed out loud at the thought of eventually being picked up by an alien spacecraft and revived. *Shit, wouldn't that be a trip?* She mocked herself, thinking about what she might say and giggled, saying under her breath, *Where the hell am I? And who the hell are you?* She thought how laughable it was; not the technology, or the space flight, she got that completely. It was the what-ifs.

Dorathy plugged away day after day, stealing moments here and there in order to talk to her beloved Alex. She adored the sound of his voice, that accent, the ruggedness, the confidence. She needed desperately to be with him, to hold him. She kept a tight rein on her emotions.

As the end of the second week approached, she was so excited about seeing Alex she could hardly contain herself. She had kept busy and purposely away from anyone who might figure out she had met someone. She was under the radar, so she thought.

Dorathy was preparing to leave for the weekend. She planned to pick Alex up at the airport and then head directly home. Just about the time she was going to call it a day, Hugo walked into her office. "Hey Dora, can I have a word with you before you head out?"

"Sure."

Hugo was almost afraid to say anything, so he chose his words carefully--after all, he thought of Dorathy as a friend. "You've been working here what, ten years now, and I have never seen you this damned happy. So, whatever it is, or whoever it is, responsible for this newfound happiness, it's okay. You won't get any argument from anybody around here, even if it's related to work. Many of us are guilty of having work relationships and, as you know, people who work here are committed to their projects and don't have much of a life outside these walls. Far be it from me, or anyone else, to judge you. We just wanted you to know that we've noticed your excitement has coincided with the arrival of Dr. Mason, and it's okay . . . really. I, for one, say it's about time you met someone. He's a lucky guy and a good match. Anyway, have a great weekend and we'll see you both Monday; gotta get those human popsicles up into space."

Stunned, all she could possibly say was, "Thank you, Hugo. I appreciate your honesty and understanding."

Hugo added, "Hell, I met my wife here, been married twenty-two years. So, I'm just sayin' it's all good and I know you will conduct yourselves in a professional manner." Then he said, with a boisterous laugh, "Besides the cat's outta the bag and everyone knew what was goin on anyway . . . so I thought I'd let you off the hook."

Dorathy's shoulders slumped. "Really? Am I that transparent?"

Hugo smiled his big, Texan grin, "Shit, girl, even the folks over in mission control knew!"

Dorathy shook her head and rolled her eye. "It never ceases to amaze me how shit gets spread around here so goddamned fast."

"Yup, we're one big happy, dysfunctional family. And ya know what? Don't think I'd change a thing."

Dorathy smiled and agreed with what he was saying—this workplace was populated by a great group of people who cared as deeply as she and Hugo did about their work and the people they worked with. She did feel blessed.

Hugo said, "Now, go get that that man of yours and enjoy life together, because you only get one shot!"

Dorathy gave Hugo a quick hug. "Thanks, boss, see you Monday." With a wave she was out the door and heading for the airport.

Dorathy practically ran to the parking lot to get to her car. She looked at her watch and smiled, murmuring to herself, "Finally I have an excuse to see what this black bucket of bolts is capable of doing!" She jumped in and sped out of the lot with the engine roaring. The volume was on high, some old heavy metal tunes cranked up to get her adrenaline kicked into high gear. When she rolled into the northbound fast lane she was approaching 125 miles per hour She thought, *I just might make it there on time.*

As usual, the Burbank airport was busy, but she had made it there with time to spare so she decided to park the car in the lot and wait by the gate. After a few agonizing minutes her phone beeped with an incoming message from Alex telling her they had landed, and he was on his way. Dorathy was pacing in front of the jet-way entry like a panther ready to pounce. Palms clammy and heart pounding; a few minutes seemed like an eternity. Just when she was about to jump out of her skin with anticipation, she saw Alex approaching.

Looking even more handsome than he had in Phoenix, he was dressed in slacks and a white linen shirt that showed off his tan and his bright hazel eyes. She leapt into his open arms and they kissed as if they had been separated for years. He looked into her eyes and said, "God, I missed you something awful." Alex kissed her again and held her close. He never wanted to leave her side again but knew he must. For now, he was going to wrap himself in her love like a warm, soft blanket after a long winter out in the cold.

"How about we blow this popsicle stand?" Alex suggested. Dorathy burst out into laughter, shaking her head.

When they reached Dorathy's car, Alex seemed shocked at first, but then said, "I would expect no less from you, and this car definitely suits you."

Dorathy paused for a second as Alex threw his bag into the trunk then asked, "Do you want to drive?"

"I thought you would never ask." Dorathy tossed him the keys then directed him home. He handled the car like a professional Formula 1 driver. She was impressed.

As promised, Athena was home waiting to meet the man who had stolen her mother's heart and who would eventually become her step-father. She was waiting patiently in the kitchen and had prepared a few appetizers and iced a bottle of champagne to celebrate his arrival. Over the past two weeks Athena had seen a remarkable metamorphosis in her mother. Dorathy had become a beautiful butterfly, shedding the chrysalis of the past and for this Athena was grateful. Alex had made her mother come alive and had given her the much-deserved happiness that was long overdue.

She heard their approach as the garage door opened, followed by the familiar growl of her mother's car. A moment later they entered through the kitchen.

Athena quickly checked her appearance with the help a small mirrored mosaic art piece her mother had brought back from one of her business trips to Peru.

She wanted to make a good first impression

They tumbled through the doorway with the large case, still arm in arm. Alex stopped still, looking from one woman to the other. Athena stood tall and was the spitting image of her mother, with large green eyes and slightly lighter hair.

He said, "Hello Athena," as he offered his hand.

Athena took his hand and pulled him in for a hug. "Welcome to the family," she said, punctuated by a peck on his cheek.

After a couple of hours of getting to know each other, Athena excused herself. "I'm going over to Kevin's for the weekend. If you'd like to get together some night for dinner, or whatever, give me a call and he and I can join you." She threw some things into a bag and was out the door, wearing a huge smile.

Alex got up from the sofa and stood, looking out through the large French doors leading to the back yard and pool. He turned to Dorathy. "Athena is a great girl. Intelligent and beautiful, just like her mother."

Dorathy joined him, wrapping both arms around his waist. "Yes, she is. She is such a wonderful daughter and I couldn't be prouder of her. I am so happy you hit it off. Not that I was worried about that, I knew you would love her just as much as she would love you."

Alex gathered Dorathy's long hair in his hands and pulled her in for a long passionate kiss and said, "How about a swim?" Dorathy didn't hesitate to begin unbuttoning Alex's shirt and then undoing his pants. He was happy to return the favor, of course.

They spent the rest of the night outside, making full use of the pool and spa and the oversized, outside lounging bed made for two that Dorathy had picked up from an upscale patio store just the week before. They woke in the wee hours under the comforter she had dragged from her bed. They gazed up at the clear night sky and wondered what was, and who might be, out there just beyond our reach.

She told him about the discovery at CERN and they discussed what life would be like in the next fifty years and what our species might be able to accomplish in the next five hundred years. Dorathy said, "It's truly amazing if you think about the world the way it was just a hundred years ago with the Saturn IV Rocket and the moon missions, and just fifty years before that, we barely had the combustion engine. Now we are sending tourists into space for vacations and mining the moon and neighboring asteroids for rare minerals. Just imagine what the Earth will be like, perhaps in just ten years from now. This discovery will change how we live our daily lives. Not just the way we approach traveling through space, but how we might live in it."

Alex responded to her musings, "I look forward to the future, our future and the future of the planet. Wouldn't it be great if we could take that technology and apply it, even in the smallest way, to our cryocapsules? I think that's something you could design and even if it was under a test application, I am sure it would catch on with potential clients. When this new discovery is made public, the world will be going crazy trying to find ways of applying it."

Dorathy pondered it for a moment. "Yes, you're so right about that. I know how I can score exclusivity on a small-scale research platform."

"How?" Alex asked, overcome with curiosity.

"It's simple really . . . money. My father's goal in his life, which I continue in his honor, was to set aside the funds for research and development of new technologies. This fits the bill. I donate the funds towards research and development, and, in return, we get the right to design and use the technology as we deem fit. It seems to me that investing a sum for the sole purpose of launching cryocapsules into deep space via space bending or whatever they are going to call it, is the perfect venture."

Alex was strongly attracted to the strength and power she exuded, and her intellect; add beauty and sexuality to the equation and he felt he was the luckiest man alive. These qualities were an incredible turn-on and he felt an urge to make love to her again with such intensity it seemed that he had fire running through his veins. Dorathy welcomed him to her immediately.

Alex and Dorathy were like-minded and carried each other's hearts in their hands; their souls seemed to be as one, forever linked together. Together there was nothing they couldn't accomplish.

When the sun peeked just over the hill, Alex kissed Dorathy and said, "Good morning beautiful, how about I make us a big breakfast?"

Dorathy yawned and stretched while she laid her body on top of Alex's and said, "As long as you're naked, you sexy man." With that Alex got up and just before he jumped into the pool Dorathy managed to get a playful smack across his firm backside. Dorathy followed him in. After a few long kisses they wrapped themselves in beach towels and proceeded into the kitchen. As promised, Alex made them a feast and served it to Dorathy, the princess that had stolen his heart.

Afterward they went to bed and slept in each other's arms. They slept like they had never slept before, finally knowing the comfort and the feeling that only comes when you know someone loves you, that that person will be there for you always; that warm, secure feeling that we only seem to have as children, curled up in our beds with our favorite stuffed toy.

The weekend seemed to pass so quickly, already it was Sunday night. Alex and Dorathy decided to grill steaks and allow Athena to come home. Athena decided to call first and asked jokingly, "So is the coast clear, can I come home now?"

Dorothy laughed and said, "Yes, honey, and bring Kevin with you. We are going to have a family dinner tonight."

The evening went well, and by the end of the night it was as if they had known each other all their lives. Kevin had to be at work early the next day, so said his good nights and went home. While her mom was in the kitchen putting the dishes away Athena pulled Alex aside. "I just want to thank you for bringing such happiness to my mom's life. I can see that you really do care deeply for her and she feels the same about you." She paused for a moment, but she had to add, "Please don't break her heart, that's all I ask. She is such an awesome person and she truly deserves a love in her life and I really think that's you."

Alex assured Athena that he would be true to his heart and that every fiber of his being was completely in love with her mother. "Look, Athena, I have spent my whole life thinking I didn't deserve happiness. Your mom has shown me a life of love that I thought I would never have and I'm not about to screw up the best thing I have ever had. Your mother is the love of my life and I plan on marrying her someday, if she'll have me."

Athena smiled and gave Alex a hug good night. Alex felt like he was home. He felt whole, he felt needed, and he felt like he had a family again. He would never want for anything again. He had everything he had ever wanted in Dorothy and the love of a daughter he had never hoped to have.

Athena leaned in to give her mom a kiss good night and whispered, "I really like him, mom, he's a good guy."

"Good night you two. I have an early class tomorrow and won't be home till after six or seven I'll probably grab something to eat between classes so, don't wait around for me."

After the kitchen was cleaned and tidied, Alex and Dorathy brought their wine out to the patio and lay in the quiet night air. They snuggled without a care in the world and drifted off to sleep. They needed to rest because they were going to have a very busy few weeks ahead of them . . . even busier than they had anticipated.

CHAPTER 7

The next morning came quickly. Dorathy woke, her head perfectly nestled on Alex's muscular and groomed chest, her arm draped across his abdomen with her hand resting on his thigh. She clutched at his hip. Alex stirred awake and said, "I love waking up with you next to me, more than that I love making love to you first thing in the morning." Needing no encouragement, Dorathy slowly moved her body on top of his, kissing his neck, his face, his eyes and finally kissing his lips. They moved as one, her long, tousled hair teasing Alex's senses like fragrant silk fabric. Clutched firmly in his fists, he breathed in its scent, gasping in pure ecstasy. Soulmates finally together and life for them had never been better. Everything seemed new and exciting and life was about to get just a wee bit more interesting.

Later, Dorathy and Alex were sitting in the car outside her building at JPL."I know exactly what you're thinking," he said. "But, if Hugo is okay with us, and this isn't the first time something like this has happened, then who are they to judge us? Today's news will be replaced by something bigger and better tomorrow."

She knew he was right—then she was hit by a memory of her college days with all the photographers and their zoom lenses lurking around to get a clear shot of her. Dorathy shook it off and grinned, "You're right, who really gives a shit anymore? You are my man, we are going to be working together and get the job done, end of story. Okay, let's get it over with."

They walked side by side and as they approached the front door Dorathy laughed and said quietly, "Well once Lisa sees us the rest of the building will know you're here before we reach my office." Dorathy enthusiastically swung open the heavy glass door for Alex. He chuckled and thought, *Well this is going to get interesting.*

Good morning, Lisa. This is Dr. Alex Mason. He will be accompanying me for the next few weeks." Lisa, wide-eyed, stood up to take in this historical event, all the while giving Alex a good once-, and even twice-, over. Before she could gather her thoughts to speak, Alex winked at her and said in a whisper, "I'm her boyfriend."

Dorathy grimaced and said, without hesitation, "Yes, he is." And completed the thought in her head, *just deal with it!*

Lisa held her hand out. "It's very nice to meet you," and thought, *I wonder if he has a brother?*

Walking down the hall towards her office, she could feel the stares boring into them. Just then Hugo came down the hall towards them and said, "Great, you're here early, we need to meet right now in my office." Dorathy looked at Alex and back at Hugo, "Yes, both of you, because I think we might be able to pull off something with your project."

Alex and Dorathy sat side by side. Hugo shut the door and sat across from them, behind his desk. "Okay, folks, just got the word a little while ago from Geneva. Looks like the bastards have really got themselves in a pickle and so much for taking their time; they've been rattlin' some cages, including ours. They seem to have cracked the mystery and got the damned thing figured out. Now they want to have an open symposium to discuss a variety of applications. They have invited top scientists from around the world to have a powwow. Dorathy, they want you for your obvious abilities as a scientist, but also, dare I say, a nice fat research grant from your foundation."

Dorathy said, "Hugo, you know what my answer will be—Lifecor and JPL get exclusivity on the technology and we get to test it first. The rest of them can line up behind us."

"All right then, Dora, let's make this happen! And Alex, welcome aboard and be prepared for a hell of a ride. I would love to go along, but I have got to get things sorted out over in Lunar Dig. Jack will be going in my place, it's more his field of expertise. I have Lucy booking hotel and transportation and if you want to take over your supersonic flying machine, knock yourself out, it's your dime. Speaking of that, Carlo will be wanting to hitch a ride. His uncle is one of the key scientists that solved the mystery to taming this goddamned particle and needs him over there indefinitely.

They sat and talked financial arrangements for a while, and Dorathy said, "This is one of those defining moments in human history and money shouldn't be a deciding factor, so my feeling is, whatever it takes to get the job done—my father would have agreed." They all shook hands.

Hugo said, "Looks like your preliminary designs for the cryocapsules will have to be scrapped, 'cause it looks like it's going to be a whole other kind of animal now. So, go home, pack, get done what you must get done and get over there ASAP. I'm assuming here, and correct me if I'm wrong, you're going to let that poor bastard Jack hitch a ride too?"

Dorathy laughed, "Oh, I suppose I will." Glancing in Alex's direction she said, "Guess we'll just have to wait to join the mile-high club."

"Jesus Christ, girl, you tryin' to give this old man a heart attack?"

Lucy was coming around the corner as they were leaving Hugo's office. When she caught a glimpse of Alex, she shifted direction almost tripping in the process, and tried desperately to act nonchalant. "Hi, Dora." There was a hint of envy. "This must be Alex. I'm Dora's friend, Lucy. It's so nice to meet you. I found you an awesome hotel in Geneva, right on the water and near the train station. It has huge Jacuzzi bathtubs, and a great view of the lake and fountain."

Alex shook her hand. "Sounds great, Lucy, should be a good trip. With any luck we can get this project off to a brand-new start. Then hopefully when we get back, we'll all have to go out for karaoke— heard you're a great songstress."

"Who me? Oh, I love your accent Alex. I would love to go to Australia one day. So, are you going to move here? Phoenix is so hot you'll like it here better. You should learn how to surf. Did you surf when you lived in Australia?"

Dorathy interrupted the torrent of questions and said, "I'm just going to step into my office and call about the plane." As Alex turned to face Dorathy, she could see Lucy mouthing over his shoulder, "HE'S HOT!"

Alex turned back to Lucy and said, "It's a pleasure to meet you and I'm sure we will be seeing a lot more of each other." Alex turned to follow Dorathy into her office and Dorathy could see Lucy gesturing, "NICE ASS! CALL ME!" Dorathy was having a hard time holding back an amused smirk.

"What's so funny"?

"Nothing, just Lucy. I think she likes you."

Alex, oblivious to the interaction, responded, "Yeah, she's a good mate."

He could hardly contain his excitement. "This kind of technology is going to change the world!" He looked at Dorathy with such admiration, such intense curiosity and had to ask, "How does it feel to be a part of this new world, to say that you were able to contribute and be somewhat responsible for its further development?"

Dorathy sat back in her chair and looked out her office window at all the cars in the parking lot and thought about her father. What would the world have been like if not for all he had accomplished with his advancement in hydrogen-fueled engines, which led the world to behave differently, to somehow bring nations to work together instead of fighting and aligning themselves over a natural resource that we never really needed in the first place. Hydrogen is the most abundant element in the universe and it was just sitting there, mocking us for our nearsightedness and greed. Her father had literally changed the course of the planet's evolution. All those who couldn't adapt to the growing pace had perished long ago and they had taken their fanaticisms with them. It had finally brought the rest of us together.

Dorathy responded, "If I can accomplish just a fraction of what my father was able to, then I trust the world can fill in the gaps and turn it into something truly amazing in the future. You and I may not be around to see the result, but I know it will make a difference in our species' future. I only hope I can effectively do my part to move us forward, and that I can live up to everyone's expectations. I would like to be able to say that I made my father proud, wherever he might be."

Alex could see that all her life she had pushed to prove to herself, and to everyone around her that she was capable of greatness. She had allowed it to consume her as if there were measuring stick against which to measure the rest of us mere mortals. He carefully chose his words. "Dora, you know perfection is in the eyes of the beholder. It's not tangible. Sometimes something is not perfect, except that it *is* perfect just the way it is." My darling, you are perfect, and I know in my heart, that for you, giving it your best shot is far better than most others' efforts at perfection."

Dorathy looked at Alex with love in her heart, but it was laced with just a bit of disappointment that he could not see the bigger picture of why she felt as she did. She needed to be more, to prove she was worthy. She had pushed herself hard all through her life to prove she was more than a billionaire's daughter. The pressure she applied to her efforts was the essence of who she was, to be more than that, and her accomplishments were her own and nobody would take that from her, ever.

She started to speak, but hesitated, then finally said, "There are so many people who would judge me differently if not for my merits. My accomplishments are mine and I would not have accomplished what I have if not for my drive to be better than I am. You might feel that perfection is overrated, but I look upon it as something to strive for."

Alex leaned back in his chair to consider what she had just said. "All right, I get it, my darling Dora, but for me, when it comes to me, you are perfect to me, as perfect can be. You need not feel judged, for one who is judgmental must be perfect, and I am nothing of the sort. If I were to live in a glass house, I would not be throwing stones at anyone."

Dorathy got up from her chair and whispered in his ear, "I love you, my darling man. Thank you for being you." She stood above him and said, "How about we get our shit together, I'll call and get the jet ready, then we'll gather up Carlo and Jack, and fly our asses over to CERN. We'll see what those bastards are up to."

CHAPTER 8

Lucca Venturini walked through the cold, dimly lit, seventeen-mile-long tunnel, occasionally stopping to listen for anyone who may be following him. The underground facility that housed the particle accelerator was deep below the surface, its curvature hardly noticeable. Lucca recalled that just over a year ago mother nature herself had revealed a hint of what his group of scientists knew was missing from the equations they had worked on for years. They now had confirmation that all along they were working with only a small fraction of the entire picture. The Standard Model, as they knew it, could never work. Now everything has changed. Pondering mankind's future, he slowly continued along the tunnel, checking the equipment as he went. After the immense power surge caused by a freak lightning storm, the particle accelerator had been powered down for repairs, but not before revealing the secrets of the universe.

Finally, their work neared completion. The Large Hadron Collider had been able to perform as it was intended, presenting us with the secrets to another existence by forcing a hole through the veil that separates our reality from the Prime Reality—that being the reality where heaven resides.

Lucca turned when he heard footsteps echoing from behind. "Hello, my friend," Hans Grobler said, running his hand along the cold steel housing. "I understand your nephew was successful."

"Yes," Lucca said sadly, "most unfortunate, but very necessary. Simon is gaining too much power and influence, and the only advantage we can hope for will result from Dorathy's removal from the equation. It has become far too dangerous that Simon is uncovering information that will inevitably lead him to the truth."

Hans's eyes were tired as his gaze shifted along the narrow passage-way, barely able to discern the curve off in the distance. "Our charade has become most difficult as Simon pursues the truth. He must not know of our mission while the amulet is in his possession. He must not realize its true power, or all is lost."

"Yes, I agree with you. Dorathy must be removed for her own safety, and the safety of humanity. We cannot move forward without her in-volvement and we are in desperate need of finishing what we have begun before it is too late. She will, no doubt, take the bait, ultimately funding our project."

Lucca sighed. Shouldering the responsibility of ending the life of someone so close to his heart was almost too much to bear. "Carlo has been following the progress of Dorathy's project with Lifecor for the last year and now has good reason to believe that Dorathy would participate herself in proving the concept of cryogenics being space worthy. All we need to do is place a tracking device, so our ship is able to detect her presence and location for her retrieval."

Lucca leaned against the housing, feeling its cold structure beneath him and grew weary thinking of the past. Attempting to ease their guilt, he said, "John was wise trusting us with the information and his intu-itions were correct, but he was slow in acting. Perhaps not wanting to see the truth of what he had a hand in manufacturing. Whoever Simon's abductor was has proved to himself to be quite elusive."

"Yes," Hans added, "and has become quite the more powerful."

Hans's train of thought shifted. "What of the amulet, how will we re-cover it? Simon has every reason to believe it holds power but has no knowledge of what the power may be. John made sure of that, but unfor-tunately was too late in realizing Simon had been compromised."

Lucca said in a more positive tone, "We need to ensure Dorathy's life continues as planned, but it has simply become too dangerous for her to remain here. Her DNA must endure intact and her presence is needed far from here. It's the only way and our small crew will see to her safety on the other side."

Hans nodded in agreement. "I suppose you are right. Simon's altered DNA has made him immortal and he will follow her to the ends of the universe seeking the truth. The amulet is useless without her, so we must separate her from it for as long as he has it."

"Yes, very true my friend . . . very true. The last year has been taxing for both of us and the journey at hand has brought us to this point. All our efforts are about to pay off and, with Dorathy's help, this mission will commence shortly."

They walked together, wondering what the future might hold. Knowing that the significance of what they were doing now would eventually shape the future for the rest of mankind. A truly daunting task.

The next morning both Alex and Dorathy were scrambling to get everything in order. Dorathy packed the files she thought she would need. Athena was going through Dorathy's closet, making suggestions on what she should take with her.

"Mom, you always look good, but you have to dress the part. You have to look like you aren't going to take shit from anyone."

Dorathy had explained to Athena what she was planning on doing at CERN. Athena was on board with her decision to fund the project there. As long as Dorathy was alive she had control of the foundation monies and, ultimately, made all the decisions.

Feeling flustered, she said, "All right, pack my black suit. It has a look about it that says power."

"Mom, black on you says a lot of things, but yeah, power is good. I threw in some color . . ."

Dorathy cut her off. "Fine, it's all good, if I need something, I'll just buy it there." Dorathy gave the contents of her bag a final once-over, zipped it closed and looked at her watch, "Shit, the limo will be here . . . ," and the doorbell rang. "Okay, got to go, honey. Call me if you need anything."

Athena kissed her mom and followed her into the family room where Alex had been waiting patiently, but he was now at the door telling the driver they would be out shortly.

"All right. I'm as ready as I'll ever be, let's blow this popsicle stand." Alex smiled, as the term had become old hat. He helped Dorathy with her bag and gave Athena a kiss on the cheek. The driver put their bags in the trunk, and they were off to get Carlo and Jack.

Alex saw the chilled champagne in the bucket built into the limo's console, pulled out the bottle and popped the cork. "What the hell?" he said. "Let's celebrate."

Dorathy asked, "What are we celebrating?"

Alex response was simple. "Life."

"To us, then, to our brave new future together and to the future of our planet."

Alex leaned in to kiss her. "In case you didn't know it, you are the most incredible woman I have ever met."

Everyone was so excited about this new technology, but tension also filled the air. She knew what she needed to do when she arrived and was a bit apprehensive. She needed to be firm in her approach, and relentless when it came to bargaining. She knew she couldn't show her cards until all the chips were on the table.

As they boarded her jet, the flight attendant was taking drink and food orders, and making sure everyone was comfortable. Dorathy stopped at the flight deck to greet the pilot. "Hi, Hendrik, nice to see you again. How's the family?"

Hendrik, with a big toothy grin, said in his thick German accent, "Ach, they are good, Dorathy, and it is good to be seeing you again."

"Hey, Hendrik, we need to make this a quick trip."

"I understand," Hendrik said. "You want I do Mach 3?"

"Yes, that would be good."

"We must refuel then, in Iceland."

"That's fine, thank you."

"Okay guys, take a seat." Dorathy was in charge now. "Hendrik is putting the pedal to the metal."

Alex was amused and enamored by his woman and said, "Honey, you sure know how to show a guy a good time and you definitely have a need for speed."

As she settled in beside him, she fastened her seat belt and said, in a very serious voice, "Oh baby, you have no idea."

The jet rocketed down the runway and immediately was throttled up to full power. The landing gear was tucked efficiently into its belly, the acceleration throwing everyone back firmly into their seats, leaving behind a vortex of clean exhaust.

CHAPTER 9

On their approach to Iceland Dorathy looked out the window and appreciated its untouched beauty. It was raw, it was a place frozen in time. The rest of the world seemed to have disappeared, as if she had travelled back millions of years when the Earth was still in its infancy. Hot gases and steam rose from cracks in the crust above a bubbling hot cauldron, reminding her of all from which she thought we had originated.

Refueling was quick and they were off again before an early summer storm could make its appearance.

After landing at terminal three at Geneva's international airport, they all gathered their things while an immigration officer took their passports and checked them through. As they walked through the terminal Dorathy admired the luxury specialty caviar and wine shops. She grabbed Alex's hand and said, "Please, remind me to stop by and pick up some wine before we depart."

Exiting the airport, they found a limo at the curb waiting to take them to the Four Seasons Hotel. Lucy had done her research and told her this was by far the nicest place to stay, with an incredible view of Lake Geneva. They could go by train or have a private car with driver. And, although Dorathy had loved traveling by train on their last trip here, she decided having a car available on her schedule would be better than working around a train timetable.

The rooms were incredible. Jack was across the hall with a city view, while Alex and Dorathy's room had a magnificent lake view. Jack said he planned to take a nap and then would meet up with them for dinner.

Carlo had gone on to stay with his uncle. Since the unfortunate assignment he had been tasked with had been completed, there was no point for him to stay stateside. Carlo's guilt over what he had done would follow him for the rest of his life. But knowing the eventual outcome and foreseeing the future eased his burden somewhat. He would forever remember the kindnesses Dorathy had extended to him. For now, the only thing he could embrace was that this was his ticket home.

When the bell captain opened the door to their suite Dorathy gushed with excitement, "Look at the view Alex, isn't it amazing?" Alex tipped the bellman as he left and shut the door behind him.

"Yes, it is." He walked over and put his arms around her waist and turned her to face him. "Yes, the view is quite spectacular. And I guess the lake is nice, too." He kissed her neck and sniffed the sweet scent of her hair. "We should check out the big Jacuzzi tub Lucy promised us. I think you need a good long back rub and a nice glass of wine before dinner."

"You know what? I think you're right."

The bath was nice, the backrub erotic, dinner superb, and the night was full of romance. They lay in each other's arms in a huge canopy bed facing a wall of French doors that were opened out to the oversized balcony. From the bed they could see the Jet d'Eau. An impressive sight: illuminated bursts of water shot more than one hundred and twenty meters into the air.

Dorathy slept, secure with her man by her side. But tomorrow was to be another day. She was to address the International Council for Science.

In the morning Alex and Dorathy dressed and decided on room service for breakfast out on the balcony overlooking the water. She called Jack with an invitation to join them, so they could sit and discuss their plan.

It was a beautiful summer day, with the snowcapped Alps in the distance and a variety of boats passing by on the lake. Dorathy sat enjoying the view and wondered how it might look even just fifty years from now; what changes to the scenery would be made with the development of this technology? Would it stay the same or would its beauty and charm be lost and forgotten as mankind shifted attention to the sky?

Dorathy and Jack discussed her approach to making her presentation when she addressed the members of CERN and the ICSU. She was impeccably turned out in a beautifully tailored black suit skirt and deep turquoise blouse.

Passing a plate of pastries to Alex, Jack said, "I think you should just spell it out, Dora. They'll fall over themselves when you make the announcement, and they'll see what will be gained over the long run. When you get up there, just spell it out. The shock and awe will wear off once they wrap their heads around the offer being presented."

Alex chimed in, "I agree with Jack, they'll get over it. Maybe not immediately, but in the end, they'll be on board."

Dorathy said with a little amusement, "I think I'm just going to wing it. I hate overthinking this. And forget about a structured speech; they just tend to screw my presentation all to hell."

Alex and Jack laughed, and both said that they knew she could handle herself under pressure.

Dorathy got up and reached for her bag. "If I don't take care of this throbbing pain in my head, I'm liable to take someone else's head off if they cross me while I'm up there." She grimaced, "And, then where will we be?"

"Can I do anything for you, honey?"

Looking at her watch, she said, "No, I'm fine, but we should wrap this up and get down to the car soon."

The amphitheater at CERN was filled to capacity. There were representatives from all over the world, including CERN's member delegates. Dorathy would be the last to speak, after the field experts had disclosed their research findings. She took notes during the other presentations, impressed by the complexity and comprehensiveness of the information. Jack was equally excited, as his field of expertise was particle physics. What they both knew, without a doubt, was that the presentation of the discovery was going to change the world.

When the last speaker left the stage, it was Dorathy's turn at the podium. She was a bit anxious, since she had never been comfortable with public speaking. She took a sip of water and, wishing it was tequila, she approached the podium. A moment or two went by and people were still rudely talking amongst themselves. She tapped the microphone with her perfectly manicured fingertip. Once the crowd had quieted, she introduced herself. "Hello. For those of you who do not know me, my name is Doctor Dorathy Rosen of the Rosen Foundation."

"I am going to get right to the point. This new discovery here at CERN has captivated our attention and our imagination. There is so much more to learn and the task may take several years to see it through to fruition. I am here to make an offer to try to speed its progress along, so to speak, at light speed. My colleagues and I represent the private sector at JPL. We are prepared to take on the cost of what will, no doubt, be a prodigious financial outlay. Our intention is to advance this discovery to the point where there are applications to daily life. Progress will be made toward the development of a new frontier for space travel. My proposal is simple, really. We receive exclusive rights to the technology—Dorathy was interrupted by a huge uproar from the crowd. She waited for things to calm down, but it seemed as if the gathering believed that what she had just said was up for a debate. She tapped her microphone a few times and said, "Please, let me finish. My proposal . . . MY PORPOSAL," she practically had to scream into the microphone.

The crowd started to hush, and she continued, "My proposal is that the Rosen Foundation is prepared to donate funds for further development, but to have all advancements from such developments be regulated by, and disclosed only to, JPL. We retain all intellectual property for the technology, and we use such technology as we see fit." Uproar erupted, as she said under her breath, "For God's sake, people."

Dorathy had had enough and said, with such authority it surprised even her, "OUI! . . . I AM WILLING TO DONATE TO THE RESEARCH AND DEVELOPMENT 150 BILLION DOLLARS!" That seemed to get everyone's attention.

One of the key research scientists from CERN yelled out, "You Americans think you are so entitled!" Another, from the Turkish delegation, stood up and said, "My grandmother always told me, "Beware of Greeks bearing gifts!"

Dorathy stood at the podium nonchalantly looking at her hand, checking her nails, for she was about to bare her claws. Dorathy took the microphone in her hand and calmly walked away from the podium so that everyone could see her clearly. She projected total confidence, signaling to the assemblage of scientists *'I will not back down, nor will I give the impression of taking cover.'*

Dorathy spoke with a calm that projected steadfastness; she would not be swayed, nor would she waver. "That is my offer, take it or leave it. The offer is only good for twenty-four hours." She tossed the microphone to the podium and walked off the stage.

The crowd became hysterical. Some were shocked at the dollar amount, as no one in history, including her father, had ever granted that amount of funding. Others were outraged by her attempt at controlling the discovery and some were simply in awe and didn't know what to think.

As Dorathy went backstage she found Jack chuckling with eyes tearing, shaking his head, "Man, Dora, you got a set of balls! Holy shit! That speech will go down in history!"

Alex was grinning ear to ear he was so proud of her. "Honey, remind me never to piss you off."

"You think they got the message? Damn, I need a drink, because I pretty much gave away my entire fortune."

Jack said, "Yup, I think it might be a good time to leave before they gather a lynch mob." A security team led them to a back door where the car was waiting.

In the car Dorathy kicked off her stilettos. "I wanted to beat that Turkish prick within an inch of his life, with my shoe!" They all laughed, including the driver.

When they got back to the hotel, they decided that having a drink and an early dinner sounded good. The concierge suggested they try a small place just up the road that had a nice terrace overlooking the lake, so they changed into comfortable clothes and met in the lobby.

Alex and Dorathy sat in the lobby waiting for Jack and marveled at the beauty of the hotel Lucy had chosen for them. The furnishings were beautifully upholstered with an ornate heavy silk fabric in powder blue;

the floors were no doubt Italian marble and brightly lit crystal chande-
liers hung above them. Large original oils framed in ornate gold leaf
were tastefully displayed on each of the lobby walls. The air was filled
with the fragrance of a variety of white flowers blooming in artfully done
arrangements that were dispersed amongst the French provincial furnishings. Dorathy was acquainted with this level of splendor but would
also have felt right at home if it had been a tree house.

Alex commented on how lovely the hotel was. "You must be accustomed to this lifestyle."

"Well, yes and no. I grew up living in nice homes and when we traveled abroad it was always top notch, but my father showed me the other
side of things and that made me understand that a person really only
needs so much and anything beyond that was just a waste. Honestly, I
would have to say the best times I spent away from home were on trips
I took with my father that were a bit more rustic. We spent a lot of those
times in tents with no modern amenities," and with a chuckle she added,
"that also means no bathrooms."

Jack appeared, wearing his best business casual attire. "Sorry for the
delay, Hugo called to get a blow by blow of the presentation today. He
sends his best and wished he had been here to see their faces when you
made your demands. He's quite confident that they will agree to the
terms."

"Damn straight they will take the offer. It's the most anyone has ever
donated to funding a project in history."

Jack was still shaking his head. "And that was the most entertaining
speech I have ever witnessed. Thank Christ you're on our side. I would
have hated to have been on the receiving end of that lashing."

Dorothy said in her defense, "Well, hell, I barely said anything."

"Oh, yes." Jack continued, "It's not what you said, it's more about how
you said it. I loved how you threw the microphone at the podium when
you were finished—nice touch."

Dorothy snorted, "Well I guess better at the podium than upside those
bastards' heads." They broke out in laughter as they left the lobby.

While dining on a nice meal and sharing several bottles of exquisite French wine, they made plans for the future of this extraordinary

new discovery. Jack said, "The idea of bending space in order to travel through it changes everything. The way I'm hearing this is that they have discovered that the stiffness of space-time may have some dependency on the magnitude of how the acceleration and snap are manifested in a physical system. The scenario within the LHC induced a very high rate of transverse acceleration. My theory is that this stimulated the quantum vacuum in a manner that opened a worm hole. Jack felt punchy. "What it really sounds like is creating a worm hole and instantaneously being pulled through." Jack suddenly found himself snorting in laughter. "It's sort of like disappearing up your own asshole."

Dorathy was taking sip of wine when she heard that and practically blew it out of her nose. "Oh God, Jack, you're killing me," she chortled and wiped her mouth with her napkin.

Jack continued, "Seriously though, can you see how big this is going to be? It's so exciting."

Dorathy added, "Hope those bastards call tonight and give us the okay, because I can't wait to get down there and start ripping into this project. Of course, I must meet with my board of directors and tell them they are out of a job after they cut a big fat check. They're not going to like that, not one bit, but they answer to me, not the other way around. They'll just have to get over it."

Alex was enjoying the conversation, listening and learning. He finally said, "So I'm guessing here, you will design around this and test it at a small scale, then get a much larger application for it later?"

Dorathy said, "Absolutely, but I plan on designing it around a cryo-capsule first. Talk about a great selling point. The cost will be exorbitant at first, but all new technology is and that never seemed to stop anyone in the past from purchasing it. Everyone wants to be the first one on the block to have something new."

Alex agreed and said, "I wonder who will be the first to sign up for it?"

Dorathy replied, "Most likely some eccentric bastard who's spending his last dime on one last adventure. But I do want to sign up for it; burial in space, forever preserved on ice."

Dorathy felt compelled to share her thoughts on the matter, the wine having gone to her head. "So, what if someone chooses this route for their final farewell, and they get launched out into deep space through a wormhole and end upon the other side of the universe, then an alien space craft comes by and says, 'Hey look, what's that out there?' And they go over and pick up your sorry ass and revive you?"

By this time the group were feeling the effects of the shared bottles of wine and feeling punchy from the stress of the day. Jack said jokingly in his best Martian voice, "Take me to your leader."

Alex cracked up. "You just spent hundreds of thousands of dollars to be frozen and shot out into deep space by means of the most current, advanced, cutting edge technology, that will change the course of the planet, so you can be brought back from the dead by an alien race and for what? So they can do an anal probe?"

Jack and Dorathy took a moment to absorb what he had just said and to realize the scale of the insanity and even perhaps the probability of what he just described, and almost fell off their chairs in laughter. Dorathy said both as a joke and as a commentary should those events actually transpire, "That's messed up." Jack and Alex continued to laugh at such a possibility.

Jack said, "You took the words right out of my mouth."

After a few more colorful metaphors, the group decided to call it a night. Dorathy was anxious to get back to the hotel and see if there had been a response to her offer. They strolled along the lakeside walkway and stopped to take some pictures in front of the fountain. It was brightly lit now that the sun had set. Dorathy was feeling a bit of a chill and Alex put his arm around her shoulders to keep her warm.

When they reached the lobby, they went directly to the front desk to see if there was a message of any kind from CERN and behold there was. It read, '*We accept your offer.*'

Dorathy was relieved. She feared she may have been too imperious, but she had drawn a line in the sand and was glad it paid off. She calmly said, "We're in."

CHAPTER 10

The next morning there was to be a brief meeting with the director of CERN and the head of the ICSU, but it didn't quite turn out that way. Dorathy wanted to personally go down to the Large Hardon Collider, and she wanted to look at the most recent data that had been collected.

Dorathy quietly said, "I will be spending a lot of time here in the next few years. I have dedicated a very large sum of money which you have agreed to accept on the condition that you abide by my demands; which are not up for negotiation. So, unless you have changed your minds, I advise that you cooperate."

It was with a feeling of triumph that Dorathy watched the two men in charge lean back in their chairs and, acting as it was a massive inconvenience, finally agreed.

Hans Grobler had been the director of CERN for the past seventeen years and he saw the resemblance to his old friend, John, as he took Dorathy's hand. A big Austrian man in his early sixties, he had intense blue eyes and sported the same crewcut he most likely had been wearing since he was a child. Hans finally stood and said, "All right, you have made your point. I will take you down now and you can meet the people who you will be working for . . ."

Dorathy interjected, "With, who I will be working WITH."

"Yes, of course. Hans sounded put off by her persistence.

Dorathy could not get a handle on Carmen Mallia the president of the ICSU. He was a short, dark haired, quiet man with a goatee, who had to be in his sixties as well, but showed hardly any signs of his age. He seemed to be studying her every move but said very little. When he finally did speak all he could muster, in what sounded like a Maltese accent was, "I hope that by accepting your *donation* we have not shot ourselves in the foot."

Dorathy answered him, "We have a common goal here; the advancement of this technology. My funding will get the job done and having me on board gives this project the much needed . . . ," she felt like saying 'kick in the ass' but said, instead, " . . . help to make this technology available in a timely fashion." Carmen Mallia nodded his head in agreement for he was acquainted with the situation.

The group was escorted to the elevator that would be taking them one hundred and seventy-five meters below the surface where the LHC resided. When the elevator glided to a halt and the doors slid open, the group was greeted by Carlo and his uncle Lucca.

Lucca Venturini was a tall, vigorous man with an athletic, muscular build, a beautiful olive complexion and a stunningly perfect face. His wavy salt-and-pepper hair was thick and tousled and his bright blue eyes shone with a deep caring for Dorathy. Dressed to the nines in beautifully tailored slacks and shirt, he spoke with just a hint of an Italian accent. He had spent a good portion of his life in the UK at Oxford, where he had studied and later was involved in a research study.

"Hello, Dorathy. My nephew has told me a great deal about you, and I want to thank you, first for your caring and the friendship you gave to Carlo. That is important to me and I will help and support you in any way I can."

"Thank you, Mr. Venturini."

"Please, no formalities. Lucca . . . just Lucca." He was having a very difficult time with the decision that had been made. Dorathy was the daughter of his dearest friend. He gained solace in knowing John would have approved; nevertheless, the pain had shown in his eyes.

After the introductions were taken care of, they proceeded down a corridor that opened into a cavernous area filled with equipment and encompassing the location where the particle beams were being smashed at nearly the speed of light. They met with countless scientists in just about every field imaginable and with interns from across the globe.

One of the young interns, a chatty young woman from MIT and about the same age as Athena, approached Dorathy and said, "Dr. Rosen my name is Rachel McMasters and I just want to say it's a real pleasure to meet you. I wanted to tell you that you have been an inspiration to me and my studies. I also want to say that I read your book *Read Between the Lines* and I found it fascinating, a real eye opener. So far removed from your expertise and yet so precise in its presentation."

Dorathy was honored, first that she could inspire anyone to do well at their chosen field and then that anyone had read her book and liked it.

"I'm very pleased to hear that, Rachel. I always hoped that the work that I have done, and the work that my father had done before me, would help pave the way for a brighter future for all of us. Now as far as my book is concerned, I wrote that when I was still trying to figure out what I wanted my major to be. I must have been about eighteen when I was doing research for a genetics class. My professor urged me to write it after a paper I had handed him—an attempt to decode our un-coded DNA. Can I ask where you found it or how you heard of it?"

Rachel said, "Well I was just going through the library at school and came across it when I was trying to find some research material for my dissertation." Rachel continued, "The fundamentalists I know disagree with your hypothesis, but the more radical thinkers agree that it's incongruous to believe that much of our DNA is junk and has no real purpose. I believe there is purpose for it, and the studies being made lead a lot of people to think likewise. That it could read as a language and may well be an encryption of some sort is fascinating, to say the least. Also, your explanation for why the human race seems to be divided the way it is, not because of the differences due to cultural upbringing, social status, or the rest of it, but that there is a gene sequence that some of us have retained, while others' sequences have degraded over the course of time and evolution . . . well it makes a person stop to consider the likelihood of your explanation when correlating it with past events in our history."

Dorathy responded thoughtfully to the young scientist. "I know my explanation was very broad in its description and many argued that

there are myriad reasons that civilization has evolved along separate paths. As time moves on, we cannot deny that the process of evolution and natural selection is taking place before our eyes. One has to ask why, when we all are made of the same stuff, it is that some of us have evolved towards technology and moving forward towards a common goal, when others feel the need to destroy and justify it that by wrapping it up in a nice package and labeling it religion. My summary of the book is that aggression is in all of us, but some of us have been able to grow past it, while others have not. That was my theory of *why*."

Rachel smiled in agreement. "I enjoyed reading it because you basically put it all in a nutshell. Anyway, I just wanted to meet you and to tell you that I hope I have the pleasure of working with you. What you are doing is changing the world and I'm glad I'm a part of what you are trying to achieve."

Dorathy shook the young woman's hand. "It was a pleasure Rachel and thank you."

The group moved on toward the Collider. Alex whispered in Dorathy's ear, "You never mentioned you wrote a book. You think I can get a signed copy of it?"

Dorathy whispered back, "It will cost you." Alex's smile held promise.

Dorathy had always appreciated the Large Hadron Collider. An impressive piece of technology, with enhancements over the last fifty years that had intensified its power exponentially. With each new upgrade, the last major one only being a few months ago, scientists had been able to slowly unfold more mysteries on how the universe functioned. The fabric of space itself was becoming more transparent to those who peered closely enough into the weave of its threads.

Dorathy and Jack were fascinated by the data collected and by the impact of what had been discovered. It all made perfect sense—it was the simplicity and the harmony of its nature that was truly captivating. The equation was of its purest form, a simple alignment of all things; truly the theory of everything coming together in a beautiful arrangement of elements.

This indeed broke the Standard Model of physics and everything that had remained elusive came together with such clarity that the Universe suddenly made sense. Dorathy was deeply emotional to have been a part of history being made right before her eyes and said, "This truly is an extraordinary discovery, this is going to change humanity."

Jack agreed. "This is exactly what theoretical physicists have been searching for since the beginning of modern science."

Alex, a physician, compared it to the discovery and development of 3D Bioprinting and Synthetic DNA. "This seems to be equivalent to finally becoming capable of creating life from lifelessness. We have always been able to find a way. With this discovery we can now venture out beyond the stars. This is just the step that will allow us to evolve to the next level of our existence."

After hours of going over the latest data the group was ready to call it a day. Dorathy was given direct access to any new data coming in and was handed all current data to examine and do what she was trained to do: design and build for the purpose of using this technology. She could fabricate a spaceship capable of traveling to the far reaches of space in a fraction of the time it would have taken with current technology.

Back in their hotel room Dorathy was standing out on the balcony overlooking Lake Geneva and thinking hard about the world they live in and the future of the human race. Alex came up behind her and wrapped his arms around her waist, pulling her in close, and said in her ear, "Penny for your thoughts."

Dorathy's gaze remained on the view. "It's amazing to be alive during this time of realization and to be a part of the human existence. Things and life as we know it will never be the same."

Alex agreed. "It's a blessing to be a part of this and it's a blessing for me to be a part of your life. I'm looking forward to all the wonderful things that are going to happen in the not-so- distant future."

Dorathy turned and gave Alex a long, loving hug while yawning in his ear. "I'm exhausted, my darling, please take me to bed." Alex scooped her up and laid her on the bed, then he settled in behind her. They instantly fell into a deep sleep. In the wee hours of the morning they were startled awake by the hotel-room phone ringing on the bedside table. Dorathy had a sense that anyone calling this early could not be the bearer of good news. She reluctantly answered, simply saying, "Dorathy Rosen."

"Mom it's me . . ." Dorathy could hear the pain in Athena's voice.

Dorathy sat up in the bed. "What's wrong, what's happened?" Alex sat up and reached over to his side of the bed to turn on the bedside light.

"It's Dad, there's been a horrible incident." Athena was trying hard to hold back the tears but was failing miserably. "He's dead Mom. Tiffany called me a few minutes ago to tell me."

Dorathy was shocked. "Athena, please catch your breath, calm down honey. Tell me, baby, what's happened to your father?" Alex watched her with concern while he patiently waited to hear where the conversation was going. Athena was sobbing out of control, and Dorathy could only make out a few words here and there. "Honey, please calm down, please. Tell me."

Athena gasped for air and tried slowly to communicate to Dorathy the fatal events. Clearly in a state of shock, Athena struggled to find the words, "Tiffany called, she found Dad dead in the garage under the car he was refurbishing. The ambulance came, but he had been dead for a while. Tiffany was shopping and came home to find him. They think it was a heart attack." Athena crying and sobbing again and said, "Oh, Mom he's gone, Dad's gone."

Dorathy, also in shock, found herself saying, "Okay, baby, Alex and I are coming home as soon as we can get the plane ready. Is Kevin with you, baby girl?"

Sniffing and weeping Athena said, "He's on his way over. Mom, please come home soon."

"Okay, darling, we'll be home as soon as possible."

Through the line, Dorathy could hear her front doorbell ring and Athena said, "Kevin's here, I've got to go. I love you, Mom."

"Love you too, baby girl."

Dorathy sat on the bed in shock. "Oh God, Alex, Steve has died of an apparent heart attack. So young and so unexpected. I can't believe what I just heard. I just talked to him last week. I know we were never on the best of terms, but . . . ," As the initial shock wore off and the news started to sink in, Dorathy broke down in tears.

Alex held her close and kissed her hair, offering small words of comfort. "Oh, my darling, you never know about these things."

Dorathy sobbed, "I cared about him, but he never really loved me. Somehow, for whatever reason, he thought I was never good enough for him. Where did I go wrong? In the end, I knew he was never going to change and that he was never going to allow me to just be me. When we split, he actually said he was never attracted to me."

Now Dorathy sobbed and laughed at the same time, "You know he actually said to me 'You might turn into an incredible woman and then I'll feel like I'd been gypped.' I figured it was his own low self-esteem. He couldn't stand being in my shadow. He'd try to 'manage' me and when I would stick up for myself, he would call me obstinate. Then he marries Tiffany with her stereotypical artificial look . . . blonde, short, skinny with no ass, big lips and big tits. The first thing that woman did was quit her job as a dental hygienist to establish a new career—shopping. I don't know Alex, I suppose he was looking for someone who would make him feel superior, but I can't help but think we were both to blame."

Alex listened and tried to make sense of her relationship with her ex-husband but thought the man must have been nuts. "That life is over now, it's all in the past and for sure I'm not the only one who thinks you are an incredible woman."

Dorathy looked up at him, face streaked with tears and said, "Yes, I am." She wiped her eyes with her hands. "I'm okay, darling, I need to just let it go. His rejection has been eating at me for far too long. I love you, sweetheart." She kissed Alex and got out of bed. "I need to make a few calls." She looked at the clock. "I'll call Jack in a while to let him know the plan, no need to wake him up this early."

After making the arrangements for her jet and packing, Dorathy called Jack to tell him they needed to leave. She had already received all contact information for the scientists at CERN and was linked into the main server to receive all new data as it came in.

Jack was speechless. "Dora, I'm so sorry. Give me about thirty minutes and I'll be ready to go."

"Great Jack. I'll call for the car and we'll meet in the lobby at 6:30."

Dorathy stood in the shower with the hot water running over her body, trying to wash the past aches down the drain. Every time she looked into

Athena's eyes, she saw her father and now her daughter's father was gone for good as well. She had never wished him harm, and had hoped he would find happiness. But she didn't think Tiffany had been what he was looking for.

Dorathy thought, how could it be that that woman could make me feel so inadequate? Was Steve really that shallow? Was it as simple as him wanting a trophy wife? Dorathy could see her reflection in the mirror opposite the shower. She had a near perfect body, full breasts, small waist, long shapely legs, and nice backside. "God damn it," she said, under her breath, "he always complained I was too tall and never thin enough . . . screw him, a size ten is not fat!" She was having a hard time keeping her emotions under control. She started to cry. The pain of the past was creeping into her like harsh weeds covered in thorns.

Just then she felt Alex's arms come around her as he joined her in the shower. He said, "I'm here for you darling, I'll never disrespect you and I will love you 'til the day I die." Dorathy looked into Alex's eyes, and knew he would be there for her through hell or high water and felt safe knowing she could be herself—that there was no need for her to hide or to try to be someone she was not. Alex loved her for who she was. That would be the last time she would shed a tear over past hurts.

The group managed to get it together in a timely fashion and were sitting on the jet waiting for their turn on the runway. Hendrik had been able to file the flight plan in record time. Once in the air they could relax and have a nice breakfast and a much-needed mimosa to take the edge off. The trip back seemed to take forever.

Dorathy stared out the window into the emptiness below, knowing Athena had Kevin to comfort her but knowing she needed her mother with her as well. Dorathy was dreading having to face this reality and the fact she would have to deal with Tiffany, who would have, most likely, some very unrealistic demands. The woman was insufferable. It seemed as if her every sentence began with I.' All Dorathy ever heard was, "I need, I want." *I'm pathetic*, Dorathy thought.

It was still early in the day California time when the plane landed. Athena and Kevin were there to pick Alex and Dorathy up, while Jack's wife Mel was on her way. Athena ran into her mother's arms and the tears started to fall again. Dorathy kissed her daughter and murmured words of comfort.

Jack said, "If you need to take some time off to get things sorted out, no worries. Please let us know if you need anything." Jack shook Alex's hand and gave Dorathy a quick peck on the cheek as the women piled into the back seat. Alex threw their bags into the back of the SUV and gave a wave to Jack. He sat in the passenger side beside Kevin.

On the ride home Athena said, "Tiffany wants to come over tonight to discuss memorial and funeral services."

Dorathy sighed, "Of course, that's fine. I'll make us a light dinner and we can go over the details with her."

"Mom, she says she wants you to pay for everything and she sort of mentioned she needed money as well so she can pay the household bills until the life insurance policy is paid."

Dorathy rolled her eyes and said under her breath, "When does it end," knowing it had just begun. But she had had the entire trip back from Switzerland to prepare to deal with that dimwit.

Later that afternoon, after unpacking and a trip to the grocery store, Alex and Dorathy sat in the spa together trying to erase some of the day's stress before having to pile on more—Tiffany was sure to cause them grief. Dorathy said, "I'm pretty well numb from everything coming at us at once—the impact of the discovery, to the news of Steve, to the frantic flight home. Dealing with Tiffany is just going to be the icing on the cake, so to speak." Alex agreed, positioning himself behind Dorathy so he could give her a much-needed back and neck rub to ease the tension in her shoulders and the pounding in her head.

Tiffany arrived at the house thirty minutes late, as usual. Athena answered the door and invited her in with a quick hug. Athena knew Tiffany had never thought much of her and could see right through the attempts at friendship as being phony and an attempt to align herself with the Rosen fortune.

As expected, Tiffany was dressed like she was ready to walk the streets of Hollywood—the seedy parts. She wore a dress that left not much to the imagination: very low cut and so short it barely covered her nonexistent backside, and a pair of platform stilettoes reminiscent of something one might find at a strip club. She was draped in every piece of diamond jewelry Steve had showered her with over the years. Dorathy grimaced when she remembered when she had asked Steve to buy her a keyring that had a little leather pouch attached to it and he had responded, "What makes you think you deserve that?" She immediately pushed that thought aside; it was not going to benefit the situation at hand.

Tiffany shimmied right past Dorathy to introduce herself to Alex. Dorathy was thinking, 'this woman is so unbelievable. Her husband still in the morgue, she comes into my home, dressed like that, ignores me and makes a beeline for Alex, and wants me to give her money on top of it. Un-freaking-believable!' Dorathy took a very deep breath and slowly let it out. "Can I offer you a drink, Tiffany?"

"Yes please, a white wine, if you have it, something good."

Dorathy moved into the kitchen and caught herself staring at the knives, but with another deep breath, rummaged in her wine cooler for a bottle of French sauvignon blanc. She murmured to herself, "As if she would know the difference." After opening the bottle, Dorathy poured a healthy portion and put the rest on ice. Grabbing a crystal lowball glass, she tossed in a couple of cubes of ice and poured herself a double tequila with a squeezed wedge of lime. She thought, *this is my much-needed tonic for tonight.*

She handed the wine to Tiffany, who took it with an overly sweet, "Thank you, you're a doll."

One would never know that less than forty-eight hours had gone by since she had found her husband dead and now this woman was gushing all over Alex. Alex had had enough and excused himself to the kitchen to see how dinner was coming along. He was a great cook and was preparing a simple roasted chicken with veggies and wild rice.

Dorathy asked him, "How long?" hoping to rush the night along.

"About twenty minutes." He suggested, "Perhaps take Tiffany out back while I cook." In other words, *get that woman away from me . . . please.* Dorathy read his mind and turned to say to Athena, Tiffany, and Kevin, "Why don't we take this out back since it's such a nice night?"

They sat around the patio table and Tiffany started to cry. "I don't know what I'm going to do without Steve. He was the breadwinner and we have so many bills to pay. If I can't come up with the mortgage payment the bank will take the house and, you never knew this, he was playing the stock market and he lost all our money. We've been living on credit to make ends meet. Now Tiffany was sobbing hysterically. Dorathy you have to help me; I just don't know what to do."

Dorathy tried to calm her down as she was not devoid of sympathy. "Look," she said, "I know Steve had a big life insurance policy, because he took my name off it when he met you. So, unless he's cancelled it, you're going to be fine." Tiffany almost screamed, "But it's only for five million dollars!"

Dorathy said, "That's more than enough to pay the house off and most likely the majority of the debit, I assume."

"But then what," Tiffany said, trying to catch her breath.

Dorathy was confused by her question. "You pay it off and life goes on."

"How will I live on what's left?"

Dorathy shook her head, having no idea where this was going.

Tiffany, in hysterics, and in no particular order, shouted at her, "Food, taxes, entertainment, travel . . . bills, Dorathy! And I have a face lift already scheduled."

"Well, Tiffany you're just going to have to get a job."

"Oh my God, Dorathy! I'm forty-two years old! Who is going to want to hire me at my age?"

Dorathy had had enough, "Look, you're just going to have to suck it up and figure it out. I'm fifty-one and I have a career . . ."

Tiffany shot back, "Oh spare me, Dorathy, you don't even have to work if you don't want to, you have billions."

"Yes, true, but I don't draw from it. My house, my car, I earned myself and so can you. Without a mortgage payment and no debt hanging over your head, you'll be fine. Christ, sell the big house, buy a condo and invest the rest."

"A condo," she screeched, "are you kidding me? I can't live in a condo!"

"Jesus Christ, Tiffany, why the hell not?"

"Oh my God, Dorathy, you would love to see me living in squalor!"

Dorathy rolled her eyes and said, "Well, this conversation isn't going anywhere. I will arrange the memorial service and the funeral . . . and pay for it. As far as I'm concerned, you can do whatever you want with your life, but I'm done."

Tiffany lurched to her feet and screamed, "You are such a selfish bitch for not wanting to help me. I can see why Steve left you." She stormed out of the backyard, through the house and slammed the door on her way out, without any further words.

Dorothy grabbed her drink off the patio table and slugged it back. "Crazy wench!"

Athena started to cry. "OH Mom, how could Dad have been happy with her?"

"I don't know, sweetheart."

Alex came out back and said, "That went well. Guess I'll set the table for four?"

After dinner Alex and Kevin cleaned up while Dorothy spoke with Hugo on the phone. They discussed both CERN and the situation with Tiffany in depth. Hugo was sympathetic and told Dorothy to take care of family matters first, then start fresh the following Monday. That would give her nearly a week to get this whole thing over and done with. Then she could finally put the past in the past.

It was a trying few days. Athena and Dorothy planned the services for Steve without much help from Tiffany. It was surprising to Dorothy how few friends they had as a couple. Steve was an only child without surviving parents and had no other relatives, so the guest list was short. Most of the people who attended were with the company where he had worked for so many years.

Athena was really the only family he had, but he had never really been involved in her life. Not because Athena didn't try, it was his choice. Dorothy would never know why, and Athena was without her father now.

Standing next to Steve's coffin, listening to the sermon, Alex kept his arm around Dorothy and was holding Athena's hand. Athena was leaning into him, holding his arm tight. Dorothy knew that they were a family and that Alex would always be there for her, for both of them. On such a sad day, she was feeling a quiet joy and felt guilty for it. She turned to look at Tiffany, dressed in a very little black dress and thought, she would eventually find her way as it would only be a short time before she met someone else and he would then take his turn taking care of her. Tiffany would be fine.

CHAPTER 11

Monday seemed to come too quickly. Dorathy woke refreshed and eager to get to work on her design for the cryocapsules. This was the most exciting project she had ever worked on, and deep down inside she was convinced that this was going to change the lives of every living soul on the planet. What she didn't know was how much this discovery was going to change her life.

Alex decided to fly back to Phoenix briefly so he could get things sorted out with the business and his house. "Darling, I won't be gone long, I just want to tie up these loose ends then I'm all yours." He added, "I'm going to get a contractor out to do a little updating on the house and sell it turnkey. It's a great place for a retired couple looking for a second home. And, as far as the business is concerned, I feel confident putting things in Stuart's capable hands. I'll arrange to fly out there every now and again, as needed. Then we can work here, together, with the team to get the project off the ground."

Dorathy knew he was right, but hated being parted from him, even if only for a few weeks. She said sadly, "I know, honey," and they kissed each other goodbye. Athena was waiting in her vehicle to take him to the airport, since she was going in that direction anyway.

Dorathy stood outside in the driveway, waving as they drove off. She looked down at her watch and decided that even though it was early she would get to work and get a head start. She went in, grabbed her things, and drove the way she had always driven . . . fast.

On her way into the building she stopped to greet Lisa and, no surprise, Lisa immediately asked where Alex was, just in case she would need to file a report with the other members of the gossip chain that they already had broken up.

Dorathy said, "Yes, we are still together. He had to fly back to get things sorted out. He'll be back soon." Lisa was always left wondering how Dorathy knew what she was thinking.

She got to her office and no sooner had she seated herself than Lucy, walking past from the other direction, noted her arrival. The first thing out of her mouth was, "Where's Alex?"

"He had to go back to get things in order, he'll be back for good in a couple of weeks."

"Oh my God, Dorathy, I heard what happened to Steve, I'm so sorry, that's crazy! How was CERN? I heard what you did over there, that's awesome. God, I wish I had been there to see their faces. Wasn't the hotel just fabulous?" Lucy took a breath, sat down opposite Dorathy and for once, calmly said, "I've been meaning to tell you, but with everything going on we haven't had a chance to visit. I want you to know that I am so happy for you—happy you met Alex. He seems like a wonderful guy." Then Lucy started to cry, tears rolling down her face, and sobbed out, "Peter and I are getting divorced."

Dorathy loved Lucy to death and jumped up to comfort her. Dorathy was beginning to feel drained by all the drama in her life. "I am so sorry, Lucy, how can I help?" Lucy sighed and reached for a tissue on Dorathy's desk to wipe her eyes. She assured Dorathy she would be fine. "Peter moved out and is signing over the house." Then, with a bitter little laugh, she said, "Well, let's face it, I'm a veteran at this. I swear I'm never getting married again!"

Dorathy had heard her say that the last time two times she got divorced. Trying to cheer her up, Dorathy said, "I know you love weddings, so how about you be in mine?"

"Oh my God, Dorathy, did Alex propose?"

"No, he didn't, yet, but I know he will . . . eventually."

Lucy came up out of her chair to give Dorathy a hug, "Oh, yay, I love weddings! Are we on for Friday night?" Dorathy knew there was a lot of work ahead of her but couldn't disappoint a best friend in her hour of need, "Yes, absolutely."

The days seemed to whiz by as Dorathy worked relentlessly, but the nights were terribly lonely. Dorathy would lie in bed thinking about all the years she had spent alone. Had Alex come along when she needed him most—was there some kind of divine intervention? She didn't care, she was happy and was comforted knowing that she would never be alone again.

Meetings with Hugo and Jack became an almost daily occurrence. Dorathy plugged away at the data and figured out a remarkable design for space bending. God, she thought, the endless bickering over the discovery and the data coming in was always so fragmented that she wanted to pull out her hair in frustration.

"Damn it, Hugo those dimwits over there are always dragging their goddamned feet. I come up with a design, I shoot it over to them and then it takes them days to tell me what they think. So, to hell with them. I know this will work and they are being so damn noncommittal."

Hugo leaned back in his chair, plunked his handcrafted western boots on his desk and said, "Shit, Dora, those bastards don't want you to take all the credit. Comes down to bruised egos, plain and simple. Look at all the folks they got workin' over there, most of the brightest the planet's got to offer. You throw a crapload of money at them to get the job done and, with their shit eatin' grins, they take it so they can do all the fine tunin'. Trust me when I say they are takin' your designs and usin' them. They figure they'll take their sweet time figurin' out how to make something they already got, better. I'm gonna have a little talk with them over there and tell 'em, 'shit or get off the pot.'"

Dorathy agreed with him and said, "Thanks, Hugo, but I know what I have and I'm telling you it's going to work." Dorathy got up and left his office, knowing if anybody could get this crap sorted out it would be Hugo. True to form, as illustrated by the sticker on his door that read, *don't mess with Texas.*

It was a happy day for Dorathy, because Alex would be at the house when she got there—home for good. Athena was going to pick him up from the airport and bring him to the house with whatever belongings he had been able to check packed into the back of her SUV. The rest of his things and his car were due to arrive in the next few days.

Alex's home was only on the market one day before he got an offer for the full asking price. Stuart was more than happy to take the reins for a while. Besides, Alex was ready for a career move. Felt he had been stagnating for some time and that he may be better suited for a research and development position at one of the nearby teaching hospitals, perhaps even UCLA. Then he would be able to see Athena in her comings and goings.

But for now, he wanted to be a part of this historic event and help Dorathy with the development of the Cryogenic capsules. They needed to redesign the actual apparatus in order to make it space worthy, while Dorathy worked on designing the method of getting them into space.

Dorathy's initial designs for rocket propulsion were a means to an end, and were not entirely scrapped since the cryocapsules needed to be launched from space after being carried to just beyond the upper atmosphere in a low orbit by means of either Virgin Galactic Launcher One or by leasing a ride via the government-owned Shuttle Service.

The cryocapsule would then rocket beyond Earth's gravity where the small liquid rocket booster would drop away and, after a timed sequence, the Space Bender would come online and the capsule would literally disappear, being snapped to an unknown destination.

But that was the tricky part.

This was not traveling through space at the speed of light, it was not even warping space to travel at the speed of light—this was a way of manipulating space, bending it to permit the ability to travel through it in an instant, as if it were a flexible fabric that could be stretched and contorted.

The how, who, and what were predictable; it was the where and, in particularly, the when that were not. Not in the sense of when will the technology be completed, but the when of a relationship to space-time. That is what truly seemed to elude human comprehension, as the theory of relativity may not be relative to the *new* Standard Model. The capsule would sit in its protected warp bubble as it passed through the fabric of space-time, creating a wormhole, stretching and contracting the space around it as it went.

Solving those problems would take a great deal of time, and finding those solutions would be a staggering challenge, but Dorathy was committed for the long haul. Her father had always said, "Where there's a will, there's a way."

Dorathy was quite a competent engineer, but her arrogance may have gotten the best of her.

CHAPTER 12

W hen Dorathy got home, Alex was already there, trying to unpack the clothes and shoes he had packed in two giant suitcases. Alex heard the garage door open and went into the kitchen to greet her. He was standing there smiling and called out, "Honey, I'm home!"

Dorathy dropped her purse on the table and ran into his open arms to smother him with kisses. "You are home, my darling."

She helped him put away his things and even moved some of her winter sweaters into the spare bedroom so he could have drawers for his socks and underwear. Being in a relationship, she knew, was all about giving and taking and a certain amount of compromise and understanding, even when it meant messing with her closet—that being her temple of sacred artifacts.

Alex was happy to do the grocery shopping and cooked a nice meal for the three of them. After dinner they all sat on the large sectional and watched a movie together like a family; Alex and Dorathy snuggled together on the chaise, feet up and propped with comfy pillows. Athena sat with her bare feet on the coffee table and the three of them passed back and forth a huge bowl of popcorn.

Alex could not be happier; he looked over at Athena and Dorathy and thought he was truly home. For the first time in a long time he had family. Life was grand and he had so many things to look forward to. A new career, a new outlook on his business; he couldn't wait to get started.

So many positive things were happening; there was only one thing left to do and that was to ask Dorathy to marry him. He wanted the timing to be right—perhaps after the capsules were ready for testing would give them a stretch of time to tie the knot. A private beach wedding at her island compound with a much-needed vacation after what would be, no doubt, the grueling but rewarding challenge of getting them up into space. Yes, that would be the ticket.

The months pressed on. Alex would spend some days at home going over schematics for the cryogenic tubes; other days he found himself at the David Geffen School of Medicine at UCLA lecturing about the advances of cryofreezing. Other days he would go on the road to promote his business, and every now and again, he would be invited to speak about 3D Bioprinting at Stanford University Medical Center. Life was busy, but he was having fun doing what he loved with a woman who had just as much fun as he, doing what she did best.

Dorathy was successfully integrating Alex's designs for the cryotube into the canister that had been engineered as part of the space-going vessel, which had the—Space Bending Device. Better known as the SBD, built into its systems. Rocket boosters with an auto-release would be attached to the vessel.

Every minute detail needed to be addressed. It seemed to be a never-ending job. The original specifications of the project were to design a way to send cryogenic capsules, which held a recently deceased person, into space. They were meant only to keep a person preserved with the same care as those patients not bound for space.

But delegates from CERN and the ICSU had other ideas for Dorathy's team's designs and cryogenic technology. Their intention to use the discovery and the designs for the device as well as the tested and proven science of cryogenics, was known only to a select few and well-guarded. Most of all, they needed Dorathy for their secret mission. This mission would change humanity and the course of life on Earth.

CHAPTER 13

H ugo had contacted CERN and ICSU delegates and ruffled their feathers a bit to see what they were up to. He pretty much demanded an old-fashioned face-to-face meeting with them. On JPL's turf.

As they approached one of the many conference rooms at JPL, one of the representatives from CERN spoke up. "What we are curious about is the technology for cryogenic freezing. We are interested in utilizing the technology as a method to transport humans through deep space to colonize distant planets that have been discovered to support life." No one was surprised to hear this information, least of all Dorathy.

Dorathy held open the office door, and when everyone had been seated, took her place at the conference table with Hugo and Jack to either side of her. A handful of delegates sat opposite and announced that they wanted access to the area where the first prototype was being assembled. Dorathy was arguing that the conveyance being built was intended to be a one-way ticket for a deceased individual. "What you are proposing requires a different design—I completely agree with what you are saying there. We would need to be able to control where this thing goes and where it ends up, that is, if you plan on sending living breathing people out there. Look," Dorathy reasoned, "the cryocapsules are a perfect platform for testing to see if it even works. *Testing*, being the key word here. The occupants are dead," Dorathy said, restating the obvious.

Carman Mallia, the quiet man with the dark hair and goatee she had met briefly at CERN, was suggesting freezing living people for the purpose of deep space travel. "What you are not getting," Dorathy tried to explain, "is that these people are not coming back!"

Carman persisted, "I understand that, but what we are suggesting is that if they are frozen, they can survive for many years, if need be. They can then be revived once they reach their destination."

Dorathy said calmly, trying not to sound condescending, "The playing field has changed with this new method of traveling through space. In the past, space travel had taken many months to reach a destination such as Mars. Solar radiation was just one of the factors that made the mission so challenging."

BINGO! At that very moment Dorathy realized that the solution to preserving the lives of space travelers was staring her in the face. It was so incredibly simple. The key word was *frozen,* not *enhanced.* Planning a mission around the thirty-year-old mentality of the Mars Mission, prior to the successful technology of cryogenics and with its usage of synthetic DNA *enhancements* were made to transport human occupants with serious long-term consequences. But this didn't change the fact that her design was for a one-way ticket to—the pivotal component—*WHERE?* Time spent in transit should be removed from the equation. And, with the new cryogenic technology, it was essentially no longer an issue.

Dorathy shook her head. "Okay, okay . . . but we still need to find out how to control WHERE these things go. What you're proposing is a whole other animal. I propose that we test it on cryogenically frozen DEAD occupants, who want to stay dead, for one final adventure into the unknown. That is what we will sell here. So, WHERE they end up will be of no concern to them. It's simple: these clients won't care where they end up, as long as they end up somewhere far from here."

It was time for Hugo to make his pitch. "Look, fellas, I know what you want, and that's doable. We need to test it on these dead poor bastards, and we have already got a ton of these folks signed up for a fantastic journey into the unknown. We stick a damned trackin' device to them and see where the hell they end up and then we go from there. We all knew goin' into this that it was gonna be a long haul. For now, what we're doin' is goin' to presenting a means to an end. You can't just point and shoot here. You find us a planet and we'll getcha there, just not tomorrow."

Hans Grobler, the director of CERN, had sent one of his science officers over to the meeting, a tall, painfully thin man with a complexion that suggested he had spent most of his life in the underground facility. His name was Edgar Heinz.

Edgar alluded to the fact that Dorathy's design was missing elements, saying, "We have been working with the schematics you have provided to us and have found some room for improvement. We are proposing that you continue your work, and testing shall continue on schedule, so then we might evaluate its competency."

Dorathy lit up. "Did you just say I'm incompetent?"

Familiar with her temperament, Edgar backed down. "No, Dr. Rosen I did not, but I believe it to be flawed."

Dorathy spoke now with an attitude, every word like daggers being launched. "Enlighten me, then."

Edgar was holding back information and he knew he had gone too far, had said too much. "We came here to see your progress and are looking forward to the testing phase. If the test is successful, then we can move forward in sharing and incorporating our findings to build on the larger scale necessitated by its future function. That is all we are trying to relay here today."

Jack finally, in an attempt to defuse the exchange, said, "Okay, now that we have all that sorted out, may I suggest we take a break for lunch and then I'll go get a golf cart and we'll head over there so you can take a look at what we have accomplished so far."

Hugo had called out for a light lunch of sandwiches and a variety of salads to be delivered. Afterwards they trooped over to the other side of the compound where the cryocapsule prototype was being assembled. Before entering the vast room, they needed to don static free bunny suits for the clean room environment.

When they walked into the negative pressure room, the first door closed behind them. A jet of air hit them with some force and was sucked out by the ventilation system before the inner doors would open.

There were about a half dozen people around doing a variety of tasks.

Earlier that day, Hugo had informed the project manager that there was to be a 'show and tell,' so the staff was prepared for the visitors.

Karen Johnson, the project engineer, was a bright young woman in her early thirties. She had received her master's degree in Mechanical Engineering from the University of Minnesota and although she had worked at JPL for only a couple of years, was more than proficient at her job. She was lovely, and very youthful looking with long, straight, strawberry blonde hair that she wore in a single braid down her back. Karen loved to wear oversized black rimmed glasses, because she thought they made her look more trustworthy.

Karen respected Dorathy immensely and saw her as a mentor. She always told Dorathy, "One day I'm going to have your job when you retire, don'tcha know."

In response, Dorathy always promised, in her best midwestern accent, "You betcha. When I retire, most likely kicking and screaming, you will most definitely have my enthusiastic recommendation."

The group approached and Karen seized the opportunity to introduce her team of assemblers, and to highlight each of them individually. Every person working on this project, as with most of JPL's projects, was an engineer. All were highly trained professionals and had worked on a variety of multi-million-dollar projects. Karen had impressed upon her team the significance of this project.

On their first day as a team she told them, "Take special care with this project because it is going to change the world. We are about to embark on a venture that will bring us to the horizon of a new frontier. There is no room for mistakes here, no margin of error. If you think you may have done something already, but you can't remember if you did it, then go back and do it again."

Dorathy had been spending a lot of time on this side of the compound. In fact, someone, she suspected Jack, had spray painted one of the golf carts black, as a joke attaching a very loud horn on the vehicle and slapping on a bumper sticker that read 'Move it or Lose it.' Dorathy drove the cart at top speed, weaving in and out of people passing on foot, shouting to be heard over her horn, "Excuse me, coming through." After a while she parked the cart next to her car in the parking lot, so she would have easy access to it from the moment she arrived on site every morning.

Introductions were made all around and Karen began her presentation. "Welcome to JPL. This is, as you can see, the propulsion portion of the apparatus. The cryogenic canister, which holds a single occupant, will fit snugly and securely inside this open area here." With a sweeping motion of her hand she indicated the eight-foot-by-four-foot rounded opening at one end of the device. Continuing, she pointed to the end of the structure where the generator for the backup freezing canister was located, and said, "This will be supplying the cryocanister with liquid nitrogen."

At another work area, Karen started by pointing out the top portion of the canopy, what the team called the *lid*. "This will be fitted as a cover to the device. As you can see, there is an inside holding area for any personal effects that someone might want to send with the deceased."

Karen sensed a bit of tension in the group and attempted to defuse it by adding, "That was my idea, thought it would be a nice touch."

Sensing the fellows from CERN had little personality and that her attempt to lighten the mood had failed, Karen said, "Moving along, over here we have the component we are all excited about, the SBD!"

Now, it seemed, she had everyone's full attention. "This is nothing like we have ever worked on before, and I'm going to hand this segment of the tour over to Dorathy." Dorathy walked up and carefully removed the outer casing to display the inner workings of the SBD. Everyone clustered together to take a closer look.

Edgar, in his usual form, said, "Most predictable design." Dorathy, still holding a screwdriver type device, wanted to hit him over the head with it, but quietly said, "Sometimes predictability is preferred when dealing with complex processes—space travel, for instance."

Carman interjected, "I think we would like to see the actual freezing canisters."

Dorathy was starting to lose her patience. "What we have been doing here, as I have been trying to tell you, is to design the system to carry and maintain the canisters that go inside. We are not in the business of preparing bodies, just the business of getting them into space. The occupants will be prepared in Arizona and, after they are painstakingly frozen to the ideal temperature, they will then be brought here and placed inside."

Carman said bluntly, "We wish to have the current technology for the canisters."

Dorathy was thinking about all the things she wanted to say, some quite colorful, but said instead, "Then you need to talk to Dr. Alex Mason. He is not part of our arrangement with you. Regarding the technology for the canisters, we work for him."

When everyone had gotten a good look at the SBD and the outer casings for the cryocanisters, or tubes, as some people called them, the group departed for their hotel.

Dorathy was drained, and said to Hugo, "There is something going on with them and I want to know what. Why the urgency to acquire the technology for cryogenics? Why the skepticism about my design for the SBD? They're dragging their feet with one and they're pressing for the other. Something smells fishy."

Hugo agreed by saying, "If it looks like a duck, walks like a duck, and quacks like a duck . . . It's duck huntin' season! Lock and load time!"

Back at the hotel Edgar and Carman had excused themselves from the group and moved to Edgar's room for privacy to discuss highly classified information. Only a small handful of individuals knew of a secondary discovery: not a discovery at CERN, but of the same magnitude. The find had been made by a Russian geneticist at a research facility in northern Siberia. The discovery had established the pace when the find had been identified, putting in motion a mission inaugurated well over two years ago.

Edgar peered onto his 3D imager and pressed a few keys—Hans

Grobler's image appeared above the screen. "Remember, this information is of the greatest importance. If news of this discovery gets out, there will be, no doubt, a disruption of power if our associates get too close to the truth. We have reviewed Dorathy's design and our best engineers have found the flaw, but we are still unable to tell the ramifications if deployed. Your task now is for the technology for cryofreezing. Dr. Mason's system works. We must get the particulars if our mission is to be a success."

Carman gazed into the screen alongside Edgar and said, "They are very close to testing the SBD. Once deployed, we will have to find a way to retrieve it. It is on such a small scale, the relevance of the apparent flaw, as a risk factor, is negligible."

Hans nodded his head in agreement. "Yes. I want you to proceed to the facility in Arizona and gather intelligence. So far, we have been unable to discover patents, or, in fact, any intellectual property related to the methodology of this medical procedure, worldwide. We cannot wait much longer. Acquire the information we need for this project using whatever means necessary to achieve our goal. This must be done quickly and quietly. Contact me when you are finished in Arizona."

The screen went blank.

CHAPTER 14

A few years back a Russian scientist, while performing the menial task of examining and cataloging ancient fossils and Neanderthal bone fragments, made an astonishing find. The discovery was made due to the fact that he was qualified for and had held a much higher position, but as the result of an indiscretion with the daughter of a security official of the Russian President, he found himself reappointed, buried underground beneath the stark, frozen landscape in a laboratory that was seldom visited by anyone of importance.

Dimitri Astana had, at one time, been a tall, handsome man with a strong, husky build. In his former years as a scientist he had first been a member of the Russian space agency, Roscosmos State Corporation for Space Activities searching for ancient extraterrestrial life by examining materials being brought back from asteroid mining operations. But one ancient relic had set itself apart. It had been unearthed many years prior and was believed to have come from a privately funded mission to Antarctica.

His involvement, which led to the discovery of code buried deep within our DNA, resulted in an offer of a prestigious appointment as head of a research team of experts in the field of cryptology. The assignment was to decipher the un-coded portion of human DNA. During this period of his life, he had rock-star status among his peers, throwing exorbitant parties to align himself with the Russian hierarchy.

Women had always been at his disposal, but when he unwittingly approached and, with much finessing, deflowered the young daughter of a high-ranking presidential appointee, life as he knew it suddenly took a turn for the worse. The only women he encountered now were either round and robust with little resemblance to what he remembered of the female species, or ancient and long dead bones from the previous occupants of this frozen hell he now called home.

One night, and it didn't matter what time of the day it was, for it was all the same in his small, dark space heavy with the scent of mildew and oppressive with the cold dampness of constant winter, Dimitri had finished his ration of vodka and was studying a sample marked *unknown*. When he placed it under a microscope, he discovered something peculiar and decided to put it aside for further study. He had ordered new, upgraded equipment and it was due to arrive soon enough.

He had been asking for more sensitive radiocarbon dating equipment and a new electron microscope, in addition to other supplies, so he might be able to accurately perform a standard microarray experiment. He said to himself, as he was slowly becoming his own best company. Those Moscow pigs must have put it all on the dog sled, including my fucking vodka. When the hell am I going to be released from this goddamned hellhole? No woman is worth all this shit."

A few days had passed and while asleep with his feet propped on his desk, fur hat pulled down over his eyes, and arms crossed to hold in his body heat, he was startled awake by someone bursting through the door. He accidently kicked his bottle of vodka to the floor where it landed and exploded, shards of glass mixing with his precious liquid, the only glue keeping him from falling apart at the seams—the only thing helping him retain what remained of his sanity.

Dimitri screamed at the middle-aged woman who had kicked open the door. Her arms held boxes stacked up to her double chin, and only her round, red nose and plump cheeks were peeking out from beneath a huge, hooded parka, the fur trim framing her full face. "Fucking stupid piz'da, you better have brought me my equipment!"

Crunching over the broken glass on the floor with her heavy, frost-covered boots, she dropped the boxes on the worktable and knocked over a tray of specimens which fell to the floor. She yelled back to him, "You stupid, arrogant pig, if not for me you would never get any of your fucking shit down here. Maybe next time you better keep your little 'khu i' in your pants."

Dimitri's head hurt too much to argue with her. He remembered that the last time they bickered she had cold-cocked him, which had rendered him unconscious, and she left him lying in the freezing snow only to be awakened by a sled dog pissing on his face.

Dimitri barked again, "Where is the rest of this shit equipment?"

The woman, having had enough of him, yelled back, "How the hell should I know? Maybe you should call them and ask them yourself, mu'dak!" The woman slammed the door behind her and stomped up the stairs, back into the freezing cold.

Kicking his desk chair in frustration and nearly falling over in the process, he decided to clean up the mess on the floor by knocking the large glass shards under his desk— then unpacked his boxes of equipment. He swore if he were ever able to leave this place, he would never talk to another woman again, unless a young one with big tits and firm ass were to approach him . . . then maybe.

Winter was approaching and the days grew short. Dimitri finally received all the needed supplies, including the case of vodka he kept outside in a snowbank, retrieving a bottle as needed, and was finally going to get his wish.

Now with all the equipment set up he could get to work. He remembered the specimen that looked odd, but he needed to find it since it had been dumped onto the floor with all the other pieces he had been examining. Dimitri swore under his breath, "Stupid whore, messed up my work."

He looked everywhere but could not find that particular relic. He had a sense that perhaps that one artifact may hold the key to his release, if only he could find it.

Dimitri had returned one evening from a local watering hole that catered to a unique array of visiting explorers and scientists that came to study this remote region of permafrost. He had stumbled home drunk after a heated disagreement with one of the many who came and went, fell down the stairs and slid across the floor, hitting his head hard against a worktable which was resting against the wall. Jarring the table dislodged the artifact that had been wedged between it and the wall. It had bounced from the table and hit him in the face. He picked it up and carefully placed it on the table while he prepared his equipment in order to study it.

It took only a short time to realize the impact this discovery would make, and he screamed with joy because he knew his days in exile were now numbered. Moscow would overlook his indiscretion and reward him by reinstating him to his former position. He could finally go back to his old life, back to the parties and women.

So, he thought.

CHAPTER 15

After an exhausting week of work and dealing with the meeting of delegates, Dorathy decided to call it a day. She was pleased that the construction of her new bathroom and closet finally had been wrapped up. Living with Alex was a joy—living with his clutter, well that was up for debate . . . but that was an easy fix and she couldn't wait to soak in her new tub with him He gave the best back rubs.

Trying to relax away the stresses of the day with bubbles up to her chin, a nice glass of cabernet and a foot rub from the man she loved, Dorathy was ready to discuss the day's events. "Oh God, Alex, I had the most bizarre meeting today. As you know the delegates came to check on our progress. Hugo and I took them over to assembly and all they really seemed interested in was the cryogenic process. We all know that since the recent developments in this new age of space travel, the global scientific community has been aggressively seeking to develop a means of transporting a team to a distant planet for possible colonization. I get that part; the part I don't get is the urgency they are projecting not only for pushing the mission to the forefront, but to have cryogenics for the purpose of transporting humans to deep space. If this new technology is going to work the way we've been intending for it to work, traveling through space will be almost in an instant. But the thing is, we are a long way from that and that's where I'm at a loss. Why the urgency, and why cryogenics?"

Alex contemplated what Dorathy had just told him while rubbing her toes with one hand and taking a sip of wine with the other. "Perhaps the importance of pushing the mission forward hinges on another aspect that, for whatever reason, is not being divulged at this time. As far as cryogenically freezing individuals for a trip to a known, or perhaps unknown destination, it's a better option than not using it for means of space travel. Over the years scientists have been studying methods of cryosleep or some method of hibernation for a long journey through space, but we all know that the time duration required for a such a long period, wasn't conducive to that type of technology, and freezing people for a mission wasn't either, due to the fact that the freezing process was too involved."

"True. The perfect example would be the Mars mission. There were so many factors to ensuring that humans would travel to Mars successfully. The biggest obstacles were *humans,* so the next best thing was to augment or enhance their DNA in order to make the long trip possible. But the unforeseen consequence of that mission was a tragic end for those poor bastards."

Dorathy spun around in the tub to encourage Alex to provide a back and shoulder rub and said, "I honestly don't know what they are up to, but I have faith in Hugo that he will get to the bottom of this intrigue."

Alex started to kiss the back of Dorathy's neck. "I'm sure he will, I would not want to cross him. By the way, have I told you lately that I adore you?"

"Yes, I think so, but tell me again."

Alex wrapped his arms around Dorathy and held her close. "I think we should go to your little strip of sand when the project is ready for testing. I think that would be a great time to get away, because it sounds like after the test phase is complete it will move to the next level quickly and we won't have the opportunity to get away."

Dorathy thought for a moment. "You know what? You're right, as usual. I think that sounds great."

Alex was enthusiastic. "Leave all the details to me, and I'll take care of it. Soon as the project looks like it's ready for launch and a date has been set, we'll take off, even if it's only for a few days."

Dorathy sighed, "That sounds heavenly."

Alex shifted and pulled her to his side and gave her a long passionate kiss. "I think we should break in this new tub properly."

They were both silent, reveling in the quiet and the intimacy they shared; the love and respect they had for one another was profound. When the water grew cold, they were so exhausted they could barely dry off and crawled into bed clinging together as if they would never be parted, that no one or nothing could ever part them. But time was creeping up on them.

CHAPTER 16

L ife had become mundane over the last year in this top-secret laboratory. The smell of biomolecular compound had begun to nauseate Henry Tinmen, but he had been chosen for this classified project for a few reasons other than that he was the top scientist in his field of study.

These reasons seemed a violation of his humanity, forced upon him by the powers that be. Ultimately, it wouldn't make a damned bit of difference to him. But as the end drew nearer, he thought of his demise and wondered if he would recall any of this life and his life as he knew it, or would he go on trapped in a soulless body forever, never knowing the peace that came with death.

Henry watched the bioprinting material being layered slowly and meticulously by the 3D printer and wondered about his consciousness inhabiting the new body being formed before his eyes. Deep in thought, he was startled when Brenda walked in, in her characteristic stealthy manner and put her arm around him. "Good morning, sunshine, how ya doin' today?"

"Oh Christ, you trying to give me a heart attack?"

"No baby, but I suppose you might be okay with that. You look tired today, didn't sleep last night?"

"Shit," Henry said with a yawn, "I never sleep anymore."

Brenda, always chipper, crooned, "I'm so sorry, baby, can I give you something that will help calm your nerves?"

Henry looked at her with a blank expression that showed the effects of his decline and his body's increasing deterioration. "Tell me how you are handling this so well?"

"I don't know, I just am. We all have to die sometime."

"For Christ's sake, Brenda. There isn't anything wrong with you, and you're just going along with it?"

"Yep. I get a brand-new body without all the imperfections."

Henry shook his head. "So, what about our souls, do you even think about that?"

"Oh, come on, Henry, you still harping on that old story? Get over it and put on your big boy pants. Think about the mission, our mission, and all of us have to be on board with this project, so get over yourself."

Henry harped, "Blah, blah, blah, the damn mission. Screw the mission, I'm sick of hearing about this mission. What if the mission is a big blunder, and what we are setting out to find is nothing but a bunch of bullshit?"

"Honey, look at it this way, if you're worried about where your soul has gone, then maybe you can find it somewhere out there . . ."

Henry cut her off. "Yeah, I know—the discovery of all things. I just hope these bastards get it right and we aren't lost in space with this soulless mission."

"Baby, the way I see it, it's another chance at life, a great adventure into the final frontier."

Henry recoiled. "Part of me thinks being dead might be better."

Brenda put her hands on her hips. "I should give you a pill for that bad attitude."

Henry snapped back, "You know if you weren't my best friend . . ."

"Your only friend," she added.

"I'd deck you."

"Oh, you don't have the strength for that." He knew she was right.

Henry sat down, rubbing his neck and rotating his stiff shoulders, and declared, "I feel like shit."

Brenda lightly touched the top of his head on her way out to check on things and said, "I know baby, you're dying."

"There you go again, stating the obvious," he said with very little reflection on the truth of her statement.

Henry caught sight of his blurred reflection in a highly polished stainless steel cabinet. Staring back at him was not the person that had once been a strong, attractive man in his late forties, it was a face that had lost all muscle tone, had bags and dark circles under his eyes and was suffering from red burnt skin that was sloughing off in patches, producing open sores that covered his frail build. He sighed, feeling beaten down, while he rubbed his bald head, peering at this stranger through half-blind and bloodshot eyes. Henry could no longer hold on to his emotions and began to weep. His life had passed him by, consumed by his work, no family to love him, no one to miss him. He would depart this Earth soon, one way or another.

Brenda entered the area of the lab where the final stages of transplantation were being prepared. This was a cold, sterile environment that reeked of the harsh truth of what they were about to do to this handful of scientists who had signed up for the *procedure* willingly, to avoid lives being held captive for crimes in their pasts.

Not one of the team members had family of any kind and all connections to the outside world had been severed. Anyone who had known them thought they had died of some sudden illness or by deadly accident. A high price to pay for a shot at immortality.

Brenda walked into the next room where another team member was sitting reading over a new memo that had been dropped off. This small space had become their comfort zone for discussing the future. A future that was a mystery, an unknown path into darkness that blurred a reality that only one's imagination could hold and bind together.

Brenda pulled a chair out from the round table which, for all intents and purposes, was the place intended for them to meet and discuss daily events, and to report to the team how the different stages of development were proceeding in their field of expertise. But no one had ever come to check on them; simple, straightforward memoranda were dropped off in the middle of the night.

"Well, I just had a visit with Henry. He doesn't have much time left; fortunately, his SELF is almost ready for transplantation. Poor baby, he's still having second thoughts about the whole damn thing. I don't get it, though; he's going to die, regardless, and having an opportunity for a whole new life—he should be elated."

Magnus, being the optimistic one of the group, leaned back in his chair, muscles flexing beneath a thin, fitted shirt. With a compassionate expression, he said in his South London accent, "Look, I know how he feels. All of us here believe one thing or another when it comes to death and the afterlife. But what we are seeking here, the true nature of this mission and what it has become, is to find the truth of our existence and protect that truth at all costs. My lady, the proof is in the pudding."

Magnus Connery was the kind of positive person that one could either relate to or pass off as being unrealistic. He could be a sanctimonious ass whose beliefs were sometimes very hard to swallow. He had managed to join this group of explorers due to his expertise as 'an international computer science intrusions engineer,' as he liked to call himself. He had become a member of the Federation of American Scientists while serving in his former position at MI6 Headquarters. During his time there, he managed a very lucrative hobby of hacking into the offshore bank accounts of some very wealthy, yet seedy, individuals. Most of whom were a colorful assortment of politicians. When he was caught red-handed, his justification was that the money he stole came from a corrupt government and that they needed to pay for their dishonesty by being relieved of their misguided attempts at power through wealth.

Unfortunately for Magnus, the government he was stealing from was his own and, as a means of silencing him, he had been detained without trial or representation.

Brenda reached over the table for the memo they had received. "Did you read this?"

"Yes, I did."

"So, what do you make of it?"

Magnus slowly stroked the three-day growth of his chin and said, "I believe, my dear, we are going to be in good company very soon."

Brenda said, with a bit of uncertainty, "He is the reason we're here; I just hope he is as smart as he thinks he is."

"But from what I know of him, he lacks a certain amount of common sense and suffers from delusions of being magnificent."

Brenda ran her hands through her thick auburn hair and scoffed, "Great, well I'm going to have to nip that one in the bud. I don't much care for that kind of attitude."

"Nor do I. But, as you stated, he is the reason we're here. His discovery could most likely change the course of mankind, and I feel a bit more at ease knowing he'll be a part of this team. No worries. If he concludes that he's in charge, he'll be sorely mistaken. As we both know, one does not want to get in Henry's crosshairs. I hope he is back to his old self." And with a chuckle he added, "When he's fully functioning in his SELF."

Brenda seemed pensive. "I hope he does get back to his old self after the procedure, because without him our mission is doomed before it gets started."

"Let's stay focused. That statement is filled with negativity. Let's not go to the dark side of things just yet.

"Magnus, honestly, stick it your ear."

"My dear woman, you must learn to control your emotions."

"God, you're a piece of work." Brenda got up, kicked the chair back under the table, and walked out of the room wondering if she could tolerate working with this cast of characters for Christ knows how long. Being the only woman on this mission had caused her to reconsider her position, but her choices were limited just as much as the others on board for this insane venture.

Dr. Brenda Hyden was the architect of the first fully functioning human constructed of synthetic and human DNA hybrid. Her involvement in the Mars colonization project had put her in the forefront of her area of expertise and she was the first in her field to apply this technology to the discipline of 3D Bioprinting. She had revolutionized the use of synthetic DNA to mimic human DNA in order to create life. She had been able to achieve what everyone in her field had deemed impossible. Her answer when criticized, "God must be a woman, as women are the givers of life, therefore it would only make sense that a woman would be the creator of life from lifelessness."

In her successive attempts to create an intelligent being from synthetic material with the upload of a dying woman's consciousness, she had been placed under a great deal of moral scrutiny. So much so that all grants for continuing her work had been stripped away and she had been ousted from her constituency. At that point she turned to the underground scientific community where her work was welcomed. As a means to finance her project, she turned to the oldest profession on the planet. She had created a handful of synthetics with the *appropriate* upload from the part of the brain that held sexual orientation and desire . . . nothing more and nothing less. Her train of thought was simple really, *just give them what they want.* She had become the perfect Madame for the perfect female, perfect in every way.

Both the fact that she was at the top of her field and that there were issues with the legalities of her situation had brought her to the attention of the creators of this mission; blackmail goes a long way.

Brenda sat in her room flipping through the pages of data provided by her would-be captives and wondered how she had gotten herself in this unlikely predicament. She was being punished for thinking outside the box.

"God damn it," she muttered under her breath. Convinced everything had been bugged, she wanted to be heard without it being obvious that she was aware they were being eavesdropped upon. "Those pricks are not giving me enough data on the alien DNA." She thought, 'I have what I need, but I want to be more enlightened on the true nature of this mission. This Dimitri character better be worth the trouble that they have gone through to get his project off the ground. What kind of person gets himself exiled to Siberia? Must have been a stupid move on his part.' Brenda finished the thought, 'Then again, most men are stupid and all of them are led around by their dicks.'

While studying the files of new data her inner thoughts were about Henry. 'How could such a good person be a part of this predicament?' They had only known each other a short time, thrown together in this heap of mishaps and unfortunate misfits.

Henry sat alone with nothing more than his thoughts and the white noise of the slight hum of the 3D printer. Feeling as if he had been drawn and quartered, pondering his life such as it was, he said aloud to the cold environment that surrounded him, "Where have I gone astray from my course in life? Oh, how one fumble turned into a landslide of effects that brought me to this dreaded place?" He chuckled at his arrogance. "Once upon a time I was full of life, full of piss and vinegar. What the hell happened to me?"

He thought back to his early days at West Point and his first love. Under his tear-stained face a small smiled emerged with thoughts of Rebecca, her short, bobbed silky black hair and big brown eyes. He laughed out loud, fresh tears flowing. "God, she was funny, always cracking jokes. Why the hell didn't I marry her?" He sobbed and said aloud to no one, "She loved me. But no, I had big plans . . . what an asshole I was." Brooding about his life up to this point in time, he said, "I had to be the big cheese."

"Is there a big mouse?" Magnus had walked in on Henry's proclamation. "Sorry, old man, didn't mean to intrude."

Henry wiped his face and said, "When you get close to the end, I guess you tend to reflect on your past."

Magnus's eyes glowed, compassion settling into the lines of his ebony face. "Yes, I imagine one would, to try and decipher if one's existence made an impact on anyone else's life, and whether it be negative or positive."

Henry sighed, "I have nobody to tell me if I have or not."

"So, talk to me," Magnus said. "It's not as if I have much else to do at the present moment."

Henry had always been a quiet, private man, and opening up to a woman was one thing, but to do that with another man somehow made him feel weak. Frail as he was, he was not a weak man, not at his core.

Magnus sensed his hesitation and said, "I know of your past and I guarantee I think you are a respectable bloke. Brother-in-arms so to speak. You were a Navy SEAL Master Chief, a nuclear physicist, and Navy pilot turned astronaut. You will hear no criticism from me."

"Damn Navy SEAL . . . sitting here sobbing like a schoolgirl . . . I never saw that coming!"

"You're allowed. What we're planning to do here requires a bit of adventurousness on our part in order to follow through with this mission."

"You mean madness, don't you?" Henry added, "We could live forever out there, seeking something that may not exist."

"Yes, but I think it's essential that we seek the truth of our existence in a positive spirit."

Henry rubbed his eyes, exhaustion on his face and his body slumped in his chair. "I'm sorry I don't share your enthusiasm, but I'm feeling wiped out and I think I'm going to lie down for a spell."

"Of course. Would you like me to have Brenda help you to bed?"

"I think I can manage, but if you could ask her to give me something for the pain, I would appreciate it."

"Will do. Chin up."

Magnus said his goodnights and he was off to his room. He grabbed a book titled, *Relativity and its Relevance* from the shelf to do a little light reading.

Henry dragged himself out of his chair and said to no one in particular, "Friggin' MI6," as he managed to stumble to his room without falling over in pain.

Once Henry was tucked in bed comfortably with Brenda taking his vitals, he asked, "How much longer do I have?"

Brenda truly cared for this man and held his hand as she said, "Not long now, baby. Don't worry, I'll be right here with you."

"How much longer until my SELF is ready for upload?"

"A few more days 'til the brain is completed, then I can get all your memories and consciousness uploaded correctly. Otherwise, I can only achieve a partial success rate. It's a fine line, really. You must try and hold on. If it's not finished, I won't have enough functioning synapses in the new brain to hold enough data for a comprehensive upload."

Henry, feeling the effects of the pain killer, gathered his thoughts. "Where are the cryogenic tubes, don't we need them?"

Brenda held his hand tight, not knowing the answer. "We'll have them soon, they're on their way."

"My SELF . . . how many . . . more . . . days?" Henry was asleep.

"Just a few my friend . . . just a few."

Brenda knew how important the cryogenic tubes were to the success of this mission, as they all did. She watched her friend sleep and pitied him for a moment, then said to him, knowing he couldn't hear her, "Damn it, why didn't they have that sorted out from the beginning? How do they expect us to survive in this dimension? That Russian bastard apparently *doesn't* have all the answers."

CHAPTER 17

D imitri had been waiting for hours in this small, remote airport that had been used to transport mail and goods between his almost abandoned village and the southern region bordering China. Now he was finally on a private, government-owned jet sitting on the airstrip waiting for the worst of the snowstorm to pass in order to safely take off for Moscow.

He was deep in thought, going over the events of the last few weeks. *I have been stuck in this frozen hellhole for far too long . . . how many years has it been? I must make sure I have constructed this theory correctly so I may claim my prize of freedom and redemption. The significance of this discovery is going to give me my old life back; the importance of it will give me the opportunity to succeed at achieving great new political status.* While he was contemplating his future, the very young and attractive flight attendant approached him from the back of the jet, "Is there anything I can do for you sir?"

"Yes." He undressed her with his eyes. "Champagne and caviar." Dimitri knew he didn't have to ask for the finest, it should be assumed.

"Right away." She walked to the galley kitchen and she could feel his eyes stripping her naked.

Although Tatianna had grown accustomed to men making advances in her years in private travel services, most of them were respectable businessmen. She said quietly to herself while preparing his request, "This one is a pig and smells like a yak. I wonder how he is so important to have justified coming out to this hell?" She snickered and added, "How stupid must he have been to be sent here in the first place?"

When she had readied his request, she put the ornate silver tray on the cart and wheeled it down to her overeager passenger. Leaning over to place the tray on the table beside him, she politely asked, "May I get you anything else before takeoff?"

He had caught a glimpse of her bountiful cleavage and made his move. He groped her stockinged leg, "Yes, there is." The implication was obvious.

She grabbed his hand and, contorting it slightly, said, "You may want to check with my father first, before helping yourself." With that, she disappeared into the cockpit and shut the door. Dimitri was going to have a long flight, alone with nothing but his thoughts.

Edgar Heinz and Carman Mallia landed at Phoenix Sky Harbor just in time. Exiting the private terminal, Carmen looked up at the darkened sky and felt the electricity in the air. Carman noted, "The dust storms here are truly amazing, but I would prefer not to get caught in one. We need to get to the car now." Wasting no time, they drove directly to Lifecor. The meeting with Alex's business partner Stuart Kern had already been arranged.

The two men walked briskly through the parking lot. The dark grey sky had turned to an eerie yellow and the wind picked up with the smell of the approaching rain in the air. Lori stood just inside the lobby entrance to greet them. "Hello, you must be here for Dr. Kern. I will let him know you are here. Please have a seat . . . may I offer you anything to drink while you wait?"

Edgar, sounding overly pleasant said, "No thank you. What is your name, dear?"

"Lori."

"Tell me, Lori, how many people currently work here?"

"She hesitated a moment and gave it some thought. "Eight . . . including myself."

"And how many have decided to come into work on a day like today? The weather is quite disconcerting."

Lori smiled and said, "Oh, this is nothing. I've seen storms with a wall of dust 365 meters tall. But today's a slow day, so it's just myself and Dr. Kern."

"So, you still have to put in a full day?"

Lori giggled and said, "I think I might get to go home early today, since it's Friday. I hope so, I have plans with a group of friends tonight."

The inner door leading from the storage area swung open. "Hello. Great, you fellas made it through this muck. Offering his hand, Stuart said, "I'm Dr. Kern, and please call me Stu."

"Greetings, Stu. My name is Ed Robertson and this Dr. Spiro Abela."

"Hello, nice to meet you."

"Edgar said, "Thank you for seeing us on such short notice. I hope we are not keeping you from any early weekend plans." With a wink in Lori's direction, he continued, "I would say this lovely young lady is eager to call it a day."

Lori shot a pathetic look in Stuart's direction and said, "A bunch of us are driving out west for a concert tonight . . . would it be okay?"

"Sure, why not? I have everything tied up well, so go have fun and see you early Monday. We have a few patients coming in then, so going to be a rather busy week coming up."

"Cool. Thanks!" Lori grabbed her things. She looked in Edgar's direction with a smile and mouthed *thank you*. "I'll be here bright and early Monday. 'Bye, Stu. Nice meeting you guys."

"Well, let me take you on the grand tour." They walked through the secure storage area with Stuart on autopilot since he had given this tour to hundreds of potential patients over the years.

Edgar was asking, "Tell me, Stu, I'm most curious about the freezing procedure. What makes the process so . . . special?"

"Special? Hmmm, well first, the canisters themselves are simple really. We use a manufacturing plant in Wisconsin that builds them for us to our exact specifications. The basis of this technology is the same technology utilized for freezing any life form and has been used for decades. The canisters are designed exclusively for our method of cryogenics, which through the years has proven to be the only successful method of freezing and reviving individuals after many years of being frozen. The freezing process is quite lengthy and involved."

The two men looked at each other and Carman spoke up. "Please, I would like to know more about the procedure. As a doctor, that fascinates me the most." With a smile, he added, "We don't want to take up too much of your time. I'm sure you are ready for the weekend."

"Certainly. I'll take you to the prep room next. That really is the most interesting part of the tour."

They entered the frigid sterile room and there was a hint of death still lingering in the air. Carman asked, "What we would really like to know is can the reviving procedure be fully automated?"

Stu was taken aback by the question and deliberated for a moment. "Yes, I believe it could be. It would take some time to engineer and construct the mechanism for such a lengthy procedure, but I believe it could be done."

"So, tell me, Stu, is this something you might be interested in doing?"

Again, Stu was thinking, *where is this conversation leading*? "To tell you the truth guys, I'm not a mechanical engineer. I know the procedure, but as far as constructing such an apparatus, I would only be good as an adviser on such a project."

At that Edgar and Carman exchanged glances. While Carman asked a somewhat more routine question to distract Stu, Edgar pulled a syringe from his inside suit pocket and plunged it into Stu's carotid artery. Stu went down, unconscious in an instant, falling forward into Carman's waiting arms.

Edgar said, without any remorse, "The effects are good for about twelve hours, so I think we have all we need. We should proceed to the airport and deposit our guest in his special accommodations on board."

Carman gently lowered Stu's limp body on the floor while Edgar grabbed a gurney that had been set aside awaiting the next patient. Both men lifted Stu onto the stretcher. Then Edgar headed to Stu's office to find the keys to the building.

Rummaging through the desk, he glanced at the framed picture sitting on a shelf next to a pile of magazines and books. A lovely young woman was holding a child with an amazing resemblance to the man they were about to kidnap. For a moment Edgar felt a pang of guilt as he thought of the child growing up without his father. He was quite familiar with those challenges. Then he turned all the lights in the building off to avoid drawing attention to the fact that something had gone awry. He locked the main door to the entrance as he exited, got into their vehicle, and drove it around to the back parking lot. The two men then wheeled the gurney to where they could inconspicuously load Stu into the waiting car. At the airport they transferred Stu's unconscious body onto the jet registered to a diplomat and took off without a hitch.

Upon arrival Stu would have no choice but to cooperate if he ever hoped to see his family again.

CHAPTER 18

The last few days had been hectic for Dorathy and Alex after the disappearance of Stuart. On the phone with Alex, Dorathy was trying desperately to hold down the fort and said with concern, "How are you doing today, my love? Still no word on the police investigation? Poor Tracey, how is she holding up?"

"I guess as good as can be expected. The detectives are here just about every day asking the same damn questions. I can't wrap my brain around this; no sign of a struggle, nothing stolen, his car still parked in the lot. The two men that no one seems to be able to locate on any database—facial recognition, the prints they lifted—all show nothing. I don't know what to think, Dora, I just don't get it. Stu's record is clean, they can't find any reason for his disappearance, and there's nothing anyone can put their finger on."

"I'm so sorry, honey. I wish I could be there for at least some support. I must get the final stages of this project completed then a firm date for launch can be set. I'm looking at another two weeks, I think."

Alex said in a tired voice, "Good, because we really need a break. I've got Mark up to speed on the business end and have hired another physician with a Ph.D. from Stanford to fill Stu's shoes. He's completely on board, but we have to go over every aspect of the freezing and reviving procedures."

"It sounds like things on your end will come to a close soon. Please tell

Tracey that if she needs anything at all to let me know. The wire transfer went through today, so she won't have to worry there."

"That's great, Dora, thank you. She's a great gal and a good mom. With Stu still listed as a missing person, and we all hope he's just missing, a claim against the insurance policy can't be made for quite some time. So that's a huge help to her and little Andrew."

"Look, we're all in this together, so if I can be of any help just let me know."

"You're an amazing lady. I love you and everyone here loves you. I'll be home soon and then we're going to our little strip of sand for some well-deserved R and R. In fact, the governor of Arizona has indicated that he would like to be here for the opening of our new branch of 'Funerals in Space' since he's paid the fees for his own future service."

Dorothy chuckled for a moment and said, "'Dead in space' is where all politicians need to be."

"That isn't quite politically correct, but I don't disagree with you."

"All right, baby, let me get back to work here. The faster I can get this done, the sooner we can leave on a little vacation."

"I love you, darling, and I promise to be home soon."

"I love you too, honey. I'll call again in a couple of days, but if you need to talk, I'm here, okay?"

"Okay, 'bye baby."

"'Bye."

As Dorothy ended the call, Lucy popped her head in. "Hey there, how's Alex doing? They have any new developments with Stuart? You know, I was thinking about the description of the two men that were there that day, don't you think by the sounds of it, that they match the description of those two guys that were here from CERN?"

Eyes wide, Dorothy stared at Lucy for a moment before speaking. "Shit, you're right, Lucy." The more the two women thought about it, the more it made sense. Dorothy put her hand over her mouth and gasped, "They were here the day before Stu went missing. "Oh crap, Lucy, you could be right, all the interest in cryogenics. But why? I keep asking myself, 'Why?' I don't want to say anything to Alex just yet, let me pass this by Hugo first. Shit, you might be on to something!"

Lucy said, "Just saying. Anyway, have you seen the new guy who started here from Deep Space Industries?"

"What guy? Roger? Lucy, NO! As your best friend, I forbid you to even talk to him. The ink on your divorce papers isn't even dry yet! NO!"

"Ah, you're no fun," Lucy proclaimed. "Well, just let me know what Hugo thinks about what I said."

"As soon as he gets back from his meeting, I'm going to have a sit down with him. I don't know why I didn't see that."

"Dora, you have too much on your plate right now, but it should be interesting. It could be an international cover up! I love intrigue." With that, Lucy was off, saying as she left, "I'm going over to talk to Roger."

Dorathy called after her, "You'll regret it!"

As soon as Alex ended his call with Dorathy, he called Athena. "Hi Alex, how are things going over there, any new news?"

"No, unfortunately. But the reason I'm calling is that your mom is almost done with the project and I want to run something by you. It's been on my mind a while and I want to know what you think."

"Sure, shoot. What's going on?"

"Well, you obviously know I love your mom to the moon and back, so what if I were to propose to her while we're at the beach house?"

"Oh My God, Alex, I love it!"

"Okay, here is the part I need to know. Which do you think she would prefer: a private ceremony on the beach with a few close friends, or a big wedding there in California?"

"I would say a private ceremony at the beach house. We could use the jet to fly a handful of people over and there are plenty of accommodations with the little bungalows. We have a small staff that lives on the other side of the island. I can arrange to have everything we need brought in from Fiji and then have a big reception back here afterwards. I really think she would like that."

"Okay, good, I was hoping you'd say that. Can you help me plan it, because I want it to be a surprise?"

"That sounds great, Alex. I love it and I know Mom will be thrilled."

"All right," he said with excitement. "As soon as we get a firm date set for the test launch, we can move forward. I'll leave it up to you to make a small guest list and inform folks about travel arrangements and accommodations. I'll take care of the wedding arrangements on the island and for the reception afterwards."

"Awesome, Alex. You're such a great guy and I really love you and I KNOW Mom loves you. We're going to have such a great time. I love weddings! So, when do you think you'll be home?"

"I'm shooting for the end of next week. Hopefully there'll be some kind of breakthrough on Stu's case."

"I know, this is so crazy! His poor wife and kid! Sorry, I've gotta get going to my next class. Love you."

"Love you too, Athena. Bye."

Alex leaned back in his chair and thought about his future wife. He said out loud, "God, I love that woman! A special lady needs a special ring." Determined to make sure that happened, he thumbed through his file of contacts and found what he was looking for. "It's always good to have a jeweler for a friend."

Stuart woke with throbbing pains in his neck and head, eyes blurred, and lips chapped from dehydration. He was lying on a cot in a small, windowless room with a heavy steel door. The room also held a nightstand on which there was a pitcher of water and a single plastic cup, and a sink and a toilet which were tucked into a corner. His clothes had been removed and he saw that a khaki, military-style jumpsuit had been left neatly folded on a chair against the wall. As he sat up the pain in his head became almost unbearable. He struggled with the pitcher of water, but managed to fill the cup and drink, spilling some of it over his bare chest.

He sat on the edge of his cot attempting to clear his head, desperately trying to remember the chain of events that led him to this small room. His memories were scattered and broken. He muttered, his words slurred, "Where the hell am I?" He clutched his head, wishing the ringing would cease its constant bombardment of his senses. He drank more water in hopes that it might help. A memory flashed to the forefront of his mind. In this fragment of memory, he recalled meeting with two men and standing in the prep room at Lifecor. Another fragment flashed of him on a small jet, landing and arriving in a cave. He could hear voices, there were dim lights, he was lying, no sitting . . . his thoughts drifted for a short while. At the edge of his consciousness, he could make out a craft . . . some kind . . . he lay down and lost consciousness, his hand losing its grip on the cup of water which fell to the floor.

The jet landed on a private landing strip that ran directly into the side of a mountain. The taxiway curved into a huge cave that had been excavated years ago. It was in the Alps out beyond the outskirts of Geneva. The jet taxied through the foggy, starless night into the cavern through an opening in the mountain that was camouflaged from all but the most intense scrutiny. It came to a halt next to a second small jet, in a well-lit area on the concrete apron. The heavy steel doors of the huge hangar closed behind them.

Dimitri had passed out from an abundance of good vodka and was dreaming of his new life in Moscow, not realizing the direction of his flight path.

"Waking up groggy, and still half drunk," he stuttered. "Where am I? What is this place? There must be some kind of mistake. I am supposed to be in Moscow! I demand an explanation!"

The flight attendant and pilot opened the jet door and two large men dressed in black combat gear walked up the steps into the luxurious cabin to accompany the new arrival off the jet.

"What is the meaning of this? Do you know who I am?" The two men were uninterested in his protestations, and forcefully jerked Dimitri out of his seat and hauled him out of the jet, almost throwing him down the steps to the concrete apron. One of the men pulled out his sidearm and pointed it at Dimitri's head. He said, with no hint of humanity, "Walk ahead and don't try anything. I won't hesitate to shoot you."

Dimitri put his arms up as he was ordered, but said to the man, "When this is sorted out, I will have you thrown back under the rock from which you crawled." The two men exchanged amused glances as they escorted him into an unmarked elevator.

When the elevator doors opened at the end of their descent, Dimitri could see the scope of what was unfolding. A large underground cavern that looked to be a huge ancient sinkhole was now a hangar that held the most advanced aerospace technology known to man. Hundreds of men and women were scurrying about finishing what looked to be some kind of spaceship.

Dimitri was escorted past the ship towards the back of the wide open space. Passing the ship on its starboard side, Dimitri looked up dozens of meters and could see that the gap at the apex of the cavern was covered with camouflage netting. A hazy moon shone through its holes.

How can this be? he thought to himself. *What on Earth is going on here*? And then he knew it must all stem from his long ago discovery. His thoughts ran wild. "They kept me contained in that frozen hell, so I could finish all my work and they could construct this, a means of reaching the destination. Yes, it all makes sense now." He said to no one in particular, "My God what have I done?"

When they reached the back-rock wall, one of the guards held his eyes close to a monitor. It swept a red glow over his retinas and the door next to them automatically unlatched. They entered through the steel door and it shut with a heavy clang. Dimitri could hear the automatic latching system taking hold. They were in a long, dimly lit hallway that led to another heavy steel door. It opened to a space that held what appeared to be offices. There was the familiar damp coldness scented with mildew that Dimitri had grown so accustomed to over the years. Just beyond the smattering of offices there was yet another door leading to a type of living quarters. Dimitri hesitated, but the men shoved him in, the door shut, and the automatic locking system engaged, trapping him in his new home.

Dimitri screamed at the top of his lungs, "You can't leave me here." As they walked away, all the men could hear through the heavy door was the muffled sound of his screams.

Hours more had passed, and Stuart came to, but this time a jolt of fear had startled him awake.

"Oh, God", he said to himself. "I remember . . . I've been kidnapped! Those men!" He reached for the side of his neck where he remembered a sharp pain before the darkness enveloped him. He felt a lump and could sense that a bruise had formed in the area.

His thoughts were clearer, and he couldn't think of any reason some-one would find value in him. He decided a cooperative state of mind would best suit his situation, if he were ever to leave this place. He put on the flight suit that had been left and drank almost all the water in the pitcher. Then he sat calmly and waited.

As minutes ticked by and became hours, his thoughts were of his wife and son, and how worried they must be by now. Wherever he was, he could only assume he had been missing for quite some time.

Just then he heard a man shouting, and a thud vibrated through the small room. Muffled by the thick door, he could not make out what the man had said, but he thought it was reminiscent of Russian. A sudden fear crept into his gut that he was certainly, as the saying goes, not in Kansas anymore.

Dimitri kicked the door hard with his heavy snow boot, knowing no one was going to come back and release him from the clutches of yet another hell.

He looked around at his surroundings, trying to calculate where he might be and who had put him there. He pulled out a chair from a round table that appeared to have been used as a gathering place for possibly a couple of people, as there were crumbs of food and stains of coffee on its surface.

There was a small fridge and a sink with cabinets. In desperate need of a beverage, Dimitri stood to open the fridge. He was disappointed to find only a few cans of soda; he needed a real drink to calm his nerves. He yelled, hoping someone would respond to his request, "I need some fucking vodka!" With a heavy sigh, he grabbed a can of cola and opened it as he sat, swinging his boots up to rest on the table. He strung together a few Russian words, muttering to himself, "Why does this shit keep happening to me?"

He leaned back in his chair, staring up at the ceiling tiles when he heard voices approaching. Through an adjacent door Hans Grobler entered the room accompanied by Edgar. With a smile that did not give Dimitri any feeling of reassurance, Hans said, "Welcome to the beginning of your new life." Dimitri thought for a moment that perhaps he could fight his way out but noticed that the men were carrying very large guns holstered inside their suit jackets.

Hans said in his thick Austrian accent, "I trust your flight was comfortable. My daughter said you had much time to reflect on the past." Dimitri's thoughts went immediately to the buxom young flight attendant.

"I apologize if I offended her."

"We will discuss your lack of manners later. What I need now from you is your commitment to your discovery. As you can see, we are planning, for a mission of true importance. My colleague will now escort you to your room."

Dimitri remained seated, not budging from his chair. "So, you expect me to just follow along with what you have planned for me?"

"Simply, yes." Hans's mood changed suddenly, and he offered a bit of advice. "You will comply, or you will be disposed of."

Dimitri contemplated his options for a moment and said, "Since you put it that way, I will play along."

"Good, but please remember you are expendable at this point in the game." Dimitri could only nod his head in agreement, for his choices thus far were limited.

Edgar said, "Follow me. I will show you to your room. Don't try anything, and do not underestimate me."

They entered the adjoining hallway where he saw several steel doors. Edgar pressed his thumb against a blue screen that must have read fingerprints and the door automatically unlatched. "I trust you will find everything you need."

Dimitri entered without quarrel and the door locked behind him. "Hey, what about some decent vodka?" His request fell on deaf ears. He looked around at his small space and sat on the edge of his cot. He thought, "I must have been a real prick in my last life."

He lay down on the bed and fell instantly asleep. His head was swimming with dreams of his discovery. How could a simple ancient relic of the past so dictate the Earth's future and finally reveal the answers to all of mankind's questions about our existence: our place in the universe.

CHAPTER 19

Dorathy woke with another splitting headache. Rubbing her eyes, she figured it was time to have them checked. She said, acceding to reality, "Well I guess it's probably time for a complete overhaul since I'm approaching yet another damn birthday. Where the hell has the year gone?"

She sat in the backyard with a cup of tea, enjoying the early morning chirping of birds, and pulled her wrap around her shoulders to avoid a chill. It was starting to look like spring, and she could feel the warmth of the sun on her face. Her mind wandered back to the time before she met Alex. The loneliness she had lived with was never evident until now. She thought if not for Athena living at home and her career keeping her busy, she would have been completely solitary. Looking at the time, she was jolted from her pondering and her thoughts shifted to the present situation—hoping Lucy's theory was correct. She stood to stretch, wishing her head would stop pounding and feeling the strain of the last few weeks. Today was crunch day with a final push to finish the project and set a date for the first launch of the prototype. She yawned said out loud. "Damn I need a vacation." She headed indoors to get ready for what was going to be a very interesting day.

Dorothy's first order of business at the office was to share with Hugo the clues that may give a bit of insight into the mystery of Stuart's disappearance. After hearing what Dorathy had to say, Hugo sent the video feed from the JPL security cameras and was able to get a positive ID from Lori. The investigation was now in the FBI's hands, in a joint effort with Interpol. Hugo was adamant that he would do some digging of his own and was going to call in some favors from friends higher up.

"I can smell some serious trouble here, Dora. This needs to go to the top. I have a buddy from college that works at the Pentagon. If anyone can find those pricks, he can." Dorathy felt confident that they would soon to get to the bottom of this. She called and told Alex the news since he was part of the ongoing investigation. He had been placed under protection by the authorities, as he too could be at risk. Alex listened carefully to what Dorathy had to say and was shocked to hear the news, struggling to ascertain the connection to Stuart's disappearance. "Why would anyone go to such extreme measures to the point of kidnapping Stu? The only thing I can think of is they, for whatever reason, needed his knowledge of cryogenics . . . but still, why, to what end?"

Dorathy agreed but didn't have any more insight to offer. "I don't know honey, but they have been a complete mystery from the get-go and they definitely have their own agenda. There is something very wrong going on with this discovery as well as the hierarchy at CERN. But I assure you Hugo and I are going to get to the bottom of this one way or another." Dorathy ended the call saying, "Be careful out there and I'll keep you posted."

Putting the phone down she swung her seat around to look out her office window, trying to make sense of what they knew so far. She was startled by the ringing of her phone. Looking over at it she was pleased to see it was the representative from Virgin Galactic Launcher One. "Hello Gary, how are you today?"

"Not too bad. How are things going in your neck of the woods?"

"On track and on schedule. We have a willing volunteer for our maiden voyage. He passed last week at the ripe old age of a hundred and nine. His family, although saddened by his loss, are excited about him being the first in the family to go into space. Apparently, he wanted to do it his whole life but was never healthy enough for the trip, so his dying wish was that he be preserved and blasted into outer space. Funny how we can cure so many illnesses but there's always something lurking around ready to claim its next victim and destroy so many dreams."

Gary considered his own health and said, "Yep, you just never know. So, what's the tentative date?"

"Well, I'm thinking end of March. I'm planning a short vacation around the sixteenth to celebrate my birthday, then we get'er done, and I guess on to the next thing."

"Yeah, I hear you guys are going to do some great things for Deep Space Industries."

"They've been doing all right without us so far, but they have a mining operation planned on a much larger scale. We have one of their guys here already working on it."

"Okay then, I'll pencil you in for the end of March, so just keep me updated on an exact date."

"Will do."

"Talk soon."

"All right Gary, have a great day."

"Yep, you too. 'Bye for now."

Dorathy pushed away from her desk and rubbed her neck and shoulders. "God, I miss my little island and need a change of scenery." With a heavy sigh she said, "The sooner the better."

After depositing Dimitri in his room to give him the opportunity to reflect on his current situation, Edgar proceeded down the hall to Stuart's room. Unlatching the door, he startled Stuart who nearly jumped out of his seated position on the cot. Stuart sat, trying to stay calm, hands clasped on his lap to present a non-aggressive attitude.

Edgar spoke in a soothing voice to appear reassuring. "I hope your accommodations are satisfactory."

Stuart was desperate for answers but all he could mutter was, "The room is fine. But please tell me, why did you bring me here," Stuart glanced past Edgar's shoulder into the hall behind him, "to this place?"

"Dr. Kern, please follow me and we will explain as much as we can."

Stuart rose slowly, not trusting this individual who had ripped him away from his family and his life. Edgar sensed the fear Stuart was unable to hide—it was clearly written in the lines of his brow. "I assure you we do not mean you any harm and you will understand the full scope of what we are doing here and why your presence is essential for our success."

As they walked down the dimly lit hall, Stuart was feeling a bit more at ease. "You know you could have just asked."

Edgar smiled. "But would you have dropped everything and departed with us willingly? Time is of the essence here."

"No, I suppose I wouldn't have."

"So, there you have it."

Stuart thought that whatever this was all about, he hoped the information they were about to share with him didn't make him a risk. "All right. I will offer you my full cooperation and I hope, in return, you may release me back to my family."

"My dear Dr. Kern, our business is not of a murderous nature. We are all scientists here, just like yourself."

When they entered the meeting room, Hans stepped forward and seated himself at the round table. He gestured to the two men. "Please have a seat. Dr. Kern, we apologize for taking you away from your life, but I promise, you will soon have a greater understanding of what we are doing here, what YOU are doing here."

"My name is Hans Grobler and I am the director of CERN. I am also a leading member of a society of scientists known as the Illuminati."

Stuart's head was spinning. He had heard about this secret society, but thought it was all a myth—a collection of fictional intrigues and embellishments. Stuart shook his head and said with a bit of a chuckle, under his breath, "You can't be serious."

"We are very serious. Serious enough to have taken you against your will."

Stuart placed both hands on the table. "Great. Can you just tell me why?"

"We want you to 'prepare' a few patients for cryogenic freezing and assist in the assembly of a fully automated apparatus that will 'revive' these patients once they reach their destination."

"Okay. I'm on a need to know basis and I don't need to know any more than what you just shared with me. I fear the more I know, the less chance I have of getting out of here."

"Very wise, Stuart. May I call you Stuart?"

"Sure, Hans."

Hans laughed out loud. "I'm happy to see you have maintained a sense of humor."

"Well, shit, it's not every day you get to enjoy a huge dose of some concoction, are flown to God knows where, and hook up with the grand poohbah of the Illuminati. Maybe I should feel honored?"

"You don't seem to be taking what we are doing very seriously, but you will my friend . . . you will."

Brenda entered through a side door leading from the prep room. "Hello Hans, Edgar."

Hans stood as Stuart turned in his seat to look over his shoulder. Brenda was obviously American, lacking the foreign accent that was apparent in everyone else's speech. "Let me introduce you to our newest team member. This is Dr. Stuart Kern, our cryogenic expert."

"Hello Stuart. I'm Dr. Brenda Hyden, the resident bio fabrication expert and geneticist. Nice of you to join us on such short notice."

"I didn't see I had much of a choice in the matter."

"Well honey, you better get used to it."

Stuart was a bit overwhelmed by her matter-of-fact demeanor and wondered how long she had been here and under what circumstances she had been appointed to her position. Brenda knew all too well how Stuart must be feeling, but she was beyond empathy and directed her next comments to Hans. "We really need to get started with Henry; I don't think he can hold on much longer. His SELF is almost completed, and the brain is close to functioning capacity, so whatever it is you need to do, I suggest you do it soon."

Stuart blinked a few times, because what she had just said made absolutely no sense to him. "Excuse me, but what the hell are you talking about?"

Hans stepped in. "We need to get Stuart up to speed on his purpose here, so may I suggest you take a seat, Brenda, so that we might enlighten him on his current situation?"

"Sure, this should be a fun conversation," Brenda said, as she pulled up a chair. Smiling, she knew the information being shared would send his mind into a tailspin. "I think our new friend Stuart will be impressed with what we've accomplished so far."

Hans said to Brenda with some hesitation, "Maybe you should explain. There is a bit I'm sure that gets lost in translation if I were to attempt an explanation."

"I'll give it my best shot," Brenda said with enthusiasm. She considered what she was going to say for a moment. "Let's see where to start. A few years ago, a Russian geneticist, whom you will meet shortly, discovered ancient alien DNA on Earth. This DNA was actually discovered within a human specimen but predates us by approximately 1.5 billion years."

Stuart's eyes grew wide and he leaned back in his chair. He put one hand over his mouth in disbelief and, muffled through his fingers said, "How can that be?"

Brenda huffed a quiet laugh as she recalled her own reaction to the news. "Yes, well you better believe it. Seems this planet was seeded, and we can extrapolate that others were as well. The thing is that the ancient DNA structure vibrates at a different frequency than ours."

"Okay, yes, I get that our atoms vibrate, but what exactly do you mean?"

"They, whoever they are, are from another dimension."

Stuart was trying desperately to grasp what she was saying. "I take it you have been able to prove that."

"Yes, without a doubt. That's only half of it though. As you may already know, about 99% of human DNA is non-coding; only 1% carries our genetic code. For decades we have been trying to accurately read the non-coded material. Decades ago, some wrote it off as 'junk DNA with no real purpose, then of course others found it in fact served many purposes, and some thought it resembled language, a precursor to Sumerian. They weren't too far off with that hypothesis. There is actually quite a bit of information in that so-called 'junk DNA.'"

Stuart was all ears and Brenda could see he was like a kid finally having proof of the existence of Santa Claus. "Jesus Christ!" Stuart exclaimed.

Brenda loved possessing this information and loved even more imparting it to someone for the first time. "Wait for it," she said with a playful smile.

"There are two things in the so-called un-coded portion. The first is a type of timed gene sequence. In the process of evolution, we have come to a point where hidden deep in our DNA, is a sequence that "clicks" on, for lack of a better term. We can excel and grasp technologies, our minds expand as we evolve . . . simply put, we are evolving to a higher state. Our brains are beginning to rewire. Some of us have been able to retain that part of our DNA where others have not. Point in fact: The Degraded Section. They, for the most part, are unable to evolve as their DNA simply won't allow it. It lacks the 'sequence' and they are gradually de-evolving."

Hans had always known there must be an explanation for the way our civilization had been so divided. He leaned back in his chair and thought about the future of mankind. He said, "You see Stuart, science has finally been able to prove the existence of a higher power, the creator of life on this planet, and what we hope to find is the existence of our cousins on other planets. What we are trying to do is to find them. Find the beings that created us in what we believe to be their image."

Brenda smiled in agreement. "The second discovery came to us a bit more recently. Stuart my friend, also written in the un-coded DNA are coordinates."

"To where?" Stuart almost shouted, not believing his ears.

"We assume to the other side of this reality . . . to the Prime Reality."

"What the hell do you mean the other side? Are you talking another dimension? A higher level? What?"

"Heaven."

"Come on, you can't be that broad. Heaven?" Stuart crossed his arms over his chest.

Hans tried to reason. "Stuart, you at Lifecor have been able to revive people that lay dead and frozen for years and, tell me, what has been the outcome? What effects have they suffered from, besides the obvious?"

Stuart slumped and hesitantly said, "The ability to transcend to another reality. Look, I'm not what you would call a religious man, but I can't deny what I have heard from our revived patients. They, regardless of their faith, report the same thing. Not a state of being, but an actual place, a planet or moon with a binary star and a ringed planet on the horizon."

"Exactly. A planet or moon in a binary system." Brenda looked at him now with one eyebrow raised.

"Okay, okay, I get it. So, you figured out a way of getting there."

"We believe we have, by creating a large enough wormhole through which to slip, bent the fabric of space-time to reach our destination, transcending to a higher dimension."

Stuart scratched his head and said, "So why do you need me?"

"Well Stu," Brenda replied, "we need our consciousness uploaded into our SELFs then frozen for the trip to the other side of this reality."

"You've lost me. Why cryogenics? What is a SELF?"

Brenda said proudly, "Putting it in simple terms, I've been able to reproduce the alien DNA with a 3D Bioprinter. We have recently discovered that the DNA found within the ancient relic vibrates at a frequency different from our existence, different from this reality. SELF is short for 'Synthetic Extraterrestrial Life Form.' We will have our essence, everything that makes us—us, uploaded into a SELF then frozen to make the trip to the other side where we will then be revived. You see we can't survive very long in this dimension we currently inhabit."

Stuart rubbed his neck and wondered if he was ever going to be able to go home. He felt as if he had just fallen through the rabbit hole, transported up through a crazy vortex and into the middle of a psychotic nightmare. He determined that if he worked quickly on the project for these people, maybe just maybe, there would be a chance to come out alive on the other end. "So, when do we get started?"

Dorathy took her usual route to the other side of the complex, bumping and speeding along in her customized golf cart. She pulled up to the entrance where Karen and Jack were outside enjoying the weather and discussing the project.

"Speak of the devil," Jack said with a good helping of excitement in his voice.

"Hi Dora," Karen said, matching his enthusiasm. "I'm going to be your new best friend. My team hit it hard this weekend and aside from a few odds and ends to tie up, we are done!"

"Oh my God, I could kiss you both! Let's go inside, I want to take a look."

After donning white clean-room attire, Dorathy inspected the inner workings of the SBD and the outer casing, and proclaimed, "Lunch and drinks are on me boys and girls!" The team applauded the successful culmination of their joint efforts.

They all sat in the back courtyard of a local tavern enjoying their well-deserved time away from work. Dorathy got up and made a quick speech as she held up her margarita in a toast. "To Karen and her amazing team of talented engineers. We all must die someday, now we can enter through the gates of heaven, skidding in sideways yelling, 'It was a hell of a ride!' Thank you all for your dedication to this project. I for one am happy it's done."

When Dorathy got home that night she was exhausted, but excited to finally see the light at the end of the tunnel. She called Alex in Phoenix. "Darling you are not going to believe this. The job is done—aside from a few minor adjustments, it's done! So, when are you coming home baby, because we need a vacation?"

Alex was surprised and excited to hear it. "All right smart lady, let me tie up a few loose ends and I'll be home in a couple of days. Is that island music I hear in the background?"

"Yes, it is, Dorathy exclaimed. "I'm already starting to get packed and in the mood. I called to make sure the beach house is ready and stocked for our arrival, and I've called Hendrik and booked the jet. So, get that gorgeous Aussie ass home!"

Alex laughed. "Can't wait, baby! I miss you so bad I can taste you."

"Oh, don't you get me going with that sexy talk, you best save it for when you're home. I am drinking and hula dancing while I pack, so I'll talk to you tomorrow."

"Okay my love, you do that. I miss you bad and have one for me. I love you, woman."

"Love you too, darling."

For the first time in her life she felt this happy, this excited. *I'm going to my little island with the man of my dreams! I think it's time to semi-retire and enjoy my life and all that I have worked so hard for; just for once it's finally my time in the sun.*

After Alex got off the phone, he started to make his plans, their plans, for a beach-side wedding. Athena was the first person to call, then Jack, Lucy, and Hugo. A sudden sadness hit Alex that Stuart, his best friend, not his oldest friend but certainly his closest, remained missing. *God where are you buddy? I hope you are okay; I promise, we will find you.* He sat in his chair and ran his hands through his hair trying to continue with the task at hand. That old familiar feeling of guilt was creeping back in.

He sat quietly berating himself, *Shit if I had been around instead of going to California, he would still be here . . . I just can't go there, and I can't blame myself. I have spent nearly my whole life buried in guilt; I just can't and won't do it anymore. Besides, I would be the one missing now.*

After speaking with everyone, with Athena's help the plans were set and the arrangements made. Alex pulled open his desk drawer and took out a small velvet box and opened it. Inside was the ring he had found for Dorathy. He thought *a stunning ring for a stunning woman. His wife.* He turned the stone as it reflected the light and said out loud, "My wife, Mrs. Dorathy Mason . . . has a nice ring to it."

Dimitri was asleep in his room snoring when he was startled awake by the door opening with a jerk. Brenda stood in the doorjamb, arms crossed, waiting for this lump of a man to stand and gather his thoughts. "Nice of you to join us down here, I've heard quite a lot about you."

"Where am I, and who the hell are you speaking to me?"

"Where you are is not as important as who is speaking to you at this moment. I am either going to be your best friend or your worst nightmare and that, my friend, is something you'd better get used to. Now get up and follow me, so we can get started on the first day of forever."

"You listen to me you stupid bitch. You bring to me the leader of this conspiracy because I am not the type of man that is accustomed to being treated this way."

"No, you listen to me, Ruskie. I don't give a damn about who you are or who you think you are, you're MY bitch now. Get your fat ass up off that cot, and follow me, *now*, before you really piss me off." Brenda grabbed him by the ear and gave it a good hostile yank and Dimitri followed, muttering some obscenity in Russian. Brenda laughed, "You wish, asshole."

At the end of the softly lit hall they entered the room where Hans, Edgar, Magnus and Stuart were sitting at the round table, waiting. Hans stood and motioned for them to have a seat. "Good, we are all here, except for Henry who is presently too ill to join us. So, let us begin with introductions for our new guest. My name is Hans Grobler, and I oversee this mission. This is my assistant, Edgar Heinz. If you require anything that is needed for this mission or for your comfort, Edgar will try to accommodate your requests. This is Dr. Brenda Hyden. She is a molecular biologist, in charge of manufacturing the synthetic bodies you all will be occupying . . . except for Dr. Kern."

Dimitri stood up to loom over those seated at the table and yelled,

"What the hell are you talking about? I want no part of this so-called mission! I made the discovery and that is where it ends for me. I told you everything I know, and I demand you release me at once!"

Hans gave Brenda a nod. She drew a syringe from her lab coat pocket and jammed it into Dimitri's neck. He went down instantly with a thud since no one had volunteered to break his fall. Without a qualm, Brenda stepped over his unconscious body and reseated herself. "Well, that went as well as expected."

Magnus added, "Maybe when you upload this irritating arse's consciousness, you might finesse it a bit to delete the most annoying aspects of his character—just a suggestion."

Brenda nodded. "Trust me, I'll do my best, he's an annoying prick."

Hans was tired of the constant bickering and he knew Henry would eventually take control of the squabbling, so he let it slide for now. "Yes, let us finish our introductions and get down to business."

Stuart sat looking down at Dimitri wondering at the madness that surrounded him. Hans yanked him back to reality. "This is Magnus Connery. Magnus held out his hand and bowed his head slightly, "Her Majesty's Secret Service, MI6 Headmaster of Intrusion, at your service."

Hans stated the obvious, "While on the other side, if perhaps they find themselves in an alien civilization, Magnus should come in quite handy maneuvering through any database they might come across." Stuart's eyes glazed over with the incomprehensible feeling of being trapped in madness where there were no boundaries between realities.

Stuart shook Magnus's hand without uttering a word.

Hans continued without skipping a beat, "We all know the importance of Dimitri's field of expertise." Hans shook his head and sighed, "He will take some time, but in the end he will comply."

Hans demanded of Stuart, "For now we need four cryogenic tubes. Can I trust you to take charge of this request?"

Stuart snapped alert to his situation. "If it gets me home any faster, I'll start the process of getting them right now. Give me a sheet of paper and a pen and I'll give you a shopping list. I'll leave it up to you on how you'll transport it all to this location."

"Excellent."

Stuart recalled an article he had read quite some time ago about the Illuminati. He wished he had paid closer attention, but he recalled a reference to *A New World Order*. He acknowledged that although he was afraid for his well-being, he was curious about this mission's outcome. And that a part of him was excited to participate in an effort that was obviously something extraordinary. It was the one thing mankind had been searching for since the beginning of time, which was also the one thing that could finally bind us together as a species. He had the distinct feeling that there was someone else running this show, someone of a higher power. With that thought a chill went up his spine as images of his demise went unchecked in the depths of his consciousness. Nevertheless, he would comply with their demands as he thought full cooperation would best suit everyone's needs, including his own and cooperation, he felt, would be his ticket home.

Stuart sat armed with standard notebook paper and pen while he and Hans discussed the engineering and construction of the tubes. "These tubes are usually on hand either in Wisconsin or at Lifecor. At Lifecor we always have a handful in stock ready to go. We keep them in a separate storage area secured by a door accessed with a key code." Stuart drew a map of the Lifecor building the tubes occupied. As he drew, he said, "This is where they are, and you should use this alleyway to enter the buildings from the rear. The code is 2063. You shouldn't encounter anyone if you go in at night. You'll need a large, flatbed truck; these things are large and very heavy, and there is a forklift inside that can be used to load them. They come to us crated for protection. You're just going to have to figure out how to get them here."

Hans leaned back in his chair to consider the best way of accomplishing the task. "Yes, I believe this can be done quickly."

Edgar had summoned the two guards to return Dimitri's limp body to his room to sleep it off. Edgar had always known Dimitri would be trouble, but perhaps with Dr. Hyden's expertise a way to alter his behavior during the procedure could be found.

Henry was lying in his room struggling to stay alive. Brenda was seated next to him holding her friend's hand. It would only be a few moments before the cocktail of meds were pumping through his body. "Hold on Henry, my poor boy, I'm here for you." Henry blinked back tears of regret and he struggled to focus on her face. Her lovely face, lined with years of personal tragedy, her beautiful, piercing blue eyes conveying her longing for a better life. Henry struggled to speak but managed only a small smile as he felt the warmth of the drugs diminishing his ability to even manage a thought.

Brenda stayed with him a while mired in contemplation of the future. Her thoughts were scattered thinking of the realities about to unfold. Her new body was being printed, perfect in every way. A heart would beat, pumping blood through newly constructed veins, lungs would expand and contract, capable of breathing air, a brain would develop to which her soul would be uploaded. Her thoughts, her memories, the essence of what made her unique; all uploaded as one would upload applications into a device, new, out of the box.

All constructed from a synthetic DNA. A replica of them: alien, but human. We are them as much as they are us.

Brenda kissed her friend's cheek and slowly stood and straightened her lab coat. "It's time to do this." She moved with purpose. Down the hall without hesitation into the lab. She checked Henry's SELF—it was complete. She made certain that all preparations were complete then called Hans to have Henry moved to the lab. As she waited, she stood in front of the glass container peering at the fully functional body of the new Henry Tinman. It was suspended in an electromagnetic absorption fluid: in essence, amniotic fluid. His new heart pumping blood, marrow producing blood cells; everything functioning protected by the fluid as if he were sitting in the womb waiting to be born.

There were strands of fine clear flexible fibers protruding from every inch of the otherwise bald head. They waved around the new Henry's head like hair moving in a current. Fluid flowing between the strands made for an elegant dance caused by the electrodes firing pulses, and twitching muscles. The ends of the filaments all came together and plugged into a portal jutting out from one end of the container. From there a connection was made to a large screen with a control board. The only connection remaining to be made was the one that would soon be linked to Henry's dying brain. His soul would soon become a permanent part of this new person who had been created in his likeness but with the core DNA of our alien cousins; the frequency of a higher dimension.

Hans and Stuart entered the lab as a technician was wheeling Henry in on a gurney. Stuart was stunned by what he saw. He knew only too well that if this technology ever became public, it would change the face of the planet. Death would become obsolete; illnesses gone, abnormalities extinct, replaced by perfection and everlasting life. They were playing God.

Stuart was not a religious man, but he knew there had to be consequences for this blatant disregard for the Divine. He said to himself, not realizing his words were audible, "How is this possible? You can't be this arrogant."

Hans responded matter-of-factly, "If God created the heavens and the Earth, he also created these beings who, in turn, created us. So why is it so wrong for us to create from them . . . from us? We can expand our minds with the coding buried in our DNA, put there by them, for us to finally discover answers to the mystery. All that we have achieved has been written within all of us . . . well most of us. It's more than fate, it's our destiny. They have given us the tools and the map, so we might join with them. You see Stuart; we are just following their instructions."

Stuart replied, "I was told once you can't believe in Heaven and not believe in Hell—the two go hand and hand."

"Stuart, being a man of science, you must embrace what we are doing here. Spirituality is real, the other side is real, and our attempt to reach it is real. Religion is man-made. Made by people hungry for power as a means of control."

Stuart listened carefully and grasped what was being said. "I get it, and I really do appreciate what you are doing here. It is incredible. Sometimes though, playing God has certain consequences—like building a ship and claiming it's unsinkable."

Hans roared with laughter. "Maybe we should christen the transport ship *Titanic.*" Stuart didn't see the humor.

As Hans and Stuart debated the ethics of what they were doing, Brenda was busy making the critical connections from the console to Henry's brain. With help from the technicians, Brenda shifted Henry from the gurney to the flat table of the transference machine, and the push of a button slowly slid Henry inside headfirst. Brenda was busy making necessary adjustments. The inside workings of the machine spun furiously around Henry's head, making pinpoint connections, picking up every electrical signal coming from the millions of synapses in the brain. It probed deeply, uncovering every thought, every feeling, every emotion, recovering every moment Henry had ever had through his life, uploading every experience that had shaped him into the individual he had become. All his joy and happiness, pain and disappointment, every achievement and failure. Memories of every moment of his life were rapidly extracted, leaving behind only emptiness; erasing everything. His brain still functioned, commanding his heart to beat, his lungs to breathe, but Henry was gone.

Brenda checked and rechecked the upload; it was complete. The machine still whizzed around Henry's bald and battered head, seeking any small shred of information left for loading. She stood slowly and moved over to him. There was only one thing left to do. She initiated the intravenous cocktail that would painlessly stop his heart. She whispered in his ear, "No more pain, my friend. I will see you on the other side." With the procedure complete the connection was broken. His brain function ceased, and his heart stopped.

Brenda regarded Stuart and Hans. "I can sustain his SELF in our reality only so long in the electromagnetic solution, so I suggest you get to work."

Stuart was amazed at what he had just witnessed; a man he had never met lay dead on a table, his essence or his soul transferred from his broken body to a new one created from a synthetic structure that presumably came from ancient alien/human DNA. Stuart put his hands on his head and then slid them down to scrub the stubble on his chin as he digested what was being asked of him and why. He looked intently back at Brenda and said, "Okay you got it." He handed the paper with the map and key code to Hans, who glanced at it and passed it to Edgar with the shopping list of medical supplies required for freezing four human hybrids.

Edgar said to Stuart, "Come with me," anxious to get the ball rolling.

Stuart followed close on his heels as they left through the double steel doors.

Edgar led them down the hall and through the doors leading to the adjacent offices. He turned and looked into Stuart's eyes as if sizing him up for the first time since they had abducted him in Arizona. "We understand you are here against your will, but I assure you we do not wish to harm you. I have been given authorization to allow you to communicate with your family. It must be kept brief and absent of any details about your assignment here. The connection will be very hard to trace, but even so, I will only allow a few seconds during which you may convey your safety and pending return. No more, understood?"

Stuart was grateful, "Absolutely!"

"Follow me." They turned down a narrow hall and stopped at a door with a retinal scanner. Edgar held his face where the scanner's red ray could identify him, and the door unlatched. They stepped into a large room that obviously had been rigged for the sole purpose of scrambling communications. Stuart was directed to sit in front of a huge screen that covered the entire wall, with consoles that took up the remaining space. This was an advanced monitoring and rerouting system. Edgar went to a console and entered his passcode. The screen came to life with an image of a global map. "Punch the telephone number of your residence on the keypad in front of you." Stuart's hands were shaking while he struggled to remember his own phone number. When he entered the last digit, the screen pinpointed its location in the western portion of the United States, further zoomed to the state of Arizona, then zoomed again to the Phoenix metropolitan outlying area. Slowly, in small increments the view resolved to a residential area and finally to a single home.

Stuart was suddenly overwhelmed with homesickness and wanted to leap through the screen to be with his wife and child but needed to gather his thoughts quickly. He could hear the ringing on the other end of the line.

"Hello," the voice sounded anxious and frail, but he knew it was his wife's even though it felt like a lifetime since he had heard her speak. "Tracey honey, listen carefully, I don't have much time."

Tracey started to cry uncontrollably, "Oh my God, Stuart, is it really you?"

"Yes, I'm fine honey. I don't know where I am, but I'm being treated very well. I don't want you to worry about me. When I am no longer needed here, I've been assured of my safe return."

"Stuart, they know who took you. Why have they taken you?"

"Look Tracey, I can't discuss anything. Just know I'm okay and I will come home."

Tracey very nearly screamed into the phone, "When? Why did they take you?"

Stuart had to think fast—how could he pass off a clue to her? But he had no idea where he was, only why. "Remember that time we hiked up to South Mountain, where I told you I love you? I love you, just remember that evening my darling."

"Stuart, I love you baby. Please come home soon. I . . ." The line went dead. Tracey sobbed, yelling into the receiver, "Stuart? Stuart! Oh my God, where are you . . . where are you?" She fell against the kitchen counter and cried. Finally, she wiped her eyes and her mind began to clear. Tracey recalled the evening Stuart referred to during the call. There had been odd lights floating over the city and never a satisfactory explanation for what they had seen that night.

Edgar said, "I hope that will suffice for the time being." Stuart was trying to hold back his emotions, his anger for being brought to this place, being forced to comply. He believed that what they were doing was important, although it walked a fine line between what he believed to be space exploration and insanity.

All he could muster was, "Thank you. At least they know I'm alive."

Edgar showed no emotion and said, "Follow me, we have much to do." They walked down the hall and exited the same door through which they had originally brought him into the complex, which seemed to be an eternity ago. They entered the elevator and went up several levels. The doors opened onto what looked to be a large warehouse that had been dug out of the side of the mountain, a huge cavern or cave. Row upon row of shelving units were stacked high to the rock ceiling.

Stuart followed Edgar through a maze of supplies ranging from food and household products to tools and machinery. Towards the back they stopped in an area separated from the rest of the cavern by a sliding glass door. A medical supplies area, the space was easily large enough to hold provisions for several hospitals. Edgar looked at Stuart as he gestured about him, "I think you should be able to find what you need in here."

Stuart looked around to get his bearings and could easily see that everything he needed was indeed there. "I'm going to need a cart or something to move everything down to where we need it."

Edgar nodded and said, "I trust you won't try to escape . . . you would not make it very far."

Stuart nodded in agreement. "No, I don't suppose I would."

Edgar returned with a flat crate cart which he parked to the side of the door. After about an hour of looking and sorting through drugs and equipment, Stuart had everything he needed to initiate the freezing process, with the final freezing to be completed inside the canisters.

Hans was sitting in his office speaking with Dr. Lucca Venturini who appeared on the video screen before him. "We have much to do still."

Hans responded, "We have the information we were looking for, and a team is already on the way to Arizona. Dimitri's latest discovery has come late, but we are able to rectify the problem now." Hans continued, "He is not going to go willingly on this mission."

Lucca had grown weary of Dimitri's behavior over the years. "Brilliant as he is, he has always lacked self-control."

Hans added, "He was just a young man when John invested in his team's research. Unfortunately, the Russian government had taken control over his work, but always remained conveniently open to our requests."

"Yes, lucky he found the link and lucky I'm a patient man."

"We both knew this project was going to have many challenges. The gravest of challenges has yet to fully unfold. Your nephew had the most unfortunate task, but we know it's necessary; she will be safely tucked away shortly."

Dr. Venturini exhaled heavily. "Yes, how ironic, that her funding this project would also lead to her demise."

Hans said with a bit of a chill in his voice, "Her own arrogance would be her undoing—very unfortunate."

"Let me know when the team has been cryogenically frozen. Also, when you are finished with Dr. Kern, dispose of his memory."

Hans kept his thoughts to himself and reflected on how he might accomplish that task. "When the time comes, I will take care of him personally."

Lucca responded, "I trust everything else will go according to plan."

Hans reply was simple. "Only time will tell if this mission actually goes as planned."

"Yes, time will tell, my friend." The screen went blank.

Hans pushed back from the desk, stood and straightened his suit jacket. He knew it was time to get things done. He exited the offices and determined that it was also time for a serious conversation with Dimitri.

As Hans entered Dimitri's room, he noticed something was not as it should be—then Dimitri attacked him from behind. The Russian was a large man, but Hans was bigger and highly trained. Hans grabbed Dimitri's arm and twisted him to the floor face down, then held him in place with a knee firmly planted in his back, arm contorted in a way that left Dimitri helpless to defend himself.

Hans said, showing no signs of exertion, "We really need to discuss your attitude."

"Let me go you fucking Nazi!"

Hans moved away from him and said calmly, "Now is that any way to talk? For God's sake, get up you blubbering idiot!"

"Why am I here?" Dimitri shouted.

Hans picked him up off the floor and pushed him to the bed before starting in on him. "For once will you just listen. Your expertise is needed for what could be the most important mission of all history. Furthermore, most people would jump at the chance to have the opportunity of a new start in life and a chance at immortality."

"I am a very important man in Russia!"

"Yes, I saw that when we had to go to Northern Siberia to fetch you from your miserable existence; very important, indeed. You must ask yourself, Dimitri, why you think you are here after such an important discovery. Could it be that the powers that be are indeed a part of this organization? The decision that you should be here came from the top, for your President is just a subservient member of a far more powerful order. So, you see, my friend, you are not as important as you believe yourself to be.

The others are here mostly because they are at the top of their respective fields, but also because each of them found themselves in a bit of a bind in their home countries. We rescued them and offered them a new start on an important mission that may change the future of our existence. So you see, you must ask yourself this question—knowing that your past life of parties and women is, to say the least, no longer viable; would you rather be part of the future and set forth on a mission that will, no doubt, be history in the making? Or would you rather make a feeble attempt to return to a life you once knew, knowing what you now know? Because, my friend, you will surely have your memory erased before you ever left this place alive. Then where would you be?"

Dimitri sat on the edge of his bed and started to sob. Hans stood in front of him and said, "Be brave my friend, for courage is the only thing that will get you beyond this horrible feeling of isolation. I encourage you to embrace what has been bestowed upon you. For your resistance to your new life is futile."

Dimitri had been whipped into submission. He felt hopeless and helpless, stripped of control over his own destiny. Imprisoned in some kind of hellish nightmare. Trapped like a caged animal without the ability to escape. His head was swimming in the horrid depths of sheer uncontrollable dread.

Hans said, "I will return, and I hope you will have made the decision to stay."

Dimitri needed to know only one thing. He had only one question to ask, his eyes swollen and trembling with the kind of fear he had never experienced, "Will we be returning to Earth?"

CHAPTER 20

After a long few weeks of working diligently to bring the project to completion, the first "FREE" (Frozen Remains Encapsulated for all Eternity), as it was christened, was being prepped for delivery to Arizona from JPL.

Alex and Dorathy were lying in the sand soaking up the late day Polynesian sun in front of her cozy beach house. "God, this is heaven, Alex. I never want to leave this place; I want to stay here forever with you. Even if a giant storm swept it all away, I would live in a tree with you." She turned to point at a tree. It was old and large with a few thick sturdy branches that spanned out to create a perfectly symmetrical canopy. "Oh honey, wouldn't it be great, I always wanted a treehouse up there. We could put a deck with an old brass telescope and spend our evenings with a good bottle of wine gazing up at the stars. Wouldn't that be wonderful?"

Alex leaned over to slip his arm under her head and kissed her. "That would be wonderful my love. I want nothing more than to spend the rest of my days living in a tree with you."

Alex had made other plans for the time of his proposal, but this seemed to be the right moment. He had been carrying the ring in his small backpack knowing she would never happen to find it there. He sat up and unzipped a small side pocket, hiding it from her view. He removed the ring from the box and clutched it in his hand.

"I have been waiting for the right moment but every moment with you, Dora, is perfect." He rolled to his feet and bent down on one knee in the sand. He took Dorathy's hand in his. Tears began to shine in his eyes. "I never thought this kind of happiness existed until you walked through my door and into my life. I love you, Dora, with all my heart. Will you please do me the honor of being my wife, for better or for worse, 'til death do us part?"

Dorathy started to sob tears of happiness. "Yes, my darling, YES!" She tackled him and lay atop him in the sand. They laughed and embraced, covering each other with kisses. The ring sparkled in the fading light of the sun as he slipped it onto her finger. They sat in the sand wrapped in the safety of each other's arms and watched in silence as the sun dipped below the horizon, covering the sea with a beautiful, eerie green glow.

Dorathy looked into her fiancé's eyes and said, "At the end of a perfect day the beginning of the rest of our life together." They kissed passionately and fell back into the sand to make love with a billion stars as witnesses to their true, unfading love.

The cryogenic tubes arrived in the cavern twenty-four hours later. They had been stored exactly where Stuart had said they would be found. The team flew in armed only with night-vision goggles and a moving truck. In and out within thirty minutes, they headed to the secret base without incident.

Stuart was busy with Brenda, preparing Henry's new SELF, when his cryogenic tube rolled through the lab doors. Stuart had coached Brenda on the stages of freezing. "Great, they're here. I'll get the first capsule prepped and ready to go. Can you handle the rest of the procedure by yourself?"

"I'm sure I can," Brenda said with confidence.

When Stuart had completed his task, he and Brenda worked together to carefully position Henry inside the tube and seal it. A renewed sense of commitment flooded through Brenda. "One down, three to go."

A bit apprehensive, Brenda stared at Henry's cryotube. She needed to confirm what she thought she already knew, and she needed to clear the fog from the tangled thoughts spinning in her mind by laying the facts out. "What we are doing here is basically removing our soul and repositioning it into our SELF. Then we die, we get frozen, and what you have been saying, Stuart, is that our soul goes to the other side . . . heaven . . . another planet, another reality." Brenda stopped to think for a moment. "We get shot out into space in a ship capable of finding its way to that reality. Then, if all goes as planned, we are revived and can go searching for heaven. With any luck, we can maintain the proper frequency and return to Earth." She emitted a nervous, uncontrolled laugh and said, "There are so many things wrong with what I just said, I don't even know where to start! Earth . . . people on Earth have been searching for answers that have eluded us since the beginning of time. We come back . . . IF we come back—what and when are we coming back to? With the time slippage will there be anyone left to report to? It ultimately seems a bit pointless, don't you think?"

Stuart thought for a good while before sharing his thoughts. "What I think is irrelevant. What I know is that man has always sought to find what lay just beyond the horizon. Without that yearning we might still think the planet is flat. As you said, the search for the answer is part of our DNA, encoded there by another, far more advanced being. Deep down there must be a part of you that wants to go on this mission, otherwise why would you be here in the first place?"

"Well Stuart," she began, "How about it, given the choice would you go?"

Stuart took a moment before answering, already knowing his answer. "If not for my family, yes, I believe I would."

A look of concern crossed her face, her eyes filled with a sudden sadness. "Your family—you must be very angry that you were brought here. Dimitri screwed up in the final hour so to speak. He's a brilliant man behind that drunken stupor, but he did figure it out, the higher dimensional frequency, thank God. Better late than never."

Stuart needed a straight answer, "Brenda, do you think they will let me go?"

Brenda sighed and looked into Stuart's eyes. She saw a good, kind man. "Hans is a standup guy and I think you will go home, but not until he has your memory wiped clean."

"What!" Stuart was distressed. "What do you mean wiped clean?"

"Listen to me carefully. I'm the only one who can calibrate that machine. The order of how things must be done is simple. I must set the machine for you then I have to adjust the machine for myself since someone else will have to perform the freezing process on me. Once they believe your memory has been erased, they will prepare you for transport back to Arizona. What if I told you to fake it? In fact, don't say a word, keep a blank look on your face and go down for the count. I want people to know what's going on here; I want our lives to count for something. Can you do that, Stuart, can you do that for me, for us? We are in an underground sinkhole in the French Alps outside of CERN."

Stuart began to tear up. "For what it's worth, thank you."

"It's not done yet buddy," she said with new-found hope.

The next morning Dorathy couldn't wait to go to the south side of the island and meet Athena and Kevin and the rest of the people who had been flown in for the small ceremony on the beach. Alex had let her in on the surprise that Athena had orchestrated the whole affair. Lucy and Roger, along with Jack, Melanie, Hugo and his wife and Hendrik and his family were all there. Lori and her father, Alex's oldest friend, and most of the crew from Lifecor made it as well.

As Alex and Dorathy entered the adjoining courtyard, Athena caught sight of them and ran over, hugging them both. "Surprise, Mom!"

Dorathy smiled from ear to ear. "How did you keep this a secret? You've never been able to keep anything a secret!"

"Oh, I'm good when I have to be. You look great, Mom, you look so happy. I'm so excited for you, for you both!"

Dorathy was bouncing with happiness. "I'm excited for me! Where's the rest of the gang?"

"Over at the pool bar, half in the bag."

"Great, let's go join them!"

Arm in arm, the three of them went tripping down the steps to the pool area. It was a beautiful day—the warm trade winds were blowing rustling the fronds of the palms in the surrounding gardens. The soft sound of Polynesian music whispered in the background and the smell of exotic flowers drifted in the air.

Lucy was the first to greet them. Holding up her glass she yelled, "To the future Dr. and Mrs. Alex Mason!" Everyone turned and cheered, raising their glasses in a toast. Dorathy was all smiles and, laughing, and Lucy jokingly announced to the bartender, "All drinks are on me, spin the bar!"

Dorathy called out, "So, can someone fill me in on when my wedding is?"

"Lucy climbed up on the bar and yelled back, "It's Saturday and it's just us special people on this tiny, little island in the middle of the big blue ocean that get to see you get married, yay!"

Jack wadded up some wet napkins and threw them at Lucy in fun. "Okay maybe I should get off the bar, although I do have underwear on." Jack bent his head as though he was trying to sneak a peek and Melanie whacked him on the arm.

Dorathy was laughing so hard she was crying. She leaned into Alex and looked into his eyes and said, "Thank you." Alex burned the image of his future wife's face at that moment into the depths of his memory because he never wanted to forget her smile, her beautiful smile.

It was Magnus's turn; his SELF was now ready for transference. He and Brenda sat up half the night, talking about their lives. He was a good man but suffered the same consequences as the rest of them. The ambition to succeed in life meant that they were alone in this world, no one to miss them and no family to love them. They had each accomplished so much, but in the end, who really cared if they left this life?

Magnus was being prepped by Brenda. He was lying on the table, his bright eyes glowing against his ebony skin, stricken with fear as his thoughts turned to the unknown voyage ahead. "Tell me again," he said, his voice cracking and barely a whisper, "what you think we will see and feel when we have gone to the depths of the unknown?"

Brenda smiled and said, her voice laced with hope, "I think it will be a wondrous place and I bet we are met by everyone we once have known and loved."

Magnus felt a comforting peace wash over him in his final moment and said, "Sounds heavenly, my dear."

She smiled back and injected a sedative into his IV line. "Sweet dreams, my friend, and I'll be seeing you on the other side very soon."

"Cheerio . . . old . . . gal," and he was out.

Brenda took the controls and started the procedure. Within a few hours she and Stuart were placing Magnus's SELF into a cryotube.

Dimitri, the last to show up at the facility, still had some time to wait for his SELF to be ready. He had reluctantly agreed to cooperate. Brenda had to baby him through detox, as he was falling apart at the seams without his precious vodka. She gave him mild sedatives to calm his nerves and she consoled him. She had started to care about his well-being and found common interests that would follow them to the other side.

"Good morning, sunshine. How are you doing today? Still having bad dreams?"

He growled back at her, "I am fine, get me some water!"

"Oh God, please don't start that macho bullshit with me again, I'm so over it! You might be able to talk to poor Stuart like that, but don't try and intimidate me with your false sense of superiority. Why don't you get yourself a set of balls already!" Just then there was a huge bang and roar from above. Dimitri almost started to cry from the stress.

"Get a grip, will ya? They're testing the rocket launchers today, you big fat baby!"

Brenda shook her head and decided she had better things to do than hang around Dimitri when he was like this. Instead she went into the lab to check on the cryotubes and how their SELFs were progressing.

Stuart was standing in front of the two canisters, mesmerized by what was taking place in front of him. "How is this possible?" he asked Brenda as she sidled up next to him.

"Bioprinting has been going on for decades; even the ability to peer into one's thoughts. I just took it all a colossal step forward."

"I know about bio fabrication. I've seen the results first-hand," Stuart said. "but not on this scale. Arms, legs, kidneys, even a few hearts, but not fully functioning bodies. Then the added factor of recreating alien/human DNA . . . It's mind-blowing."

"It's not really, Stuart. You punch in the right sequences and inject the proper bio-codes into the molecular solution; it's not any different than punching a few keys on a keyboard, putting paper in a printer and ink in a cartridge and pressing start."

Stuart looked at her in amazement. "It is very different, Brenda; you're creating a human being!"

"Well someone was going to eventually figure it out, why not me?" As she walked away, she said in dramatic fashion, "Remember, it's written in the stars."

Stuart took a chair, spun it around, swung his leg over the seat, and rested his chin on its back. He sat deep in thought, contemplating what the next fifty years would bring. What was it going to be like when he became an old man, in what kind of world would his son be living? He prayed that Brenda was right about the sequence of events that would lead to his release. But deep down he thought if not for his family would he really consider being a part of this mission? Maybe.

After a couple of days of planning the ceremony and celebration with Athena and relaxing while enjoying everyone's company, Dorathy's wedding day had arrived. It was a balmy, late afternoon and Dorathy was standing in front of a full-length mirror dressed in an elegant but simple white dress that had small pearl bead embellishments on the bodice. Her hair was loosely pulled up with fresh island flowers adorning her black hair. Athena came up behind her and, as mother and daughter peered into the mirror, said, "Mom, you're beautiful and you look so happy. Alex is a great man and your soulmate. I can see it the way he looks at you, he loves you so much. I'm so happy for you, Mom. You deserve to be happy."

Dorathy was tearing up, "I love you, baby girl. I want you to be happy in your life. I'm so proud of you and the woman you've become. Kevin is such a sweet young man. I know that the two of you are happy together and that pleases me so much."

Athena leaned in and kissed her mom on the cheek. "Happy birthday, Mom. I love you."

Dorathy smiled as she watched Athena walk through the courtyard, past the yard and down the steps to the beach to stand at the white lattice altar which had been decorated with tropical flowers and pink ribbons. Guest were seated in white chairs on either side of an aisle of sand. Alex stood at the end of the aisle in the front of the altar dressed in white linen, hands clasped in front of him. Standing next to him was his old buddy, Bob. Alex couldn't help but think about Stuart being held captive and how much he wished Stuart were with them today, but at least they knew he was alive and well. He felt guilty but knew Stuart would be happy for him.

Dorathy approached Jack who was waiting for her just inside the courtyard. He had graciously agreed to walk her down the aisle. "You look beautiful, my dear friend. Beauty and brains—Alex is hell of a lucky guy."

"Jack, I think I'm the lucky one." They both smiled. A young native man started to play his ukulele as she linked her arm through Jack's, and he escorted her down towards the beach.

Jack placed Dorathy's hand in Alex's, gave her a kiss on the cheek and turned to seat himself in a chair next to his wife. Athena stepped forward with a huge smile on her sun-kissed face and took Dorathy's bouquet. The trade winds were blowing a fragrant breeze, waves lapped gently along the shore. It was a perfect day.

After they recited their vows to one another, concluding the ceremony with the traditional 'I Do's' everyone clapped and congratulated the newlyweds. Dorathy hugged her friend Lucy and without fanfare handed her bouquet over as she cautioned, "Just, please, wait awhile."

Lucy giggled and whispered back, "Oh Dora, I'm just using Roger for sex."

A large catamaran had been docked, waiting for the party to arrive for a sunset sail with cake, open bar, hors d'oeuvres and live, traditional Polynesian music. The view of the tropical jungle and its jagged peaks was spectacular as they sailed around the calm waters of the lagoon of Rosen Island.

After the sunset sail the party continued at the pool bar till the wee hours of the morning. Alex and Dorathy decided to stay the night at the secluded, over-water bungalow and had snuck off at the height of the party. When they reached the end of the walkway Alex scooped up Dorathy in his arms and carried her over the threshold to a bed that had been covered in red rose petals and a variety of fragrant local flowers. He playfully threw her onto the bed. He laughed as he said in a pirate's voice, "You're my wench now. I'm here to collect what's rightfully mine."

Dorathy was giggling from too much champagne and cried in a high-pitched voice, "You need to tie me up first, you dirty scoundrel!"

Alex looked around the room and found the silk cords that had been used to tie off the decorative drapes of the bed.

Dorathy laughed and kicked her bare feet, trying to sound like a damsel in distress, "Oh please don't . . . please don't stop!"

Alex threw off his clothes and gently tied her wrists to the headboard. He said solemnly as he looked into her eyes, "I love you, wife."

"I love you, my wonderful husband."

They made love until sunrise and slept wrapped in each other's arms until the warmth of the day woke them. Dorathy draped a sarong around herself as she got out of bed to greet the first day as Mrs. Alex Mason. Alex was sleeping soundly as she leaned in and kissed his cheek. She ran her fingers through his hair and whispered, "I love you, my darling." He smiled, eyes still closed, "I love you, too."

Dorathy noticed that someone had delivered a covered tray of fresh fruit and croissants packed in ice along with a pot of hot water, still steaming, for tea and French pressed coffee. She gathered it up and took it to the back deck, which overlooked the crystal-clear water of the lagoon.

Dorathy sat and turned to see Alex coming out of the bungalow to join her. "I could get used to this," he said. Dorathy burst out in laughter at the sight of him wearing her hot-pink, floral print sarong tied around his waist. He looked down at himself. "What? I think this is a great look for me."

She cocked her head to assess his sense of style. "Yes, I think we could both get used to this way of life and maybe we should start seriously thinking about it."

Alex raised an eyebrow and lowered himself into the lounge beside her. "You're serious, aren't you?"

"Yes, I think I am. Why not start enjoying our lives together free of stress, work, business travel, etcetera, etcetera? I like my job at JPL, but I'm ready for a change."

Alex sat back in the chair and looked out over the water. "You're right, we can do whatever we want to do. If we get bored, we can do something else. Dora, you're right baby, we have our whole life ahead of us, why not make the most of it?"

"Damn straight! I'm going to hand in my resignation to Hugo after this project gets off the ground, pun intended. Right after the test launch."

Alex leaned in to seal their plan with a kiss.

Dimitri was terrified as he lay on the table waiting for Brenda to give him his sedative. "Please, Brenda, I'm sorry for the harsh words I have said to you in the past, forgive me." He was crying uncontrollably now. "I don't want to die; I am afraid of what might happen to us!"

"Shhhh, listen to me. We are not going to die; we are going to live forever in perfect bodies. We are explorers; scientists working together to find the meaning of life. I'll be right behind you and always beside you. Don't worry, my friend. I'll look after you and I will always care for you." Brenda ran her fingers through his hair and kissed him on the cheek, smiling down at him she injected the IV and . . . Dimitri was out.

Outside the lab Hans sat at the table with Stuart. "I am not an unsympathetic man. I have a family and regardless of what you might think of me, I am a man of my word. You, my friend, have been working diligently with my engineers so they may build the automated reviving mechanism and I will send you back soon enough, but I must first be assured that your knowledge of this place be permanently erased from your memory. With luck you will retain the memories of who you are, maybe your family as well. You see I must secure the safety and secrecy of this mission. The truth cannot get out about what we are doing here and the technology we are using and why. The world is not ready for the truth, not yet."

"Look, I know it's useless for me to try to assure you that your secrets are safe with me, so I won't even try. I'm just grateful you aren't going to shoot me."

Hans laughed at Stuart's comment. "My friend, I am a lot of things but a murderer I am not."

Stuart remembered what Brenda had instructed him to do and played along. "Dr. Brenda seems to be the brains behind all the memory uploads, so I guess I feel somewhat at ease knowing she's the one operating the machine." Stuart understood that secrecy needed to be maintained and the mayhem that would result if the truth were to get out. "I believe what you are doing is beyond most people's comprehension, but slowly people will be ready, then what?"

"A new world order is on our horizon," Hans said. "In order to achieve success, we must manage things with finesse and go slowly. The team will eventually find their way back with proof of why we exist, and how our existence is relevant to the rest of the universe. That is our goal."

Hans stood up and said, "Come with me. Before I erase what you know of us, I want to show you what we have been building." Stuart jumped up out of his seat, curiosity getting the best of him. Hans led him down the hall to the elevator and punched in a key code. As the doors closed behind them, Hans punched the button that read 'Hangar Level One.' Above that, another read 'Hangar Level Two' and one above that read 'Surface.' Stuart was now sure that Brenda had told him the truth about their location. The elevator came to a stop and the doors slid open to reveal secrets.

Stuart's eyes grew wide as he gazed upon a massive ship. The color of the material was like nothing he had seen before. A dark, gunmetal gray, but where lights shone upon its surface it glistened like the sun on water—an iridescent, almost transparent ruby red.

Hans said proudly, "Welcome to the future of space travel."

Stuart followed him out of the elevator into the giant hangar. "I've never seen anything like this."

Hans said, "No you wouldn't have, it's been years in the making. Completely self-sufficient, it utilizes applications engineered from our most recent discoveries on negative vacuum energy to propel it. It is complemented by the device that is capable of bending space by contracting it and expanding it as the ship travels through by creating a wormhole. It can regenerate its fuel source and sustaining life by gathering matter from space and turning it into useable energy. Thanks to Dr. Rosen's generous donation we have been able to fast-track its fabrication."

Stuart reached up and stroked the cold underbelly of the ship as they walked slowly beneath her expansive girth. He almost felt as if an electrical charge was flowing through his body from his fingertips and he noticed the hull change color where his hand came to rest on the strange metal. It was a pulsing bright red as if it were alive. Stuart asked, "What type of metal is this?"

Hans chuckled. "My friend, it is not metal at all. It's a type of absorbent, organic membrane. Just one of the many discoveries from secret expeditions."

"It's alive?"

"Yes, an alien life form. Completely impenetrable; attached to the outer hull of the craft by a nutrient-enriched skin. The material adhered to it and started to grow around it. It is best suited in space, but it seems to adapt easily, thus making it ideal for space travel and visiting other potential worlds. There is still much to do, but the project is progressing well, with your help. One day, in our lifetime I hope, I believe we will have all the answers to that which has created much controversy over the millennia. Our goal is simple; it is to create a new world with a new order of things."

As Stuart continued to caress the underbelly of the ship, he had the sensation it was somehow trying to communicate with him. He was amazed by what was being accomplished in this hidden underground facility.

Stuart was justly overwhelmed by the information he now possessed. He knew it would be a matter of time before his release and deliberated about how much, if any, of what he knew of this place he could safely share with the public. He knew the chaos that would result if the truth were revealed. He felt that he alone must deal with the knowledge he carried; skepticism would be his enemy, knowing the truth would be his burden.

Everyone had thoroughly enjoyed their little vacation to the outskirts of Fiji. But it was now time to get back to work.

Dorathy and Alex had flown into Arizona for the grand opening night of Free. They had come up with the name together as they both agreed that once dead a person's soul could finally have the freedom to explore the mysteries of the universe, the body would be preserved forever as recognition of the person having ever existed. So, 'Frozen Remains Encapsulated for all Eternity' conveyed accuracy in describing the project.

The test subject was a man that had led a long life, but not a very healthy one, and had died of complications at the age of a hundred and nine. It had been, to say the least, a good life worth living. Charles Wembley, or 'Charlie' as his friends and family knew him, had wanted badly to take a trip into space but his health had prevented him from doing so. His last wish was to be frozen for the trip he had always wanted to take but was never able to do.

Alex was finishing up the final prepping of Charlie's cryotube for his long journey. Dorathy had been feeling melancholy thinking about his dying wish, thinking about a man she never met who had always dreamed about going into space but never having had the opportunity to realize his dream while he was alive.

Space was truly the final frontier and Dorathy thought how extraordinary it would be to travel the stars someday. She had been blessed with the opportunity to experience space firsthand when working on the 'Space Hotel.' She thought that to look upon the Earth from space made a person reflect on their place in the universe. How small our world was and how alone we must feel occupying this small blue planet so far away from anything, or anyone, else.

She walked down the corridors of stainless-steel tubes regarding the names on the plaques and wondering about each person that lay within . . . what were their dreams, what had they accomplished and what had they wanted to do, but never had the chance?

Dorathy bent down and the long braids adorned with pink silk ribbons from her wedding altar fell forward over her shoulders. She examined one plaque which read simply 'Ivor "Wizard" Hurn, RAF.' She smiled at the thought of the man inside that had gone by the name Wizard, obviously a fighter pilot. She wondered about him and the life he had led. She concluded that he must have had a pretty good life with a name like that. As she continued to walk, she thought about her own life. *I have done some pretty goddamned, good, fun stuff. But it's time for me to do what I want to do. I'm done proving my worth to everyone else, it's finally my time to shine. My time for some adventures with the man I love.'*

She saw Alex coming toward her from the far end of the warehouse. She smiled and blew him a kiss, when suddenly she was struck to her knees by a sharp pain in her head that drew the breath from her lungs and blinded her with bright, flashing bursts of light. As her vision narrowed, she could see Alex running, calling her name. Dorathy was gasping for air, but couldn't understand why she couldn't draw in a breath. Alex was by her side screaming, but she could no longer hear his voice. She looked up at him as her vision faded and managed to murmur, "I will always love you . . . test it . . . on me . . . love." And she was gone.

SECTION 2

CHAPTER 21

Dorathy awoke lying in a bed of clover. The tiny, neon pink flowers scattered through the emerald green seemed to glow with shimmering specks of ruby, as if the blossoms had been sprinkled with a fine dusting of small grains of gems.

She was trying desperately to clear her head when she heard a dog barking. The dim sound was a memory from her childhood, and it was becoming louder as she struggled to her feet. Standing, she rubbed her eyes as she looked to the sky. She felt dizzy for a moment—she was seeing double. Two suns shone upon her face and on the distant horizon was a blurred image of something she couldn't comprehend.

She turned to see a little dog barking happily, leaping through the high grass and clover, bounding towards her as fast as his little legs could manage. Dorathy started to weep as she crouched down. Zwicky leaped into her open arms, licking her face wildly and whining from joy to be reunited with his beloved Dorathy. She kissed the top of his curly, cinnamon-colored head and his black button nose. "Oh, my little Zwicky, I missed you so much my darling, little pup." She hugged the small poodle close and stood to find her father and mother walking toward her. Dorathy called out, "Mom, Dad, you're alive! Zwicky's alive! How is this possible? Where am I? What happened to me?"

Her mother cupped Dorathy's face in her hands. Dorathy looked deep into her mother's eyes and saw a glow within; the outline of her face seemed to emanate an aura of light. "My precious girl, I'm so sorry I was never there for you. I left you when you needed me the most and for that I am very sorry."

Dorathy was weeping with an inner peace that she had not even felt with Alex. "I never stopped loving you, Mom."

"Oh, my darling girl, please forgive me."

"Mom, I missed you so much. Dad, where are we?"

Dorathy's dad hugged her close. "My little girl, all grown up. Only a moment ago you were in high school and now you're here."

She placed Zwicky on the ground and asked, "Dad, where is here? Where are we?" Her father looked past her into the distance and Dorathy turned to look in the same direction. She suddenly realized her vision was clear as she gazed upon a huge, distant ringed planet hanging low on the horizon. She gasped at the beauty and the splendor of it.

"Oh my God, Dad, I know this place, I've heard of this place . . . I died, didn't I?" With a whimper she said, "We're dead."

"No, my darling angel, we have transcended. We have merely moved on to the next level of awareness." Her father saw the look on her face, the anguish; she was suddenly overcome by grief. "Dad I was finally happy."

"Yes, I know, we were at your wedding. Alex is such a good man and Athena has grown up to be just like her mother."

"You were at my wedding?"

Her mother spoke with happiness for her daughter. "Such a beautiful bride and Alex looking so handsome in his white linen."

Dorathy started to cry. "Alex, my poor darling husband, and Athena—they'll be heartbroken."

Her mother brushed Dorathy's hair out of her eyes. "Don't cry angel. They will be here shortly, and we will be together again."

"Time doesn't exist here, Dorathy." Her father added, "Time as you know it has slowed to a stop here; we only just got here. But knowing, that is what remains with us through all time."

Dorathy looked as a sudden realization hit her. "Yes, I know, I feel we are from a greater force than one individual. We are from the beginning of all things, we are from them, the first ones from before this time, from before any time. Dad, this is an alternate reality . . . a higher level, a different realm."

Dorathy's mom responded, "We come from this reality, this 'other side,' then we came back to it when we passed. We can see the other side as if we were only separated from it by a thin veil. Look, my darling girl, look with your heart and you will see."

Dorathy closed her eyes and opened them to see Alex standing in front of her on the airstrip in the blazing New Mexico sun. His head was bowed, and his hands rested lightly on her cryotube. "Oh Alex, my darling man," she murmured as she reached out to brush the tears away.

"Mom, I want to be with him."

"Darling you can be with him whenever you want, but he will be here before you know it. Don't fret my dear girl." Her mother kissed her forehead, "Don't worry, life as you knew it is short."

There wasn't a dry eye in the room. Athena bravely gave the eulogy for her mother and then sat beside Alex, whose head was bent, and shoulders curled as he twirled the wedding ring placed there by his beloved wife little more than a week ago. Alex was devastated by his loss. Unable to contain his anguish, his eyes were red and swollen. He wanted to stand and speak about what a wonderful woman he had married, but he was a broken man. Everything that made him whole was now gone. He gathered his strength and with as much composure as he could muster, slowly stood and took the podium, grasping at it as he bowed under the weight of his grief. He shook as he spoke while clutching one of Dorathy's braids still bound by the pink ribbon. "Dorathy was an incredible woman. She helped so many people by giving them the means to expand their horizons, to venture beyond their boundaries, to hold on to their hopes and to realize their dreams. I was one of those fortunate enough to have been a part of her life. She was my life. She was, and always will be, my wife."

Alex could no longer hold on to his composure. He broke down as Athena got up to lead him down from the podium.

Jack, Lucy and Hugo each took their turn to speak of friendship and kindness. Many whose lives had been impacted by Dorathy had gotten up to speak. One after another they stepped up to the podium to tell a tale of how much better their lives were because she had been a part of it.

Later at the wake, Alex sat in a chair in the corner of the room, staring blankly out into the backyard of Lucy's home. He was winding Dorathy's long braid around his hand, around and around, holding his grief at bay. If he were to stop caressing the braid, he feared he would stop breathing— then he thought it may be a far better thing than to live through this torture. Athena touched his shoulder. "Alex, can I get you anything?"

He looked up at her and saw Dorathy's face. "No, I'm okay."

Athena dragged a chair closer to Alex and asked, "Can I sit with you?"

Alex quietly responded, "Sure."

"I got the call from Lifecor today. Mom has been placed into the capsule and is ready to be shipped to New Mexico to be launched by Virgin Galactic Launcher One on Saturday. Hugo, Jack and Lucy have said they want to be present, so I've arranged for the jet to take us all there. Lifecor is taking Mom in the transport plane as the weight is more that we can handle on the jet."

Alex looked pained at the thought that Dorathy wanted this for herself. "Athena, if she stays here with us maybe one day they can fix her, maybe." His voice trailed off. He knew her massive brain aneurism could not be repaired, not soon anyway. Athena took the hand that still clutched Dorathy's braid. "I have my braid in my diary. I hold it sometimes as it gives me comfort knowing I, we, still have a little bit of Mom still with us."

Alex looked down at the hand holding his. "You have your mother's hands." He started to weep. "All I have left of her is this braid of hair." He looked up at Athena. "Her long hair would not have survived the freezing process completely intact. His gaze drifted. "They wanted to shave her head. I told them, 'absolutely not, just cut the length.' So, they cut her braids off."

Athena held him close as he sobbed. They sat and wept together. Athena finally said, "Alex, I hope you continue to live in the house. Kevin and I are thinking about getting our own place anyway. We've set a date for the wedding. Alex, will you walk me down the aisle?"

Alex looked up and said, "I'd be honored, Athena. I know I haven't been around very long, but I hope you can look at me as your family and that you will allow me to be a part of your life."

"Alex, you will always be a part of my life and I want you to know that I will always be here for you."

He smiled and gave his stepdaughter a kiss on the cheek. "I love you, my Athena."

"I love you, too, Pops."

When the wake was over Athena and Alex drove home in silence. Alex opened the door to the house, and he could almost smell dinner cooking and Dorothy's voice calling out, "Baby, you're home," with a big hug and a kiss to follow. He could still discern her sweet perfume lingering in the air. Reaching the kitchen, he fell to his knees in anguish and cried, "I can't believe she's gone . . . I want her back, Athena . . . I can't go on . . ."

Athena tried to be strong for him; she needed to be his rock. "Oh Alex, I know, I miss her too, but she wouldn't want us to be like this . . . she would be saying right now, 'Get over it and live!'"

"I know she would." But he couldn't handle the pain. He got up slowly and settled at the dining table as Athena poured him a strong drink. "I'm sorry, Athena. I wish I could be strong like you. I don't know if your mom ever got around to telling you, but she was going to hand in her resignation after the launch; we were going to start a new life for ourselves."

"No, she didn't. Oh, I'm so sorry, Alex. I'm sorry for you and I'm so sad for Mom. She was never happier. Alex, you gave her the happiness she was always seeking. I'm so thankful you came into her life even though it was for a brief time. She died happy. Thank you for giving that to her."

Alex threw back the remainder of his drink and choked on his words. "I need to lie down for a while."

She leaned in and gave him a kiss on the head. "I think I'll do the same."

It was April fourth and it was already very warm. Alex, Athena, Hendrik and his family, Lucy, Roger, Jack, Mel, Hugo and his wife had flown into the Virgin Galactic Space Port to watch Dorathy's launch. There was a media frenzy beyond the gate, reporters trying to position themselves to win access to the story of the year.

The cargo plane carrying Dorathy's cryocapsule had arrived as scheduled, with Karen the design engineer from JPL. Wafts of steam drifted from the exhaust ports around Karen, who was busy checking the outer casing and making minor adjustments. They winched the capsule onto a custom-built gurney to maneuver it to the hold of Launcher One.

Alex and Athena approached, and Karen reached out for a hug and said, "I rode in the back with Dorathy all the way here." Karen continued, her voice cracking with emotion, "She was such an inspiration to me, such a brilliant engineer. I'm so sorry for your loss. She's all set to go so I'll give you some time alone with her before we load her in. I understand there's room for a passenger in the cockpit, which one of you will be going up?"

Alex said, "Athena and I discussed it. I'll be taking that seat."

Karen nodded in acknowledgment. "You'll have a great view up there—almost in space, but not quite; that honor goes to Dorathy." Karen patted Alex on the shoulder and squeezed Athena's hand before she walked away.

Athena bent over and kissed the capsule. She laid her hand on top and said, "Oh Mom, I love you so much and I miss you desperately. I hope that your journey into the unknown is filled with happiness and adventure. I know you're in a good place with Grandma and Grandpa. I put all the little things that were in your keepsake box in there with you so you will always have them. I promise to make you proud and every time I look up at the stars, I will think of you." Athena wiped her eyes and patted the cold metal one last time before walking away.

Alex put both hands atop the metal casing. "I love you, my darling wife. You are and always will be the love of my life. I will always treasure the time we had and look forward to when we can be together again." A soft warm breeze dried the tears that spilled down his face as he spoke his final words to his beloved. He kissed the casing and entered the launcher aircraft.

The captain helped Alex into his flight suit and got him situated in the passenger seat while Athena walked back to join the others on the tarmac. Dorathy was carefully placed into the cargo hold of the aircraft with the help of Karen and the flight engineers. Everything was set to go.

Athena and the others watched through the heat shimmer rising off the airstrip as the aircraft barreled down the runway. It took off with tremendous force, bound for the edge of the Earth's atmosphere. Dorathy's spacecraft would rocket away past Earth's gravity and then her creation would bend space and take her into the unknown.

Everyone waited in the heat and felt the ground shake as Launcher One sped past them down the runway and took off at a steep angle. Minutes had passed like the slow ticking of an old clock. Athena, blinded by the sun, looked up and saw her mom hurtle away with fiery rockets blazing over a perfectly formed rainbow from a passing storm. The sonic boom that followed had shaken her. Her mom was truly gone.

Alex looked out his porthole and could make out the curve of the Earth. He could hear the captain speaking over the earpiece built into his helmet. "Launcher One is a go. Mark, five, four, three, two, one. Release."

Alex whispered to himself, "Safe travels, dear wife."

"Release confirmed, remote activate now." He felt the capsule disengage and felt the rumble from outside the aircraft. He placed his gloved hand on the porthole and watched as the red tail flames of the capsule whisked his beloved Dorathy away. Away, faster and faster she journeyed into space, into the unknown, into the abyss. Only a few moments had passed before a yellow flash sent out a shock wave that shook their craft just as it began its descent to Earth—back to life, back to emptiness and loneliness.

Inside the Space Port Karen excused herself from the group and found a secluded location where she could use the satellite phone that had been sent to her. It had only one number programmed. She pressed the button and a foreign voice spoke briefly, "Is it done?"

"Yes, goddamn it. I did it, now wire me the money!"

"You'll get your money as soon as we verify her location."

Karen spoke, spitting with anger, "Good luck with that. She's just gone through a wormhole that closed behind her. I did as you asked and attached your contraption, now wire me my money."

The line went dead, and the phone started to heat up in her hand. She could smell the fumes from overheating wires and melting plastic. She tossed it in a large trash bin and skirted the media horde surrounding Alex and Athena as they attempted to exit through the other side of the terminal to board their jet.

Stuart woke with the throbbing headache that was quite familiar to him. He found himself lying in the bushes under a shade tree, in the rear parking lot of Lifecor, wearing the clothes in which he had been taken. There was a thermos standing next to him. Desperately trying to stay awake, he managed to prop himself up against the base of the tree. He drank from the thermos, cool water soothing his parched mouth, until it was almost gone. He needed to get to his wife. Holding onto the tree for support, he slowly stood erect and leaned against it for a moment to gather his scattered recollections. Recalling his last moments in the machine that was to erase his memory he knew now Brenda was true to her word. Remembering what she had said to him prior to the procedure, he lay still and unreactive. There was whirring from the machine as it spun around his head. When the sounds ceased, he maintained a blank stare and they had drugged him, assuming that Brenda had set the machine accurately in order to completely erase Stuart's memory.

He struggled to gather his strength to cross the parking lot to the building. He used the stucco wall to support himself, clawing at the wall and dragging himself along. He finally reached the front office.

Stuart tumbled through the front door and fell to the floor. Lori, startled by the commotion, looked up from her work at the front desk and screamed loudly, "Stuart! Somebody help, its Stuart!" She ran to kneel at his side.

Stuart held up his hand, his voice cracking, "Don't call the police."

Just then, one of the technicians pushed the door open with force. "What the hell is wrong, Lori? Holy shit!" He yelled back into the offices, "Hey Kent, get the Doc out here pronto. It's Stu!" The tech came to Stuart's aid, stumbling to his knees in the process. "Hey buddy, you're safe now. Lori, get him some water. Shit! And get the Doc in here!"

Lori did as she was told and went running into the back offices yelling, "Stu's in the reception area!"

Kent and Stuart's replacement came running in to his side. "Okay, lay him down and give him some space. Someone get the oxygen from the prep room." Kent jumped up. "On it!"

After a few moments, Stuart's head started to clear. "Don't call the police. I'm going to be fine . . . don't call the paramedics. Call my wife . . . and call Alex."

Lori placed the call to Stuart's wife Tracey first. "Oh my God, Tracey, Stuart's here! No, it seems like they drugged him, but he's fine."

Lori then called Alex. The phone rang and rang, until finally Athena answered, "Yes?"

Lori was talking so quickly she was falling over her words. "It's Lori, I'm Lori. Calling to . . . your . . . Stu's back! Is Alex there?"

It took a moment for the information to process, "Yes . . . yes, I'll wake him. Hold on." Athena ran to the other side of the house and banged on the bedroom door. "Alex wake up. It's Lori on the phone, Stu's back!" There was no response. "Alex!" Athena yelled. She opened the door, but Alex wasn't there, and the bed was left unmade as it had been for days. The French doors were open to the patio and Athena looked into the backyard to find him curled up under a blanket on the oversized lounge bed her mother had bought. She walked over in her bare feet, the decking cold and damp from the morning dew and held out the phone. "Alex wake up. It's Lori, Stuart's turned up."

Alex rolled over, his hair a matted mess and his beard overgrown. He looked up at her with bloodshot eyes framed in dark circles. His voice cracked as he fought to come fully awake and took the phone. "Lori, Stu . . . is he okay?"

"Yes, he seems fine. The Doc is looking after him now."

After a long pause Alex said, "I'll get the next flight out. Are the police there?"

"No, he refuses to call them."

"All right . . . please tell him I'll be there as soon as I can."

CHAPTER 22

B renda was lying, nervous, on the table. The two technicians that had acted as assistants during the past procedures were now in control of her transference. "Okay then. The system has been programmed; all you have to do is start it."

Felix smiled down at her. "Don't you worry Doc, I got this."

Brenda looked up at the young technician who had become like a son to her over the time spent in this underground facility. She took his hand and palmed him a note. Her eyes brimming with tears she whispered, "For my mother."

He nodded his head and Brenda could see from his expression he would carry out her last wish as he inserted the needle and started her IV. She was out in only a moment. The mechanism slowly slid her body into position, and it started to whir slowly around her head then gained speed. Everything seemed to be functioning normally when unexpectedly the machine was spinning out of control and the unit started to shake violently.

Hans jumped out of his chair and shouted, "Don't turn it off! We must let it run its course or she will be lost!" After several long, agonizing moments the machine came to a grinding halt. Felix frantically checked the console and said, "According to this, the upload was successful."

Hans walked over to review the display. Somewhat familiar with the programming, he punched a few buttons on the screen and said, "It appears that the program has run through its entire cycle. Continue, finish the job." Felix selected a needle filled with the lethal concoction and inserted it into the IV. Brenda's journey was complete. Hans looked concerned as he said to Felix, "Whatever's done is done. Commence the freezing process."

The following day Hans had all four canisters moved adjacent to the ship to prepare for the final installation. The remaining components were then connected to fashion fully automated revival units. As Hans oversaw the progress on the ship's interior, Edgar boarded to tell him that he had received an important call in communications. "They're holding for you."

Hans sat in front of the monitor and regarded the familiar face of Lucca staring back at him. He asked Lucca, "Have you been able to verify her location?"

"No, not from here. But I believe once the ship has entered the Prime Reality, they should be able to home in on the beacon." The gentle voice continued, "Yes, I believe her untimely death, such as it was, has led our advisory to believe she is long gone, and he is hopefully satisfied with her end. We still get most of the Rosen wealth, which is convenient and most beneficial to our cause. John would have agreed with what has been done."

"Hans leaned back in his chair wondering what their friend would have thought of his only child's death being planned as it was. He said, "Ultimately, he would have agreed with our method to ensure the continuation of the bloodline. After all is said and done, she will come to realize the importance of this mission on a more fundamental level."

Lucca sighed in agreement and with a heavy heart asked, "And what of Dr. Kern?"

"I took care of him. He won't even know his own name."

"I hope you're right, but I think even so anyone listening to him will think he has gone mad."

Hans sounded determined when he replied, "We are in the final stages and with a timely departure there won't be any need to worry about the Doctor one way or the other."

"Yes. I trust you will keep me apprised of any changes to our schedule. My source at the Pentagon tells me they are digging a little too deeply for my comfort. INTERPOL has also done their fair share of scrutinizing our activities. This mission needs to be concluded. It is just a matter of time before they establish your location."

Hans agreed. "Understood. By the time they put it together, we will be long gone, and all evidence of our technology will have vanished."

"You have two weeks; I trust it will be done."

Hans responded with assurance, "Yes, we are very close to completion."

Lucca rubbed his tired eyes, "Good then. Godspeed." And the meeting was over.

Lori picked Alex up at the airport, and when she caught her first glimpse of him, she was stunned by his appearance. As she gave him a hug, she could feel his ribs through his shirt. "Oh, Alex it breaks my heart to see you like this."

He had no response, he simply picked up his case and threw it into the trunk of her car.

Alex ran his hand over his thick overgrown beard said, "How is Stu doing?" Lori knew it was pointless to ask how he was coping with his loss. It was apparent to anyone who looked closely enough how he was coping—not well. He had been struck down, his soul crippled by the pain, so she let it lie.

"He's resting at home. The police and INTERPOL want to question him, but he refuses to talk about it to anyone. He just keeps saying he needs to talk to you, especially after he heard about . . . Dorathy." Her voice trailed off. That subject may be too much for him to bear.

Lori tried to cheer Alex up, but failed miserably. He stared out the car window, alone with his thoughts. Would he ever recover from this loss? He looked like he had been shattered into pieces by a blow far too great, the wound far too deep.

When she dropped him at the Kern home everything seemed surprisingly calm. Alex walked around the house into the backyard and found Stuart and Tracey playing with their son. Stuart tried desperately not to look alarmed by Alex's appearance; he clasped Alex's arm for a moment then pulled him in for a solid embrace.

Tracey decided this would be a good time to put their son down for his nap. Tracey gave Alex a rub on the shoulder and said with affection, "It's so good to see you Alex. I'm so sorry for your loss . . . such a tragedy." That was all she could muster, afraid anymore said would be too much.

When they were alone Stuart said, "Buddy, looks like we've both been through hell. I'm relieved you're here because what I must tell you is going to blow your mind and it can't be discussed openly. What are you drinking these days? By the looks of it I'd say anything goes well with what's ailing you, my friend." Stuart retrieved a bottle of what he thought might do the job and set it and a glass filled with ice on the table. Alex poured to the top thinking he was going to need every drop.

Alex took a long draught, letting it slide smoothly down his throat and settle. Liquor had become his pain killer of choice. "Now tell me, Stu, what the hell is going on and where the hell have you been? Who the hell took you and why?"

Stuart poured himself a tall one as he spoke. "Cryogenics. They needed me to freeze four of their people. Your technique is the only one that has been successful. I realize this is your method and it's something you don't put out there for all to know, but I don't think they intend on using it on a commercial level."

"That's fine, but who the hell did they freeze and why?"

"Oh man, are you ready for this? Crap, where do I even start?" Stuart took another slug and ran his hands through his long, unruly hair. "Shit, I don't even believe what I'm about to say, but here it goes.

I hope you're ready for this. One of their team members is a Russian scientist who discovered an ancient specimen under the ice in the Antarctic. It was alien DNA, but that's only the half of it."

Alex shook his head while he thought it through, but he couldn't think of a connection between that and the events at hand. "Hell, you got my attention, get on with it."

"Here goes—the alien DNA is human and predates us by one and a half billion years!"

Alex looked at Stuart as if he had gone mad. "Are you kidding me? You're telling me we, Earth, were seeded somehow?"

"That's exactly what I'm—they're—saying. But look that's not such a farfetched idea; scientists have been speculating for years that's one possible theory to explain our origin."

"Yeah, I know. So now they have proof; guess that sorta throws the whole creation theory out the window, and it doesn't say much for Darwinism either."

"Well listen to this—it gets better. It appears there is a gene sequence buried in our un-coded DNA. It's 'time' coded!"

Alex slammed his drink down on the table. "Christ, people have been trying to figure out for years why the majority of our DNA was coined 'junk'. In fact a few years ago I read about a Russian team having deciphered it as a type of language. Didn't see anything else, after that came out."

"Yeah well, this Russian guy was part of that team and he's the one who broke the code. Get this, not only is there a timed sequence for the development of technology embedded in there . . . but also coordinates."

Alex leaned back in his chair and although he thought he knew the answer, asked, "To where?"

Stuart looked at him and knew exactly what he was thinking, "The other side, man—the *other side.*"

Alex scratched at his scruffy beard, "Jesus Christ!"

"No, l don't think Jesus lives there. It's deep space, and not in this reality. They called it the Prime Reality."

They sat in silence. Alex needed time to take it all in. He swirled his drink around, staring blankly at the ice cubes and finally asked, "Who did they freeze and why did they need to freeze them in the first place?"

"I hope you're ready for this one. Four scientists that were . . . shit . . . I don't even know how to describe it . . . they were 3D printed out of synthetic alien DNA!"

"What the hell are you even talking about? What the hell? Stu we've been friends for a long time, but I think you might need your head examined. Are you losing it?"

"Nope. I'm telling you they 3D bio fabricated entirely new bodies constructed of the same material, synthetically, as the alien DNA; right down to the exact molecular structure, vibrating at the same frequency. They then had their consciousness—their souls—uploaded. Everything was uploaded into their new bodies then I froze them for the trip."

Alex reacted to the information Stu was throwing at him. "We don't have that kind of technology!"

"Not us, but they fucking do, I'm telling you! You gotta believe me!"

"Who the hell are 'they'?" Alex shouted.

Stuart exhaled, his shoulders slumping, not knowing how Alex would take the information he was about to share. He said, bluntly, "The Illuminati." Alex stared directly into Stuart's eyes for long moments looking for the truth. "Alex, you know I'm telling you the truth. Alex, they have a ship and it's almost ready to fly. I helped them design an automated system to do the reviving once they reach their destination."

Stuart added, "The Illuminati are an international network of scholars, heads of state—the wealthiest one percent. Their interests are far-reaching, and they are thoroughly imbedded in the global economy. It wouldn't surprise me to find at least one of them on the board of the Rosen Foundation."

Alex's eyes went wide, his emotions wild. "And what if Dorathy's death wasn't from natural causes? God, could it be possible, could they have wanted her out of the way? And what of Athena?"

"I don't have those answers for you Alex. I simply don't know. That part's just speculation."

Alex's head was spinning. "If they have the technology to do what you're saying, they can heal and revive Dorathy! Oh my God! Alex dropped his drink, sending shards of glass across the patio and stood, suddenly flinging the chair backwards into the grass.

"Where are they? Where were you? You have to take me to them!"

"I don't know exactly. All I know is that I was in a huge sinkhole in the French Alps outside of CERN! And I only know that much because Dr.

Hyden told me before she was tasked to erase my memory. She didn't affect the erasure because she wanted people to know; to know of their sacrifice."

Alex was frantic. "We have to go there now! There are ways of finding them with satellite topography, infrared, drones . . . something, anything . . . I have to try!"

"Alex, Dorathy's gone. She's well into deep space. How the hell are you going to find her out there? And if you did find her, how the hell are you going to get her back? You got to think it through!"

"Stu, I will stop at nothing. Athena and I would give every dime of what's left of the foundation to get her back. I need your help, but I'll do it alone if I have to, I've gone it alone before."

"You know I've got your back, but I don't know how much help I can be."

"Can I count on you? Because we have to leave for CERN now!"

"All right. I'm with you, buddy, but I think this is bigger than both of us."

CHAPTER 23

A day later they were sitting in Dorathy's jet on their way to Washington D.C. to meet up with Hugo, who had been there for a conference. Athena insisted on joining them after hearing the details of Stuart's abduction. Kevin had not been pleased when she insisted on going without him. He was forced to wonder why she was adamant in her decision to leave him behind. He could sense there was something not quite right, something she was hiding and that for whatever reason she needed to do this alone. He knew Athena would eventually reveal whatever it was and did not push the issue. He knew well enough to let it be. Athena was after all her mother's daughter.

"Please, Alex, tell me everything I need to know about what happened to my mother. I can't just sit back and let things play out however they may. Anyway, you guys might need me. A woman's touch can go a long way. I may be young, but I have a lot of my mother in me so you're just going to have to deal with me!"

Alex had to smile. He could hear Dorathy coming through loud and clear. "There's no doubt the apple didn't fall too far from the tree."

"Indeed, I didn't. And as the head of the Rosen Foundation, I need to know what's going on. I also need to know more about the members of the board. A few have been there since my grandfather was in charge."

Alex put his hand on top of Athena's. "We'll get to the bottom of this and I promise you, I'll stop at nothing if it means getting your mom back. If there is the remotest chance, I will find a way."

Athena looked up at him and her eyes started to well up. She knew it was a longshot but hoped that Alex would be able to pull it off. "I know and I'm here to help however I can."

Hendrik's voice came over the intercom. "Dr. Mason, you have a call on the secure line."

Alex rose from the plush leather sectional. As he looked out the window of the jet, he could see a storm brewing over the central plains—he figured somewhere over Kansas. He sat at the desk across the aisle from his seat and picked up the receiver. "Alex here."

"Hi compadre. Hugo here. Hey y'all, we need to meet in a private locale. I've been doin' my fair share of diggin' around these parts and with the help of a buddy of mine have come up with a cast of some pretty interestin' characters. With the info Stu gave me I was able to run it in for a touchdown. When you folks land let's plan to meet at the Lincoln Memorial Reflecting Pool on the National Mall. I'll be feeding the pigeons near the Washington Monument end of the Pool. I'll fill you in then on what I came up with."

"Right, Hugo, sounds good and thanks."

"I loved Dora like one of my own. There isn't anything I wouldn't do for her or for her family."

The jet landed on time at Dulles International Airport, where the group climbed into a private car to take them to their destination. Hugo was already there taking in the view of the Washington Monument, which was beautifully reflected on the perfectly still water of the pool. The sky overhead was a clear blue, making the water look like a window into another reality. The cherry blossoms that had replaced the shade trees of the past were in bloom, casting a pale pink haze of light onto the stark white of the stone obelisk.

Athena called out and Hugo was jolted by her resemblance to Dorathy. "Hey y'all, good to see you again. Alex . . . you look like hell! Athena you're the spittin' image of your mother, breathtaking. And you must be Stu. Nice to finally meet you. Let's find a quiet place to chat."

The group walked toward a tree in full bloom, its leaves rustling in the warm spring breeze. Hugo looked around to make sure no one had been following them. "This bench seems to be as good as any."

"Athena darlin', what do you know of your grandfather?"

She was caught off guard and answered slowly while thinking back, "Well, not a whole lot, he was killed soon after I was born. Why do you ask?"

Hugo pulled a file of photos out of his briefcase. "I was able to get copies of these."

Athena examined each one carefully. "These are all old pictures of my grandfather and his original board of directors."

"Yes. Now look at the last one."

Athena shuffled through a dozen or so until she came upon a photo that had been zoomed in on a gold ring. Athena deliberated for a moment then recognition brought her head up. "I remember this ring. I've seen pictures of my granddad wearing it on his left ring finger, and so did this man." She flipped through the photos, stopping when she came to an image of a group of men. She pointed to a young, balding man that was standing to the far right of the group. She squinted and said, "You can almost make it out, he's wearing it here."

Hugo looked as if he was about to burst. "Athena honey, do you know what it means?"

"No not really. I think it has something to do with my namesake and Greek Mythology."

Hugo looked into her big green eyes and said, "There's an owl sitting on a book. It's the 'Owl of Minerva,' also known as the 'Owl of Athena.' It's the original insignia of the Bavarian Illuminati."

Stuart leaned back against, crossed fingers at the back of his head as he always did when he felt his ideas have been validated. Alex turned pale with alarm. "Hugo are you telling us that somehow the Rosen Foundation is involved with this madness?"

Athena looked as if she was going to faint. "Oh my God, this man in the photo has been on the Board of Directors for many years!"

Hugo gently put his hand on Athena's to calm her. "There's a lot I've been able to uncover concerning your grandfather's involvement with this secret society, although much of the information available to the public is pure horseshit. I found loads of conspiracy theories, but what truth I have been able to gather from Intel at Langley is that your grandfather was part of the Bilderberg Group, where the top 1% has been operating behind closed doors since 1954. Many members of this group are in fact part of the Illuminati.

Hugo inhaled on a whistle. He chose his next words carefully. "How I see it is that the Illuminati and the Bilderberg Group are about a 'New World Order' to use science and the progression of science to control religious conflicts. They've joined with the Russians, who appear to have cracked a code in human DNA. They've found etymology that seems to lead from what looks to be very much like a precursor to Hebrew, all the way back to before the Sumerian language. Your grandfather was a part of that sect and I believe he was killed by a rogue agent of the opposition."

"The opposition being who?" Athena asked with desperation.

Hugo leaned back against the cold wooden planks of the bench. "The opposition have always been religious fundamentalists. Given the information Stuart has provided, I think it's safe to say that the Illuminati are well on their way to confirming the origin of life on this planet as well as the mysteries of the afterlife, the truth of which has heretofore been shrouded in the holy cloth of religion."

Stuart's eyes became suddenly clear. "Athena, can you imagine how the world would change if they were to bring back proof of the order of the universe? The meaning of life itself?"

Alex whispered to himself, but he came through loud and clear, "A New World Order."

Hugo went on to clarify for Athena. "It comes down to the almighty buck, I'm afraid. A mission of this scale didn't come about at wholesale prices. I'm pretty sure they wanted the whole kit and caboodle for themselves, so they presented their proposal like a carrot on a stick to your mom, which means they either need to get you on board with their plan or get rid of you. Sadly, your mom's demise may have been on the agenda."

"Oh, Jesus." Athena slumped over and put her face in her hands. "What are we going to do, how can we fix this? Are they capable or even willing to bring my mom back? What if I give up control of the Foundation and trade it for my mom . . . if that's even possible, given the fact that she has been sent into a part of space unknown to us?"

Hugo edged in, "We put a trackin' device on her capsule and lost contact when she crossed over down through the wormhole. That was pretty much what we expected to happen. But what we do have is her last known trajectory.

Now my guy at the Pentagon has a pretty good idea of where their secret operation may be located. He's been tryin' to get permission from the higher ups on redirectin' a spy satellite, so we can get a closer look at the area. We can go to CERN and do our own sniffin' around and see what we come up with while he tackles the local bureaucrats and hopefully cuts through all that dang red tape. But for the time being all this info has been labeled classified. Christ, if all this bullshit got out the holy rollers would be chantin' on the streets in front of the goddamned White House."

Athena looked at Hugo, feeling a tiny bit of relief. "Does that mean you're coming with us?"

"Hell yeah. I called Jack and put him in charge back at JPL. Y'all are goin' to need me. I have some military pull and security clearance." As one, the group looked at Hugo, perplexed. "Well ya didn't think JPL only worked on privately funded projects solely for commercial use, did ya?" Hugo looked around and saw blank looks on their brows and reluctantly announced, "Oh, for Christ's sake. I work for the Department of Defense, so this convoluted space mission to change the 'Order' of things is right up my goddamned alley."

Athena looked at Hugo with new-found respect. "Awesome."

Hugo thought to himself while he scratched his head, *What the hell am I getting myself into?* He placed the wide-brimmed Stetson back on his head and said, "Okay, you folks get back to the jet. I'll swing by to pick up my things from the hotel and meet you there pronto."

Alex held out his hand. "Thanks, mate. It's good . . . thanks . . . right . . . see you in a bit."

Hugo departed with his usual long stride, his handcrafted boots striking the concrete with a strident beat. Alex said, "That is a big man . . ."

Athena interjected, "With a big heart."

Stuart observed to no one in particular, "Most likely packing big guns."

Over an hour ticked by as they waited patiently for Hugo's arrival. Hendrik appeared from the cockpit and announced Hugo was about to board and that he would open the cargo hatch and assist with his luggage. The group was stunned at Hugo's appearance when he boarded the jet. Alex reacted to it saying, "Shit you weren't kidding when you said you had military ties!"

"Thought I'd go the extra yard and put on my uniform. It might get us a little further through the door at CERN."

Stuart shook his head. "Sir, you are full of surprises today . . . Green Beret?"

"Army likes to call us Special Forces."

Stuart held out his hand. "Thank you for your service. For what it's worth, I'm glad you're coming along. I think I can speak for us all when I say that we all feel a little bit safer with you on board."

Athena stood, head cocked to one side and arms crossed and a small smirk on her face while she examined him head to toe. "I've always loved men in uniform."

Hugo laughed his usual roar. "This old guy still got it."

CHAPTER 24

With a late start, the sun was just peeking up over the mountains, casting a shadowy red glow upon the snow-covered peaks as they made their final descent into Geneva. Athena stared out the window as she did all through the night. Alex sat beside her and leaned in to kiss the top of her head. "My darling girl, we will get to the bottom of this conspiracy. I don't want you to worry; we'll find out what has happened to your mom and, with Hugo's help, stop what has been set in motion."

Athena eyed him with an intent look. "Mom must have known about my grandfather's involvement with the Illuminati. How could she not know given the fact she named me Athena? My name is the very essence of the Illuminati . . . the Owl of Athena . . . just a coincidence? She donated billions of dollars to the cause! Merely a write-off, or was it a way to advance this New World Order?"

Alex leaned back and responded to the pain and confusion in her eyes. "I have a hard time believing your mother would have kept that kind of secret from me. We openly shared every thought, every feeling without hesitation. If she was involved and there was foul play, then she obviously had been opposed to their beliefs. Sweetheart, your mom's very essence was about bettering mankind and exploring the universe, therefore I have to think she contributed to the cause and not the effect."

Athena sighed heavily. She straightened in her seat, twisting her neck so it cracked to relieve the strain from hours of deliberating on the future, her future, and its ominous veil of uncertainty. Alex rested his hand on her shoulder to comfort her. He could feel she felt she was bearing the weight of the world. "Think I'll get the guys up. Hugo sounds like a rabid wild boar straight out of the Outback and he has obviously slept well."

As they disembarked Athena felt a lingering chill in air scented of fresh snow. Hugo was already down, freeing a very large case from the cargo hold. He hefted it without difficulty and placed it in the back of an SUV that had been sent to meet them.

Athena's curiosity got the best of her as the group climbed into the back seat. "Hugo that case of your looks a bit suspect . . . to say the least."

"Darlin', ya didn't think I'd come out here to a gunfight holdin' a knife, did ya? Besides, I know you can handle yourself, you did quite well when you and your mother joined me at the gun club all those times."

Stuart let out a distressed moan. "You can't bring guns into a foreign country. How do you expect to get them through . . . ?"

Hugo cut him off before he could finish the question. "Diplomatic Immunity. This is a government mission and you are part of my team."

Stuart clearly lacked any confidence that being considered a diplomat would save him from trouble. "Great . . . I feel safer already," he said, just a little sarcastically.

After they had checked into the hotel and had scattered to their assigned rooms, Alex stood on his balcony remembering how he held Dorathy close while admiring the view. Where the sun had been shining then it was now replaced by the frosty gray pall of a late season storm that obscured the sky. Athena joined him, pulling her coat collar up around her ears to protect against the wind whipping up from the lake. Alex stood frozen, white-knuckled hands clutching the guardrail. "It doesn't seem that long ago that your mother and I stood in this very spot talking about what a wonderful future mankind was realizing with the advent of this new technology of space travel. I don't know if I'm as hopeful as I once was."

"Mom believed that technology would move us forward, that in time we would work together as one with the purpose of bettering ourselves. That we would finally abandon our pettiness and replace war with aspirations for the common good of mankind."

Alex turned to look into his stepdaughter's eyes. "Then perhaps what they are trying to stop is the natural progression of disasters to come. Maybe instead what they are trying to do is only the first step towards a global unification."

Athena thought about what he was saying. "When you put it that way, it sounds brilliant. Think of how much more we could accomplish if we weren't all wasting time on spiritual, political and racial differences. No lines, no borders, and no boundaries!"

Alex, disappointed, said with a heavy sigh, "Unfortunately, I think we are a long way off, and I'm not sure the Illuminati have a grasp of what the ramifications will prove to be. Perhaps not one giant leap for mankind . . ."

Athena sighed as she too looked out over the lake. Both stood quietly in deep thought; the only sound was that of the wind howling. Trying to control the dark strands of hair blowing across her young face with one hand, she reached for Alex's hand with the other and squeezed. "We should go, the others will be waiting."

Lucca Venturini was sitting at a desk in his usual secure location at CERN. "It seems our secret is out."

"Just as well," Hans responded. "If they decide to go public with our mission, the team will be well on their way before anyone can investigate. We only need to delay their efforts."

Lucca continued, "Certainly. But in the end my hope is that Athena will come to understand the importance of this mission and the significance of her bloodline. It might give her a greater understanding of the order of things."

Lucca thought of his old friend John going to the grave never having known the depravity of his old friend, Simon, and how his mind had been co-opted by a lunatic that would stop at nothing to destroy all John and their brotherhood had accomplished in their determination to change the world. "I know our adversary has not figured out the importance of the Amulet and what part Dorathy is to play."

Hans replied, "It would be prudent though for us to assume that at some point he will recognize its significance."

"Yes," Lucca agreed, "Simon or shall we say what is left of Simon, will eventually learn its secret, but only Dorathy can wield its power. Dorathy is out of danger and eventually she will discover the rest of her kind. Together with our crew they will find the path and not to worry, the Amulet will find its way back to its rightful owner and their mission will be completed."

Hans looked into Lucca's wise old eyes and together they felt that familiar anguish over the loss of their friend John Rosen so many years ago. Having recited his promise dozens of times over the years, Hans repeated it now, "We made a vow to protect the Rosen heirs."

Lucca sadly conveyed what Hans already knew, "John was my mentor; therefore, I take responsibility for Dorathy's safety. Her life cut short here on Earth so she can know the life she was destined to live. Perhaps someday she will make that realization."

His thoughts turned to earlier years. "Dorathy knew of her father's involvement and had been supportive of his many quests over the years, but she withdrew after John was found murdered. She distanced herself from the fear that she would be unable to protect her daughter from our opposing faction." He leaned back in his chair. "It saddens me, for her life had taken such a turn towards true happiness and we have stripped it away. An unfortunate, untimely death of such a brilliant young woman. One day Dorathy will have the chance to finish what her father started many years ago, and Athena will continue our efforts when she realizes it was her grandfather's wish that she take her position amongst us."

Hans reminded Lucca, "Athena will not be turned easily, not if she is made aware of what happened to her mother. Not even if she were to believe it was all part of a plan to keep her and her abilities safe from the grasp of our poor, tortured soul Simon."

Hans was tired and wanted desperately to put this phase of the mission behind him. He pressed to change the subject. "If your theory is correct her capsule will arrive well after our team's arrival."

Lucca rubbed his eyes, weary. The science was still untested. "That is our prediction, although we are unsure of the time slippage. Dorathy's interpretation of the discovery was to create a small rip in the fabric of space-time through which to slip, but our team saw it quite differently."

"The ship has extraordinary capabilities and either way gets them to the destination, but I cannot help to think what kind of world they will be coming back to . . . if they come back."

"The world we leave behind for them is now up to us to fashion. That, above all else, is the essence of this mission's success. They will do what they have set out to do; we must also do what we have set out to do, what we started so many years ago. We may not see the fruit of our labors, but our children's children might." Lucca gazed down at the gold ring that had been handed down to him by his grandfather. He ran his finger over the small owl perched on a book and said, "Yes, generations of men and women have carried the burden of continuing in our ancestors' footsteps so that one day we might finally be able to achieve our goal of global contribution, our One World Order . . . our New World Order.

"Well said, my friend, Hans said to reassure Lucca. "We will be ready to launch within the day. I believe Athena and her friends have likely found our location; there have been far too many people searching."

Lucca took a sip of the tea that had grown cold and said, "Yes, this charade of ours to keep Simon away and out of our secret plan has gone on far too long and I am not sure how much longer we can keep him from discovering this facility. He has grown powerful, but fortunately Dorathy gave up most of the Foundation's wealth to our project before Simon had a chance to react. I will keep you apprised of what transpires and now I think it's time for a little tour."

Hans was feeling like an old man and rose from his seat to stretch tired muscles. "Yes, I think a tour is in order." Hans thought about Dorathy and the power within her DNA. A heavy burden to bear, but he felt at ease, confident that Dorathy could face her challenges and success would be theirs.

CHAPTER 25

After unpacking and getting a bite to eat, the group was on their way to CERN. Hugo, seated in the front seat of the black SUV, turned and said, "I took the liberty of arranging a meeting with the directors of the establishment. Seems to me our arrival is no surprise; they are practically rolling out the red carpet for us."

Athena sat back in her seat. "We can only hope they come clean with what they've been up to."

Stuart, focused on his driving, interjected, "I don't think honesty is one of their virtues." Alex was deep in thought trying desperately to make sense of everything,

Athena sighed and fidgeted in her seat. It was all too much and was beginning to take its toll. "I don't know what to think anymore. Mom had been suffering from headaches for about a year or more, so maybe someone was dosing her gradually with something that caused her to have an aneurism?"

Hugo shifted in his seat. "Everyone has enemies. Who has been the greatest enemy of the Illuminati through the centuries?" The only reactions to Hugo's question were blank expressions.

Stuart said, "Up until recent events I thought the Illuminati were an ancient myth."

"It's easy really," Hugo said calmly, "The Vatican." Raising a bushy eyebrow, he continued, "Maybe not the Vatican directly but possibly a rogue agent. The Illuminati are a powerful group as I've already noted so someone from an equally powerful group."

Athena looked directly into Hugo's eyes. "There is something you're not telling me."

Hugo replied, "Yes, I have my own theory regarding the mystery of your grandfather's death. The investigation has never been conclusive. The Vatican was the enemy of the Illuminati centuries ago, but that's far too obvious. I believe it to be a radicalized individual with Vatican ties. John Rosen was killed in Switzerland during a Bilderberg meeting. I found an underground society operating in Switzerland. They claim they are the descendants of the Knights Templar that escaped persecution and they renamed themselves 'The Knights of Christ.' They are firm in their belief of religion over science. The Vatican and religious beliefs have been losing appeal over the last few decades while people embrace advancements in technology. When the Vatican and the Knights caught wind of what CERN had discovered and then the Rosen donation to the advancement of that technology, someone decided to put a stop to it."

Athena was becoming weary. "If the Vatican or these Knights of Christ killed my grandfather, do you think they killed my mom as well?" Athena's patience was wearing thin. "So, what I'm hearing is that they, whoever they are, want to turn me against the Illuminati, and the Illuminati want what, my loyalty?" Athena began to sob, "I wish we never accumulated all this wealth. I have spent my entire life looking over my shoulder, questioning the intentions of everyone I have ever met, trying to prove to others that I was worthy, and never knowing if my friendships were genuine. My mother suffered the same consequences, and for the first time in her life she finally found happiness, only to have possibly been murdered because of it!"

Alex put his arm around Athena and pulled her close as she cried. "Oh, my poor girl, I'm so sorry, I promise we will get to the bottom of this."

Athena sobbed uncontrollably, heaving and gasping, "I want my mother back and I'm tired of being strong."

Alex kissed the top of her head and wiped the tears from her face. His emotions were stretched thin as well. "We have each other now and we'll get through this together."

Hugo stared out of the windshield. Snow had begun to fall, flurries drifting against the glass as it collected in mounds of slush. "Athena darlin,' we will get to the bottom of this. Me and Alex and Stu here, we won't let anything happen to you—they gotta get through us first."

Athena reached into her purse for a tissue. "I don't know what I'd do without you guys, I'm sorry for breaking down."

Hugo tuned to face Athena. "You are exactly like your mother, strong and spirited."

"Yes, and I'm extremely stubborn."

Alex chuckled. "I loved that about your mom."

Hugo laughed. "Ha, you have no idea . . .'"

Stuart announced, "Guys we're almost there, so what's the game plan?"

Hugo reached into his briefcase and pulled out diplomatic passes. He handed one to Stu and then passed the rest into the back seat. "They're expecting us, so may I suggest we keep our cool and our wits about us. Athena, can you reach the case from where you are?"

Athena turned to kneel on her seat and reached into the back for the case. When she flipped it open, she let out a huff. "Holy shit, Hugo, you weren't kidding. You do like your guns."

"Hand me the Glock, and you take the others."

Stuart craned his neck to investigate the back. "What do you have for me in there, an AK?"

"Don't be ridiculous Stu," Alex said as he cocked his head to see what was in the case, "that leaves you with a semi-automatic."

"Cool, I always wanted to shoot one of those."

"On second thought," Hugo said, "Athena, you take the semi and give Stu the smallest one . . . over on the right. And Athena, make sure Stu doesn't shoot his damn self by accident."

"Hey, I've fired a gun once," Stu announced.

"Yah, amigo, and what kinda gun was that, a bb gun?"

"The group started to laugh at Stuart's expense and defending his dignity he responded, "No man, a double-barreled shotgun."

Hugo couldn't stop himself. "Knocked ya on your ass didn't it?"

"Ah . . . well yeah, it sure did. In my defense though, I was left unsupervised."

"Athena, take the ammo outa his gun will ya?"

The group concealed their weapons and draped their government-issued IDs around their necks. As they approached the building, Lucca Venturini was already walking towards them. "Welcome, I trust you had a nice uneventful flight. It can get a little bumpy up there with an approaching storm."

Lucca didn't waste any more time. "Ah, Dr. Kern, I see you made it home safely and with your memory intact."

"Yes, how fortunate for me that one of your team members wanted the world to know what you are planning on doing here."

Lucca replied with a small smile, "It's unavoidable my friend. The truth about our existence on this small planet will no doubt be out in due time. I must personally thank you for your involvement."

"Not that I had a choice in the matter."

"For that you have our sincere apologies. But let us go inside so we can discuss our future."

Lucca escorted the group into one of the buildings. "Please follow me." As they entered through the main door, they saw men and women going about their daily routines. He said, wondering how the information about to be shared would be received, "I would like to show you something in the main auditorium."

Alex recognized the room as soon as they entered. It was the auditorium where Dorathy had stood in front of the science community to offer her deal. The large room, its rows of seating resembling lecture halls at numerous universities, was now empty and seemed to demand silence as if it were a place of worship.

"Please take a seat," Lucca said in a hushed tone. "I think you will find this . . . enlightening." The lights dimmed and a large image came alive on the main stage. Athena shifted in her seat and as she glanced down, she noticed a golden flicker on Lucca's left hand. It was the same ring worn by her grandfather and the young man in the photo. Lucca caught a glimpse of Athena's reaction to the sight of his ring and smiled to himself—he felt he now controlled the cards.

Slowly the screen came to life. One by one, old forgotten photos of John Rosen as a young man faded in and out, showing Athena her grandfather in a new light. These were photos taken long before her birth, photos she had never seen before. These photos were being shown only now to reveal the true nature of John Rosen's and Dorathy's involvement with the Illuminati.

Athena frequently peeked over at Alex during the presentation to see if there was any truth to what they were watching, but she could tell by his expression that he was just as perplexed by the images. Athena suddenly stood. "Please stop, I don't want to see anymore." Lucca pressed a button on a key fob. The screen went blank and the lights came up, illuminating the room back to its original cold glare.

Lucca shifted in his seat and carefully chose his words, "My dear girl, my intent was not to upset you but to shed light on your family's involvement in this organization. Your grandfather, as you could see, was closely involved with the science that has moved our planet forward. He dabbled a bit in the 'derogated section,' but he too came to realize that the population needed to be 'controlled.'

Athena became exasperated. "My mother . . ."

Lucca coolly cut her off. "Your mother was involved with our attempts to depopulate the planet. We were rapidly approaching ten and a half billion inhabitants, how many more do you think our small planet could support? The needs of the many, in this case, do not outweigh the needs of the few. John set forth his objective to better what was left of mankind knowing most of the population was on a self-destructive path. My dear, don't you see what is happening around us? Your grandfather knew that it was just a matter of time before the current population would experience another cycle of de-evolving. The derogated section was just the beginning. Most of the human race is doomed. It is written in our DNA."

Athena almost screamed her response at him. "What the hell are you talking about? Are you insane? Depopulation sounds a lot like murder!"

Lucca wore a weary smile. "Most of our current attempts have failed. Presently we are not planning to cull the herd, we are planning to leave the herd behind. Initially, when the derogated section started to fade away, we were heavily involved with alternative fuel sources, trying to clean up the mess humans had made of the environment. We then moved to genetically enhancing our food sources to feed the population. Then came your grandfather's involvement in 3D Bioprinting and medical advancements, which again exacerbated the problem of over-population. I do believe that is when our purpose shifted from trying to take care of everyone to taking care of a chosen few. You see most of us are destined to become an endangered species. This will create the dawn of a new age for mankind and with it perhaps colonizing another world; a new world populated with evolved enlightened members of humanity. Just as the black plague brought forth the Renaissance, the breakdown of our DNA will bring forth human transcendence."

Alex drew a long breath. "I do know this much about my wife; she was excited about the future. In her own way she was telling me all along what you have shown us here today, but without coming out and saying, a 'New World Order.'"

"Yes, Alex you are correct. Dorathy withdrew from active membership when John was found dead."

Hugo now demanded the truth. "Who killed John Rosen and why?"

Lucca rubbed his tired eyes. "Hugo, I think you already have the answer. There are many members of religious factions that wanted to see John Rosen dead for the reasons I have revealed today, but we believe the assassin to have been a loner acting on his own beliefs. He committed this horrible crime and escaped capture. He still lives and could in a sense have been responsible for Dorathy's death."

"Still lives?" Athena said, sounding confused. "How do you know he still lives?"

Lucca paused a moment and decisively said, "He was one of your grandfather's . . . experiments."

Now all eyes were on Lucca and although he suspected he had already said too much, this was his opportunity to divulge the truth about what they were doing and why.

"Back then John was creating life with 3D Bioprinting. Not just body parts for transplantation, but trying his hand at creating a new body and attempt to transfer one's consciousness. Not much different than what we have now been able to achieve with our SELF. His experiment was not quite successful and the individual to whom he had given life has been faced with a painful unending existence. You see, he is somewhat immortal. This person has stolen the body of our dear Simon and has managed to alter his DNA to resist the aging process. He cannot die unless of his own doing and his religious beliefs will condemn him to eternal damnation if he does. This demented individual managed to manipulate his way to our brother Simon and has been residing within his mind for many years."

Stuart interjected, "So this Simon character really has someone else lurking inside his brain?"

Lucca nodded his head. "Yes, he wanted to even the score by infiltrating our exclusive society and kidnapping Simon; and with an upload of his immortal soul, resides within him. He uses the technology he stole from us and reengineered it to perfection to maintain his youth and his appearance. He has become quite powerful and will stop at nothing to find the truth of our mission. In his possession he has the world's oldest artifact and is desperately seeking the knowledge of the power it possesses. He knew the artifact had a special purpose but has not figured out what that might be. He only knew that whatever powers it had could only be harnessed by John Rosen and his offspring. The purest of our alien ancestors. Thus, he believes we are the product of Satan himself, and God himself has placed him on this path. It is why he has claimed membership in, as you must already know, the Knights of Christ."

Everyone saw how it was all starting to connect.

Stuart, having witnessed their technology, observed, "Although you have the means and the science to create life you are still looking for 'the other side' or some might call it 'Heaven.' The way I see it, you are using science to prove its existence, not using science to prove it never existed at all. To me that sounds a lot like faith."

"Yes, we have faith that there is an afterlife. We want to not only prove its existence, but how and why it exists in order to finally lay to rest the quarrels over religion."

"Buddy, *quarrel* is a hell of a way to describe the damn Holy Wars which spanned thousands of years!" Hugo was becoming animated now as he was remembering his time served in the Middle East. "Those jihadist bastards were shooting and beheading innocent people on the streets, there and on our shores, screaming, 'Death to the infidels,' all in the name of Allah! You bringing back proof is supposed to fix that? There's an old sayin where I come from, "You can't fix stupid!"

Lucca had to laugh. "Yes, my friend, I would have to agree with you there. Our goal is to prepare mankind for the truth and slowly those who fail to evolve from religion superseding logic will simply die off as evolution has proved in the past. We know now that it is the case, 'directed panspermia;' we were seeded by an ancient alien species and buried in our DNA is the sequence to evolve past this barbaric behavior. Some of us will fully evolve in time, and our job is simply to help it along. And the ones who don't have the gene sequencing will no longer be allowed to carry on as they have."

Athena, recalling what she had been told in the past, mused, "That part of our civilization either evolves or they are simply left behind; left to their own devices. The rest of us continue on with the goal of working together for a better future for all of us."

Lucca looked upon Athena now as he would if she were his own daughter. He reached over and put his cold weathered hand on hers, "Think of the possibilities mankind could achieve if we were to come together in the realization that we have a purpose in this life and that purpose is greater than just an individual's needs."

Athena's eyes started to well up, as she knew her mother had adopted this way of thinking. "My mother worked hard at her career, she gave her time and her wealth, and she strived to better herself and the lives of those around her so that they would have the means to contribute to society. If my mother taught me anything in life, it is that with hard work we could achieve anything and that there was nothing gained by having everything handed to us. This from a woman who never actually needed to work at anything, or for anyone."

Hugo straightened his uniform and said, "I understand you boys have been busy, and now that we all know a little bit about the whys, I want to hear more about the hows of this mission. How the hell do you put together a mission of this size and importance and hinge it on faith?"

Lucca looked over with assurance. "We have, without a doubt, uncovered the information buried in our own DNA that is needed to complete this mission. We have broken the code and have successfully deciphered it as coordinates on the other side."

Hugo shook his head. "Tell me this then, are these directions to another dimension, or to another world?"

Lucca responded, "Both. Upon reaching the other side the team must find the starting point from which the map had been sent."

Hugo closed his eyes and turned away in bewilderment. "What if these poor bastards you're sendin' out can't find their startin' point within the other side, then what?"

"I have complete confidence that they will."

Hugo was skeptical. "Somethin' tells me that we aren't getting the whole story about how you plan on findin' the place where we all seem to go when we pass to the other side."

Lucca had the look of a man who held the secrets of the universe in his coat pocket. "In time my friends, in time . . ."

CHAPTER 26

The following day, after a long discussion about their mission, the group was sitting on the runway ready for departure. It would be a short trip to their destination in the middle of the Swiss Alps.

Hendrik looked over the flight plan, scratching his head. "Ms. Rosen, this is highly irregular, but if you are confident that these coordinates are correct, then I will get us there without incident."

"No worries Hendrik, many other jets have landed here, so I know we will be fine in your quite capable hands." Hendrik punched in the coordinates. He thought that if someone else was able to fly into the side of a mountain then so could he. Having served time in the UNSC Defense Force, Hendrik was more than qualified.

Within minutes they were on final approach to the secret facility. The spaceship carrying a team of SELFs was ready to depart this reality for another dimension. Their mission was to bring back proof of the existence of not only the other side, but of an ancient civilization that was responsible for creating life on Earth. It had been considered quite an enormous task for such a small, select few. The clock was ticking.

After landing they taxied into the huge hangar that had been excavated out of the side of a mountain. Inside were two smaller jets parked side by side. The base had been connected to an ancient sink hole that had been turned into a modern facility. The Illuminati's sole purpose was to build the most extraordinary spacecraft ever imagined, with a crew of the most advanced specimens of humanity ever conceived, on a mission that would change the face of the planet if they were to succeed. This grand plan was a collection of scientists from around the world working together to achieve the goal of a greater existence, a new world order; all members of this exclusive secret society.

Athena, Alex, Hugo and Stuart descended the stairs from the private jet; Hendrik was happy to stay behind knowing they were in Hugo's capable hands. Hugo had given him a small communicator in the event things went south. Hendrik could prepare for immediate take-off and assist, if need be, with the arsenal of weapons at his disposal. Over the years, Hendrik's quick thinking and military training had extracted members of the Rosen clan from many sticky situations. He had filled a variety of job descriptions; pilot was just one of his more menial tasks.

At arrival they were greeted only by an open elevator door. The elevator sat waiting for them without escort. Its open door invited them to enter to access the secret chambers below. The group looked around at their surroundings, unsure what might be waiting below the surface. They gave one another uncertain glances, then accepted the silent invitation and entered.

When the doors slid open after a short descent, Hans Grobler was waiting for them and loudly, almost eagerly, said, "Welcome my friends to the Rabbit Hole. I assure you that what you are about to see will change your thinking about our place in the universe."

When Stuart caught Hans's eye, he noted a glimmer of surprise and fear. "Nice to have you back under different, more positive circumstances," Hans said, wishing he were more prepared for Stuart and the others' unexpected arrival. Stuart was suddenly very uneasy with Hans, and it wasn't merely the fact that he was back in this place. Something was terribly wrong, but regardless he felt comforted knowing they were armed just in case Hans had other plans for their small group.

They stepped out onto the main floor and gazed up in amazement. The ship capable of existing in multiple dimensions was sitting on its launch pad as steam vented from its underbelly like the hot breath coming from a beast ready to sprint.

Athena observed a familiar face approaching through the cloud of steam, his hazy appearance coming into focus from under the ship. "Hello Athena, nice to have you join us for the launch of a new era for mankind."

Athena's body language spoke volumes. Arms crossed tightly around her chest and a chill running up her spine, she gasped, "Simon, what have you done with my mother?"

"Yes, never skipping a beat, just like your mother. Simon has almost disappeared from existence and is only a distant voice now in the void at the back of my thoughts. Your mother's demise and then her involvement in this fruitless endeavor to the tune of 150 billion dollars. It was a smart move on her part, although she contributed that boost to the mission's success unknowingly. As far as what happened to your mother, I believe her untimely death was orchestrated to assist in this mission."

Simon Bedford had been a strikingly handsome man, with a piercing gaze and bald head, a man who should by all rights be well into his eighties. He looked to be in his forties. Under his strong form was a fierce opponent with a mind as sharp as a whip and eyes that shone with intelligence.

"My dear Athena, all those years I had been with your grandfather carrying out his wishes. Along the way I grew more powerful, almost capable of snuffing out this constant nagging in my brain from your dearly, almost departed Simon. My only endeavor had been to rid the world of your kind, but you see curiosity had gotten the best of me over the years. Your grandfather had an artifact in his possession that had an evil glow when I pried it out of his dead hand. Your mother's DNA, as I discovered over the years, also has the ability to wield its power, therefore preventing me from extinguishing her myself. Fortunately for her she has been safely tucked away. You see your mother, no matter how she tried to pull away, will always be a member of this illustrious group. Now I have something for you." Simon reached into his coat pocket and pulled out a gold ring. "This needs to be passed on to the next generation. It belonged to your grandfather and I claimed it after his death. You are now its rightful owner. Poor girl, lucky for you your DNA is degrading like the rest of the mere mortals."

Athena snatched the ring from his grasp, blinking back tears and trying desperately to hold on to her composure, but she found herself snapping back at Simon or whoever this person was, "What have you done with my mother?"

"Believe me when I say there were many who wanted your grandfather and your mother eliminated, but I discovered they possessed a power and with it the capability to leave our mortal disabilities behind. "Your mother's abilities, as I recently discovered, posed a great threat to our religion. I now know I needed her to destroy the evil power within your grandfather's crystal trinket. But her involvement has changed the playing field with this new discovery, a discovery that could finally prove once and for all the origins of mankind and by doing so pull our civilization into a dark abyss of faithless creatures."

Athena's head began to spin, and she began to shout at Simon with an anger that was welling up from her depths. "Do you know who killed my mother?"

Alex pulled her gently away. "Dora wanted no part of any of this madness. Your words are lunacy!"

Simon shook his head. "Why would she? She wanted to separate herself as much as possible; admitting to it would have defeated the purpose. But she could not change who or what she was. The power she possesses is evil and for that she should have been eliminated."

Alex felt his heart fill with a rage that he could barely contain. He asked through gritted teeth, already knowing the answer, "Was Dorathy murdered?"

Simon, with his years, had an inner strength that shone through his eyes. "Oh yes she was indeed killed, for she has the power to change everything." Simon gave an evil, condescending laugh. "As you already know, the man responsible for John's death still is quite a threat to this project and all the individuals involved with its success. The truth finally comes to the surface," he said as he gazed down at Athena. His crazy gaze locked on to her. "My dear . . . and the truth shall set me free. So many have tried to apprehend me, but I continue to elude. You see, my altered DNA is nearly impossible to trace, forensic analysis always comes up empty-handed. As for Simon, he has been living in purgatory within my mind. And the members of your pitiful illustrious group shall soon come to their demise!" Simon pulled out a weapon that had been hidden by his coat.

The hair rose on the back of Hugo's neck and with lightning-fast reflexes, he un-holstered his own gun. Simon was expecting his attack and fired first, grazing Hugo's head, causing his cap to fly off his head. Hugo shoved Athena, knocking her to the ground. Simon had taken aim at her, but she spun on her side and drew her weapon, managing a clear shot to Simon's shoulder. Alex and Stuart were slow to react but managed to shoot off a few rounds in Simon's direction as he ran for cover.

Alex rushed to Athena's side, dragging her behind a forklift where Hugo, Hans, and Stuart had taken cover. Stunned at what had just happened, Alex shouted at Hans, "You set us up!"

"I did not, but I'm sure I can tell you who did!"

Stuart grabbed Hans's elbow. "Is there another way out of here? We can't let him escape!"

Hans pointed in the direction Simon had fled. "Beyond that door there's a cargo lift to the surface, and he will no doubt try to make his escape there."

Hugo activated the small communicator in his ear. Athena gave him a knowing glance. "Hendrik can cut him off top side!" Hugo was on it, but Hendrik, as usual, was one step ahead of them.

Simon was hunkered down, the bleeding from his wound already slowing as his body rapidly repaired itself. Simon was muttering unintelligibly, stammering as if he were possessed by another soul that was trying to come to the forefront of his consciousness.

Desperately gathering his thoughts, he decided to make a run for the doors to the cargo elevator. He stood and fired in their direction, a fast-steady flow of hot ionized bullets flying in every direction, sending them for cover. He shouted tauntingly over the pop! pop! pop! of his semi-automatic, "I have something you want, something you need." He wedged himself against the door jam, just out of range for a clear shot. "You have nothing without it," he called as his inner voice reminded him, he had nothing without Dorathy. Simon rapidly punched at the buttons trying to speed the slow descent of the lift.

From above Hendrik was hastily making his way to the opposite side of the huge hanger and heard the grinding sound of the doors sliding open. He hid behind an aircraft wheel, ready to make his move. His senses on high alert, he felt a shift in the air, the sudden wave of purpose coming from behind. He turned to defend himself from attack, but he was a split second too slow. The last thing he saw before darkness claimed him was the door sliding open to reveal the icy stare of his would-be opponent.

An old woman, reddish hair liberally streaked with gray, eyes as blue as the sea, was standing above Hendrik's limp body motioning for Simon to hurry. "I told you the girl was useless to us." She pulled the amulet from beneath her coat collar. It remained the same lifeless black, with not a hint of light emanating from it.

Simon clutched at the crystal that hung from her neck, smearing his bloodied hand over its surface. "I failed!" He fell to his knees. "Oh God in heaven, I failed you!"

The woman lifted him up off the cold concrete. "Come with me now, there will be another chance. With great patience there will be a time to undo what has been done."

The elevator conveying Hugo's group made a slow ascent to the surface where the sound of small jet engines could be heard in the gray clouded sky. They rushed over to where Hendrik was slumped, blood flowing down the side of his face. Athena patted Hendrik's shoulder as he groaned from pain so bad it blurred his vision. Hugo helped him to his feet. "What the hell happened and who blindsided y'all?"

Hendrik leaned against the aircraft. "I don't know, I just remember the scent of perfume." He stood and winced in pain. The wind had picked up, blowing a drift of snow, dusting their clothing.

Hans said, "We need to go below and see to your head. There's much for us to discuss." Hans, although shaken by the events that had unfolded, felt compelled to share his knowledge of what had happened to Simon so many years ago. As he bandaged Hendrik's head wound, he thought of the time that he and John had discussed their suspicion that somehow Simon had been compromised.

"John was skeptical at first; he refused to accept that the man who had been like a brother to him would ever be capable of such a horrific act of deception. You see, John had secretly funded a project of soul trans-ference from a living breathing human into a bioprinted copy. He knew there would be moral and religious ramifications if the technology were ever to be released for public knowledge. There was a bit of quandary over how to navigate through the logistics of such a project, so John had pulled the plug on the whole damn thing. But it was too late. An individ-ual with whom he had worked on the project decided to go it alone but had infiltrated the Rosen Foundation and our brotherhood and a way to embezzle the funds needed and in doing so learned of our intentions."

Hugo was scratching at his two-day growth. "You mean to tell me he body-snatched Bedford and was privy to all material that would have been otherwise deemed classified?"

Athena added, "My grandfather knew there was something going on because I heard my mother mention his journal and something about the Antarctic and monks they had gone to see once before I was born. Mom rarely talked about her dad—I guess I never asked much because she seemed so disturbed by his murder."

Alex was tired and still shaking in his shoes, never having been shot at before. He demanded, "Someone please tell me more about what is going on!"

Hans tried to explain. "This technology has become old hat and has been successfully used unannounced to the public for several years now. The first manned Mars mission utilized bioprinting astronauts to the specifications required to endure the effects of space travel and adapt to hazards presented by long periods of time in an unprotected environment."

Alex spat out, "The public believes that the colonization of Mars is being accomplished by 'human' astronauts, not by some kind of hybrid!"

Hugo added what he knew of the Mars mission, "And what of those poor bastards? They're stuck up there now, unable to adapt if they were to return."

Hans chuckled, amused at Hugo's passionate response, "My dear friend, science has pushed mankind to evolve; what we are doing here is part of the evolution of mankind. The group of scientists on Mars knew the risk and chose to go regardless of the outcome. Those brave souls have paved the road for further missions into space, including this one. So, don't be too hard on us."

Hans continued as he proudly gestured to the spacecraft, "This is our future: mankind's future. All we have accomplished through the centuries brings us to this point in time where man can leave the confines of our universe to reach past our own reality."

The group fell silent, with only the sound of the ship's exterior throbbing like the beating of a beast's heart and steam blowing in gasps, reminiscent of a racehorse ready to leap out of its gate.

Hans sensed that his guests were in awe of what had been accomplished and felt no need for further concealment. "Come. Let me give the tour of man's greatest achievement." With a nod, Hans took control of the panel and in an instant a hatch appeared where there had been no defining markings or creases to show that a door had ever been placed there. It was at the lowest part of the ship; it seemed to be only a wingtip suspended merely a foot above the cold concrete floor. Hans directed the group with only a flicker of his eyes. He stood at the entryway to allow his guests to enter first.

Athena put her hand to rest on the outer skin of the craft and was shocked at the sensation of it responding to her touch, but she didn't falter as she stroked her hand gently over the surface as if she were petting a large gentle beast. She whispered to herself, but also to the creature that had been positioned in this grand scientific achievement, "Remarkable. So . . . alive."

"Yes, actually it is . . . alive that is." Hans spoke softly as not to alarm his creation. "Bio-material, not from this world, but from deep space. From exactly where, we have no clue. Found under the Antarctic ice. We acquired it, studied it, and found it could, indeed, multiply if encouraged to do so."

Alex shook his head to clear his thoughts. "How do you encourage a bio-material to . . ." He stopped short. "Do . . . actually . . . do anything?"

Hans responded with a smile, "We asked it to."

Hugo, with his typical out loud pondering, exclaimed, "I'll be goddamned! You mean to tell me this ship is made from some type of intelligent bio-space-stuff you guys picked up from under the ice, then grew it and stuck it to this ship?"

"That is exactly what I'm saying. And, for the record, it is far more superior than bio- space stuff, as you so eloquently put it. It's a sentient being, capable of far more than I think we will ever be able to ascertain. So please show it some courtesy and respect."

Hugo took a deep breath—things never ceased to amaze him, and he said softly in a non-threatening voice, "A ship grown in a lab . . . I'll be damned." But only with his first stroke across the hull did he realize the full scope of this creature's existence.

Everyone stroked the ship lovingly as they entered, fearing if they didn't relay a modicum of respect or managed to upset it somehow, it might lash out at them in some wild display of anger for being used in such a manner. One by one, they entered, touching and caressing as they went. The interior had all the comforts of a home away from home with advanced secret technology that no one, including Hugo, could imagine.

Stuart immediately saw his handiwork lined up in a row. The crew of this mission lay in stasis, ready to be awakened after a long journey into the unknown. "The people you coerced for this mission are giving up quite a lot and they wanted to be recognized for their sacrifice."

Hans smiled. "They will, in time they will. That time is not now. We are ready to launch and by the time you find anyone to listen to you about this mission, we will all be gone. This ship and her crew will be gone, and all evidence that anything ever happened here will be gone, I assure you."

Athena spoke softly, calmed by her new friend's presence, "What you are doing here could unite us as a species. Why keep it secret?"

"Oh Athena, my dear. When faced with things we don't understand our species reacts in fear and fear propagates aggression. Simply put, humans are not ready to accept what this crew will no doubt find. By the time we find the truth of our existence, maybe then we will have evolved enough to embrace it and not fear it. To pursue it, not to destroy it."

The group followed Hans to the control room where there was a fully functional cockpit, but none had ever seen the likes of this on any air, or space, craft. Hugo, ever bold, queried, "How the hell do you fly this thing?"

Hans said, "You don't. You see, any navigation is done with mind control."

Hugo asked, "So what . . . the pilot tells the ship where to go, and how to land?

"No, my friend, the other way around."

"Oooo-kay," Hugo sounded annoyed. "Now you mean to tell me that the ship tells the pilot how to fly and the pilot does what?"

"The pilot merely tells the ship where he wants to go, or the direction he wants to go— the ship adjusts for airspeed, turbulence, or any other unforeseen problem that may arise. The pilot, having already charted a course, communicates his intent to the ship and the ship carries out his request with the best approach possible."

"Well shit, that's a hell of a navigation system!"

Athena half listened as she sat in the belly of this ancient alien being. She felt a closeness, almost a bond being formed with this unlikely soul. She whispered to it, "Please find my mother and bring her home," as she slowly stroked the inner surface of the ship.

The gentle beast read her thoughts and emotions. It responded to her, every intelligent atomic particle stored her request and it was now bonded to her DNA with the touch of her hand. It took a small part of her to take on its long journey into the unknown.

A few hours later Athena, Alex, Hendrik, Stuart, Hugo and key members of the staff that had not already departed from the underground facility stood in awe as the ship hovered silently when the mechanical anchoring mechanism released its grasp.

A technician keyed a few commands into the remote guidance system and the ship rose slowly through the opening that had once been covered with camouflage netting. The craft was gone in an instant, rockets propelling it to the upper atmosphere. Moments later only a flash of gold could be seen in the now dark sky and a thunderous boom echoed through the snow-covered Alps. It was gone, going faster than anything man had ever built, bending the space around itself. It was a ship of dreams . . . but, after all, it wasn't really a ship.

CHAPTER 27

A fter a long journey home Alex was sitting in Hugo's office at JPL. He desperately wanted answers to what had happened to his wife. Exhausted and feeling helpless, he demanded, "Now what Hugo? What do we do with this information?"

"Damn, Amigo, I don't even know who to call about this convoluted bullshit! And when I do figure out who to discuss this with, they're gonna think I lost my damned mind!"

Karen Johnson had come in after hours to check on her next project and noticed a light on down the hall. She stepped closer to investigate and heard Hugo's voice bellowing over the dim humming of monitors in adjoining offices.

"John Rosen created this hybrid psychopath who's now running loose and could be responsible for Dora's death. They launched this ship with technology that was made possible by Dora's donation."

Alex was maddened by the thought. "What would be the point of having Dora dead? She donated most of her money and her expertise to get this new technology jump-started to mainstream. She was no threat! If anything, an asset!"

Karen pressed herself against the wall next to the slightly ajar door into Hugo's office. Sweat collected on her brow. Her thoughts ran wild with the true nature of what she may have been a party to.

"So exactly my point. Alex shook his head in despair. "Why kill her?"

Karen's head was throbbing; she had to speak up. She gathered her composure, knowing her involvement could cost her career. But she admired and respected Dorathy, and she had to come clean so they might get to the bottom of what had happened to her.

Karen wiped her brow with the back of her hand and straightened her coveralls. She pushed the door open. "I think I know what happened to Dorathy."

The two men jumped out of their seats and a moment later Hugo said, annoyed, "Please, elaborate for us, since you've injected yourself into our conversation."

Karen looked down at her feet, biting her lip, very uncomfortable. She cleared her throat. "I was contacted several months ago and asked to place a tracking device on the cryotube, long before Dorathy died." Tears welled up in her bloodshot eyes. "Men from CERN offered me a huge amount of money, so I did it. It wasn't ethical, but I really didn't see the harm. The person inside was going to be already dead and we were putting our own device on it anyway . . . I just didn't see the harm."

Alex's and Hugo's thoughts were spinning. Alex spoke first. "Why would they do that? The first patient was to be an elderly man, nobody of any importance to them. Besides, as you pointed out, there was already a JPL tracking device installed."

Karen's voice started to shake as it became clear to her. "The tracking device they wanted me to install worked on a higher, more complex frequency. It was designed to be used by someone already in that dimension, not by us on Earth."

"So . . . so what?" Alex tried to maintain his composure.

Hugo leaned back in his chair rubbing his tired eyes and whistled, "Oh man, those rat bastards!"

Alex's breathing became labored, his thoughts clouded, "What? Where are you going with this?"

Hugo sat forward. "Look, who would be the greatest asset to their mission? They get her out of the way, protected from this Simon character, AND get her expertise for the mechanism they installed on that damn ship. You heard the man, Alex. Dora helped design that thing. They get to where they're goin', come out of stasis and bingo! They have a bleep on a screen with instructions to pick her cryotube up. If ever there was a single person who could be their greatest asset and a key to their mission's success, it's Dorathy Rosen."

Alex's head was spinning as he attempted to digest the information. "But how would they know Dora's wishes were to be placed into cryosleep and placed in that tube?"

"It's not a stretch of the imagination to say that if Dora were to die suddenly, she would want to be the first to go. It was her pet project—both of your project; she would no doubt want to be a part of it."

"Alex's eyes grew wild. "Oh my God, that means they are going to fix her—revive her . . . she's going to be alive!"

"Hold on there, buddy. I've seen that look in your eyes before. You're here, and she's there and, may I remind you, way in the hell out there!"

Alex stood up, looking at Karen now. "If I go, can you duplicate their tracking device?"

Karen felt like she was being sucked into some kind of nightmare. "Yes, I believe I can."

Alex could think of nothing else but being reunited with Dorathy. "How long before you can get another cryotube built and ready for launch?"

"Weeks . . . a couple of months perhaps."

"Get it done!"

"Hold your horses, pal!" Hugo was feeling railroaded. "I can't authorize that!"

"Last I checked, Hugo, I was paying you for my project. This is still my project and I'm still a paying customer and Karen still works for you, correct?"

Hugo sighed deeply and nodded his head in agreement. "Yeah, my friend, you got it. Don't think I have to remind you that for you to pull this off you have to die."

Alex said quietly, "I'm already dead."

Alex turned and said a hasty goodbye and headed home in a rush, unsure how Athena was going to respond.

Hugo was tired and rose slowly from his chair. "Karen, after this project is done, you and I have to have a long chat about your future at JPL. Given the current situation you will resume your status as project engineer, but under no circumstances are you to discuss what you have heard or reveal any part of the application of the tracking device, the purpose of the rush to get another one built ASAP or, most of all, who the next passenger will be. Don't cross me girl, not on this, not if you don't like the idea of saying in your next career, 'May I take your order?'"

Karen was grateful for the chance to redeem herself. "I'm so sorry, I will make it up to you . . . ," her voice trailed off as Hugo walked past her and out the door of his office.

"Close the door on your way out."

CHAPTER 28

A lex pulled into the driveway of the home they shared as a family, reluctant to get out of the car. He knew the discussion he was about to have with his step-daughter was not going to be easy. He thought how could he depart this world knowing how much Athena loved him as her own father, knowing how much she had been through with the loss of her mother. How could he ask her to let him go as well? He had to try to make her understand. Somehow, he had to make it work, he had to find Dorathy alive and bring her home.

Athena was scurrying around the kitchen preparing dinner. "Hi, what took you so long? Hope you like chicken Marsala." Athena glanced up and their eyes locked. "What's wrong, Alex?" He only shook his head in response. "Would you please tell me what's wrong?" Athena grew impatient, "Tell me damn it!"

Alex placed his hands on her shoulders. "Your mother is alive . . . going to be alive, and I have to try and bring her home."

"What the hell are you talking about?" Athena's head was spinning. "What do you mean alive? What is going on with you?" Athena turned the stovetop heat off. "I really need you to start making some sense right now." She yanked at his arm and dragged him over to sit at the dining table. "Now talk to me and tell me what's going on."

Alex ran his fingers through his thick hair. "Look, what I'm about to tell you has to stay here. You can't jump up and take matters into your own hands, not this time."

Athena begged, "Alex, please just tell me."

He scratched at his unruly beard. "This isn't going to be easy, but you have to know what I'm planning to do." He waited a moment before he continued, trying desperately to make sense of what needed to be done. "Your mom may have been murdered by our friends at CERN. We don't know how, but I think we know why."

Athena searched Alex's eyes for the truth, but truth was all she saw, and it began to frighten her. "Alex, what are you thinking of doing? Because I can see the wheels in your head turning."

"I have to go find her. I have to try, Athena; will you let me do that?"

Athena pulled away from the table, frightened. Alex didn't have to spell out what he was planning. "No, Alex you can't, you can't do that . . . I won't let you!" She started to sob, "I can't lose you too, Alex!"

"Honey, it's the only way. I wish the circumstances were different, but you've got to see I have to try! It's the only hope she has and even if the chance is slim to none, I can't go on knowing I may have been able to save her and did nothing.

Sweetheart, you're young and have your whole life to live. If there's a way to bring us back safe and sound, I'll do it. But if not, you continue on with your life knowing I did everything to get your mother back." Alex's voice started to break. "Get married to Kevin, start your own family— your mother wanted that for you, I want that for you. Please Athena, I can't do this without your blessing. You have Kevin and his family and all your friends to lean on. You have to tell me it's okay."

Athena sobbed, rubbing tears from her eyes. She was being torn apart, completely gutted. How could she give Alex her blessing? She felt that was something she was incapable of doing. Losing her mother, now losing Alex on the slim chance that she could get them both back alive. Then she realized that a slim chance was all the hope she needed. She said, "Okay . . . Alex I love you . . . go find my mom." She got up and hugged him tight, asking through her tears, "When, when are you going."

"Soon. In a few weeks."

Time marched along and as promised Karen upheld her end of the deal, working day and night to get the cryotube ready for launch ahead of schedule.

Athena and Kevin were by Alex's side on the jet to Phoenix. The thought of cryogenics and what was about to happen bounced around in Athena's mind. "Alex don't you think it's ironic that you started your company in Phoenix?"

He contemplated her question. "I'm not sure I get you."

Athena continued, "You know the myth . . . the rising of the Phoenix, life after death, being reborn from the ashes."

Alex's mind was fading in and out and he was having a hard time concentrating, "Oh right, guess I never thought about that." He said, "Consequently it was never part of the equation, but maybe I should rename the company 'Phoenix'; it has a nice ring when you think about it in those terms."

Athena smiled. "I can do that if you want."

Alex chuckled, "Sure, why not? Has a bit more intrigue and interest than 'Lifecor.'" They both laughed, trying to push aside the thought of what was about to take place.

When the jet rolled to a stop and Hendrik opened the jetway, he held out his hand and with tears welling up, pulled Alex in for a manly hug. "I will look after her while you are away. I hope you can find our dear Dorathy. Godspeed to you."

Alex looked into Hendrik's ice blue eyes and nodded. There were no words he could manage to string together. With that they departed.

Alex lay naked under a thin sheet. The room was cold, and he was shivering, mostly out of blinding fear of what was about to happen. Athena sat holding Alex's hand and Kevin stood behind her and rubbed her tense shoulders, while the sedative Stuart had given Alex kicked in. Stuart was disturbed by what his best friend wanted him to do. "You know at the federal level I could go to prison for murdering you."

Shuddering while he spoke, Alex replied, "Nah buddy, the legal documents are ironclad, and this is a right-to-die state. It's all good."

Stuart looked pale and frail. "'Good' is not the word I'm feeling right now."

"I know buddy, but you know I have to do this, so let's get on with it."

Stuart looked into Alex's dazed eyes and with a heavy heart said, "Go find your lady. God, you always were an asshole."

Alex winked at him and turned to gaze at Athena who was still holding his hand. "Just remember one thing, you are my daughter and I love you. You and your mother are my whole life." His gaze shifted to Kevin. "You're a good man son, take care of her and be kind to each other." Kevin, trying to be strong, assured Alex he would always be there for Athena.

Athena leaned down and kissed Alex gently on the cheek. "I love you, Pops." She then looked up at Stuart and nodded. Stuart reluctantly injected a strong sedative and said softly, "I'm gonna miss you man."

Alex's eyes closed with a flutter and Stuart proceeded to the next step, rapidly lowering his body temperature and stopping his heart.

Alex was gone.

Athena sobbed and broke down in Kevin's strong arms. Together they left the cold room. Athena stumbled, feeling the Earth moving under her feet, sending her swaying. Her heart ached as she grasped Kevin, feeling the walls closing in on her. They departed down the hall, Athena crying uncontrollably. She could not bear to witness the following procedures.

Alex felt a warm breeze and the sensation he was not alone, that somehow Dorathy was by his side kissing him gently. He was between awake and asleep, having a wonderful dream of being back at the beach house and napping the afternoon away in their favorite hammock.

"Alex, darling, what are you doing here? Couldn't stay away could you? Oh, my darling husband what have you gone and done?"

Alex woke suddenly, his face was being licked vigorously by some small creature. He opened his eyes to see a small tan poodle sitting on his chest staring back at him. As his vision cleared, he saw his beloved wife lying beside him in the cool grass, her dark hair shimmering in the late day sun. He put his hand against her cheek. Every movement and every touch seemed to glow. "Dora, how I missed you!" He pulled her close and kissed her, tasting her lips. "I needed to come and find you, to save you and bring you home with me."

"This is our home now. We will never be apart again, and soon Athena will be here with us as well."

Something snapped awake in Alex and he struggled to emerge through a heavy fog into the clear of day. "No. Dora, you have to listen to me, and you have to try and remember what I have to say. You are floating in space." Alex was having the hardest time finding the right words, his thoughts were a jumbled mess in his head. "They . . . your father's friends . . . the society . . . they are coming for you, but so am I Dorothy. You must remember this . . . Don't let them leave . . . when they revive you, you have to make them understand . . . I'm right behind you. Can you remember that for me? Don't let them leave me behind!"

Dorothy wrapped her arms around Alex and held him close. "I'm never going to leave you, my darling husband." He held her close and breathed in the soft fragrance of her hair.

Suddenly Dorathy felt a painful sensation come over her and lifted herself to look into Alex's bright eyes. "Alex . . . ALEX!"

"No! God no, not yet!" he yelled.

A vortex opened behind her and for a fraction of a second Alex saw his wife's lifeless body lying on a table in a distance that seemed to stretch until it distorted, and the image dissipated. As the image fragmented it carried Dorathy with it, ripping her from his arms, her scream echoing in the emptiness.

He screamed after her, "Please, wait for me!" But she was already gone.

Alex clawed at the grass, hoping that his turn would come momentarily. From behind, he heard a familiar voice, "Alex, you were right."

SECTION 3

CHAPTER 29

"Dorathy Rosen, can you hear me?" Brenda brushed the cold, damp hair from Dorathy's face. "Hand me the oxygen."

Henry did as he was asked. "Should we start warming her up?" Dr. Brenda Hyden shook her auburn head, feeling a stress she had not felt for quite some time, "No, not yet. The heat will put her into shock. We have to make sure all the preserving fluids have been drained. Bring up her brain scan." Brenda looked concerned, "Okay, the repairs look like they have been made. Shit, hand me that vial, I need to give her another injection . . . it's going to take her a while to assimilate our blood."

Henry looked down at Dorathy and couldn't help but see a striking resemblance to a life he almost had long ago, a life that he lost in the pursuit of a pointless existence.

Suddenly Dorathy's frozen eyes flew open and she started to gasp and cough. Brenda spoke calmly but was terrified that she had somehow forgotten something. "Help me turn her on her side." Henry pushed from one side as Brenda pulled from the other, rolling her on the table. "That's it Dorathy, cough it all out, get rid of it and that should be the end of the preserving fluids." Dorathy groaned in pain, her lungs on fire with every breath she drew, every muscle in her body contracting, shuddering and shivering. Death warmed up was the overwhelming situation she now faced.

Dorathy's mind was playing tricks on her. She tried to speak but could only emit the faintest of squeaks. She was racked by indescribable pain.

"Okay, I think it's safe to slowly warm her up." Brenda punched a key on the control pad and the table started to mold around Dorathy's body, enveloping her in a gel-like casing. The warmth the table provided, although still far below her normal body temperature, felt as it was fire licking along her nerve endings.

Henry reached for the hands Dorathy held clenched across her chest and held them firmly in his own. "Hey, it's going to be okay."

Dorathy peered through her half-frozen corneas and tried to make out the image of the man who was holding her stiff hands. She managed to speak in a whisper, "Alex is that you?"

"Deep breaths kiddo, don't try to talk . . . calm deep breaths," he said in a soothing voice, as he adjusted her oxygen mask.

Brenda gave Henry a knowing glance. "I think she's out of the woods for now, so I'm going to give her a sedative."

Dorathy drifted to sleep, her mind going back and forth, unable to rest. Her body was numb to the onslaught, but her mind was in turmoil.

Brenda and Henry entered the common lounge area of the ship. Dimitri sat as he always did, his feet up on the table. Brenda sat down next to him, knocking his feet off in the process. Magnus sipped his evening cup of tea. "So how is our newly acquired patient doing?"

"Well, she's alive, Brenda announced as if she wasn't quite sure how, given that they gave her a transfusion with blood they had each donated, along with the injection of the nanobots repairing her damaged brain tissue.

Henry spoke, concern in his voice, "She will start to transform as she takes on our synthetic DNA. She will adapt."

"Oh, yes," Brenda said with a hint of resentment and reminded them, "as we all have. Unfortunately, she was not privy to her purpose on this ship or this mission and something tells me that she may have objections."

Dimitri placed his feet back onto the table in a sign of defiance. "It will be good to have someone new to talk to after all these years of me being bored with all of you. I think we should have a drink to celebrate."

Brenda rolled her eyes, "Shit, Dim, you'd celebrate a fart!"

"Enough, you two," Henry said, taking command. "While we're out here we need to reload this ship and you know what that means. I say we head out as soon as our guest is up and functioning." There were groans and sighs abundant. "We all know the risks, but until we find another source, we need to do it, and do it carefully. Suck it up, people."

Dimitri hissed, "Screw that. I about lost my ass to those damn creatures."

Brenda said, "No loss there."

"Ha! You love me, you can't live without me, I'm your big Russian man toy."

"Piss off, "Brenda murmured under her breath, knowing her circumstances were less than stellar.

Henry had grown accustomed to the banter between Brenda and Dimitri over the years. "Dim, with your analysis of the creature's DNA do you feel we have a better chance of delivering a sedative if we come in contact with them again?"

"I feel it will work, but it has to be delivered at a close proximity to the creature's mucus membranes in the mouth."

Henry sat next to Magnus, grabbing a sandwich from the plate on the table. "Brenda, any thoughts?"

"No, he's right. I just don't want to have to get that close in order to find out if it works or not." Brenda continued, "But I don't see we have a choice. We're here, and we need to do this so we can follow up on the next clue our scaly little friend, Jobar, gave us."

"Jobar might be sending us on a wild goose chase." Magnus spoke through the steam rising from his mug.

"He's been in this sector a long time. If what he says is true, we might be able to find some viable clues to our elusive portal." Henry was hopeful when he thought about any chance of finding the ancient relic that had been left for them somewhere in space, a long time forgotten. "It's not like we have anything better to do, folks." Brenda nodded in agreement and sat back in her seat.

Henry continued, "Now back to Dr. Rosen. If, or should I say when, we find this portal, her expertise will be much needed to align this ship's Space Bending Device to match its trajectory. Hope she's up to the challenge."

Magnus cleared his throat. "When the poor woman wakes from her long sleep and realizes what has happened to her, I think she will be more than happy to try her best to accommodate, as she has just as much to gain from our success."

They heard a scream coming from the med lab. Henry was first to jump up and the rest followed in his wake.

They found Dorathy awake and struggling against the table that had immobilized her in its warm grip. "Someone please help me," she sobbed, her eyes dilated, wide with fear, her complexion as gray as death.

"Okay girlfriend, relax, we're here to help," Brenda soothed. With the push of a button the table released its grip on Dorathy.

In a raspy voice that she could barely muster, Dorathy said, "Where am I? I want my husband, please help me."

"Calm down, Dora. May I call you Dora?" Henry asked, trying to sound non-threatening and hoping to calm her nerves.

"Where am I?"

Henry held her hand that was warm and very much alive. "Can you sit up?" Dorathy struggled, attempting to draw her wits about her. With help from Brenda she sat on the edge of the table wearing only a thin gown that was now wet with cold sweat.

Magnus handed her a cup of hot tea. "Here, take this my dear, it will help."

Henry attempted to break the ice. "Our friend Magnus here thinks tea is a cure for everything."

Dorathy looked from face to face and locked eyes with each of them before accepting her hot tea. She sipped it slowly, an odd, unfamiliar taste lingering on her tongue, her senses trying to ascertain her current circumstances. "Where is this place? Where am I? What happened to me?"

Henry glanced at Brenda for help, but she only nodded back for him to continue. "You may find this hard to absorb. Tell me, what is the last thing you remember?"

Dorathy struggled to regain her memory. She looked around in hopes that something looked familiar. Her eyes came to rest on the cryotube that was resting quietly in the back corner of the med lab. Her eyes grew wide as memories started to flood in. "That, I built that."

"Good," Henry said in a comforting voice. A few seconds later Dorathy reached up to her head, but the moment was gone. "I can't remember."

Impatient as usual, Brenda spoke up, "Honey, you died. You died and you were cryogenically frozen for a long trip into the unknown. Can you remember any of that?"

Dorathy wore a blank stare, but slowly a shimmer of light broke through. "That was my project . . . my husband Alex Mason . . . I was just with him."

"Yes, you died, and he was with you," Brenda was saying.

Dorathy shook her head. "No, I was just with him, just a moment ago . . . we were on the other side. I died." She said, her voice cracking as reality sunk in.

The group looked at one another and with that statement they were reminded of their mission. That the place existed and wasn't just a myth or legend. It was real and tangible and was waiting for them to discover it.

Dorathy put her cup down and ran her fingers through her damp hair to find it had been cut unevenly to her chin. "Please help me up."

Brenda helped her to her feet, the floor reacting to the touch of her bare feet. Dorathy looked down at the strange sensation. Brenda grabbed some coveralls from an adjoining shelf and held them out. "Here, put these on." Brenda helped her dress and walked her over to the cryotube.

Dorathy stared down at her creation, memories flooding in, and spoke, "You revived me . . . how far did I come? Who are you?"

"Well girlfriend, that is a long story."

Dorathy spread her hands over the hull of her creation and noted the amount of deterioration from a constant bombardment of solar radiation. "How long was I out there? This place . . . I don't . . . recognize it." Dorathy turned her gaze to Brenda's almost-too-perfect face then back to the three men, "Who are you?"

Henry rolled over a chair and sat straddling it, "My name is Captain Henry Tinman and I'm the commander of this ship. This here is Dr. Brenda Hyden and those two scruffy individuals are mission specialists Dimitri Asania and Magnus Connery. We were sent here on a . . . search mission in the year 2063 . . . approximately twenty Earth years ago. I gotta ask, what the hell took you so long? We had instructions to pick you up, which tells me you left Earth some time before we did, yet you only just arrived."

Dorothy's head started to ache and she propped herself up against the cryotube. This convoluted nightmare hadn't even begun to penetrate her thought processes. "I don't understand, why are you here—for me?"

Magnus approached with his bright-eyed, utterly positive composure. "My dear, we were sent here to find the origins of human life and you just happen to be the only person who can get us there. You are of great importance to the success of this mission. Our instructions were concise: pick you up and we have ourselves a mission specialist in space warping with certain inherited capabilities."

Dorathy wanted no part of this madness, "I . . . I just would rather go home." Somehow, she knew the moment the words came out of her mouth that this crew was not able to grant her that request. She searched each face for support, but there was none to be had.

Henry said, to offer a bit of comfort, "Well, the way I see it, we have a little bit better chance at finding our objective now that you are on board. Then your wish to return home . . . ," he shrugged.

Dimitri laughed. "You are stuck with us, and we are stuck with you. Hope you are a good cook."

Henry came to his feet and held out his hand. "Welcome aboard. Speaking of food, it's probably a good idea to get something in you." Dorathy reached out her hand and accepted this band of characters as new friends, friends that in a short time would be her family.

They sat for hours after dinner telling Dorathy of the worlds they had encountered and the beings that occupied them. Dimitri talked of his discovery in the un-coded human DNA. "You're telling me we have coordinates buried in our DNA. Then what you have been looking for is a starting point in a higher reality, a prime reality for humankind?"

Henry shook his head. "No, not just humans . . . we used to think that but now we know that almost every being we have encountered, regardless of its evolutionary track, carries the same code. What we have learned is that the beings that left us the code have also left us a portal. That is our starting point and that is what we and countless others have been looking for.

"The reason we were engineered the way we were, is that it was be-lieved the beings that created us came from a higher existence, a different dimension; the specimen that was found was governed by a whole dif-ferent type of matter that vibrated at a completely different frequency. A mission to the Antarctic found evidence proving the theory of directed panspermia; the intentional seeding of Earth. What Dimitri discovered buried in the specimen was alien DNA, but it wasn't alien at all; it was us, it was human, but it predated us by over a billion years!

"Ever since this discovery, scientists have been pushing to find a pat-tern in our un-coded DNA. The thinking was how could over 99% of our DNA be nothing but junk? There had to be something more to it; to think it had no real purpose other than offering some assistance to the coded DNA was unreasonable. Dimitri's team thought it seemed to have a pat-tern that resembled language."

Dimitri explained, "My team could see there was a pattern and kept trying to decipher it as a hidden message. It was believed to be similar to ancient languages, but finally one day it became clear to me; it wasn't a cryptic message at all, it was star coordinates!"

Brenda added, "We have traveled into a higher dimension. Everything here vibrates at a completely different frequency than it did at home. Our reality now is the same as from the DNA that seeded our planet."

Dorathy asked, "And what of the people of Earth? If we came from this DNA, why are we so different?"

"In one word," Dimitri said, "evolution."

Dorathy was struggling to absorb and assimilate all the information being presented. She knew only too well her father's involvement had paved the way for them being here and felt responsible. She knew the Illuminati would stop at nothing to gain control over the planet; this mis-sion would be their turning point for world dominance, a New World Order. Dorathy was saddened by the thought of her father and the bru-tal way he had been killed. She tried to explain, "The Illuminati were paving the way to control the planet, and eliminate the ones that were de-evolving and threatened an everlasting peace."

Brenda shook her head. "No, you have it wrong, they weren't looking to control the planet, they were looking to leave it. The planet was rapidly approaching a breaking point with overpopulation. Advancements in technology had caused a tipping point for our species, and simply put they were planning to jump ship. They felt it's the path towards evolving past what we are now, to what we can become, to get to that higher existence. We can move one step further up our evolutionary track so that we might become like the beings that created life eons ago. That is their New World Order. Quite literally."

Dorathy knew she was right, and a sense of grief settled in with the realization of their circumstances. "Our home and everyone on it might be gone by the time we're done with this quest . . . it might already be gone."

The group had mused over that often through the years. Henry spoke. "So we press on, we find this Holy Grail. It's out there and we are not the only ones looking for it."

CHAPTER 30

Jobar was a wise old fellow from a flat, swampy world. Its beautiful, sprawling cities covered the landscape with a dazzling display of eco-conscious architecture so as not to detract from the surrounding natural beauty. Slightly larger than our own Earth with denser gravity, this ancient planet and its tropical climate accounted for Jobar's short stature and the brown leathery skin that had evolved over time into a layer of protective cooling scales. Home for the harvest holiday, his work this season took him four sectors away. Space mining was becoming harder and harder these days with all the regulations being imposed on independent contractors, but he managed to save and put enough aside so that he didn't have to worry for a while. Jobar was happy to have time off to spend with the friends and family now gathered around him at the dinner table.

Jobar's brother was an annoying fellow, shorter than most, with opinions that made those around him groan in either disgust or anger. "Tell me, Jobar, how can you afford to take this much time from work? I think your work council contracts reek of favoritism!"

Jobar grew tired of Patsup's insinuations. "You know what it's called? It's called hard work and professionalism. That's what keeps me busy despite the fact our minister has made it nearly impossible for self-employed miners to make a decent living." Jobar knew he had just opened a can of worms he did not wish to open, not now, as he hadn't the strength to talk politics with his brother, especially not on Harvest Day.

Patsup slammed his mug down on the table. "There you go again attacking our minister, and he had a lot on his plate to fix once your warlord got voted out!"

Jobar countered, "Our minister has had plenty time to mend a few loose ends, but instead he's managed to unravel the whole economy!"

Jobar's sister stood taller than most at almost a meter and a half, and shouted down at her brothers, "Both of you shut your mouths. I will not have this discussion tonight, not at my table!"

When Mares spoke, everyone listened. She was not to be messed with. It was said she was a whiz in the kitchen and was skilled at wielding a knife. She was known to throw her knives in anger and was a good aim. Mares sat and poured herself another mug of ale. "That's better. Now eat before it all gets cold." Her children whispered amongst themselves and started to giggle. Mares gave them a death stare and they straightened up immediately. "Tell me Jobar, have you seen the Travelers lately? I haven't heard you mention them for a while."

"Yes I ran across them in the Dorian sector. They were on their way to intercept an addition to their crew, a female who had died and had been cryogenically frozen to preserve. They had instructions to intercept with aid of a tracker."

Mare's eyes widened. "A woman from their home planet? It seems so unlikely that they can find a person coming from their past and their part of space, yet they have such difficulties for returning themselves?"

Jobar shook his head. "No Mares, they are unable to reverse their course. They are basically lost and all the star charts I have given them have no resemblance to their home. But what worries me the most is their ship and their safety. There are unscrupulous sorts that would kill to take that ship of theirs."

Mares rolled her eyes. "Here we go again, and there is nothing wrong with the ship you have . . ."

Jobar cut her off, "No woman. Their ship is unlike any I have seen . . . it is made from the Otherlings!"

All eyes were now wide and fixed on Jobar. He continued and everyone around the table hung on his every word as his tone became almost a whisper, "They say they grew the substance after finding it during a secret expedition. Their planet was seeded by the Otherlings in their part of space, no doubt delivered in a protected shroud, which I think is what they grew their ship from."

Patsup was skeptical. "You say their ship is from the Otherlings; no one has ever proved their existence, let alone believes a ship can be made from their essence. I call *danca dung* on the whole thing! I doubt they even exist at all."

Jobar reached for more ale so he might endure the evening with his narrow-minded, foul brother. "Then tell me why we all have the same code, with the same instructions. Why, for so many countless years, people have been searching for the portal? I, for one, believe the Travelers' ship will find it."

Mare's good friend Shepa, with her scaled skin loose with age, patted Patsup on the back. "I think that what Patsup is saying is the Otherlings sound more like fiction than reality. An ancient myth and a bed-time story for children . . ."

Patsup chimed in, "A waste of time if you ask me."

Jobar thought, *what narrow minds*, and said, "Absence of proof is not proof of absence . . . and I see more proof than the lack of."

Jobar's best friend Coolie, who had been a miner for as long as he could remember as his father before him, calmly said, "The portal is out there, it is cloaked . . . not visible by detectors; its golden beam only can be seen once you have crossed its path. Many mining ships have traveled through its wake and suffered substantial damage caused by the collision. Metal has been twisted and elongated, bent and fused. Oh, I guarantee it's out there and from the sounds of it our friends will find it."

Patsup rolled his eyes and wished the night would end, growing tired from listening to the nonsense.

After everyone had gone home and the table was cleared Jobar sat on his sister's front deck looking up at the stars. It had been a long time since he had seen them from this vantage point, and he thought how much more there must be out there. His only wish was he could find the ancient portal in his lifetime.

Night after night, Dorathy lay in the small bed in her little cabin. Other times she sat going through the personal items that had been placed in the cryotube with her prior to her launch. Athena and Alex had carefully placed photos and other mementos in the storage compartment of the tube—they even put the small wooden box containing the ashes and some fur from her little dog of years before.

She sat alone with only her thoughts and a handful of belongings. Everything she had and loved was now gone, separated by vast distances and time. She was stricken by the grief of having had her life stripped away. She needed to gather and control her emotions and try to grasp her situation.

She could still hear Alex talking to her, telling her something very important, but his voice was becoming a dim chime of a bell through the mist of her mind. A ship leaving its port for the vastness of the deep oceans. She missed her family; she missed her life. But now she was given a new life with new people and she was planning on grabbing onto it, for she knew her journey had just begun and when she was done her family would still be waiting for her on the other side. She wondered how she was going to get there—would it be through the back door like she and Alex once discussed? Anything seemed possible considering her current circumstances. She sat and wondered why the group had deemed her so important for this mission that they had killed her and then arranged for her retrieval.

She gazed in awe of the technology surrounding her. The ship was a living, breathing creature that had stumped even her ability to comprehend. She lay awake at night, talking to it as if it were a friend, "So tell me, do you run on dark energy, or are you able to just gather up hydrogen particles and somehow use that as fuel? Hmmm . . . somehow I think you totally understand exactly what I'm saying." She stroked the wall next to her bed and it gave her comfort during the long lonely nights, almost as if a big furry dog was sharing her bed. "I think I'll name you Ruby . . . think I'll bring that up with Henry . . . it's bad luck for a ship not to have a name."

The next morning Henry was performing his normal exercise routine of martial arts with a holographic image when Dorathy asked, "You want a real partner to work out with, or is the hologram doin' it for you?"

Henry laughed, "Okay, sure show me your moves."

Dorathy stretched while remembering her time spent training in the Far East. She went after him with a couple of approaches that he successfully blocked. She smiled and figured that since Henry was a former Navy Seal, she could probably go at him with everything she had, and he could hold his own. She cracked her neck and said, "I'm a little rusty." At that moment she attacked, and Henry found himself on his back smiling, "Ah, so that's how it is."

Dorathy bit her lip. "Sorry." She offered him a hand up that he took and put her on her knees in the process. She smiled. "I should have seen that coming!"

They continued, the difficulty level increasing with each blow. Henry was not accustomed to sparring with a woman. Normally he and Magnus were sparring buddies, so he had to be careful not to inflict injury on Dorathy. Just then, she kicked him square in the mouth and his lip began to bleed. "Oh crap, I'm sorry!"

"Nope, don't apologize. I wasn't paying attention and out there, like the place we're going, you've got to be alert or you can die really quick!"

"Speaking of that, I want to go out there with you guys. I don't want to stay in the ship."

Henry refused her request. "Those things are right bastards, like some kind of prehistoric- looking, thorny-winged apes with huge sharp teeth and claws to match."

She hesitated a moment. "Why don't you shoot a couple of them— won't that scare them away?"

Henry shook his head. "Nope, just seems to piss them off and they come back with reinforcements."

"So, these are intelligent beings?"

"Oh yes, highly intelligent, on a fast evolutionary track!"

"And you have to go down there to gather more of those poppies?" She queried, pointing to a container in cold storage.

"Yes. We learned years ago that the demand is ever growing, and the price per kilo has skyrocketed. We were given a tip about this planet years ago when we came to the aid of a mining ship in distress. When we run low, we come back to restock so we have something to trade for goods and supplies. We've found a few much smaller sources that are slowly being tapped out, but this planet has an abundance of high-grade product—albeit with the downside of having to deal with these mean bastards flying around."

Dorathy insisted, "I can hold my own."

"I gotta say no, not this time . . . maybe next time. You stay on the ship with Brenda, help her track their approach. Two sets of eyes are better than one."

Dorathy said reluctantly, "All right . . . whatever you say. You're the boss." Henry could tell Dorathy had an adventurous spirit; considering the circumstances surrounding her involvement with the Illuminati and eventual death and reclamation, she had maintained her composure, not giving in to fear and anger over the situation that had been forced upon her.

Henry, in an attempt to stimulate interest, said, "When we're done gathering up a fresh supply of poppies, we're headed to a deserted planet in search of a good lead on an ancient map that has some real promise. Our buddy, Jobar, is going to meet us there."

Dorathy smiled wide with excitement. "Oh excellent! You know I can't even wrap my head around this sometimes . . . I am on a mission in deep space with extraterrestrials and other planets capable of supporting life . . . a lot of life, on a dozen planets. How is it that for countless decades we searched and were able to reach deeper and deeper into space without a hint of advanced intelligent life on other planets, and here it seems endless?"

Henry shook his head. "The only thing I can come up with is that though our planet was seeded intentionally, these beings came from another part of space, a higher dimension or reality. We are now in their part of space. The specimen Dimitri found gave all indications it had traveled through a wormhole. We can't be sure though. We only know that we, humans, are part of something much bigger than ourselves and that we share a common ancestry with most of the beings we have thus far encountered. Whoever is responsible for planting the seeds of life, I guarantee they are still out there somewhere and so often we have been close to finding the answer. All I can say is that the clues have kept us going over the years and I think this ship of ours has some real significance to finding the other side and the Otherlings, as they are called by the peoples of this reality. I just wish we could make the connection."

Dorathy pondered for a moment. "Let me ask you this, have you found anything out there that resembles the material this ship is made out of?"

"No, nothing. We have been told countless times to watch ourselves with our ship, as there is a wicked faction that would stop at nothing to take control over it. As you can imagine, the power it possesses may hold the key to finding the road to the other side."

Dorathy spoke with some hesitation. "This ship is more than bio-material you found. It's alive and I feel it has an intelligence and that it is certainly aware of us."

Henry agreed. "Yes. My hope is that when we are close to our goal it finds a way of communicating with us."

Brenda broke into their musings. "Good morning, my brave young souls. Are you ready to do battle with our flying, furry friends?" Brenda always seemed to be in a good mood, as if everything was right in her world.

Henry threw his sweaty towel at her and whispered some obscenity under his breath, as Dimitri rounded the corner and said, "Easy for you to say wench, you stay on the ship and the men have to do all the dangerous work."

"Hey, I would watch who you call wench," she said with one brow raised, "because I might not be able to see a couple of these bastards coming after you, or my com may not have a good connection. There are a lot of things that could go wrong out there."

Magnus had been reading incoming messages from fellow space

trotters while sipping his morning tea. Peering over his cup, he shared one of the messages with them. "Jobar has indicated the need for two cases of the poppies and wants to pay us with multi-system credits."

"Excellent!" Henry seemed less grim for the first time in a long while. "Finally, we can purchase what we need without all the drama."

Dimitri laughed. "What's wrong, Henry? You don't like being an interstellar drug dealer? My uncle pushed drugs for years, he was a very wealthy man in Russia. But one day he sold to the wrong person . . ."

"Yes," Magnus said. "I do recall your Uncle Vladimir's unfortunate accident . . . he found himself very dead after selling a bad batch that resulted in the drug overdose of a particular young woman."

"Eh, she was a prostitute."

Magnus continued, "She may have been one indeed, but she was also the daughter of a government official. I seem to recall she was the same woman with whom you had a . . . relationship, that consequently landed you here with us."

Brenda laughed. "I see. Bad luck with women seems to follow your family around."

Dimitri muttered something in Russian under his breath as he kicked his feet up on the table.

Henry had had just about enough, "I'm going to lay out a plan here and I want it to go smoothly and by the numbers. We all know we've got to land on the night side and come in slow and quiet." He punched a key on the console and a holographic image of the planet's surface appeared. "We land here in this clearing. A good supply is growing in this wooded area here," he said as he pointed to an area where the holographic image widened and became clearer. "The only problem is it's right next to these trees here and that is where our little friends live. We need to be very careful and very quiet!"

Dorathy's excitement was barely contained and she laughed with joy. "This ship is going to land? You can breathe the air? The poppies are . . . narcotics? Oh my!"

Her crewmates looked at Dorathy with a bit of envy. They had all once had the same enthusiasm years ago, but it had soon turned to simple survival mode. Henry clapped his hands with authority and said, "Okay, crew, let's get our gear prepped and ready to go in one hour. I want to get this shit over with and without incident."

The crew moved with purpose.

"Hey Dora," Brenda called. "Come sit by me and I'll show you how we track these bastards."

Dorathy moved into the cockpit and sat in the seat beside Brenda. She was still amazed by the technology her donation had helped develop.

"I had been working on this space bending technology . . . ," Dorathy's voice trailed off. "What now seems a lifetime ago."

Brenda reached for Dorathy's hand. "Look honey, what's done is done. And as far as your family is concerned and everyone we left on Earth; it WAS a lifetime ago; they're all gone now."

Dorathy was stricken with a sense of sadness and loss. "Thanks, sometimes I just feel so . . . lost and helpless."

Brenda nodded. "Considering what we have all been through, I think we do okay for ourselves." The two women had begun to develop a bond that would last through to the other side.

CHAPTER 31

Their ship landed with quiet stealth; no rockets blasted, no landing gear locked into place, nothing but a shift in the air and a whiff of electrified ozone. Over the years the crew had become better acquainted with their miraculous ship and its amazing abilities, stripped of all the cumbersome apparatus that had been in place so many years before.

Dorathy contained her excitement so that she was able to concentrate on the task at hand. Brenda had set up the commlink for her and then the motion detector monitor. She knew what she had to do and, not unlike some of her other projects she had worked on in the past, lives depended on her accuracy. But this time it wasn't a design of hers that had to be space worthy as so to offer safety to the occupants, this was the life or death of a friend by her direct involvement.

Dorathy bit her lip in concentration as the outer door opened and the men departed, wearing night vision gear and suits that controlled their heat output and weight in a low gravity environment. The air was only tolerable, but they had the means to adapt to most of the planets they visited.

Brenda spoke into her commlink, "Okay guys, so far so good. I see the heat signatures of only eleven of those bastards in the trees to the west. There may be more out of sensor range but right now there is no movement, so the little monsters must be asleep."

Brenda looked over at Dorathy and nodded her head at the screen. "See how they are in small groups, one group per tree? Families usually consist of two adults: a male and a female, and two to three youngsters, with an additional two or more young adults that haven't left the nest yet. During our last visit here, I noticed only the males come in for the attack, but Christ it happened so quick I had a hard time keeping track of what was going on."

Henry, Magnus, and Dimitri kept low to the ground and were moving in slow motion, careful not to draw any attention. The grass was tall in the clearing and offered a bit of camouflage as they made their approach to the trees. Henry looked up and pointed so the others could see. Hand gestures were their only form of communication out here as the creatures' hearing seemed to pick up the slightest variation in night sounds.

Up in the canopy to the west they could see five family members sprawled out in the high limbs of the trees, in nests they had built from dried twigs, branches, and grass, and another six in the trees just beyond. As the men walked deeper into the forest, more groups appeared in the trees to the west and directly above their path. The poppies grew on the north side, around the trunks at the base of the trees. The flowers only bloomed at night, with an eerie, purple phosphorescence that was an indication of when they were at their peak chemical concentration.

Henry motioned forward at a purple glow of ground fog directly in front of them about ten meters in. He hated the idea of being surrounded by these creatures, but the glow was becoming brighter which meant there must be an abundance of crop ready to be picked.

Dimitri shook his head and pointed to the east. Magnus and Henry looked in that direction and counted at least twenty more creatures. Henry knew the odds were stacking up against them, indicating they needed to act quickly and do what they came here to do. Henry motioned to press on. Reluctantly they went but moved with purpose.

They made it to a small clearing and to their delight found a wealth of poppies ripe for picking. They promptly started to fill their bags with their gloved hands, as handling the poppies with bare hands would allow the toxins to penetrate through their skin. Masks covered their noses and mouths, so not to breathe in any of the spores.

Brenda's voice came in on Henry's earpiece, "Ah yeah . . . looks like a night watchman is circling in towards your direction, get what you can and exit out to the north."

Henry mouthed 'damn!' He motioned to the men to tie up the bags and pointed in the direction to depart.

Dorathy said to Brenda, "I don't like this, there are two more circling in, one from the north and one from the east."

"Oh, shit!" Brenda used an open channel. "Okay guys, you need to get out now. Stay low and come straight out the path you went in on. You have three watchman circling in from above."

Dorathy was frantic. "Brenda, what the hell are they going to do? They're surrounded!" Dorathy was watching the monitor closely when she noticed movement in the trees where groups of the creatures had been sleeping. "Brenda! They've been alerted somehow, there's movement!"

Brenda said to the men, "Get the hell out of there, pronto!"

Dorathy couldn't bear the thought of them being out there armed only with small side arms and dart guns. Even though the darts were soaked in a sedative, it had in the past been slow to take effect.

She stood and moved from her seat. "I've got a plan!"

Brenda yelled after her, "Whatever you're going to do, you better do it now!"

Dorathy snatched a side arm and slung the holster around her waist then grabbed night vision goggles, her earpiece and a cartridge of flare rods. As she passed a nearby table, she scooped up the nunchucks she had used to fine-tune her skills only the day before. With a final mental run-through, she was out the hatch and running across the field of tall grass. She cut to the north to draw the attention of the night watchman there, hoping that the others would follow to investigate.

Dorathy was lightheaded from the lack of suitable air but knew her body would adjust with the synthetic DNA pumping through her veins. By the time she was far to the north, Brenda caught on to her plan. "Okay girlfriend, I gotcha. Take that flare rod and throw it directly up the tree line when I give you the word. Looks like two of them are flying your way. They're coming now. After you toss it, double back. The guys are going to need help! Shit, throw it now—long and high due north!"

Dorathy did exactly that. She could see more of the creatures flying in to investigate. Then she was off and running south, straight along the edge of the forest. The men were about to break free from the cover of the trees thirty meters in front of her, when she looked up to see movement everywhere in the limbs high above. She hesitated for a moment to ascertain their direction and ran into the forest diagonally, so she would come in behind the men.

There was a screech from behind and she dived down to the ground just in time as one of the creatures flew over her head and landed directly in her path. Dorathy jumped to her feet and came face to face with an alien creature that resembled nothing she had ever seen on Earth. Large, canine teeth filled its maw and horns extended from its head, along its back and down its tail. Its long arms were tipped with three talons and its short muscular legs ended in feet that were comprised of three long, curved talons and an opposable thumb with an additional claw. It extended its leathery wings, making it look far larger as it advanced on her, spitting and hissing, twitching its wings and standing tall at close to eye level.

Dorathy knew what she needed to do and shot her sidearm, leaving the creature lying on the ground shuddering in pain. She was off running again and she could see the men ducking and sprinting through the trees in front of her. Dimitri was bringing up the rear, shooting up at the creatures as he ran, to no avail.

The sound of the shooting woke the rest of the tribe and they were descending from the trees in droves. Dorathy ran up to them one by one as they swooped in for the attack and used her nunchucks, sometimes knocking one right out of the air. She rendered the creatures unconscious with skilled, precise blows to the head. She saw Henry was down and had a creature ripping at him. Running to his side she struck a solid blow to the back of the creature's head. Henry, although injured and bloodied, was able to break free and rolled from under the creature.

Dimitri shot past them while Magnus went back to pick up the bag he had dropped making his escape. Dorathy yelled, "Duck, Magnus!" And he hit the dirt. Dorathy ran towards Magnus to help, but he had already flattened out his opponent.

They had run past the tree line and were now out in the open. Dorathy was helping Henry across the grass and in front of them they saw Dimitri go down with a creature on his back. Dorathy aimed and fired her gun at the creature's vulnerable underbelly. It went down with a whimper.

With the trees no longer there to protect them from an onslaught the creatures were now flying after them in a swarm. Dorathy yelled, "Magnus take Henry and the bags to the ship, I'll draw them away from you," Magnus didn't argue, he could see she was armed and capable. Dorathy ran away from the ship, waving a lighted flare and screaming, "Over here!"

Her plan worked and she could see her friends boarding the ship. Waving a flare, Magnus had returned after depositing Henry in the ship. Dorathy sprinted over to pick up a bag of poppies that had been dropped along the way. She could hear one of the winged apes coming in for her and turned just at the right moment to slam it out of the air. One after another they came.

Just as she made it to the ship, she found herself surrounded. Magnus came to help, but there were too many. Several attacked him and he could not beat them all off. He ducked for cover, throwing himself through the hatch of the ship.

Dorathy was on her own, as they closed in on her slowly. Unexpectedly, the ship shot out an electrified rod of plasma that laid her assailants out on the ground in a heap. Shocked but alert, she leapt over their unconscious bodies and dove through the hatch. Magnus grasped her arms to pull her all the way in. The hatch slid closed and the ship rose, swiftly climbing to altitude.

Magus held Dorathy as she tried to maintain her composure. "Holly shit! What just happened?"

"Good question Dora, because we have never seen that feature of this ship. We had no idea it had such capabilities!"

Dorathy leaned against its inner hull and hugged it. "Thank you!"

Brenda yelled back over her shoulder, "Magnus, you need to take over in the cockpit. Henry is not doing well; I have to tend to his wounds."

"Right-o, on my way."

Dimitri stumbled up to Dorathy as she was taking her seat at the table to check herself for any wounds. "You need a shot of vodka to calm your nerves."

Dorathy accepted readily and took a good long gulp. "Not bad." She watched Dimitri to size him up. She was not impressed by him. Brilliant scientist, yes, but his misguided attempts at rock stardom led her to believe he was all talk no action, and he had proved that with his cowardly behavior.

"So, tell me Dimitri, were you ever a track and field guy in your youth? Perhaps a sprinter?"

"Me? Never. I was too busy at university for athleticism, but I was known to chase the women." He burst into laughter at the thought. "But maybe I think they were chasing me."

Dorathy smiled. "I guess that's why you were the first one to the ship . . . being chased, that is."

Dimitri caught her sarcasm. "Hey, those creatures down there can kill. Damn right, I ran to the ship!"

"Oh, absolutely," she said with anger, "you outran us all."

"Hey lady, when you have been out here as long as we have then maybe your opinion will matter, but now I think, not so much." He threw back his vodka and slammed his glass onto the table as he got up. He peered down at her. "You know something? You are not as smart as you believe yourself to be. You are here, with us, after all."

She watched him leave the room. His comment hit home; she *was* here with them. She had an overwhelming grasp that it was her arrogance that had landed her here. She was in the depths of space and time, only a mere speck in the universe. The void she occupied was endless and she thought she could control it, manipulate it and bend it to her wishes. She was stricken by its ability to prove her wrong. She thought, *how dare I try and command such an immeasurable power?* She sat alone with her thoughts and her glass.

Magnus had taken the ship into orbit and came to sit beside her. "You were stupendous out there, and we owe you our lives."

Dorathy tried to shake off her regrets. "You would have done the same for me."

"Certainly, but you handled yourself out there with a forceful spirit I have not seen in very many women. Considering your circumstances, I would say you are adjusting very well. I am happy you joined us." Dorathy thought a moment about his words and sighed, thinking of her old life. Magnus knew what she was feeling. "I know this life was not your choice but how many of us get a second chance at something truly remarkable?"

Magnus winked, feeling an attraction to Dorathy. "Henry is being tended to and will heal quickly; he asked for you." Dorathy slugged the last of her drink and headed to the med lab.

She entered the med lab and saw Brenda closing the last of Henry's wounds. "Hey Dora," he called, "shit, I knew you could hold your own, but where the hell did that come from? Remind me never to piss you off! You gave those bastards a real ass-kicking; hell of a woman."

Dorathy sat beside him, laughing the stress away. "Well a girl's gotta do what she's gotta do and it looked like you guys needed a tad bit of help. Besides, who the hell was going to fly this thing if something happened to you?"

Brenda giggled. "Sure as hell wasn't going to be me. I'll leave you two warriors to compare battle scars." Brenda slapped a bandage on the back of Dorathy's shoulder on her way out.

Dorathy craned her neck to see where she had been bleeding. Henry was enthralled by her. "I once knew someone a lot like you . . . back in the days of the Naval Academy." His voice trailed off as he thought of Rebecca. "It was bad timing," he said with some regret lingering in his voice, knowing timing had nothing to do with him throwing in the towel on their relationship. It was his compelling need for advancing his career that took precedence. And for what?

Dorathy winced in pain and couldn't tell if it was her injury or the longing to have Alex by her side. She missed him desperately.

Henry patted her knee. "I get some comfort knowing that the ones we loved are long gone, even though it seems as if it were a short time ago. They are gone, a long time dead and here we are trying to find . . . the back door . . . I think that's how you put it once."

Dorathy looked around the ship and thought about the possibilities. "You know, if someone, had told me a couple of years ago that I was going to end up here with you, in this ship, in this situation, I would have thought they were out of their minds. Yet, here I am, sitting here in this spaceship, talking to you . . . I just don't assume anything anymore . . . kind of surreal."

"Yeah, I guess it is." Henry reached over and brushed the bangs out of her face. "Well, we have work to do before we meet Jobar at our next destination. You should get some rest."

Dorathy watched as he left the room. "Absorbing what Henry had just said, she felt guilty for having the feelings she was having for him at that moment. She brushed it off as stress to her unpredictable and incredible, circumstances.

CHAPTER 32

A s he did every morning, Magnus sat at the console with his hot tea, reviewing messages from their 'business associates'—smugglers, fellow portal hunters—typical morning banter. "Jobar and Coolie are meeting us at an old mining outpost. He sent the coordinates: 'You will know it when we see it' was his only message."

Dimitri started in with his usual annoyances. "That midget better not be wasting my time with another one of his wild chicken chases."

"Goose . . . goose chases. Get it right, will ya?" Brenda whacked him on the back of his head.

Henry often wondered how his band of misfits ever made it this far. Taking a deep breath, he said, "Coolie and Jobar have in their possession an extremely rare, old map. They have not been able to ascertain its origin, but by the sounds of it, whatever is down there has been there for many centuries and it is all that remains of this ancient civilization. Apparently, the folklore of this place says there is an inaccessible cave with walls covered with writing that has never been deciphered. The place is uninhabited, and no one has been able to gain access to this ancient city."

After what the group had just been through, uninhabited sounded very good. Dorathy was energized at the thought of seeing something this spectacular. "You know, I might be of some help down there. I spent a lot of time in the 'Degraded Section' back on Earth. My father taught me how to read some of the ancient hieroglyphics buried deep in the old tombs. There might be some similarities considering that the code buried in our own DNA resembles language from that era."

Dimitri shook his head. "No, I disagree. Any chance that we may come across ancient text that is remotely recognizable is very slim. Yes, the code resembles language; some of my colleagues saw a mathematical equation to the pattern, arranging letters to form a word; this is very different."

"So you're saying, Dorathy continued, whoever buried the code in our DNA wrote it to be read as a language in its simplest form—mathematics. A map of sorts, I guess not much different than the map we put on Voyager so many decades ago."

Dimitri pondered Dorathy's input for a moment. "So, your theory is whoever wrote the code must have left a similar form of language along the way? Perhaps, he said cocking his head in thought. Then, if that is the case, I may be able to decipher it."

Dorathy smiled. It must have taken a lot for Dimitri to acknowledge she might have a point. "Well two heads are better than one," she said, before Magnus proceeded to share his thoughts.

"If I may, we are all assuming that because the word *ancient* is being used that ancient, the way we perceive it, is what we will find. We must assume whoever wrote the code was indeed far advanced, thus their perception might be a bit different from ours."

The group fell silent for a moment. Henry ran his fingers through his hair. "Yeah, I see where you're going with this, 'ancient' is irrelevant, it could mean far more advanced than our comprehension, but still ancient to whoever wrote it."

Henry sat back in his chair. "Guess we'll figure it out once we get down there."

Magnus leaned in. "Not to worry old chap. If the text is written in some type of code, it may well be written in binary." Magnus now wore a confident smile. "If so, then I'm the guy to read it."

Brenda sat with her arms crossed. "Well aren't you a collection of smart assholes . . . did it ever occur to you that maybe it's a bunch of stick figures painted on a wall?"

"They burst out in laughter. Henry clapped his hands. "Okay let's get down to the outpost and collect our friends. We can get to the bottom of this map and hopefully find some clues."

Henry guided the ship down in a remote landing area where they could see Jobar and Coolie waiting—Jobar handing an old timer a bag of credits and watched as he mounted his trusty ride of scales, long matted fur and hooves, shoving the payment into his saddle bag, and trotted off with a yank of the rains. The ship came in slowly for a landing; Jobar and Coolie pulled their coat collars up over their faces as it stirred the dust up around them. Jobar and Coolie had been patiently waiting for their arrival on this cold desert planet.

Henry went to the hatch to greet them, watching Jobar approach with heavy packs in hand, they boarded the ship with a bit of a stumble. "Good of you to join us," Jobar said, raising a bottle of some home-grown spirits. "Thought we would come early and take care of some logistics first, before we go off on this little quest of ours. But let's get down to our first order of business—were you able to get the shipment of poppies we wanted?" Jobar and Coolie noted Henry's face and arms. "Looking at your injuries," Jobar said, "I would say you made a valiant attempt."

"Yeah, those sons of bitches gave us a bit of hassle, but we filled your order. I just hope we don't have to go there again any time soon."

"I promised a fair price. We would get the poppies ourselves, but there are too many legalities to contend with. You know the inconsistencies with the laws in our sector—some deem it legal for medicinal purposes, others see it as an illegal substance. At any rate, I don't need the hassle, so here are the credits I promised you," Jobar said as he handed Henry a bag.

"You want me to bring them over now?"

"No, best we leave them on board. Can't trust the locals around these parts. It took a handsome price just for us to park our ship here for a couple of days."

Henry had to laugh. "You guys are always buying yourselves out of trouble. Got to say Jobar, it's always a pleasure; and Coolie, it escapes me why you're always hanging out with this loser."

Jobar smirked, "Well, you will think more highly of me when I show you what we have in our possession."

Dorathy, Magnus, Brenda, and Dimitri welcomed them aboard. Brenda, wearing her usual smile said, "Hi baby. Long time no see. How ya doin'?"

Jobar gave her a hug around her waist. "If I weren't so old, we could run away together."

Brenda laughed. "Why you little devil, I would take you up on that to get away from these assholes I been hanging out with!"

Jobar turned his attentions to Dorathy. "Well, hello my dear, so nice of you to join this ragtag gang of derelicts."

Dorathy was enthralled by Jobar and Coolie, and she was at a loss for words during her first intelligent alien encounter. Jobar held out a scaly hand with its three well-manicured fingers and after a momentary hesitation Dorathy took it in friendship. Not knowing exactly what to say, she said, "I have waited all of my life for this moment."

"Well, my dear, I hope we don't disappoint."

Coolie saw the effect that they had on Dorathy and held out his bottle. "Here take a swig."

Dorathy obliged and took a mouthful of the concoction, swallowing with a cringe. "Oh wow, that's some strong stuff you got there."

Coolie laughed. "I make it in my yard at home. It's highly illegal in our sector, so we can just keep that our secret."

"Absolutely," Dorathy said, grinning from ear to ear, already feeling the effects of the fermentation.

After stowing their gear, they gathered around the table to look over the map they had had newly acquired. Jobar pointed to the old crumpled map he had won in a recent game of chance. Jobar said with a huge smile, "The poor fool I collected this map from did not have a clue what he had in his possession; of course, I played the sore loser as I relieved him of it." Coolie and Jobar smiled at each other and as Jobar pointed to the map he said, "We have faith that you hold the secrets to this map. Since the day we met so many years ago, I have had a gut feeling about you. Your ship is just one of the missing links that we have been searching for all these years."

Henry looked at the map more closely, "Looks like it's a trail map, but where is it?"

Jobar said, "It is at the center of the planet we are now going to. If what I think is true from stories I have heard about this place, your ship will allow us to gain access where others have failed."

The group passed the map around the table and listened to the tales of its possible origin. Jobar continued with his tales, as if he were telling ghost stories around a campfire. The others listened and felt in the depths of their existence that maybe they were right, perhaps they were closer to their goal than ever before. Henry sighed deeply, saying, "No one wants to get to the bottom of this mystery more than all of us do, so let's get moving. I'm anxious to see what's out there." Henry and Magnus moved to the cockpit, adjusted the controls, and departed for yet another adventure.

As the ship approached the cold rocky planet, the crew was amazed at the constantly moving ice below. It made Everest Khumbu Icefall pale in comparison. Mountains of ice pushing upwards from the pressure, creating crevasses that seemed to fall away into a black abyss.

Dorathy peered into the cockpit while Henry guided the ship towards the south pole, his mind connected to the mainframe. They were now one; his commands were being carried out as the ship read his thoughts.

Dorathy gingerly stepped into the cockpit and took a seat. She was perplexed at the sight ahead, and said, "How could this planet have ever supported life?"

Magnus sat in his seat to the right of Henry. "My readings show a hot molten core at its center." He continued to scan for any variable that seemed out of place.

Magnus's voice trembled with excitement. "I think I have something! There! He pointed to starboard. "A huge crevasse . . . wait, no . . . my readings show an entrance . . . definitely not natural." The ship turned and hovered for a moment while Magnus took readings for size and depth. "Okay Henry, we can proceed."

The ship abruptly turned in a back flip and dove into the darkness. Dorathy was holding on to the restraints that held her firmly in place. She was in awe of the ship's capabilities and apparently the rest of the crew and their guests shared her opinion. It seemed to be capable of a vast array of actions; even more emerging since Dorathy's arrival.

The tunnel they were now traveling through seemed to have been cut through the ice and rock with such accuracy that its surface was left smooth as glass. Downward they went into the blackness, with only the glow of their exterior lights reflecting off the curved mirrored walls.

Down they went, the exterior temperature reading started to climb. Magnus smiled. "It's a balmy eighty-two degrees. Simply lovely. Another hundred meters and we will be in the clear."

Henry slowed their approach. "Okay gang, coming in for a landing." The ship's exterior lights shone bright in all directions so they could get a good look at their surroundings.

Jobar and Coolie were celebrating their arrival. "We were right. Your ship has the ability to enter where none in the past have been able to gain access."

It was an enormous cavern that seemed to extend endlessly; the light of the ship could only illuminate so far into the distance. Below them was an ancient city that had lain in ruin for several millennia. Dorathy had been rendered almost speechless, her mind desperately trying to assimilate what her eyes were showing her. "Oh my God! In my wildest dreams I never would have thought a place like this could exist."

It was an ecosystem completely detached from the planet above. There were mountains of rock that climbed into the ceiling. Waterfalls were cascading, melted from the ice that came from above. Tropical forests grew without restraint, the air thick with the fragrance of sweet flowers.

"How can this be? she asked. "How can all this be here underground, how can all this even exist?"

Just then there was a light that slowly grew brighter as if dawn was approaching. Growing in brightness, it came from all directions, slowly illuminating everything as far as the eye could see. The group, mouths gaping, faces pressed against the transparent shield of the forward cockpit, looked on in amazement as the ship slowly traversed the middle of this immense cavern.

Magnus pointed. "Over there I see a clearing near that lake. We can land there." The ship spun around and landed in a grassy area on the banks of a crystal-clear lake being fed by water cascading from the sloped, rocky incline above.

Henry disconnected from the ship and slowly got up after releasing his restraints. "Okay gang; let's go see what we can dig up around here."

They hauled out their gear and sat along the bank of the underground lake in its remarkable, untouched environment. Henry looked around and could not ascertain from where the light originated. Jobar looked around in amazement. "This place is much more than it appears. Whoever built this lost city had the technology to capture the light from its distant star and direct it and magnify it as a means of sustaining life deep within."

Each member of the group all had the same question, "How is this possible?"

Jobar raised his three-fingered hand. "We passed through an undetectable force field that protects this underground paradise from the vacuum of space. That is why I requested we take your ship. My hunch was correct—your ship would have access, as I believe somehow you are tied to this ancient city."

Henry gasped, "And what if your hunch was wrong? We would have slammed into the force field and crashed!"

Jobar looked at Coolie. "I don't believe your ship would have attempted entry if it sensed it would not be able to gain access through the forcefield. For this reason, not many have attempted to come here; fewer still want to come this far off the beaten track. Many believe this place to be cursed."

Dimitri laughed. "Cursed? Look around, it's paradise."

Coolie shook his head. "No, my friend, don't let its appearance fool you, many have died trying to find the key to the Otherlings. But this secret map will take us to the cave. With what we find in the cave and your ship capable of making the journey to the other side, together we can find the Otherlings. I am certain of that."

The group packed supplies of food and water for three days, a portable shelter, ropes and climbing gear, and they departed.

Jobar, holding the map he had acquired only weeks ago said, "We were much younger, and early on in our quest when we heard of this cave. To make the trip now, so many years later, gives me hope that you hold the key to the encryptions and will make all the years waiting worth the effort."

The group hiked for hours through the ruins of the ancient city vacated long ago. They were astonished by what they found along the way. What looked to have been a modern city that once held a thriving, advanced culture had been left to rot in the elements. The forest had taken most of what was left. What remained was the high, intricate, gleaming towers that rose over 300 meters. They pressed on, approaching the thick forest at the base of the mountains. Up they climbed, over sharp, jagged boulders from an ancient landslide, blazing a trail to the base of a grand waterfall that reached up to the ceiling of this enormous underground cavern.

Coolie pointed, and out of breath, said, "There is a cave on the back side of the falls. A narrow path leads to the entrance and looks very dangerous; one bad step and you could be swept away over the edge."

Everyone felt as if their legs were going out from under them. They sat on an edge of a huge boulder at the edge of the pool close to the base of the falls. They had noticed a small area of bubbling water being heated from the core below with the cool mist hitting their faces from the falls of melted ice from the surface, crashing down from a thousand meters above. A beautiful rainbow had formed over the pool from the light shining through the mist. Dorathy was not about to miss an opportunity like this; tired, hot, and dirty, she stripped down to her skivvies and dove into ice cold water that took her breath away. She swam towards the rocks and felt a band of warm water from the natural hot springs wash over her.

"Oh God, this is wonderful!" she yelled, over the loud crashing of tons of water hitting the pool and rocks below. "You're all missing out!"

Henry looked at his dirty, sweaty crew, and decided it was a great idea. He stripped down and joined her near the falls. For a moment his thoughts drifted to another place and time far in the past when he and Rebecca were in love. Thoughts of the woman he should have married and started a life with had haunted him for so many years. Both young and stationed in Hawaii, they had taken a day for a quick getaway. Oh, how the memories now became crystal clear to him. Henry couldn't help himself and wrapped his arms around Dorathy's waist as a playful gesture. Dorathy pulled away gently as thoughts of Alex came back to haunt her. She knew he was long gone but couldn't dismiss the feeling that they had only been apart for a short time. Conflicted, she swam towards the bubbling pool and motioned for him to join her.

The hot spring bubbling and churning along with the coolness of the icy water made for a comfortable relaxing spa. They leaned against the smooth boulders, eyes closed, dreaming of another moment in space and time—memories of the loves they left behind.

Dorathy reached out and held Henry's hand: a gesture of friendship, a gesture of the mutual attraction they shared.

Dimitri broke the silence. "Ah, yes, this is the way we are supposed to live."

Henry released Dorathy's hand. As much as they wanted to stay in this place forever, they were on a mission and needed to hit the trail hard before it became dark. Once dressed and rested they began their ascent using ropes and climbing gear. Jobar, holding the old, weathered map took the lead, his squat frame climbing slowly up the switchback trail with Coolie on his heels. The team anticipated a slow ascent and was grateful for it, as none of them had the endurance to scale this trail at a faster pace.

Coolie tugged on the rope as he fell backwards. Fortunately, Henry had blocked his fall and Jobar had secured the rope to a thick branch of a tree growing out from in between the rocks and boulders. Breathing laboriously, Coolie stopped and wheezed out for Jobar to stop, "I . . . need . . . to . . . rest . . . awhile."

They could still hear the crash of the falls, but it was out of sight and they were no longer getting the refreshing mist in which to cool off. They all leaned against anything they could find while keeping their footing. The view of the city from this angle was amazing, but Dorathy's eyes settled on something peculiar.

"Hey guys, look over there," she called out, pointing into the distance. Above the city something looked like it had been carved into the side of the mountain. Everyone turned to look in the direction she was pointing, but nothing looked out of place or familiar to the others.

Closest to Dorathy, Henry looked down to the end of her arm and saw what she had spotted, but couldn't determine its significance. "Yes, I see it, two horizontal parallel zig zag lines." Everyone now saw it clear as day, carved deep into the rock.

Henry asked finally, "Do you know what it means?"

"It's the zodiac sign for Aquarius. Literally speaking, the dawn of a new age; to carry us into the next level of awareness." The group pondered what she had just verbalized so simply and eloquently.

"Holy shit!" Brenda gasped under her breath. "I think we're on to something, but what really gets me is the fact that that symbol is *here.*"

Dorathy was also perplexed and knew what Brenda meant. "Yes, a Greek astrological sign . . . what in God's name, is it doing, HERE?"

CHAPTER 33

The New Western Ordinance had long been established as the sector's government, controlling the comings and goings of the different planetary civilizations which had elected ministers to self-govern.

Prime Minister Kore Athanatos was at the top of the heap. An elderly woman from a distant planet, her species was known across the sector as being non-indigenous to her world—myths had formed over the millennia that her planet had been settled by beings from another part of space. The legend was that a group of nomads arrived in an enormous ship to the once sparsely inhabitant rocky world and through the centuries the two species had evolved together as one.

Over the years Kore had grown weary trying to ascertain the origin of her species, but it was a fascinating story that compelled her to investigate her people's ancestry. Every time she came across a clue to their existence, she would take the time to investigate, but always ran into the same dead ends. As she grew older, the issue seemed less and less urgent, but still always nagged at her; she had always believed she was a part of something much larger than herself.

Time had overtaken ambition and age had crept upon her like an old withered vine. She was growing tired of her routine responsibilities and was always seeking a way to escape her onerous duties. She was frequently vulgar, with a nasty disposition, both obvious to all in the grimace permanently affixed upon her wrinkled face. Her attitude prevented her from becoming anything more than what she had become.

Kore sat upon her throne in her enormous office, surrounded by an elegance that was in sharp contrast to her character. Her assistant entered the room, carefully carrying the Prime Minister's cup of hot morning brew. Kore lit an herb stick and she silently drew in a lungful of smoke, its toxic scent filling the room with a smoky haze. The chemicals coursed through her veins, slowly lifting the veil of exhaustion from her eyes. The old woman peered out the wall of windows from the highest level of her precious capitol, the New Western Ordinance. The gray sky seeped into the room with a cold dreariness that was relentlessly cursing the sun, delivering an everlasting somber mood.

Kore read through the requests of the NWO ministers and came upon one that sparked enough interest for more than a mere second, just enough time to contemplated it a bit more closely.

Someone had reported a rumor to one of her many offices, which resulted in the request to initiate an investigation into a group of *Travelers*. It was said the transient ship was not carrying origin papers. This was deemed a criminal act and her Deputy of Foreign Affairs was scrutinizing the request. She leaned back in her seat and read every word, assessing the urgency of the request. The hairs at the back of her neck tingled with an excitement she couldn't ignore. Kore spun on her seat and demanded, "Prepare my ship for immediate departure. I'm leaving for the outer rim."

Standing with a jerk, she sent the heavy throne back against the windows, causing them to tremble. Reaching for her cloak, she pulled her pointed black hat down over her thin and graying straw-like auburn hair. "I want to get to the bottom of this. Something tells me this is no ordinary circumstance." Kore stomped away down the hall on her skinny booted legs swinging her walking stick, dragging her crisp uniform cloak behind her.

Arriving at the ship, she observed that her handsome pilot had already entered the coordinates of the last-known whereabouts of their transient suspects. She climbed into the seat opposite him. "I suggest you don't wake me on this journey, I need my rest."

Silas could only muster, "Yes ma'am, I'll wake you once we have arrived." He was grateful she was deciding to sleep, as he couldn't stand
having to converse with such an ill-mannered creature during a trip of
this length. Moments after departure he looked over in disgust to see
that her head had fallen back at a contorted angle; she was snoring, drool
collecting at the corners of her mouth.

The ship came to a soft landing at a docking station for deep-space
mining operations. Kore woke with a snort and straightened in her seat,
wiping her mouth with her sleeve. Silas was an impressive pilot and had
already exited the ship to enter their arrival into the log of arrivals and
departures. As she exited down the gangway, the hot, swampy humidity
hit Kore like a thick damp cloud, and she winced in pain as her joints
started to seize in the moisture.

"Damn this horrendous, miserable place! Where is the flight controller? I want him to meet me here at once! I will not be kept waiting and his
superiors will hear of this massive inconvenience!"

A squat individual came scurrying up, bowing down low and tripping over himself while stammering apologies, "Hello, Prime Minister
Athanatos. How nice of you to come in person over this matter. My name
is Patsup and I am here to assist you with location of the derelict ship. I
have good information . . ."

"Enough with the pleasantries!" As she unbuttoned her stiff collar, she
grumbled at him, "Damn this cursed heat! I want the logs, just give me
the damn logs!" Patsup did as he was instructed, eyes blinded by the intensity of the rainbow of colors radiating from a pendant that hung from
a chain just under her cloak collar.

"Please follow me, Madame Prime Minister, and I will show you the
log entry. The information I have of the travelers' whereabouts comes
from an insider . . . let's just say someone with whom I have constant
contact and is a very reliable source."

"Enough said! Give me the log so I may ascertain their whereabouts
and be on my way from this Hellish climate." Patsup handed her the
information she demanded, and she snatched it from him with her
clammy hands. "Anyone else know of this information?" she quizzed as
she shook the memo pad at his round face.

"No ma'am, that is the only copy, as I thought you would want complete control over this situation."

"Good," she sneered. "I will be taking over this investigation from here. Therefore, I do not require any further involvement from you."

Patsup stuttered for a moment as he thought his help might get him a promotion. "Please, if you require any more information, don't hesitate to contact me and . . ." His voice trailed off.

Kore snapped back, "I don't need any help from the likes of you. I suggest you go back to whatever rock you crawled out from under and leave this matter to me. Now scurry off," she instructed as she swung at him with her walking stick.

Patsup hung his head in despair as he departed. "Oh my, what have I just done? "Eh . . . ," he shrugged off his feelings of remorse, "Jobar and Coolie have it coming to them with their grandiose adventures in search of some stupid myth. Serves them right."

Kore practically pushed Silas out of her way as she climbed up the gangway. She was now struggling with a limp from the effects of the intense gravity and the relentless moisture on her joints. She turned and slapped the memo pad hard against his muscular chest. "Enter this data immediately into the navigation system and get me off this hellhole."

Her pilot had grown weary of her unpleasant disposition and snatched the pad from her. He followed her into the cockpit, wishing this mission would end soon. He entered the log and with great disappointment read he was on yet another long journey. He prayed she would once again feel the need to sleep, as he could not bear to be in her presence any longer.

Kore screeched, "Where are we to go now?"

Silas, losing his patience with her foulness, was short. "The outer region, to an abandoned mining planet. Very few inhabitants."

"Oh for the love of Hell, when will this madness end?"

He was thinking the exact same thing for a very long time.

CHAPTER 34

W hen they found the symbol carved on the side of the mountain, the group was reenergized. The thought of being able to decrypt whatever may have been left behind so many years ago encouraged them to climb higher at a much more rapid pace. It had become a driving force, and they pressed on for hours without a break. Twilight was upon them and their lanterns were not supporting a safe journey, so they stopped for the night on a level clearing just off the track.

They ate their rations in silence, trying to predict what may lie ahead in that mysterious cave. One by one, they laid out their bedding and fell asleep with images of what they might find floating in their mind's eye.

Dorathy sat with her back against the rock wall, looking out over the city in the twilight.

She pondered how she came to this place; what made her so special that she would find herself doing exactly this . . . at this moment in time? Time . . . time had no meaning to her now. She would not age at the same rate and life on Earth would go on exactly as it would, regardless of time, regardless of her placement in time. Everyone and everything she loved was now just dust in the wind.

Henry pulled his sleeping pad over to Dorathy. "You look like you need someone to lean on."

"Yes, I suppose I do. You know, I keep asking myself, why am I here and what purpose do I really serve?"

Henry shook his head. "I honestly don't know. We had instructions to come fetch you once we got a signal from your tracking beacon. You were regarded as an *asset* that needed to be protected at all costs. So here you are . . . with us. I'm truly sorry about that." A smile lingered on his lips.

"You know what? I'm okay, and amazingly enough, I accept this new life as a great adventure, a journey I guess I had to make. My husband and daughter, no doubt, lived their life. My husband, Alex, was with me on the other side for just a moment and then I was gone, but I can still smell him, I can still feel his presence. I have on occasion, had very real dreams, so real I swear I can reach out and touch him. Dorathy smirked—he and I discussed once about this being a *side effect*, of being temporarily in 'suspended animation' and brought back to life." She felt an overwhelming sadness wash over her.

Henry reached out and held her hand. "I'm glad you're here with us. For such a long time I've been feeling . . . dead . . . no heart, my soul lost to me." He looked into her eyes. "Since you joined us, I have to say for the first time in a long time I feel alive. Thank you for that."

Dorathy looked back, wondering why on Earth he was chosen for this mission and what may have happened to him and the others to have elected to be a part of something this amazing, this . . . crazy and magnificent. Whatever the reasons, she thought, she was happy to be a part of it. She slept, feeling safe with him by her side.

Morning came quickly. Brenda woke, hearing Dimitri snoring, as he so often did. With a little shove, she said, "Turn over, you're snoring again." He did as he was told, muttering something in Russian. "Yeah, whatever you say, sunshine." She wondered how she ended up with him. He was a brilliant scientist after all, but it was wearing on her to constantly have to keep his ego in check. With a heavy sigh of acceptance, she also knew her options were limited with her current circumstances.

Dorathy awakened with her head comfortably snuggled on Henry's chest feeling safe and warm as if he had been Alex. Realizing where she was, she sat up ramrod straight and the moment was gone.

Coolie and Jobar were already packed and ready to go, like excited children ready to open their Christmas boxes. "Come on, you lazy house pets," Jobar said as he nudged Magnus with his foot. "We have much to do still."

The group, moving slowly, packed up their gear and with a bite to eat in hand, continued the hike upward towards the crest of the falls. After several hours they approached a wet, slippery, natural rock trail with a narrow passage up its side. The mist made it hard to see, but far below they could see where they had started, the pool as small as a bathtub. Looking up, they could make out the cave only several meters away through the cascading water. The noise was deafening, and they had to yell to be heard.

Jobar shouted, "Be very careful here, one false move and . . . ," he pointed down.

Single file, they traversed the narrow path, backs against the wet mossy rock wall, making sure they had a firm hold before making the next step. Upward they moved, Jobar and Coolie in the lead, Dimitri, Brenda, and Magnus close on their heels, with Dorathy and Henry bringing up the rear. Henry was taking special care of Dorathy.

Finally, they came to a clearing just beneath the falls. Somehow, they had to break through the tons of water crashing over their heads without being swept over the edge.

Dimitri volunteered, "I am the biggest man here. I will take the rope and secure it to the other side." He tied the rope securely around his waist and handed the other end to Magnus and Brenda and down the line, "Just in case I fail, be ready to catch my fall!"

Dimitri prepared himself and lunged in a quick forward motion. He lost his footing as the water hit him in icy cold waves, crashing down on top of him like a tsunami. Brenda and Magnus pulled up on the rope, while Dimitri clung to the rock wall, tucking his head so the water could roll off his back. He managed to muscle through to the back side of the falls.

Shaking the water from his head and body, Dimitri caught sight of a strange, dim glow from deep within the cold, musty and wet entrance. He untied the rope from his waist and secured it around a huge boulder against the side of the cave, fastening it tightly. He gave three tugs on the rope to indicate he was ready to help them across. Henry attached his end of the rope, clamping it firmly in the crevice of the jagged rock wall and, one by one, they entered what looked to be an ancient labyrinth.

Coolie yelled, excitement in his voice, as it carried and echoed deep into the cavern, "Follow me!" They trod carefully over the slick wet surface as they advanced deeper into the cave. The glow began to illuminate their approach. "Watch your heads, looks like you will have to crawl for a while."

Jobar laughed. "Sometimes it's good to be short!"

The narrow passage opened into a huge, cathedral-sized room. Droplets of water on the stone ceiling shone like stars on a dark cloudless night, twinkling with the movement of air across their surface. Dorathy gazed in amazement and pointed up with her light rod, "The constellation Orion! Beautiful!" Her voice echoed in the void.

At the farthest point of the cavern was an enormous pyramid that stretched to the ceiling, a glowing eye balanced at its familiar apex. The rock wall opposite the pyramid rose twenty meters high and displayed a beautiful carving of a majestic owl, perched on top of an open book holding an olive branch in its talons.

Dorathy almost fell backwards in disbelief and astonishment. She gazed around at it all as the reality started to sink into her existence like an anesthetic, leaving her numb and void of any cognitive awareness. Finally, she whispered, "My God, they did it."

Henry nodded his head. "Yes, it would seem they have managed to do what they set out to do . . . but when?"

Dorathy read Henry's mind. "When indeed."

Jobar and Coolie had smiles on their faces and were practically jumping with wonderment. Jobar begged, "Do you know the meaning of it all?"

Coolie added. "Yes, please tell us!"

Henry paused as he gathered his thoughts. "All this that is here, came from our world, our part of space, a secret society that predicted the fall of our way of life. For generations they were painted as evildoers that wanted to take control of the planet. They knew that our planet and most of its inhabitants were doomed, that our civilization would perish. They didn't want to control it at all, they wanted to gather the best of the best, those who could bring the most to the table and leave the planet to the rest of the growing de-evolving population. They figured it was just a matter of time and whoever was left would most likely extinguish themselves in one fatal event."

Dorathy continued, "They wanted their New World Order. A way of life where everyone thought the same way and wanted the same things. My father was part of their organization . . . and so was I for a while. Her voice trailed off.

Henry now looked at Dorathy in a new light. "I didn't know that of you. You were deemed an asset to this mission for your engineering skills and we were told to protect you at all cost. Your untimely death was necessary for this mission, and having to pick you up the way we did was an added convenience."

Dorathy felt a well of anger rising in her as she snapped back, "My death may have been convenient, alright, but not to me! I stepped away from their madness a long time ago. They wanted to use their 'investments' to leave behind humanity and I blindly fell into their trap so I could stamp my name on what had been the greatest discovery of mankind! I wanted to take it, manufacture it and put it into production, then take the credit for being oh so brilliant to have been the one to advance mankind into the new era of space exploration! The bastards played me like a deck of cards! And my arrogance allowed it!"

Henry took a step back. "Your father was John Rosen, wasn't he?

Dorathy now looked at Henry as a stranger. "Yes, he was. Why? What do you know of my father?"

Henry shook his head, wondering what he may have just stepped into. He looked at Brenda for support. "He was murdered . . . by . . . a hybrid. By a member of your Board of Directors."

Dorathy stared down Henry in distrust, for how could he know this about her father and how could he know about what her father had written in his journal, his suspicions about Simon, before her father was killed. Simon was a trusted friend; he could never have done that. Henry's words caught up to her thought process: "What do you mean a hybrid?"

Henry continued, "Simon was not who he had appeared to be."

Dorathy crossed her arms, holding herself, as she suddenly felt desperately alone. "And how do you know this?"

Brenda stepped forward. "Because I was the one who was forced to download the consciousness of an unknown man into Simon Bedford's body and mind. That is the man who really killed your father." Brenda thought about that awful day. "I was blackmailed, and he threatened to kill my mother if I didn't do it. He wanted to take control of the Rosen fortune to manipulate you and the rest of your unwitting followers."

Dorathy was taken aback. "Oh my God, my father's suspicions were correct. I always had such a hard time believing Simon could have done such a horrible thing, but the investigation showed nothing."

Brenda added, "Simon's consciousness is still intact somewhere deep within his brain. It's as if he was overwritten by a foreign entity. Simon's body was ultimately made immortal by use of synthetic DNA and Simon has been trapped in a kind of purgatory hell . . . not alive and not quite dead. A constant battle is being waged between Simon and the man who took control of Simon's mind and body."

Dorathy's eyes glazed over and she shuddered at the thought of such a horrible existence. She thought of her father and his goals of establishing the New World Order and this unknown man who had tried to stop it. Now standing peering up at the pyramid, proof of their success, it was clear this man had failed. She looked up to the All-Seeing Eye as it witnessed the rise of the Illuminati's power. "They found the way to create their New World Order and here is the proof." They peered up at the pyramid of ages, their gaze resting on an inscription upon its surface that read, *Novus Ordo Seclorum,* meaning *a new order for the ages.*

Jobar and Coolie were astounded by the information, but what was truly astonishing was the lack of communication within the team. They stood and looked at each other while listening to all the madness that was utterly confusing to anyone not of the human's world.

Jobar finally said, "Back up just a moment please . . . did you say New World Order?"

Henry's gaze slowly drifted from Dorathy down to Jobar. "Yes, what of it?"

Coolie shook his head. He knew where Jobar was going with this train of thought. "No way, Jobar. There cannot be a connection . . . can there?"

Jobar hesitated, momentarily, while he collected his thoughts. "The established government that has been controlling this sector, and many others, has a very similar name as you already know. But what intrigues us is that its name and its origin have been under debate for centuries. Its very existence has been highly suspect."

Henry realized at that very moment. "Of course, . . . it has to be some kind of offshoot created by a faction of the Illuminati that settled here. Some of them must have stayed behind while the rest continued their mission. They emerged as the governing force, aligning the sector's inhabitants, overthrowing any authority that may have been here initially and replacing it with their New World Order . . . or New Western Ordinance."

Jobar and Coolie were not surprised by the realization. Jobar said, "It is all starting to make sense now. Most of the worlds in this sector and others don't even recognize the fact the NWO came to us from beings from far off and they brought order where there was war and chaos." Jobar continued, "This *lost city* whereabouts has always been speculated about amongst seekers. The frozen planet above us has very little to offer and is so far off the beaten track, that simply put, no one really cares anymore, and a long time forgotten. Regardless of its allure of inaccessibility of the secrets held below, and no one knows of this cave and for those who may have wandered upon this map as we did, they would have never known its true meaning unless they were a true Portal Seeker."

"Yes, Coolie added, "Just another cave with meaningless inscriptions left behind by a long- forgotten civilization. Everyone thinking there was nothing left of any real significance." He continued, "I'm sure there have been a few poking around for clues and trying to make a connection over the centuries, but no one has been able to say without a doubt that it all started here inside this frozen rock."

Dorothy nodded. "Yeah, like the lost city of Atlantis. Everyone thinking they had found it here or there, but no one could ever say without a doubt, they had found it or whether it ever had actually existed in the first place."

Jobar insisted, "Many people have tried to find the origin of this map and its significance, but all have given up. None of them ever had you to enlighten them . . . you hold the answers to this place and its mysteries that have eluded us. I am confident now that we can find the portal!"

CHAPTER 35

The tall grass brushed against her knees as Athena approached Alex. She repeated herself. "You were right Alex; you were right about everything. "My mother was killed by the Illuminati."

Alex tilted his head in disbelief. "Athena, my God are you all right?"

Athena chuckled. "Well other than the fact I'm dead, I'd say I'm doing pretty well now that I'm here with you."

Alex got up and hugged her a long while. "How long have I been away?"

Athena smiled, "Just a minute or two . . . but my whole life . . . I missed you so much Alex."

Alex was aware of his circumstances. "I know time has marched on, but it seems so insignificant, as if time doesn't even exist here."

Athena cocked her head to one side. "Yeah, I know, sort of weird, as if time never existed. We know it has marched on relentlessly but in a flash it's gone. Shaking her thoughts, she backtracked. "Look, I need to tell you what has happened while you were away." Athena lowered herself into the grass, crossing her legs.

Alex followed her lead and sat next to her. "Tell me, my sweet girl, what has transpired?"

She shook her head. "God, where do I even start? Alex, Mom was needed for this mission not because of her brilliant engineering skills but because she holds the key to a device—she was the chosen one. Her DNA carries *the code*, a code buried beneath the code the Otherling left with us. Not all of us have it, but she does, and she can find the path to this place."

Alex leaned in. "What are you talking about?"

"Listen to me Alex, they are leaving Earth behind. Our planet and everyone left behind is doomed and they know it. They are in search of the beings that they believe put us here."

Alex shook his head. "No. Why kill your mother? Why not just take her if they needed her so badly?"

"Alex listen, her DNA . . . they would have had to alter her. Her DNA is intact, but she is alive because of her donor's blood. She is a part of them now. "But she can survive in either dimension. She holds the key Alex . . . she is the key."

Alex looked like someone who had been punched in the gut. "Oh my God, Athena, my worst nightmare . . . she will find her way back to us and I will be with whoever picks me up—gone for a lifetime."

"Alex a lifetime isn't that long, but perhaps there is a way . . . maybe they will find you before they find the gateway to this reality. Space is a pretty big place Alex, finding the road here will be difficult. We must believe that it will take some time.

"Yes", Alex said, realizing his dilemma. "Time is something that seems to be irrelevant."

CHAPTER 36

Her voyage to the outer region was a grueling one and Silas's toler-ance level was dwindling. Kore swore a slew of obscenities yelling, "Get me down to this hellhole of a rock so I can get to the bottom of this convoluted derangement!"

Soon after touching down on this small, cold, desolate planet a local scavenger came to investigate, approaching on the back of a domesti-cated rock crawler with shaggy fur and weathered scales. He shouted, "Hey! You can't park that pile of rubble here, we're about to excavate this area for remnants!"

Kore exited her ship, her cloak blowing around her as if a dust devil was approaching. "I can do as I like, and I can have you arrested for trespassing!"

At that moment he saw the emblem on her ship. "Oh! Pardon me . . . I was not aware . . ."

Kore cut him off sharply. "I am looking for a ship that came here recently, and if you can tell me where it has gone, I will forgive your behavior."

The old-timer shrugged his shoulders. "We don't get many ships here anymore, which is why I think you might have interest with this one. "Two scruffy-looking deep space miners that came here a day ago with the sole purpose of logging in. I allowed them to stow their ship on the abandoned airstrip about ten clicks from here. Another very strange ship, the likes I have never seen before, came in for a brief landing and before I had a chance to investigate, the two miners boarded it and they left . . . very unusual for these parts."

Kore's impatience was begging to rise as if lava flowed through her veins. "I will ask you one simple question and you better have the correct answer for me, or you will regret it. Where did this ship go?"

The poor old scavenger did not possess the answer she was looking for but did have a clue to offer. "I believe they were on a 'Portal Quest.' They logged in and requested to be logged off. They left in the other ship . . . of course I responded with a demand of my own and the old miners paid handsomely."

Kore bit back her temper. "If you are unable to tell me where they went, tell me where you THINK they went . . . and I will reward you by leaving you with your life intact!"

He nervously rubbed the dirt and sand from his goggles. "I think they went to the eighth planet of this system. It's an icy rock, but has been deluged with 'Seekers' over the years and these fellas seemed to fit the description of Seekers in search of the same old fairytale. No one ever finds anything but the *tunnel* and no one ever has been able to break though the force field to gain access to the interior of the planet. Many have tried but failed miserably. Others have tried to climb down through crevasses in the ice but have lost their lives in the process. Years ago, I made a nice little profit taking adventurous clients to *The Rock*, but the place has lost its allure and now not too many are even aware of the fascination it used to have. Too bad . . ."

Kore cringed at the thought of yet another journey. She stared out into the approaching twilight, the planet's moons just rising over the horizon. "If you are wrong about this you will regret it!" She turned on her heel and marched back into her ship.

"Take me to the eighth planet of this forsaken sector!" Silas punched the coordinates into the console without uttering a word. Over the years Kore had heard stories of the mysterious Travelers and the theory of their origin. She sat in the cockpit staring out into the vast nothingness as the space around her bent and became distorted. She tapped her long jagged fingernails on the hard surface of her seat controls and said, as if anyone was listening, "Maybe now I can finally get to the bottom of this." Silas glanced over and then continued with his tasks; he thought it best to ignore and only answer when spoken to, not wanting to give a hint of what they might find. He had a feeling about this with thoughts of a distant past slowly creeping in on him. She sat back and crossed her arms. "How much longer?"

Silas took control of the ship. "We are on final approach and dropping into orbit momentarily."

She leaned forward against her restraints. "Take us down. I want to get a good look around."

The ship was hovering just a few hundred meters above the surface when Silas motioned to the console and said, "I'm getting a reading that shows there is an opening to the interior of the planet on the southern pole."

Kore's mind was churning over the data coming in on the panel in front of her and she hesitated. "Prepare for a slow descent, enter with caution at sub-speed. That desert dweller spoke of a force field." Silas did as instructed, all sensors on maximum. The ship started to advance down into the darkened tunnel, exterior lights reflecting off the surface of the frozen rock. She was clutching her seat waiting, when without warning the ship shuddered as it bounced upward and sideways, hitting the smooth rock surface of the tunnel, scraping metal against rock.

Kore screamed, "Level her out and back away! Is there any significant damage?"

Silas ran his hands over his console with lightning speed. "No, everything seems to be in running order."

Kore sat and pondered the idea of blasting their way through the force field but was sure that technique had already been attempted. She growled, disappointed. "We will wait here for them to exit; I want their ship and you'd better not let them get away—I want some answers!"

Silas was one of the best pilots in the New Western Ordinance and was well-respected throughout the fleet. Most everyone he knew admired him for his talent, exceptional good looks, and his intellect, but when it came to his duty as Prime Minister Athanatos' personal pilot everyone pitied him. All were at a loss as to how he secured placement in service to such a horrendous creature. It was rumored that a dubious past had something to do with it, despite his untarnished career record. Silas sat in his cockpit with an uneasy feeling. His mind drifted to the past, images haunting him as they crept over him. He thought of what he must do; his long wait was coming to an end.

His response was a simple, "Yes Ma'am, I will do what is necessary."

CHAPTER 37

H enry and the rest of them could put everything together now. It was apparent what had happened so long ago.

They approached the pyramid, its large glowing eye looming above them and seeming to follow their every move. This cold, unnerving place was permeated with a smell of dankness from a long-forgotten age. Walking closer to the pyramid, they could begin to make out inscriptions carved into the stone blocks. Dorathy peered at its apex and saw an antiquity that she had seen as a child in a picture of ancient Egyptian artifacts. The stone was thought to have fallen from the stars as an iron meteorite. Upon entering the atmosphere, it had transformed into a perfectly shaped pyramid. The image of the slender neck bird carved into its surface was peering at her. A haunting image, it represented a stellar religion among the ancient world. It represented the rise of the Phoenix and, with it, the rise of a new civilization.

Dorathy ran her hands over the inscriptions at the base of the pyramid and started to read the words written so long ago. Jobar and Coolie were patting each other on the back and hugging their traveler friends with excitement and joy, for they were closer to solving the mystery of the Otherings and the portal than anyone had ever been before.

Jobar was giddy with happiness. "You can read what has been written here . . . this is a day that history will remember! For this language is foreign to us and we are sure no one else has ever been here in this cavern besides us."

"My God", Dorathy said as she proceeded to read,

We ventured out among the stars looking for the creator who had entrusted us with the code of ages. We, the survivors of humankind, departed our Earthly home on a grand quest, the quest to end all quests, for we have arrived and flourished.

The chosen ones have stayed behind to ensure their mission will continue. Our brothers have moved forward to continue the quest of order from chaos whilst we wait for the key to the holiest of places. Indeed, we search for the path of all our species. The path is the way, and the way to the gate is just beyond, but forever far. The path that leads us to the great beyond is paved with golden luster. it leads to our placement in the cosmos and we are carried by its essence in the blood of the original creator. It is all knowing and will protect the chosen one, she is the key. Beneath these walls lie the fruit of the many seeds planted long ago. They are the true Illuminati, the ones who had sacrificed the most and we are forever in their debt.

We will meet once again old friends. fear not, for time is meaningless, forever is redundant.

Dorathy and the others could not believe their eyes as they each read the carvings on the stones placed there eons ago. Henry read it through a few times and turning it over and over in his mind, finally said, "This place is a tomb for the ones who were left behind, and there must be a way in." Everyone else seemed to be coming to the same conclusion.

Brenda shook her head. "Yes, that much is true, but it also leads me to believe there is a key here to finding the other side." She then read aloud part of the encryption, *"The path that leads us to the great beyond is paved with golden luster. It leads to our placement in the cosmos and we are carried by its essence, of the blood of the original creator. It is all knowing and will protect the chosen one, as she is the key."*

Henry said as he leaned against the cold, stone surface, "The way I hear it is we need to be looking for a path—'golden' perhaps refers to the particle beam."

Jobar said enthusiastically, "Deep space miners over the years crossed the path created by the portal. All have said there was a brilliant yellow beam that bent the space surrounding their ships as they unwittingly crossed through the wake it had left behind. The turbulence it had created caused much damage to the ships as they traveled through."

Dorathy obviously knew every facet of her Space Bending Device and was attempting to ascertain the type of damage caused by crossing the wake of the particle beam leading to the path of the portal. "Amazingly," she said as she thought of her creation, "this same technology has been used, but is it just coincidence that the same type of technology is what gets us through to wherever it is we are searching for? Or does it differ somehow?"

Henry was left contemplating her train of thought. Breaking the silence, he said, "Somehow it must be the same, since it's how we came to be here. Somewhere there must be a way to amplify it, to somehow push the envelope to the next level." Henry shook his head to clear the cobwebs, seeing something that caught his eye and redirected his attention, "Hey anything under all that scrub?"

Magnus had wandered off, trying to clear encryptions that had been covered with moss and vining plants. Brenda and Dimitri joined Magnus and working together started to remove the large vining branches that had been blocking one side of the pyramid.

Magnus realized they had stumbled across what seem to be a door of some sort. "Hello, what do we have here?" he mumbled as he cleared away craggy old vines. "Looks like a passageway. Its keystone is marked with the imprint of a human hand."

Everyone gathered around to see what Magnus had discovered. "This must be the entrance to the tomb," Jobar said, climbing onto an ancient stone block that had partially come away from its structure, allowing him to get a better look.

Coolie was trying to finagle the hinges that kept the stone door closed securely in place. "Maybe we can find something to smash through the entrance."

"Highly doubtful, my mighty little friend," Magnus said, "This is solid rock. Having the proper key is the only way we are going to get through."

Brenda grabbed Dimitri's arm. "Bend over, let me get on your back." Dimitri saw the look in her eye and did as he was told. As she balanced herself, she placed her hand on the print in the keystone. "Hmmm, definitely a woman's hand." She jerked her head in Dorathy's direction. "I have a thought girlfriend, I think you need to try," she declared as she climbed down.

Dorathy stood with arms crossed. She had a sinking gut feeling that Brenda might be right, but didn't want to acknowledge it. Reluctantly, she climbed on Dimitri's back and hesitated for a moment. Her head was swimming with thoughts of something horrible happening once she placed her hand onto the stone.

She looked at Henry for guidance, and he took her left hand to steady her. Slowly, she matched her right hand to the imprint, and it was a perfect fit. She shrugged, looking down at Henry. "Nothing . . . wait . . . the stone it's starting to heat up!" Withdrawing her hand, she could see a strange glow coming from beneath the rock imprint. "Oh Shit!" She scrambled off Dimitri's back and they both lunged out of the way.

There was a deep rumble as the mechanism that controlled the entrance came to life. The door pushed back with a scraping sound and as it did, air and dust blew out from the opening. The door slid open, revealing a staircase leading down a dark narrow passage-way.

"Christ!" Dorathy said under her breath. "What the hell is that all about?"

The group stood and stared at her in amazement. Finally, Magnus said, "You, my dear, are apparently the 'chosen one.'"

"What the hell?" she yelled, as she stood with all eyes still fixed on her. "Why the heck am I so goddamned special? This is really starting to freak me out and I don't like it—not one goddamned bit!"

She was starting to hyperventilate. "If you assholes think I'm going down there, you're out of your damn minds . . . no freaking way!"

Henry had developed a calming ability when dealing with Dorathy from the day they revived her. Her emotional outbursts were a part of her make-up. "Look Dora, for whatever reason, and God only knows why, you possess a special ability and purpose for this mission. The only way we are going to get to the bottom of this craziness is if you follow us down there. Dora, you know I won't let anything happen to you and I will be right next to you always."

With a heavy sigh she realized he was right. "God, will someone please tell me how I got to this screwed up place and time. This shit really blows!"

Brenda put a loving arm around her friend. "You know I love you, but you really need to just suck it up, for all our sakes.

Dorathy pondered her highly irregular position in the universe and concluded that the likelihood of her ever having a normal life had ended a long time ago. "Yeah . . . ," succumbing to her irregular set of circumstances, she said, "whatever you say . . . still freaks me out though."

On that note, they all fumbled to turn on their light rods and started down the steep stairway with Henry in the lead and Dorathy close on his heels. As they went deeper into the tomb, the lingering scent of mildew and stale air that had been trapped deep in this catacomb over the eons filled their senses as a reminder of how much time had passed. The stone walls were moist from condensation, but the stairs themselves were fabricated from some type of metal. Dorathy found it hard to resist touching the walls as they descended; somehow it made the situation more real, assuming she wasn't having a delusional nightmare.

Down they went, finally reaching the bottom, the stairway's structure terminating in the center of what appeared to be catacombs from the time when there was a bustling modern civilization hidden deep in the core of this frozen planet. The rock floor had been polished to a reflective shine and the curved wall had clear heavy glass and metal doors securing each of twelve ancient sarcophagi. It appeared the tube-like casings had been positioned there eons ago. As they took their last step from the staircase to the smooth rock floor, a flickering of lights from above came slowly to life and illuminated the room with a soft eerie glow.

Dorathy looked down and pointed to the writing she saw carved into the stone floor. She read it aloud,

"The BLOODLINES have laid to rest their original kind. Our altercation over the years has allowed us to continue. We are leaving this place behind to start a new life amongst the civilization we have engineered; to govern the masses of the displaced ones.

Where there was chaos there is harmony, and we will continue the work we were sent to do. The peoples of these worlds will live as one and flourish.

"Well there you go, that was the beginning of the New Western Ordinance," Jobar said. "There have been legends over the years, mostly conjecture and a lot of hearsay, but there it is written in stone; passed down from generation to generation, its true meaning lost over the millennia. This truly has been an epic day." He shook Coolie's hand. "Finally, the truth of the powers that be. The hierarchy of our installed government has been around for countless generations—this proves without a doubt that they came from this place, from your world."

"Seems like," Henry said. "Also, by the sounds of it they had been altered to somehow live long enough to see the job through."

Brenda wondered, "If they had been altered for the trip here as we were, perhaps they had fine-tuned the method over the years not only for longevity, but procreation. They had to have found a way to not only create synthetic DNA, but to have it passed on to their offspring."

Dimitri added, "They must also have broken the code buried in our DNA and found the originating point in space. We must possess that information if we are to have any hope of finding the portal."

Everyone agreed and Dorathy concluded, "If ever there was a place for the answers we are in search of, I would say, that place is here. All the clues must be here, we just need to find them, and I think the first place to look is in this final resting place. What better way to find heaven than to ask the dead for directions."

The group stood in the center of the circle of tombs, all upright, standing at attention, gathered together as if they had been the Knights of the Round Table. There was a slight humming of the lights from above and air passing through the stairwell made a low howling sound that gave it a feeling that their spirits were watching from beyond the veil.

Magnus brought out his scanner to see if it could tell them anything unusual about the area they had just entered. As he looked at the data streaming in, he raised an eyebrow. "Fascinating."

Henry wondered what he was referring to. "What?"

There seems to be information encoded in each container. It's redundant and cycles into infinity."

Dorathy was attempting to wipe dust from a surface that seemed only too familiar to her. The glass was thick and pitted, preventing her from seeing inside. "Infinity indeed, life never ending . . . death is not the end, it is only a beginning to another form of existence." They nodded as they understood her meaning.

She wiped enough dust from one of the closed glass tombs to reveal a scanner just to the right of the door. "Hey look at this." Dimitri had also been clearing off the dust from another tomb, "Yes, there is one over here, too."

Henry approached Dorathy. "Well try it, see if your hand works for these as well." Dorathy

clasped her hands together as anxiety started to build. "Hey, I don't want some mummified shit show to come tumbling out at me!

Henry put his arm around her waist and pulled her to him. "I'll be right here. Now try your hand."

She slowly extended her hand and placed it on the panel. A light began to glow. "You know, I really don't like being in the position of be all end all of this mission."

Henry said in her ear as he looked over her shoulder at the console, "Well, get used to it."

They all gathered around to see the information glowing on the panel. Magnus attempted to read the data, "Seems to be dates, perhaps a reference to this individual's date of birth and death, but the language is unfamiliar."

Dimitri looked at the panel and then flashed his gaze at Jobar. "This seems to be an ancient text form from your planet."

Jobar, standing on his tip toes, the glow reflecting off his leathery skin, said, "Oh my, you are right. It is very familiar to me, but I cannot read it completely."

Magnus said, "I'll scan them all to see if we might find similarities that might give us some insight as to where they have gone and whom they have left behind." He pulled a data pad from his backpack and started to log the first entry by connecting to the mainframe. "Okay, this might take a little while, but nothing ventured nothing gained. Once the information from each capsule has been downloaded, it will show any consistencies, so let's continue. Dora, after you, my dear." Dorathy dreaded being in this position, but at some point, she knew they would get to the bottom of it all.

A couple of hours later all twelve of the tomb's occupants' data streams had been logged. Henry approached Dorathy. "We need to get a good idea of what we're dealing with so we can ascertain where it was the rest of them headed off to. Then I want to go up and get another look at the carvings on the pyramid."

Dorathy wiped her eyes with her shirt tail. "Well, so far the best we can tell there are twelve family names . . ."

Brenda interrupted, "twelve bloodlines."

Magnus agreed, "Yes, based on what we've surmised, logic would suggest they'd be the original bloodlines of the Illuminati, but these are twelve separate DNA codes."

Brenda shook her head. "You're not getting the higher meaning of this, my friends. The Illuminati have thirteen bloodlines. I'm betting, regardless of this gathering of some type of intergalactic counsel, I'd guess that these twelve represent the purest form of the Otherlings and the thirteenth bloodline is Dora's."

Dorathy's eyes grew wide as she looked down at her hand. "Oh no . . ."

"Yes . . . it's all making sense now. Regardless of your lack of active participation, your family . . . your father, is the thirteenth bloodline. You seem to be the Key Master of sorts and these twelve I'm guessing might be some type of Gate Keepers. Whatever secrets they may hold in this tomb, you carry the answers."

Dimitri and Magnus had started to review some of the data they had collected. They were huddled together with their backs against the wall with Jobar and Coolie nodding off on either side of them. Dimitri yelled, "Stop! Yes, there it is, a code written within their DNA!"

Everyone gathered around the data pad as Dimitri magnified the image to 3D. "This is going to take me some time to decode, but I am positive we have what we were looking for."

Henry clapped his hands together. "Okay, we got what we came for. Let's get topside and take images of the writing on the pyramid, then we'll get a fresh start down tomorrow morning."

On that note, the group packed their gear. Dorathy stretched and walked over to one of the canisters, wishing she could get a look inside. She ran her hands along its surface, trying to determine if there was something she was missing. It all seemed very strange to her, yet oddly familiar at the same time. She scraped her hands over the entire glass and metal casing and felt some grooves through the layers of dust and muck. She started to brush away at it vigorously, until she could see the image with more detail. "Look at this, seems to be a bird of sorts." She continued to expose the insignia. "Yes, it looks like the Phoenix rising from the ashes."

Henry squatted down to get a better look. "Yeah, you're right. I wonder what that's all about?"

Dorathy shook her head, knowing its significance to the Illuminati but also aware of its symbolism in Greek mythology. "Rebirth from death. Oddly enough, its meaning is the same as cryogenics." Henry gazed into Dorathy's weary eyes and knew her journey would be a long one.

Slowly, they departed the room of tombs. The lights flickered off as they climbed the staircase. Dorathy wondered how many more centuries these tombs would lie undisturbed and who else in the future would have the ability to enter, if anyone at all. The ages seemed to have passed this place by. They climbed up in the darkness, each step measured by countless eons of loneliness; untouched.

Dorathy looked up at the keystone as Dimitri got down on all fours. She climbed up on his back and placed her hand on the stone imprint. The stone door closed slowly with a heavy thud. She helped Dimitri up off the floor. "Well, I guess that's it. We follow the next clues, see where it takes us."

Dimitri said, already clearing vines from the pyramid, "Yes, I am eager to get back to our ship so I can start working on the code."

Jobar waved his hand at the wall, "Hey, look at these stones. They have some kind of symbols carved into them."

Dorathy bent forward to get a closer look. "I'm guessing, but they look to be some sort of constellations. Nothing I recognize, but then again, we are in a completely different part of space, God knows what they reference. Not to mention that," she pointed up, the constellation of Orion, his belt gleaming brightly with his sword slug to his side, "I have always been fascinated by him hovering in the winter sky . . . but why is he here in this cavern?"

Henry looked up and wondered the same thing as the image loomed above his head. "I have a feeling we will eventually find the answers. Everyone, look around and take images of everything, no matter how insignificant it seems."

After a couple more hours of cataloging, they were spent and made camp for the night in this mysterious place. They found comfort knowing they were nestled in their past, among the familiar eerie glow illuminating the cave. The All-Seeing Eye watched over them and the Owl of Minerva majestically kept guard with its wide glaring eyes and long talons, ready to swoop down on any threat that may lurk in the shadows.

The day's events had drained them of energy. Eating in silence, they bedded down for the night. Dorathy sat looking up at her Owl and said to Henry as he lay by her side, "I never thought in a million years that I would one day be sitting *here*. My father's ring had that exact insignia engraved onto it. And there it is staring back at me. Life can throw you some real curve balls." Dorathy chuckled as she continued, "In an odd way, I'm grateful to be here, no matter how bizarre this experience has been."

Henry rubbed her back. "Look, life has a way of working itself out. I could say the same thing about my own life. I often have to ask myself, how the hell did I get here? I was a nuclear physicist on a black ops mission. The Pentagon gave us the go-ahead and I carried out my orders. I wanted to pull the plug on the whole damn thing, but I didn't, and I lost two good men. Then I dug my way out of the middle of that shithole

Degraded Section. Our mission was to radiate the place to depopulate the area. I couldn't morally do it, thought if I did, I'd lose my soul . . . but, I followed my orders. How can a person exterminate other human beings simply because their behavior is so different? God knows, with all the shit they dished out over the centuries the bastards had it coming. The people there are de-evolving . . . almost as if they weren't firing on all pistons . . . you know what I mean."

Dorathy looked down at him, glued to his every word. "Yes, I do know what you mean. I wrote a book about how they seem to be missing the ability to evolve. My father and I spent a lot of time trying to help, in the end they all but threw us out for our efforts. Tell me, Henry, how did you come to be part of all this?"

"Well after my unanticipated return, they had to shut me down. I knew too much . . . apparently it was a one-way mission and I had received a large dose of radiation. I was dying of radiation poisoning and so here I am, in this cave, thousands of light years away, with you, Dora. You know though, when I look into your eyes, I sing to myself, *'Every little thing, gonna be alright.'*"

Dorathy started to sing the old tune, *"Don't worry, about a thing, cause every little thing gonna be alright."* They shared a laugh. If only for a moment their spirts were lifted. Dorathy yawned and Henry motioned for her to lie down next to him. They slept as if they didn't have a care in the world.

The long journey back consisted of further investigation of the city long forgotten, but offered nothing more in answer to the mystery; everything of importance had been taken along for whatever journey the citizens had departed on, and anything left behind had little more to offer.

The team arrived at the ship, muscles aching and exhausted, but with a renewed sense of purpose to their mission, eager to discover what they hoped had been hidden in the data. Jobar and Coolie, as much as they wanted to stay, needed to get back to their homes. Their holiday season was ending, which meant it was back to work for them. "You will keep us apprised of your findings?" Jobar said, continuing, "I wish we could stay and help, especially now that we have learned so much. If you find anything worth investigating, you must let us know. This search has been a part of our lives for so many years, to be so close to finding the answers is very exciting."

"Don't worry, my friends," Henry said reassuringly, "When we know something, we'll contact you immediately. "You both have been a great help . . ."

Coolie interjected, "We have been a great help to each other, and we know we are very close to finding the answers that we have been seeking for such a long time."

The ship began its ascent up over the city, the light glowing dim as night was approaching. Dorathy looked out over the citadel one last time, sensing that somehow, they were not done with this place, that somehow, they had missed something. The ship hovered for only a moment and then shot up into the tunnel.

Magnus was receiving a ship proximity alert reading as they crossed over the threshold of the force field. "Hey guys looks like we have company. I'm reading a ship to the port side as we exit."

Jobar was craning his neck to see the image of the ship. "Oh no, that appears to be Prime Minister Athanatos' ship. What in The Maker is she doing out here? We have to escape them, or it will mean big trouble for all of us—you being undocumented aliens, and not to mention our cargo!"

Dorathy shook her head as tears welled up. She huffed the laugh of someone who had a sudden realization of how immensely convoluted her existence had become. "Puts a whole new spin on the term 'illegal aliens.' And our cargo . . . well shit, if that isn't the funniest God damned thing I have ever heard. Who knew that one day I would be an 'Illegal' trafficking drugs across borders? Man, you just can't make this shit up."

Jobar looked confused by her attempted humor. "This is a serious matter, not to be taken lightly, and we MUST make our escape!"

"Cool your jets, I'll get us out of this," Henry said as his mind was piloting the ship, preparing to activate the space bending device.

Magnus checked his readings. "Ready to make the jump on your mark." The ship was just clearing the surface.

"Punch it!"

Silas was suddenly getting a reading from the fast approaching ship, his fingers flying over the controls. "They are coming out hot. Engaging the graviton beam now."

Prime Minister Athanatos screamed, "Don't let them get away. I want them captured alive, use the blast gun only to disable them!"

The foreign ship was just clearing the surface; Silas's eyes were ablaze by the sight, engaging the beam with lightning fast reflexes. The beam wrapped the ship in a brightly charged field and it shuddered momentarily. The outer hull changed from its stealth black and now to a brightly glowing red. A fog lifted from Kore's memories, for this ship had a familiar shape and she knew immediately the importance of it. "My holy hell, could it really be . . . that ship comes from the other side of our existence. Get me that ship! She pounded a fist on the console beside her.

Suddenly the travelers' ship shot an electrified field of bright blue in all directions, frying everything on board Kore's vessel. Silas played his hands across the controls to block the other ship's path of escape, but it was useless. Smoke filled the cockpit with the smell of melted fuses and ozone. Kore shouted obscenities directed not only to her pilot. "Damn you! You will regret this! Their would-be captured prey bent the space around them, and they were gone in an instant only leaving a golden flash in their wake. Silas leaned back in his smoke-filled cockpit; his suspicions were correct about the origins of this transient ship.

"Damn that was close!" Brenda, feeling exhilarated, said louder than she knew.

Jobar and Coolie were obviously shaken. Coolie gasped, "That was Prime Minister Kore Athanatos's ship. "Why was she out here in the outer region?"

Jobar shook his head. "Makes no sense . . . how could she know what we were up to and why would she care? We are just simple miners. We need to get to our ship before she figures it out, so we can make our escape!"

Jobar grasped at the back of Magnus's seat. "That electrified field was amazing. Where did you find such a technology?"

Magnus looked at Henry with one brow cocked. Henry glanced back at Dorathy. "Seems that our ship is full of surprises these days."

Jobar and Coolie looked at each other, confused by the whole damn thing. Jobar stressed the need to get back to his precious ship. "Well, whatever you did back there I hope it's enough to have disabled them long enough." He gazed around their self-aware ship. "Although something tells me we are in the clear for the time being."

Magnus looked over his shoulder. "I have a feeling you're right my little friend."

They landed back on the old mining outpost with Jobar and Coolie collecting their precious cargo and parting ways just in the nick of time. As Jobar piloted his ship away from the small mining operation, he could make out the old timer running down the airstrip in distress, waving for them to land. Jobar ignored the old fellow as he put the ship in fast ascent.

Coolie asked again, "Are you sure he can't track us?"

"Not to worry, I gave him false documents when I paid him off."

"Oh my," Coolie said with despair riddling his voice. "I hope you're right about this, because if she tracks us down, we're finished!"

Jobar pondered the circumstances for a moment and said nothing. Thoughts of the wrath of his sister Mares were almost as bad as thinking about the wrath of the Prime Minister. He glanced to his side where the crate of poppies had been thrown in their haste to make an escape.

Coolie saw the determined look on his face. "Yes, and what about those poppies? You have gotten us in quite a pickle, my friend, and the sooner we get rid of those the better I'll feel."

Jobar rolled his eyes. "You will feel better when you have your half of the credits in your hand. Why don't you have a drink? It might make you a little less irritating."

Coolie bit his lip and reached for his bottle. "One day this shit is going to catch up to us."

"Coolie, my friend, no matter how much crap we have done together you can't say we were ever bored out here."

Coolie slugged down another gulp of his fermentation and thought about it as he handed the bottle to his oldest friend. He began to laugh. "The shit we've pulled off . . . hell, wouldn't have it any other way. A couple more operations and we can finally retire."

While sharing their thoughts on the last couple of days, they arrived at their destination. As Jobar slowed to sub-speed he caught sight of the ship waiting for them. Coolie sat back in his seat trying to stay calm. "I hate dealing with these gangsters."

Jobar looked Coolie in the eye. "Look you really have to learn to relax. They can't see you sweat, or we're toast; now go get our blast guns." Coolie did as he was asked, then took a long hard swig on his bottle, cursing under his breath.

The other ship slowly drifted to initiate the docking procedure while Jobar pulled the large crate of poppies over to the airlock. The link secure, Jobar pulled the lever on the inner hull door to the airlock passage-way.

Dressed in fur coats with crudely sewn thick-hide pants tucked into tall boots, two tall, thin and pale humanoids waited on the other side of the hatch, their guns drawn. "You're late," the elder of the two said. Jobar made no move from his position blocking the entrance to his ship, his awkwardly large blaster gun pointed upward with one hand, and the other on the lever of the airlock. Coolie gave a hard shove to the heavy crate and it slid to rest at their guests' feet. The elder of the two gangsters motioned for his companion to evaluate the quality of the cargo. He opened the box and cradling one of the poppies, took a small whiff of the fragrant flower. His bloodshot eyes rolled back into his head and he muttered, "It's prime product." Clearly no stranger to the effects of the poppy, he reached into his coat and jerked out a bag of credits. Jobar flinched, stopping just short of pulling the trigger. The man laughed loudly, baring his stained and broken teeth. "Easy there little fella," he sneered as he tossed the bag of credits to Coolie. Coolie quickly counted the credits and nodded. "Not to worry little man, it's all there. Once again you have come through with excellent product. I need not remind you that you don't know us."

Jobar said arrogantly, "We are just as guilty as you, so likewise. Our business here is finished, so if you don't like the coldness of space, I suggest you get off my ship. He tightened his grip around the airlock lever.

"Now that's not very hospitable." The man could sense Jobar was getting nervous. But it was not worth aggravating him any further, particularly since Jobar had the upper hand and could easily blow them out into space. "Until next time, my little friends." They turned and walked the short narrow passage of Jobar's ship's airlock opened the hatch to their ship, disengaged and were gone.

Jobar was at the controls where he had already plotted his course and punched it in with a firm hand. They made their escape before their business associates got any ideas about engaging in foul play to maximize profits by taking their ship.

CHAPTER 38

K ore sat in the darkness of her cold mountain home, her beloved feathered and furry winged creature sitting loyally by her side. She rarely gazed into the night sky. It had become a constant reminder of how many worlds existed in the far reaches of space. She had spent so much of her life trying to discover the truth of where she had come from that she had withdrawn from others and turned within for comfort. All were inferior to her. She believed she had a special purpose in this life, if only she could find the missing pieces of the puzzle.

She had taken out the old images that had been stored away for so many years and spread them around her. Sitting on the cold stone floor with a stew bubbling over the fire, Kore brushed away the dust with the sleeve of her cloak and stared at the images that had been passed down from generations a long time dead. She didn't have even a clue about who these people were, where they were from, or when, but today she had a glimmer of hope revealed to her in the shape of a ship that was familiar to her. She rapidly flipped through the images and came to rest on one in particular. "Ah, there you are my pretty." She adjusted the lenses on the end of her long nose, and she ran her fingers over the image. Somehow, touching it gave her hope of finding the truth. "Yes, there you are in all your splendor. Who are you and where did you come from? I must find you if I am ever going to get the answers I need." She hit a button and the picture expanded to 3D imagery, slowly rotating in the smoky air of her cold dark room, glowing black and red, the wing tip moving over her head. Her beloved pet, startled at first, reached up but only managed to grasp at the air as the image distorted momentarily by his attempt. Kore patted the top of his head as he reached for her hand. "For all the creator's damnations you have just stepped into my world and I will possess your secrets, my fleeing friends." She looked down and smiled as her gaze met the yellow glow of her companion's eyes lovingly staring back at her.

"We depart on a journey tomorrow, my love." Feathers and fur ruffling, the creature jumped up and down, baring his teeth in a smile and clapping his clawed hands in excitement. He was rarely allowed the simple pleasure of leaving his bleak surroundings.

CHAPTER 39

After hours of reviewing data from the lost city, Dimitri rubbed his eyes and leaned back in his chair putting his feet up on the table and sipping from the bottle of the concoction Coolie had given them. Magnus returned with his usual cup of hot tea. "You know my friend that shit will kill you."

He muttered a reply that sounded suspiciously like an obscenity. "I have been dead before and you know sometimes I think that would be better than what we are doing out here in the middle of fucking nowhere."

Magnus gazed at him over the top of his cup, steam hazing his vision, "Yes, I do recognize the fact we are on an impossible mission but given the alternatives at the time our options and our lives had become somewhat limited, to say the least."

Dimitri shot back, "Yes but we would be a long time dead by now enjoying whatever kind of life waits for us on the other side."

Magnus laughed. "You are forgetting one key element . . . we ARE on the other side."

Dimitri frowned for a second and laughed his big Russian laugh and chided him by saying, "You are so smart, no wonder you were MI6." Magnus shook his head with a smile as he caught the implied insult.

Brenda sauntered in and knocked Dimitri's feet off the table. "What

the hell is so goddamned funny? Aren't you two supposed to be analyz-
ing the data?"

Dimitri slapped her on her back side. "Hey, woman, we have been at
it for hours; we need a break!"

Brenda took a seat at the table, grabbing a glass off the counter and
pouring herself a shot of the backyard moonshine. "Well, tell me what
you guys have so far."

Dimitri, with a heavy sigh, punched a few keys on his console and a 3D
image of his work appeared hovering over the table. "This is un-coded
DNA data I retrieved from the tombs. Each one is different, but somehow related." He added, "There is a pattern here, but I have not been
able to ascertain which order to read the data. I have tried repeatedly to
connect the individuals' patterns but they just don't match up."

Magnus scrutinized the images floating over his head while sipping
his tea and suddenly noted that something appeared repetitive but almost superfluous. He hesitated momentarily, running it through his
mind before speaking, not wanting to give Dimitri any evidence that he
was lacking in intellect. He wasn't quite sure what it was he had just spotted but deemed it important enough to mention regardless of Dimitri's
onslaught of insults over the years. He stood and pointed to the area in
question. "That there seems to be a primmer of sorts."

Dimitri stood as well and looked closely at the data hovering in the
room. He punched a few more keys and the image pulled away to show
all the data on a smaller scale. A wide smile formed on Dimitri's face as
he slapped Magnus on the back. "My friend you are not as dumb as you
look." Dimitri rapidly punched at the console as the data turned in on
itself forming a perfect cube. Dimitri enlarged the image, so it took up
most the room in which they were sitting. Inside the cube all the data had
connected to form a map.

Brenda gazed upon the map and knew the significance of this sudden
discovery. "Well boys I think it's time to celebrate!"

Henry and Dorothy were enjoying a quiet game of chess, sipping their
drinks and becoming slower to make each move. They were giggling and
throwing chess pieces at each other when they heard the commotion in
the other room. Henry came to his senses quickly and jumped up, with

Dorathy bringing up the rear. "What . . . what's going on back here?" Henry stopped short with Dorathy almost knocking him down from behind. They both took in the image floating in the room.

"Jesus Christ, you've done it!" Henry exclaimed, shaking his head to clear the effects of the alcohol. They all stood there gazing up at the stars and twelve planets floating in a dusty cloud.

Dorathy leaned against the wall. "My God, could it be that simple? There has got to be much more to this?"

Henry grabbed a chair and flung his leg over it. He leaned his chin on the back rest and said, "Look, this is great but what is the meaning of it? Twelve random points in space; we need to find the starting point."

Recalling the water droplets on the ceiling above the pyramid and how the constellation of Orion had shone brightly, Dorathy asked, "What about Orion? Perhaps there is a real significance to those markings on the pyramid." The group sat and pondered the path of the map and wondered the actual meaning of it.

Dorathy finally spoke, "The Illuminati had a thirteen-step, unfinished pyramid with the All-Seeing Eye looming over it. It was believed that their work would go unfinished in their lifetime on Earth, and it would continue in the afterlife. This pyramid has twelve steps and has been finished with the Benben stone. This stone vanished during the Great War; it was believed it had been blown to smithereens with the rest of the ancient world artifacts. The carvings on the stone show the symbol of the ancient Illuminati with the figure of the Phoenix etched on its surface. Each step there displays what looks to be a star constellation, all except the top where there is now the Benben. The All-Seeing Eye has been placed over a completed pyramid where before it had been placed over it unfinished."

Dorathy continued, struggling to find an answer as she spoke, "To me, this represents the completion of their mission. But I see another message here as well. When I was a kid, my dad took me to one of the first pyramids ever built, the Pyramid of Djoser. If memory serves, there were thirteen false doors with one true door on the southeast side. My point being that these positions in space could be considered false doors. I have no doubt this map was left for us to find our way to wherever they have gone. Look I'm grasping at straws here, but if there are thirteen 'bloodlines' and only twelve steps where there should be thirteen steps in the Illuminati Pyramid, my guess, and I'm only stating the obvious here, is that somehow my DNA holds the thirteenth point to this map."

The group watched as Dimitri stood and walked over to Dorathy. His hand reached out and he carefully plucked a strand of hair from Dorathy's head. "Almost every aspect of your DNA at this point has been altered by the donation of our blood when we revived you, but obviously not enough to change the effectiveness of what still remains intact; your hair."

Dimitri took her hair and his drink and stopped at the refrigerated storage locker for a snack on his way to the lab. "This might take a while . . . no one bother me!"

Magnus got up and made himself a new cup of tea and then headed to the cockpit. "I'm going to contact Jobar and tell him what we have discovered, perhaps he can determine the proximity of the points on the map, and maybe ascertain the significance of the carvings."

Brenda yawned and rubbed her forehead as she stumbled to her room. "I'm going to sleep off this hangover. What the hell does that little shit put in that bottle?"

Dorathy stretched her neck, rolling her head from side to side. "I think that sounds like a good idea."

Henry could sense the tension building in her. "Come on then, I'll give you one of my famous back rubs."

Dorathy smiled. "That sounds really nice," and she grabbed his hand and led the way.

Dorathy was carefully going over each image of the markings on the pyramid. "These have to be star constellations. Look how the size of each varies in size to represent brightness or magnitude. The biggest question is, from where would each configuration be visible?"

Henry was slowly spreading a fragrant oil over her tense shoulders. "You really need to learn how to relax."

She ignored his request. "Perhaps each constellation represents the sky above each planet." Henry was only half listening to her ramble on about stars and configurations—he was thinking of something much more intimate.

Dorathy swung around to face Henry and asked, "Are you even listening to me?"

"Dora, of course I'm listening to you and it's all very interesting but I'm tired of searching for something we may never find."

Dorathy looked at him, wide eyed in shock by his declaration. "Don't you *want* to find the place we were meant to find?"

Henry shot back, "And where may that be . . . heaven, hell, Earth, some other God forsaken place . . . who the hell knows where and how long it will take." Henry leaned against the wall at the head of her bunk. "We've been out here for years and I was pretty much over it when we picked you up. Then here you are, and now, finally, we are getting somewhere, but I'm just plain goddamned tired."

Dorathy tried to put herself in his position and became sympathetic to everything he and the others had been through to get them to this place and time. "I know, trust me, I really do, but we are finally getting somewhere and everything you have been through would all be in vain if we just gave up now."

Henry sighed, while rubbing his eyes, knowing the effect of the alcohol was clouding his vision and sapping his energy. "I know you're right Dora, but sometimes I just feel like I need a break . . . a vacation from all this bullshit."

Dorathy squeezed in behind him, pushing him forward away from the wall. She grabbed the oil and commanded him to remove his shirt. "I think you need this more than me." She gently rubbed oil on his back and shoulders, noticing his muscular frame and his skin, perfect except for rapidly healing scars from the wounds received during the last poppy mission. "Isn't this where you got mauled by that ape creature only recently?" she asked as she massaged oil into the wound.

"Yeah," he said, distress in his voice, "the advantages of being synthetic."

Dorathy craned her neck to see the progress of her own wound, received on the same day. "I see what you mean."

Henry laughed, amused by the irony. "If we do happen to stumble across Earth in all our searching for the other side, we will die in a very short time, thus getting us to our destination all the timelier." Dorathy also had to laugh at the irony.

Dimitri was finally getting somewhere with Dorathy's DNA when Brenda quietly entered the lab after an unproductive nap. Dimitri looked up at her over his equipment and said, "She holds the answers to what we have been seeking."

Brenda sat down opposite him. "So, what *are* we searching for?"

Dimitri shook his head. "Who the hell knows anymore? We were used as test subjects for an impossible mission based on pure speculation . . ."

Brenda cut him off. "Pure faith."

Dimitri glared up at her and took a swig from his bottle. "Yes faith, faith that there is another side of existence somewhere out here? So, which is it?" He continued, "A supreme being, a higher dimension, another planet, a Multiverse? And don't even get me started on that one!"

Brenda reached over and grabbed his hand. He lifted hers to his mouth and kissed it. Brenda looked into his sad eyes. "Look baby, we are alive, we have each other . . . and this mission . . . well, it's not really a mission anymore . . . it's a discovery and it's what our lives have become . . . we're just along for the ride."

Dimitri dropped her hand. "I just want some kind of normal."

Brenda sneered back, "This is the new normal so get over it."

Dimitri felt beaten but knew she was right. "Hey maybe we can just find a nice place to settle down somewhere out here."

"You're more screwed up than I thought!" Brenda shot back. "And do what Dim? Sit around on our asses? Besides we're wanted by the so-called government around here and **here** is where we are finding answers." Brenda continued, "The bastards knew there was something here and sent us. We didn't just happen along . . . remember Dora appeared in the same space and approximate time . . . they rigged the whole goddamned thing." Brenda kicked away from the table. "Pull your head outta your ass and figure this shit out!"

She left, Dimitri holding his head in his hands calling after her, "And then what?"

Magnus sat in his seat in the cockpit, looking out at the stars while he established a communication link. He thought . . . so far away, yet so very close. Over to the right he could just make out Jobar and Collie's home planet. Somewhere below, far off he knew from his position amongst the stars, was the dim spec of light that was the sun of the planet of poppies. He wondered how Earth's sun might appear from this tiny ship in the vastness of space . . . would it even be visible here; would it be part of some kind of folklore or mythology of some long-forgotten civilization? Murmuring to himself, Magnus said, "Guess it would depend on your vantage point in space . . . that could be anywhere . . . eh . . . and nowhere."

A crackle of static jolted Magnus from his train of thought as Jobar answered, excited to get the call, "Hello my friends how are things going?"

"Yes Jobar, I think we are on to something. I'm going to send you images of the stone carvings of the pyramid and what we found buried in the occupants' DNA. Seems that we have a map of sorts."

"A map! Oh yes, send it right away!" Jobar was at home in his study, his hand firmly clutching his deep space communicator. "What do you think the relevance is to the map?"

Magnus walked Jobar through his thought processes. "I'm not sure but the markings on the pyramid appear to be star constellations . . . hmm . . . an arrangement of stars seen from a certain point in space."

Jobar pondered a moment. "Are they the same stars appearing different from different perspectives or different all together?"

Magnus's eyes grew wide. "What did you say?"

Jobar repeated himself, but Magnus cut him off. "Do you have the images and the map?"

"Yes, I have them now; I will go over them and . . ." "Yes, yes . . . contact us in your morning . . . got to go old chap." Magnus switched off and sat, contemplating what he knew of celestial navigation, but it was not his area of expertise. He calmly walked down the hall to Dorathy's room.

Jobar stared at the images, still gripping his communicator and looked in awe at what seemed very familiar to him. "My heavens, I think they found it!"

CHAPTER 40

K ore was sitting at her desk with her beloved pet sitting at her feet wearing a harness and his favorite red cap propped on top of his head. She had decided to take a leave of absence from her mundane daily grind and was clearing her desk and her schedule. She had Silas taken out of his typical work rotation in order to be at her beck and call, his penance for allowing her prize to escape.

She looked down and cooed, "Nikko my love we are going on a dreaded trip to track down this Patsup fellow." Nikko cocked his head to the side as he tried to process her intent. Her gaze shifted as her assistant entered her office. "I have moved your appointments and have your ship ready for departure."

"Good." Kore glared at her pretty young assistant, "Now get out of my sight." Her assistant knew better than to think she was going to get any praise for having done her task in such short notice. She turned on her heels and thought how nice the next few days were going to be with Prime Minister Athanatos's absence.

Kore boarded her ship with Nikko in tow. He started to pant and whine, pulling against his harness. She gave him a firm tug, and he squealed and cowered in fear that she might punish him. She growled under her breath as she handed him off to Silas. "Take him, I don't have the patience for this nonsense."

Silas did as he was told and felt repulsed by this strange creature. He bent down and Nikko put his arms around his neck and smiled his gnarled toothed grin. Silas turned his head as Nikko's breath was nearly as offensive as his owner's. Together they boarded with the creature in his arms.

Kore screamed, "Put him down and get me to the planet Alger, we are going back to the deep mining docking station. I need to have a conversation with that flight controller."

Silas propped Nikko on a jump seat in the back of the cockpit and lowered his tall athletic frame into the pilot seat and with nimble figures he punched in the coordinates. He glanced to his side to see Kore watching his every move and wondered why she had chosen to keep him after he allowed the travelers ship to escape. For a moment Kore wished for younger years and shrugged off the pain of loneliness as she turned the other way.

Silas took the controls and effortlessly guided the ship to a high orbit as they lurched into the blackness of night. "Arrival time will get us to our destination at shift change."

"Excellent, we should easily be able to track Mr. Patsup down for questioning."

Nikko was pawing at the back of Kore's seat and she reluctantly gave in to his request for comfort. "Okay, come sit on my lap you silly creature." Nikko climbed up and leaned into her as she stroked the hair out of his eyes. "See it's not so bad."

Kore was in a pleasant mood and felt somewhat at ease with her strapping young pilot. "Tell me Silas do you have a family of your own?"

He was caught off-guard as in all the time he had served her she never asked about him on a personal level. He lied, "No ma'am."

Kore smiled, "No women in your life?"

Silas was getting uncomfortable at this line of questioning and asserted a quick and simple, "No."

She felt pleased and sad all at the same time. Slipping into her own thoughts of a family she had lost at a young age and her descendants she knew she had, proof in the images she had kept with her over the decades. The images had been passed down to her by the parents she never knew. Discovering her past was something she needed and had spent most of her life trying to find the answers to. Always wondering who the people were in her album, he said under her breath, "Today I will get my answers come hell or high water."

Patsup rose early after a sleepless night and decided going to work was better than tossing around in bed. His brother Jobar was once again planning to be off-planet which was no doubt going to be yet another wild "portal" fiasco. He wondered how Jobar and Coolie for all these years managed to make such a good living that afforded them to live the way they did, having such expensive ships, nice homes, and always off on some adventure. This was something he had always wanted for himself but was never able to provide, which left skepticism on how honestly they made their living.

Patsup with his morning brew in hand sat at his desk when the flight manager burst into his office. "Prime Minister Athanatos's ship is due to arrive anytime, and she has requested a private meeting with you!"

"With me?" Patsup almost choked on his hot concoction, "Wy me?" Suddenly he grew pale as he feared he had done something incredibly stupid in a moment of weakness and out of pure spite. He buried his face in his hands. "You need to cover for me, tell her I've left unexpectedly on a family emergency, no tell her I have left the planet, I have no family!"

His flight manager said in shock, "You want me to lie to her?"

"Damn it all to hell, tell her whatever you want but I'm leaving!" Patsup got up and grabbed his jacket, nearly knocking over his flight manager in the process. "You never saw me!"

Patsup ran to the hangar where his little ship was being stored, boarded and took off without logging out, not having a clue on where to go.

Kore's ship dropped into orbit and came in hot for landing as Patsup hurtled into space without any direction. When the coast was clear he contacted Jobar and told him to do the same and why.

"You did what! What the hell is wrong with you, have you lost your damn mind? Why in God's creation would you jeopardize my future, our livelihood, are you insane?"

Patsup was nearly sobbing, "I can't stand how everything comes to you so easily and always going on adventures with Coolie, you never once invited me on any of your trips."

"Oh, for holy sakes, you are always preaching to us how stupid we are for seeking the portal, so why would I ever invite you along? Regardless, now we could be fugitives thanks to you!"

Patsup cried, "I'm sorry . . . what am I going to do?"

Jobar had to think fast. "I'm going to send you coordinates, I will be leaving here shortly. Thank the maker Mares is off-planet and hopefully we still have a home to go to after all this. Do you know how annoying you are?"

Jobar contacted Coolie and brought him up to speed. "Oh my goodness, tell me he didn't!"

"For heavens' sake just get over to my ship, meet me there as soon as possible! We need to figure this out and the sooner the better! The last thing we need is the Prime Minister crawling up our asses!"

CHAPTER 41

Magnus walked up to Dorathy's door, hesitated momentarily and knocked. It was no secret to the crew that there was an attraction between Dorathy and Henry, but for whatever reason they were both trying to hide it. Magnus thought it made no difference at this point of the mission, as it really was all about survival up until now. He did wish he could have someone to lean on, loneliness creeping into him like a cold fog obscuring his view of what was important, forgetting what it was to be human.

Henry moved to the single chair of her small room while Dorathy invited Magnus in. "Dora, sorry to interrupt, but I think I may be on to something with these images of the pyramid."

She motioned for him to sit next to her on her bed. "Please, tell me what you have. It seems we could all do with a morale boost."

Magnus nodded in agreement. "Yes, and I think we might be getting close to our objective. I have been shuffling through copies of the images taken at the lost city. We all agree that these markings represent constellations, but what if I was to say that perhaps they represent the same constellation seen from a different perspective in space."

Dorathy looked closer at the markings, her senses a bit sharper than they were a few hours ago. Her eyes grew wide. "Yes . . . yes of course you're right! Look, they each have the same number of stars and are represented by its absolute magnitude, which means how bright a star appears at a standard distance of 32.6 light years. The carvings are precise in detail and I can figure out . . ." Something caught Dorathy's attention as familiarity set in. "These are all the constellation Orion!"

Henry got up and joined them on the side of the bed. "Look all seven stars are here, each one with a different magnitude depending on the view from the perspective from which they are seen."

Dorathy jumped up. "I'm going to the main lab, and I want to pull up the map again." They all hurried to the lab and Magnus brought the views up on 3D imaging. "Okay we have these twelve random planets. And something tells me when Dimitri is done extracting the information from my DNA there will be a thirteenth . . . just a wild guess. I think I can find these planets if I can decipher the seven stars' alignment to the planet by using their absolute magnitude to that particular planet. It's not much to go by, but it's what we got."

Dimitri lumbered into the lab, looking tired and disappointed as he downloaded his work and a new image appeared. "Yes, you are right; your DNA didn't solve anything, it just added to the problem. We now have thirteen rouge planets to figure out."

Dorathy looked up at the images floating over her head and said, "Thirteen false doors, just like the Pyramid of Djoser."

Henry looked puzzled. "I don't follow."

Dorathy leaned against the inner hull of the ship, feeling it throbbing against her back as she pondered. "Essentially we are looking for a gate or a portal . . . a door. If we find these planets, perhaps we find the door." She lifted the images of the carvings and held them up in the air. "We find the planets by aligning them to these stars."

Brenda startled awake as she heard the commlink buzz with an incoming call. "Oh for heaven's sake now what?" She turned on the light and rubbed her eyes, not having a clue whether it was morning or night. "Shit, they must all be in the lab." Brenda growled under her breath, "Wish someone would pick that up . . . damn. Hello Jobar, how are you doing my little friend?"

"Not very well, not well at all . . . we need to meet with you right away to discuss the map and our current situation."

"Okay, well come on over. We're just hanging out in our usual place . . . you know . . . in the middle of freaking nowhere."

Jobar sensed her irritation and thought he should not give his friends any more of Coolie's spirits. It was becoming apparent they could not handle the strong drink. "Okay Brenda we will be there shortly."

"Yay, I can hardly wait," she said sarcastically. She hung up and rolled over.

The group worked on local star charts they had been given years ago by Jobar. After a few hours without success Dorathy yawned, "Well gang, I'm whipped and I'm turning in. I have no concept of time; all I know is I'm tired and I'm going to bed."

Manus agreed and pushed away from the table. "Sounds like a good idea." He followed Dorathy out of the lab and stopped her at the door. "Goodnight my dear."

"You too, Magnus." She smiled as she closed her door.

Magnus was too tired to think about his solitude and turned in.

Dimitri tried to follow suit, but before he could escape, Henry grabbed him by the arm. Talking in a whisper Henry asked, "Hey Dim, what do you know about cloning?"

Dimitri shrugged his shoulders. "Enough."

"Look, if I gave you some DNA can you do it here on the ship?"

Dimitri looked at him sideways. "What are you talking about . . . you want to clone a woman for that English prick?"

Henry smiled. "Can you do that?"

Dimitri laughed. "Seriously?"

"No", he chuckled. "I want to cheer Dorathy up by cloning the little dog she had as a kid. His cremated remains and a baggie of fur were with her in the cryotube, so can it be done?"

Dimitri thought for a moment and ran through a mental list of equipment available. "Yeah, something small like that, yes. No problem. It will give me something to do and get my mind off all the other bullshit." Dimitri smirked. "Don't tell anyone, but I like little dogs, they are good women magnets."

Henry grinned. "Chick magnets."

"Yes, chick magnets," Dimitri said, remembering his old days. They both smiled with thoughts of their previous lives

Kore took Nikko firmly by his harness and led him out the hatch of the ship. Thick air hit them in the face while the gravity reaped havoc on her joints. Nikko squirmed, trying to climb back into the cool air of the ship. Kore grumbled under her breath, "This had better be a short trip."

The flight manager sat in Patsup's office trying to come up with an excuse why Patsup was no longer on planet, cursing him for leaving him in such a bind. Kore was coming straight for him, making a beeline from the nearby air strip. He pondered what he was going to say and decided the truth was his best option, but the less said the better.

She kicked in the door. "I want to speak with Mr. Patsup, where might I find him?"

The flight manager peered over the monitor, pretending to be busy. "Patsup is off-planet."

Kore's eyes grew wide and her face a splotchy red. "Off-planet! I was told he would be here and there was no scheduled departure!"

"He had an emergency."

Kore's eyes narrowed in a cold stare from beneath her hat. "Then you had better tell me where he has gone!"

"Sorry to say he left in such a hurry he didn't log out, must have been pretty upset and very urgent for him to have done that."

Kore knew all regulatory ships had trackers on them. "Then you better find out his tracking frequency and give it to me."

The flight manager hit a few keys and brought up the information. "I can transfer this to your ship, but it is a short-range frequency as it is not a commercial vehicle."

"Damn you, man! How is this possible? How can he have a private ship?"

All the flight controller could do was shrug his shoulders. "It's a very old ship and in need of repairs. Frankly I don't even know how he got it off the ground."

Kore's anger grew to almost the point of boiling and she wanted her answers now, but knew it would have to wait. Frustration was building and her patience growing thin. She turned on her heel. "I will be back, and next time I won't be as accommodating."

Kore boarded her ship with Nikko in tow. She commanded Silas, "pull up the tacking frequency of the ship and transfer it to all our patrol ships in the area. Someone is bound to come across it."

Silas silently did as he was told, wishing the day would end, knowing his resolve was rapidly approaching.

Kore stared out over the airstrip and thought of the ship in her images. She said to herself, "Where are you my friends, and what mysteries are you hiding? Oh I will find you, wherever you might be hiding, I won't stop until I find you."

Coolie met Jobar at the main mining airfield, where all commercial ships were logged in and out in the arrivals and departures department. Jobar had been an independent miner for years and knew his way around the system. Coolie sat in the co-pilot seat, aware of what he had been doing. "Jobar, one day they are going to get wise to your little contraption."

Jobar shook his head. "By then I'll be retired, so I'm not too concerned." His little invention worked like a charm by sending out false coordinates for his destination and he had rigged the ship's tracker long ago. Occasionally he would comply with regulations as not to bring attention to himself, but today was not one of those days.

Jobar sent Patsup the coordinates. "We are going to pick Patsup up first. He will just have to leave his ship adrift; I don't want it anywhere near our friends as it is no doubt being tracked."

Coolie interjected, "He will not like that plan—if Kore puts a trace on his tracker, they will find it and confiscate it."

Jobar shot back, "Well, he should have thought of that before he hung us out to dry."

Coolie shook his head. "I sometimes wonder about him."

Jobar rolled his eyes in agreement. "I sometimes can't believe the same blood flows through our veins."

A short while later, Jobar's ship dropped into empty space and waited patiently for Patsup to arrive. Once there, Jobar locked with Patsup's much smaller ship and opened the airlock. He scowled at Patsup who stood there with his head hung low. "You are more trouble than you are worth. Hurry aboard, as I'm sure we don't have much time."

Patsup stopped. "What about my ship?"

"Leave it!" Jobar demanded. "We don't have time for this crap. They have no doubt put a trace on it."

Patsup knew he was right and hurriedly joined them on Jobar's ship. Jobar quickly shut the airlock door and disengaged. Coolie was already at the controls as they headed for their friends' usual spot in the middle of deep space, far off the beaten track. Jobar looked back at Patsup sitting quietly, regretting what he had done. "Look, from here on out you need to keep your mouth shut! I mean it, if you even hint to anyone about this trip I will kill you myself!"

Patsup's voice cracked, "What about Prime Minister Athanatos?

"We will have to deal with her later . . . she currently isn't looking for Coolie and me, she is looking for you because she thinks you can lead her to our friends' ship and I will not allow that to happen. We will have to find a way to distract her and I suggest you think of a way out of this mess. Jobar was far beyond angry and was now hovering around, furious. He needed to put some space between himself and his brother. "I'm going to get some rest before our arrival." Coolie was already snoozing, head propped against the hull of the cockpit with the controls on auto pilot. Jobar, still seething without the ability to restrain himself, spat in Patsup's direction. "If you were not my brother, I would kill you where you stand, here and now! Completely unforgivable!"

Patsup lowered his eyes in regret as he thought of how many family members he had put at risk with his little stunt. He struggled with a solution to Kore's involvement, knowing she would stop at nothing.

Brenda stretched and yawned, not ever knowing what day or time it was. To her the years had blended together in one nightmarish reality. She wandered into the lab. The lights were dimmed, and the thirteen planets still hung in the eerie silence. Sitting for a moment, she looked at the scale and although clustered together, she knew the planets must be light years apart. She stood and moved to the center of the images floating over her head, looking in every direction. Peering into the space surrounding the planets at every angle, all she saw were distant, faint stars represented by dim lights twinkling at the edges of the image. It was then that something familiar caught her eye, three stars in a row, yearning to be found. Brenda whispered, "Well I'll be goddamned!"

Brenda now shouted at the top of her lungs as the rest of the stars came into play, "Damn, I'm so goddamned smart! Rise and shine assholes, I'm your new best friend!"

Dorathy, nestled in Henry's strong arms, shifted in her bed. "What is she going on about now, God what time is it . . . oh my head . . . what day?"

Henry glanced at his atomic watch he never really paid that much attention to, as time was no longer a constant. He rubbed his eyes. "Guess I better go check it out, being the commander of this ship and all."

Dorathy chuckled, "Right, you keep on thinking that, but I think that ship has sailed."

Henry could only smile.

Henry and Dorathy were met in the lab by Magnus and Dimitri, Dimitri stubbing his toe as he stumbled in. "What the hell is wrong with you, woman?"

Brenda stood within the 3D image, waving at them from her spot in the middle of the planets hovering at eye level. "How much will you give me if I tell you I know where these damn things are? At least I think I know where they are. That confirmation is a job is for Dorathy. After all, she is the astrophysicist amongst us. Come over here girlfriend and take a gander."

Dorathy did as she was asked, curiosity getting the best of her. Brenda took a step back. Dorathy knew Brenda was not easily excited and, as their eyes met, Dorathy was compelled to view from her vantage point. Brenda pointed in the direction she wanted Dorathy to look. After a short moment, Dorathy's eyes grew wide. She stepped aside then moved to the outer edge of the image, and then stared back in the opposite direction. Dorathy spoke softly and was very concise. "Magnus, can you shrink the image of the planets, leaving the surrounding stars at scale?"

Magnus did as he was asked without even taking a breath. The image shrank down to where the planets looked as they were, but just a smaller version of their original scale. Dorathy shook her head. "No shrink it more . . . a lot more." Magnus looked up and could see where she was going. He brought it down as far as it would go. The planets disappeared and all that remained was a dusty cloud with a few specks of light shining from within. Dorathy gazed upon the vastness of space condensed into a small 3D image that hovered in all its glory that filled the very room they were sitting in.

Dorathy saw the vision in her mind's eye and had been suddenly transported to a time when she was a kid looking into the cosmos through her telescope in wonderment, "My God," she said, her voice barely a whisper, "Of course, thirteen rogue planets discovered ages ago. These planets are in the Orion Nebula."

Henry stood from where he had been seated. "Are you positive?"

"Yes, come here and look." Henry went to stand next to her. "You can even make out the Trapezium Cluster," she said, pointing to a small grouping of young stars. Dorathy strode to the opposite side of the room with her back against the wall. "If I were Earth, this is the view I would have of the seven main stars. The nebula is the center star of Orion's sword, which is also the furthest point in the constellation. We peer into space from the nebula . . ." Dorathy made haste to the cloudy cluster, looking back to where she had been. "The configuration is not quite the same but you can still almost see the similarities."

Magnus took a deep breath. "I hate to be the one to point this one important fact out, but we still don't know where the nebula is from here. Wherever *here* is . . . exactly."

Everyone took a moment for that to sink in and to consider the utter unimaginable vastness of the space around them. The silence in the room was only matched by the vacuum that lay inches away.

Everyone sat in silence as the excitement had been blown out of the room, when the commlink buzzed from the cockpit. Brenda, her shoulders slouched, said, "I'll get it, its Jobar, he called earlier and said he needed to meet with us . . . something terrible had happened."

Dorathy sat and said, "Even if I had all my equipment at my disposal it could take a lifetime to find our vantage point."

Henry buried his head in his hands. "Well that's good because we were designed to last several."

Brenda sat at the pilot seat looking out at the billion specs of light. "Hello Jobar, how are you doing?"

Jobar sounded distressed. "We will be there shortly; we have much to discuss. I have my brother with us; he has done something incredibly stupid. I do have information regarding your map, but I don't know how helpful it will prove to be."

"Fine," Brenda replied. "We're here in our usual spot."

Having docked with their unusual ship many times through the years, it had become second nature to Jobar. "We will do our docking procedures in a few moments, could you be ever so kind and please have some hot tea for us?"

"Yeah sure, no problem . . . and by the way we need to get some supplies soon."

"Yes, we will discuss that further when we arrive . . . it may not be so simple anymore."

Brenda frowned at the commlink, wondering what that was all about, and thinking that *simple* was not the term she would have used. "Okay, whatever you say." The signal went dead as she sat and thought about what kind of trouble they must be in.

Well whatever . . . she thought as she made her way back to the main lab. "I'm going to make some tea, anyone want any? Jobar, Coolie and Jobar's brother are coming aboard. Guess they have a lot to tell us concerning the map and the kind of trouble they seem to be in. The group's spirits were at an all-time low and now the thought of more bad news coming from Jobar was almost too much to bear

Henry slouched in his chair and tried to sound optimistic. "Look, he says he has information about the planets. They have been a great asset over the years, so let's hope he has something useful for us."

The ship shuttered a moment as the airlock engaged. The inner hatch slid open and the three entered. Jobar and Coolie embraced their friends as Patsup took in their ship. Jobar grabbed at Patsup, "This is my younger brother. He has been a non- believer to the existence of the Otherlings and to the portal, but now maybe he has changed his tune.

Patsup gasped, "Your ship . . . it's alive! Its shape is extraordinary, and it undulates as if it were breathing space!"

"Yes, it is . . . we believe it converts energy from dark matter and other exotic matter it comes across. It keeps us safe and warm on the inside and protects us from hazards coming from space. It is also multidimensional. Henry was very proud of their ship and spoke as if he were its father. "Also, carbon dating revealed it to be as old as the universe itself."

"Astonishing!" was all Patsup could muster.

Brenda finally pleaded, "Come into the lab, I have your tea steeping."

They walked towards the rear of the ship and entered the main lab. Patsup tripped over his own feet, looking up in astonishment. "Oh my, what have you gotten into?"

Jobar cut Patsup off sharply. "What we discuss here is never to leave this ship!"

"Yes, I know." Patsup whined, "You have already told me a dozen times in the last ten minutes."

Jobar lost patience easily when it came to his brother. "Go sit down AND don't interrupt!"

Magnus poured their tea and a cup for himself and stationed himself at the console. He switched dimensions of the scale of the holographic image floating over their heads and the planets all came into focus, hovering in a cluster surrounded by dust and gas. "Here are the thirteen rogue planets. By the looks of them, they consist of gas, water vapor and possible amino acids. Now when I shrink the image you can see where they are positioned amongst the stars in that area of space. We are familiar with this part of space because it is where we are from."

Jobar pinched his chin with the look of utter confusion by the image that now hovered over his head. "My friends, I am at a loss for I don't have an explanation for what my eyes are showing me here in this room. We know those planets and their location, but what troubles me is the surrounding space."

The group looked at on another, bewildered. Henry spoke first. "I don't get it Jobar, what are you talking about, what's wrong with the space?"

Jobar and Coolie looked at each other and both shook their heads. Coolie said, "Well simply put, we have never seen any of the outlying stars that you have illustrated here." Jobar continued, "Those stars are not supposed to be there."

Everyone in the room wore foggy looks. Dorathy began to speak but hesitated while she struggled to find the right words. "Okay, give me a moment here. What you are saying is, you know where this nebula is and the planets within . . . but you are also saying, that everything else is . . . gone?"

Jobar, collecting his thoughts said, "Gone would indicate that they once existed. what I'm saying, but I'm no oracle, is that those stars that you have indicated have **never** existed."

Coolie added, "We learned about the nebula as you call it in school." He went on to recite, "It is the most distant place in the universe and shines in the night sky marking the edge of creation in the blackness of space. It stands alone like a beacon in the darkest of skies."

Dorothy's mind was racing, trying to make sense of it all. "Everything here in your space is teaming with life in relatively close proximity. The image that we got from the lost city is an accurate description of our space, the space from which we came . . . you are telling me that the same space around this nebula is . . . dark?"

"Yes", Jobar said without hesitation. "I cannot explain it." Jobar looked down at his feet, feeling as if he had aged decades over the last few hours and his heart sank. "My friends, I know where these planets are and, regardless of how their appearances differ from our world to your world, does not change the fact that they are on the other side of our known universe. And to complicate matters, they have been deemed restricted and completely off limits."

Coolie added, "None of our ships are even capable of making a journey of that length . . . it would take forever!"

Henry was taken aback. "What do you mean restricted . . . by whom?"

Coolie sighed. "By the New Western Ordinance, eons ago . . . not that it mattered as no one could ever possibly make the journey there and back. We know it as Restricted Space due to our profession as deep space miners, but it was never an issue."

Dorothy sat back in her chair, taking it all in. "Excuse me for stating the obvious, but this ship and my cryotube got us all here, so this ship can take us back."

Henry cut her off. "I'm sorry Dora but they're right, we were all frozen during the duration of the trip. You saw the condition of your cryotube, it looked like it had been out there for centuries. Time, the way we know it, just doesn't exist here. The Illuminati came here ages ago to start their New World Order and a whole new civilization along with it. My guess is that they used the same technology to make the trip and were also frozen . . . they had to have been. These guys are deep space miners, they have reached the limits in their profession."

Dorothy hung her head as tears formed. "I can't even guess what significance there is to these thirteen planets. All I know is, if miners have crossed paths with the golden beam of the portal then someone is using it."

As one, the group stared at Dorathy's proclamation and looked at each other as their mental wheels began turning. Jobar spoke first. "Who would be using the portal and how could anyone have found it?"

Dorathy shook her head, her face streaked with tears. "Just a thought, but the Otherlings would be my guess."

Patsup's eyes were wide and alert. "Oh no, something tells me we are going to attempt a crazy pilgrimage to the edge of space through the dreaded dark matter!"

Dorathy's eyes flashed, "What did you say?"

CHAPTER 42

Kore sat alone in her cold darkened home with only her thoughts to guide her. How many years had she contemplated the existence of their New Western Ordinance? The founding fathers were said to have come from some unknown place in space and with them they brought order to the cosmos. Wars among the races had ended, replaced with technological advancements; worlds had prospered. The proof of their origins she now held in her hand.

She looked at Nikko lying in his bed and whispered, "What secrets lie in that long forgotten, frozen rock?"

Nikko looked up at her and cocked his head to the side, ears perking up as she spoke. Her thoughts were racing through her mind. *I need to find a way in, but how?*

Finally, the call she had been waiting for came. As her communicator beeped, she hastily grabbed for it. "Yes, is this the director of antiquities? Yes . . . yes, I have something that you might find very interesting. I have had it in my possession for quite some time and no one else knows of it. Yes, tomorrow works. I will bring the item and my old log of images. I need not remind you the urgency of this matter and stress our confidentiality agreement. Do not cross me or you will pay for your mistake."

The appointment was set, and she ended the call. Staring at the glowing embers flickering in the darkness, she thought about the mysteries hidden away. Why now, after so many millennia, do these strange travelers show themselves?

Kore fell asleep in her large, old crumpled chair, her legs tucked to the side, her heavy blanket over her ears. Nikko grabbed the iron rod and stoked the fire as he had watched his master do a thousand times before, and bathed in its warmth, he curled up in his bed. Tomorrow, he somehow knew, was going to be different from the rest. He had felt something change in his master that he had not seen before—he felt it was positive and even without the ability to verbalize, he somehow knew things were going to become a bit more interesting.

Morning came too quickly for Nikko. He lay in his bed with his thorny head down, his eyes following Kore's every movement. "Get up, it's time to eat your breakfast, my sweet little boy, we have a very full day and I don't want you whining for food later." Nikko stretched, and hopped out of his warm bed. He made his way to the table, dragging his blanket behind him. He dreaded mornings, as they were chilling to the bone, the air thin and dry at their high elevation. Kore's old stone home was built like a fortress at the peak of a jagged mountain which was covered in snow most of the year. The thick fog would roll over the mountains and settle into the valley below covering everything with a cold damp drizzle. The skies above were grey and overcast, the sun barely rising over the peaks this time of year. It was a desolate harsh environment and only the hardiest of species managed to survive.

The dishes cleared, she grabbed her cloak, helped Nikko into his sweater, and the two climbed into her antigravity mobile. It was a small craft that seated two occupants, the driver in front and a passenger in the back with a small space in the rear for stowage. Nikko wished he had the ability to fly on his own, but he had been born with very small and malformed wings. Kore had acquired him from a keeper when his mother abandoned him as an infant. His savaged larger undomesticated species came from only one distant planet. Most systems had placed the planet under interdiction due to its indigenous crop of opioids.

Kore and Nikko sat in the dark, dingy office amidst the musty smell of old books that lay in heaps, covered in dust that had collected over the decades. The Director of Antiquities had held the position for quite some time. He was a man who preferred the old ways of doing things and regarded technology as a burden. He collected his books and artifacts and cataloged them in his journal, never finding the time to properly arrange them. Dim winter light struggled to shine through his fogged picture windows, making the dust motes floating through the air glimmer and casting long shadows over his cluttered desk. Prime Minister Kore Athanatos was not accustomed to waiting for anyone or anything, but she would make allowances this one time as she desperately needed answers to the mysteries she held in her possession.

The quiet, old curator pushed his way through his office door with his robust backside, arms laden with the stacks of folders and image books he had acquired from an abandoned underground storage locker that had lain untouched for years. "So sorry, Prime Minister, for my tardiness, but I had to spend most of the night digging through old files pertaining to your request. I do think you will be pleased with what I have found."

Kore was not known in this sector for her patience or her tolerance but today was not the time to voice her opinion; she simply wanted answers and now after all her years of searching, she finally had a clue to the artifacts she had held for so many years. "Enough with your excuses. Please sit down so we can continue with our business without further delay."

From the neck of her cloak she pulled a small crystal pyramid amulet that was hanging from a heavy chain made of an unknown metal. Inside the amulet was a red and dark glowing matter that had been preserved in a vacuumed environment for millennia. The curator's eyes grew large at the artifact that was suspended on the chain she held. It was hypnotic as it swung by the chain—it was the missing link he had been searching for his entire career.

"My God, do you know what you possess?"

Kore studied the item she held. "If I knew, I would not be here waiting for you in this dirty dingy antiquated office. But please, enlighten me for the love of hell, because I have been searching for answers for many years and am at my wit's end. So tell me before I have you taken off to the gallows!"

Kore pulled the chain over her head and handed the item to the curator as he adjusted the magnifying lens he had flipped down over one eye. "This substance is mystical and has given our scientists plenty to theorize about over the centuries. What you have is the substance that is believed to have created our universe, so you can only imagine its importance to . . . well, to be blunt, to all of mankind. This is truly the most remarkable archeological find since . . . well . . . since . . . a long while. This, my dear woman, is most likely the product of the Otherlings!"

Kore rolled her eyes. "Oh please, spare me from these ancient fairytales. I did not come all this way for you to tell me a bedtime story."

The curator sighed and leaned back in his old leather chair. "Regardless of what you may think, I am telling you the importance of this discovery." He held her artifact up as the light shone through the crystal relic casting a rainbow of colors in all directions, the substance within glowing red as the sunlight hit it.

"So, tell me, Prime Minister, how did you come to possess this capstone?"

"How I came to own this item is none of your business. What I want to know is what the meaning of it is." Kore turned to lean down in order to remove her image book from her bag. She placed it down with a thump atop the dusty desk, causing a cloud to form. When she activated it, the holographic image appeared hovering, filling the dusty room with a hazy 3D image of the travelers' ship. "So, tell me Doctor Hoffman, what do you make of this?"

Hoffman peered up at the image filling his small office. He sat there, ram rod straight in his seat, and was rendered speechless.

"Nothing?" she pressed, "You must have some idea of this ship's origins."

My God, woman, you are full of surprises," he exclaimed as he smiled broadly in her direction. Kore was not accustomed to anyone ever smiling at her, especially of the male species and this made her feel vaguely uncomfortable.

In her most feminine voice, she begged, "Please, Dr. Hoffman, what do you know of this ship?"

Meanwhile Patsup thought as the words left his mouth and he looked at his older brother and Coolie, and spoke with alarm in his voice, "You cannot possibly be serious about this. Dark matter is where our religion states Hell and its residence exist; to cross over, one would have to have the blackest of hearts." Coolie and Jobar rolled their eyes as they did not possess the patience for Patsup's silly superstitious beliefs.

Jobar closed his eyes to clear his flailing mind. "My friends, regardless of what my narrow-minded brother believes the journey cannot be made, it is simply too far away."

Dorathy shook her head in defiance. "We can't just give up on this!" Pointing to Jobar, she said, "You both have been searching for the portal most of your life! I'm telling you it exists, the Otherlings and the other side exists, and we now have the *proof* that it exists. I'm betting the answers we all have been searching for are on those thirteen planets!" Dorathy sounded desperate. "There has got to be a way of traveling through your *Dark Matter* that makes time irrelevant in space travel; gravity slows time, dark matter has mass . . . we have to start thinking in unconventional ways. Assuming we are in a five-dimensional space, we have to stop thinking in four dimensional terms; there is so much more to it, we just have to stretch our imagination and find a way!"

The room fell silent as each of them reflected on the possibilities. Brenda got up and rubbed her neck. "Look everyone, I think she's right . . . I'm not saying we have the answers or that we will ever find an answer, but she is right. We've spent several years out here getting to know the place but thinking in terms we are familiar with—we need to start thinking differently because the playing field has changed."

Dimitri added, "The playing field was always different, we were just playing the wrong game."

Henry sighed, "Well, hell, we've gotten this far, and things seem to present themselves when we least expect them, so let's try and figure it out."

Jobar stammered, "Before everyone gets excited about the possibilities, we have to address one more issue: that being my younger brother and his stupidity." Patsup hung his head in embarrassment as Jobar continued, "My dear brother has brought you to the attention of Prime Minister Athanatos and that is why she was lurking just outside of the Lost City waiting for us. No doubt, she will attempt to determine the significance of the planet and try to gain access. It is rumored that she is a direct descendant of as we now know is your original New World Order and you, my friends, will have a much harder time gaining access to all nearby systems. Fear not though, we can find ways of eluding her."

With all that they had been through, this seemed like a minor difficulty. Henry shrugged his shoulders, "Well, that's the least of our problems . . . and so what? If she gets suddenly interested in the Lost City, she'll have a hell of a time gaining access to any of it. Even if she does, it won't hold a hell of a lot of meaning. Sounds like it has the same degree of validity as the thirteen planets; they are there and everyone knows they're there, but no one really seems to give a damn. To me, this plays in our favor, she'll spend most of her time trying to find us and not trying to find the significance to us being here. All we have to do is avoid her . . . go under cover. Which brings us to our next problem—we are running low on supplies."

Jobar scratched his head in thought. "Okay, I know of an undeveloped planet. Many have raided it for its natural resources without much of a fight from the indigenous people who live there. I doubt very much anyone would be looking for you there. It will be very easy to hide your identity since the natives are fully cloaked when outside. Its star's radiation is far too intense and can be searing at times, but regardless food grows in abundance there. Anything else you might require I can get . . . it is the least we can do for you."

"Henry stood, stretched his back and clapped his hands. "Okay people, let's move like we have a purpose; everyone put a list together of what we need in supplies from your department. Hey Jobar, they take cash or credit there?"

Jobar squinted his brows together, "Sorry . . . what?"

Henry laughed, "Never mind."

Dr. Hoffman gazed at the image floating over his head, while he searched for the right words. "This ship has had very little documentation attached to it. Whilst digging around I only found one article pertaining to a top-secret mission of pure scientific discovery that involved a small crew chosen from our direct ancestors. They were sent in a ship constructed of a biological material that had signs of intelligence. The ship and its crew were sent into a higher dimension for one purpose: to retrieve an individual who had the code to access our mysterious thirteen planets embedded in her DNA."

Kore stared down at the doctor. "Absurd. What foolishness are you going on about? Our so-called ancestors came here thousands of years ago! This ship and its crew, whomever they are, could not possibly be from our past!"

The doctor sat back in his chair and crossed his arms on top of his round, protruding belly. He looked up to this fabled ship. Pointing to her image book with a confident smirk on his face, he said, "What you have in your possession, although not an original image album from the time, certainly bears an uncanny resemblance to the images I have from the ancients that came to us so may eons ago."

Kore stopped short in her questioning, her curiosity getting the best of her. "You have an original image of this ship in your possession?"

Feeling he had the upper hand, Dr. Hoffman simply said, "Yes, yes I do."

Her eyes wide with excitement, Kore demanded, "Where . . . you have to show it to me!"

Hoffman leaned forward with a smug smile on his lips and a spark in his eyes. "I will show you what you are seeking, but I want one promise from you in return."

She glared back; she was not very often in a position of helplessness. "Look my dear Doctor, I will take the information I need with or without your help . . . I would prefer that we work together," clearing her throat and hissing, "as a team."

Dr. Hoffman gleamed with approval. "Okay then, I will arrange to have lunch brought to us before we depart."

"Depart? Where do you have the information I seek? Kore was growing impatient and wanted answers. "Why is this information not here?"

"Prime Minister, this is not the type of thing we have out in the open, the information you seek is classified."

"Classified!" she screeched. "If it is classified why have I not been made aware of it?"

Hoffman said, looking through his magnifying lens, his one eye appearing walleyed, "I was called in decades ago to make an assessment on an ancient artifact that had been dug out from a dried lakebed. I was taken there so I could inspect it and cataloged what had been found and since that day it has been secured, its location secret, and I believe it to still be there. The reason I am sharing this information with you, other than the fact you have in your possession something of importance that could explain its significance, is that you, my dear lady, strike an unnerving resemblance to one of the occupants of your transient space craft."

Kore was rendered speechless. All her years spent searching for her ancestry, always having dead-end results; now she had a new twist to the core of her existence. She stared at the good doctor for what seemed to be a lifetime, finally gathering her thoughts, "How will we gain access to the information we seek?"

Hoffman was excited with pleasure from merely the thought of having the power to please this woman. All had deemed her in such unfavorable terms, but he knew that under every hardened façade lay an individual with a torrent past. A past that had sculpted the person she had become. Dr. Hoffman reached over and patted her rough weathered hands that had been gripping the edge of his dusty desk. "I believe you have the authority to get us in, if you act as if you are quite aware of its existence." Hoffman winked, "Act the part."

A sideways smile lingered on Kore's lips and her eyes sparkled as she dared a glance into her cohort's eyes, finding herself feeling young and attractive for the first time since she was a young woman.

Dr. Hoffman and Kore sat staring up at the image before them, both contemplating what the other wanted in return. Hoffman broke the silence that had enveloped the room. "This ship has always been thought of as lost, and its occupants from a place far away. I'm sure you are familiar with our questionable origins as there has never been any real proof of our evolution. I believe you are one of the few, being a direct descendant."

She sat, arms crossed, wondering how much Hoffman knew of their past. "The reason I am here is to know what you know about this ship and my little capstone, not to question how or why I have these artifacts in my possession."

Hoffman knew he was entering dangerous waters and knew that only with her help would he ever find the truth. "Okay I will share with you what I know, then perhaps you might find a reason to share with me any further information that might be advantageous for you to do so."

She pondered a moment and held out her hand, "Okay Dr. Hoffman, I trust you and I have come to an understanding."

Hoffman reached over his desk and clasped her frail hand in his as he leaned in and kissed it. "You can call me Allen."

She recoiled. "You can give me my amulet back."

CHAPTER 43

C oolie and Patsup disembarked, leaving Jobar to act as guild for the group's supply mission. Jobar gave his oldest friend a quick hug. Pointing to Patsup he said, "You do exactly as Coolie says, no questions asked. Get back to my home and remove all references to what we have been up to over the years, take the credits out of the safe box and destroy anything else that could lead anyone who might be looking. And tell our sister not to worry, the less she knows the better . . . tell her we are taking another vacation."

Patsup whined, "What about my job!" Jobar cut him off sharply by whacking him upside his head. "Your job now is to assist us and to do as you're told . . . forget it all . . . your old life is gone!"

Coolie grabbed Patsup by the sleeve and pushed him into the airlock, looking back as he switched the locking mechanism. "Be careful my friends, I will get this done thoroughly and in a timely fashion and will contact you shortly." There was a brief shutter as Jobar's ship disengaged and hurried on their way home.

Jobar look liked a man who had been beaten but was not down. "Okay my friends let me see if I can find a way to disguise ourselves as not to stand out . . . this should go smoothly without any hitches."

The group stood at the hatchway, preparing to disembark donning tattered looking cloaks that Jobar had assembled using blankets and old bits of coveralls and other remnants he could find lying around. Their bodies were covered from head to toe with just their eyes exposed. Jobar required that they wear goggles of some sort to not only protect their eyes from the harsh sunlight, but also to cover their eyes and faces from being seen, as the indigenous people had their own unique appearance. Brenda and Magnus were chosen to stay behind to watch over the ship and the mission in case something was to go wrong and they needed to lift off at a moment's notice.

Dorathy was clutching her sack and adjusting her goggles on her face as Henry opened the outer hatch, the solar radiation piercing the air where they stood. Brenda blocked the light from her eyes with her hand. "Good luck guys."

The land was stark and dry and devoid of anything that resembled food. The ship was hidden in a valley that appeared to be an ancient riverbed. Jobar assured the group that no one ever ventured out this far from the village. The group hiked for what seemed to be hours, taking in the desolate scenery, when at last they ascended over the cusp of the steep incline where they could now see the small village and the green farm land that stretched for miles surrounding it.

Dorathy peered out towards the horizon with an eerie feeling of déjà vu brewing in her gut, her eyes wide. "How is this possible . . . what type of irrigation have they developed to farm this land and what of the plants, how can they survive this intense radiation?"

Jobar explained their methods of creating water from the atmosphere from within the soil. "As far as the solar radiation, I guess life just seems to find a way to adapt. I fear this planet is doomed and before long it is highly likely the atmosphere will boil away in time."

Henry, looking at the village said, "Jobar, won't we be out of place and cause the locals to become curious of our being here?"

Jobar shook his head. "No, this place is not unfamiliar with visitors, but they are a rowdy bunch of settlers and can become bored very easily. We should make haste and get what we came for and be on our way quickly."

Henry looked at Dimitri and Dorathy. "Okay gang let's get in and out as fast as we can, we have more than enough credits to purchase what we need. Jobar will do the negotiating for us so follow his lead."

Approaching the village, they could see the market area and steep dirt roads leading up the mountain to the north. Most of the villagers had built their homes into the sides of the rocky outcroppings and caves using a system of lava tubes, creating a community that used the mountain as protection against the solar radiation. The air was still, and they could smell the peculiar scents of local grown fruits and vegetables lingering in this parched oasis.

Dorathy tightened the scarlet-colored scarf around her face to hide her identity and protect her altered skin from the searing sun. They walked through the village careful not to make a great deal of fuss and avoided prolonged eye contact with the locals. Jobar acted as interpreter and buyer, filling their huge back sacks quickly.

A stiff wind picked up suddenly and they could see a yellow darkness was fast approaching from the east. "Jobar said, almost yelling to be heard over the thunder echoing in the distance, "I was afraid this might happen, as we are in their monsoon season when massive dust storms are known to happen in these parts."

Henry shook his head motioning to his commlink. "I will have Magnus prep the ship for lift off and come get us just out of sight over behind the tree line."

Without warning, Dorathy's scarf blew off from around her face and she hurriedly chased it down as it whipped from one stall to the next. She now realized she had exposed her identity to the locals as they were packing their stalls in the wake of the approaching storm.

From behind Dorathy felt a firm grip as heavy hands wrapped around her waist, pulling her up and over his shoulders. Screaming to be heard, she dropped her sack of goods and successfully fought her way free when she felt a sharpness in her thigh and her world narrowed to blackness; nothing left but her scarf fluttering in the wind, impaled on a nearby post, and spewed vegetables on the dusty ground.

Henry had caught a glance of Dorathy as her scarf blew off and saw as she dashed to retrieve it. The very next thing he saw through the scurrying crowd was her scarf high up on a support post connecting the now wildly moving shade awnings. Henry pushed past Dimitri and Jobar only to find her sack spilled on the ground. He climbed up on a table to the objection of one of the locals and searched wildly for her, yelling her name as his voice was drowned in the wind. Henry reached up and grabbed her scarf, yelling at the local trying desperately to communicate the whereabouts to the owner of the brightly colored scarf.

Jobar and Dimitri ran over to investigate; they could see the horror in Henry's goggled eyes knowing something had happened to Dorathy in the last few seconds. Jobar started yelling to the local as she was hastily packing up. She yelled something back as she picked up her cart of goods and vacated with the others. Jobar shook his head in despair and yelled, "She saw her, but she was too busy to see what had happened. She said something about a mating ritual that perhaps she had been *chosen!*" Jobar bent over, his mind reeling as his heart sank, and put the vegetables back in her sack as he hoisted it over his shoulder. "We have to go now; these storms can be very dangerous. We will have to look for her later . . . there is not much we can do now!"

The wind was howling, and the dust was coming at them with such ferocity that if it weren't for their cloaks and goggles, their skin would be sand-blasted and eyes blinded. They slowly pushed their way to the other side of the tress as the ship came in for a landing, hovering almost motionless above the ground before gently landing in the dust whirling around them.

The hatch opened as they stumbled in, shaking the dust from their bodies. "Brenda looked past them outside with a puzzled look on her face. "Where the hell is Dora?"

Dimitri removed his goggles and scarf and calmly spoke. "She has been abducted by one of the locals."

"What! What the hell are you talking about!"

Henry put his hands on Brenda's shoulders. "She was taken . . . the storm came and there was a lot of chaos . . . and she was there one second and gone the next."

Brenda yelled now, "God damn it, we have to go back and get her!"

Jobar shook his head. "There is nothing we can do for her at the present time, we have to wait for the storm to pass."

Well shit . . . that could be hours!"

Henry walked past Brenda with Jobar and Dimitri following with their bags of goods, Brenda running after them saying, "Fuck you all, we land this fucking ship in town and come out firing . . . someone is bound to spit her out!"

Magnus heard the commotion and came into the main lab. "What the hell is going on back here?"

Brenda explained the situation and he said, "Well my dear they are right, we will go fetch her when the storm passes and best to do this in the cover of night."

"Brenda relax," Henry said. "She's a smart cookie and we all know she can handle herself—she is probably already working out her escape plan."

Doctor Allen Hoffman and Kore enjoyed each other's company while they sat for a quick bite to eat in the privacy of his cluttered office. Kore put a plate down for Nikko to enjoy. "You have been such a good boy." Hoffman loved animals and Nikko could feel his warm heart and jumped up on his lap for a scratch. "Hello fella, I must say he is an unusual choice for a pet."

Kore remembered the day she obtained him from an animal keeper who was considering having him put down due to his deformities as an infant, but she would not have it; she took him in and nursed him back to health.

Their meal finished, the three departed in Hoffman's personal transport ship for the underground storage facility. Kore was amazed, as this location was always been known to her as just another one of the many government installations. She never paid much attention to the conspiracy theories surrounding it. Many believed it to be far more interesting by saying it was a secret installation where the New Western Ordinance kept top secret advancements in technology and other speculative items.

The base was in the middle of nowhere, on a long time dried lakebed in a high desert valley surrounded by jagged mountains. On the outside, only a few tattered old hangars were visible clumped alongside an air strip that looked as if it were only occasionally used. There was no sign of any activity as they came in for a landing.

Kore smiled and laughed on their approach. "You mean to tell me that the rumors about this place are factual?"

Hoffman smiled, "My dear, never judge a book by its cover. The surface is just a façade to lead people to think nothing of importance is happening here when in fact lots of incredible things are being stored here."

After landing they noticed a single red light high up on a post shining bright as a warning not to proceed. The three of them approached an old airshaft with nothing but a heavy metal door concealing the entrance. Kore and Nikko were close on Hoffman's heels and Kore asked, "Allen where are you taking us, this seems very peculiar."

"Remember, act the part," he said, feeling confident that she could get them past the guards who were no doubt waiting within.

Hoffman pulled the door open, surprisingly finding it to be unlocked and only a single armed military personnel standing guard in front of an elevator shaft and a man sitting at a console who looked up at them, noticing Kore's insignia on the front of her cloak. A surveillance monitor from the ceiling cast down a circular beam that engulfed them in a bright green field of energy that left them immobile. Nikko screeched, trying to release himself from its grip and Kore hissed, "What is the meaning of this, do you know who I am? I demand you release us at once! We are here on official business and I will have you demoted for your lack of obedience!"

The man at the console seemed unaffected by her threats. "Standard procedure ma'am. As soon as I can verify who you are you will be free to establish contact with a controller."

Before she could protest any further the beam flickered out. "Okay madam Prime Minister, a controller will be here shortly to escort you to sublevel one where you can discuss your being here."

"This is absolutely unacceptable and completely unnecessary." With her taking another breath to voice her defiance the elevator door hissed open and with it a cold draft filled the small space that sent a shiver up their spines. Inside was a single occupant who wore an irritated stern look on his face, his body language showing his disapproval. Hoffman feared that perhaps he had been over-confident in the Prime Minister's authoritative ability to get them to sublevel fifty-one.

Kore was not accustomed to this type of procedure and usually had the upper hand with her demands; regardless, she held her head high and did not sway from her status that she had held for so many years. "I am Prime Minister Athanatos here on official business and this is Doctor Allen Hoffman, Director of Antiquities for the NWO History Gallery."

The man seemed unimpressed and agitated by the unexpected arrival of his unwelcomed guests. Sounding bored he responded, "I know who you are, the question is why you are here, and we will address that downstairs so come with me."

Kore went to protest to his behavior but refrained and they entered the elevator. The door hissed shut, leaving them in an eerie red glow as they descended. When the doors opened, they found themselves in an area that held countless offices with people buzzing around doing their daily routine. Kore's was confused as to where all the employees had come from as they followed their escort down a brightly lit hall. The starkness of the surface facades was quite effective in leading most to believe there was nothing of importance in this abandoned base.

Finally, the man came to a stop and opened the door to what seemed to be his office. "Please take a seat." They both sat, leaving Nikko curled up at Kore's feet.

The controller sat at his desk and asked, "So please tell me why have you shown up unannounced at this military facility? We don't get too many visitors here, not because we are so far removed from civilization but simply put, it is strictly off-limits. So, for you to show up as you have, I sure hope you are here for good reason . . . otherwise this is going to be a very short trip."

Kore was not one to mince words. She read the badge and insignia on his uniform. "Captain Simms, I am looking for information. It has been brought to my attention that you have in your possession artifacts that are important to my case."

Simms leaned back in his seat, "Oh really and what case might that be?"

The conviction that had driven her to this point in time was not about to leave her now. "My case, is to the find the true origins of our civilization." With that she pulled out of her bag her image book and slammed it on his desk and switched it on.

Captain Simms, although caught off-guard, clasped his hands on top of his desk and looked into Kore's eyes without a blink. "Where did you obtain this book?"

She was quick to respond and snapped back. "It does not matter where I got MY book, what matters is that I have it and I want answers!"

Simms rapped his fingers on his desk momentarily while he thought of his next move. "Well Madame Prime Minister and Doctor Hoffman, we have a bit of a problem here."

Kore looked at Simms with a piercing glare. "The only problem I foresee is your attempt at holding back the information I seek."

Simms smiled. "I need not remind you, of all people, there are procedures for this type of thing; you can't assume to have the clearance necessary to proceed any further than my desk. You don't honestly expect to . . ."

Kore reached into her buttoned-up uniform cloak and presented her amulet and Simms suddenly lost his words. Her words were concise and filled with a threatening undertone. "What I assume, is that you **will** cooperate."

At that moment Simms knew he was losing the upper hand. Every person who had gained access, instantaneously had their arrival documented in several departments in endless government offices, all in the name of security. "I cannot authorize you to proceed to the sublevel you are requesting."

Kore smiled. "We both know what this is and its importance, nor can you remove it from my possession. Simms knew she must have thoroughly covered all her bases with the Doctor's help. She chose her words carefully. "I have all the clearance I need to proceed, not only for what I have in my possession and the firsthand knowledge of what is being kept from public awareness, but with my governmental position as well. I am warning you, do not attempt to stand in my way."

Simms blurted out, "This is a military facility under the military's jurisdiction and . . ."

"And, Kore interjected, "under the control of the government to which I am appointed, therefore you are not in charge, I am. Your hands are tied Simms, now take me to sub level fifty-one."

Dorathy's senses were foggy as she struggled to gain consciousness. She reached for her eyes, only to find she had been chained at the wrists. She groaned in pain, her head throbbing, her ankles tied to some type of bed. Vision blurred she could make out that a faint light was filling the space. As things moved into focus, she saw she was in a type of adobe construction with wooden carved furniture tastefully placed. She felt a draft that chilled her skin and realized most of her clothing had been removed. She felt suddenly terrified as she came to grips with her situation. She whispered to herself, "Oh my God, where am I . . . where's Henry?"

As the drug wore off, she started to struggle against her restraints and could see she would require a key for the iron cuffs that had her held firmly in their grip. Her ankles had been tied with rope to the corners of the bed. "Think," she said to herself. She heard the heavy footsteps of her assailant approaching. With adrenaline pumping through her veins she knew she needed to outsmart her captor if she had any hope of coming out of this unscathed. What came around the corner shocked her to her core. This male specimen was big and bulky, skin hardened like some type of exoskeleton, with an outer rib cage that came down to a disproportionately narrow waist and hips. His huge penis hung partially erect, his testicles adorned with piercings and jewels. Dorathy struggled to remain calm, her breathing becoming erratic. She sobbed to herself, "This can't be happening! Stay calm!" She decided her best bet was to gain this creature's trust just long enough for him to unchain her. She turned her head to the side as she wiped away her tears on her bare shoulder when she spotted the key on the table beside her. She took a deep breath and gathered her thoughts and put on the best come- hither face she could muster.

Her bulky male companion seemed very thrilled with her positive response as he slowly moved onto the bed between her bound legs. Dorathy motioned with her eyes towards the key on the night table and gave her wrists a shake and looked into his large glowing eyes that laid in his head like pools of black oil. She spoke in a sultry hush, "Come on big guy, what fun would it be if I can't do anything for you." She knew he didn't comprehend her words but felt he might just get her meaning. She just prayed it would work and that he had the same sensitivities most men had in their groin area. As he buried his head in her neck, she could feel him becoming aroused against her thigh. She caught a glimpse of a heavy stone vessel on a stack of shelving parallel to the side of the bed. She moaned, "Come on now, unleash me," as she rattled her chains once more, and he leaned over and grabbed the key and she smiled at him, blowing him a kiss. He groaned something incomprehensible and slowly unlocked her wrists and gently released her, then slowly moved backwards and untied her ankles. "Be patient," she said to herself, planning her attack.

With one quick motion she pulled him towards her and threw his back to the bed, straddling on top of his waist and stroking his chest to gain more trust. Slowly she began kissing his hardened skin and ran her fingertips over his exposed ribs almost retching in the process. He groaned in pleasure as she worked herself down and moved into position for her attack, slowly and gently centering herself between his knees and leaving him spread eagle on the bed. She smiled at him and gathered her strength and with all the force she could gather kneed him in the groin, "Not today asshole!"

He screamed in pain with the look of anguish and surprise sketched on his contorted face. He moved to lunge at her, but she had already grabbed the stone vase and smashed it into his temple. He laid bleeding and momentarily unconscious, a greenish blood oozing onto the blanket. She grabbed what clothes she could and ran out of the room desperately trying to find the way out. There were no windows and she deducted that she must be in one of the structures that had been built into the side of the mountain. She ran from room to room and finally found a door, practically mowing it down as she made her escape.

She found herself alone in a tunnel with lanterns that dimly lit her path. She threw her cloak over her head that Jobar had fashioned for her and ran through the tunnel in her bare feet. As she moved along, she realized this was no tunnel, it was a maze of interconnecting lava tubes. The coarse black walls extended down deeper into the mountain. She stopped to get her bearings, trying not to breathe as she thought she heard distant voices. She realized the sounds were getting closer and she started to run. Every time she would come to an intersection she would stop to see if she saw a way out towards the surface. Knowing perhaps if she stayed on course, she might have a better recollection of how to find her way out or perhaps better yet it might take her out to the other side of the mountain. The voices were growing louder now coming from behind. She started sprinting, her feet being cut by the rock. She turned a corner to find a dead end. "Fuck . . . fuck, fuck!"

Panic started to set in as she could see the approaching lights and the voices speaking in a language she could not even begin to comprehend. She slowly backed up against the smooth rock wall, eyes wide with fear. As she pressed back, her knees shaking, she suddenly felt the cold surface tingle up her spine and out her limbs and she fell completely through the stone surface. She was now lying flat on her back, her head throbbing as it had bounced off the hard ground, almost rendering her unconscious. She shook off the pain and rubbed her eyes as she thought they were playing tricks on her. She scooted back and the rock wall was morphing from transparent to solid and back to transparent. She could see her captor with a bloodied rag around his head and a torch clutched in his hand, and a couple of his equally frightening looking companions, one of which had a lasso of rope slung over his shoulder. She dared not move as she gazed at the shifting rock, afraid that she could be seen from the other side, but just as swiftly as they had appeared around the corner, they turned tail and left the way they had come.

She slowly stood as darkness filled the room. She groped for the side of the cavern, not being able to even see her hand in front of her face. She finally met the cold stone wall and felt a tingling sensation in her fingertips. Slowly the cave became illuminated in a soft warm glow. As her eyes adjusted, she looked back at the wall she had fallen through and it was solid rock, but she dare not touch it as she feared it would somehow alert her attackers.

She walked to the end where it came to a small opening. Dorathy bent down to enter the small room that looked to have been carved out of solid rock with a precision that indicated this was not the handiwork of this pre-industrialized civilization. As her eyes adjusted to the dim light, she started to make out precise laser cuts in the wall. "My God, what is this?"

Her eyes grew large as its implication became clear. Depicted in the carvings was unmistakably thirteen planets, each having a pyramid being aligned to a point in space that looked to be part of a constellation, and within each pyramid was a puzzle piece. Dorathy ran her fingers over the carving absorbing its meaning. The end of the pictogram was what looked to be an unknown entity of light and in its hand was a type of crystal capstone or talisman. It was placing it on the finished product of the puzzle pieces forming a pyramid. Shooting from its apex was a beam of light opening a hole in space. Dorathy whispered to herself, "That's it, holy shit that's the answer!"

Dorathy heard an echo of voices coming her way but now she heard her name being called. She stood up straight, banging the top of her head on the rock ceiling. Running towards the wall she touched it gently then applying pressure she felt her hand slip though the cold stone. She closed her eyes and stepped forward, stumbling out the other side just as Henry, Jobar and Dimitri rounded the corner, weapons in hand. Henry rushed for her, holding her in his arms. "Thank God you're safe! Holy hell, that a girl . . . I knew you could take care of yourself!"

"Henry, I found the answer to the thirteen planets! There are pyramids on each which contain pieces of a puzzle and a crystal cap stone! It's all carved into a small cave on the other side of this wall! Watch!" Dorathy placed her hand on the wall and pushed. Nothing happened. She tried again but with more force . . . again . . . with the same conclusion. "I swear to you I was able to walk though this wall!"

Jobar said, "You found the Hidden Message!"

"Yes!" she shouted. "It's in there!" She pointed to the rock face.

Dimitri interjected, "Not now . . . we need to go!"

"He's right." Henry agreed. "We got to get the hell out of here! Come on!"

The group wound around the lava tube till they got to the surface. On their way out, they picked up sacks of supplies they had stolen from one of the locals. They had already stunned him and knocked him out cold, so they thought as he was nowhere to be seen, no doubt he has altered the rest of the villagers to their presence.

The chill of night sent shivers into Dorathy as she collapsed from the pain in her feet and the trauma she had endured finally registered. Henry handed his sack to Dimitri as he scooped up Dorathy in his strong arms. They hurried down the dirt trail from the local residences and ran to the ship waiting in the cold dark of night, almost invisible in the blackness.

Brenda stood waiting just outside and ran to them, helping Dorathy aboard and carting her directly to the med lab. Henry jumped in the pilot's seat with Magnus by his side, the hatch closed, and they lifted off without a moment to spare as they could see lights coming on and a line of villagers rapidly approaching, torches in hand.

Kore stood and leaned over Simms's desk. She was in command now and had voiced her demands to her subordinate. "Now that we have an understanding, you will take me to sublevel fifty-one."

Simms leaned back in his chair knowing he had been beaten, thinking this could go one of two ways: Either show her what she is requesting and he gets reprimanded, or the problem goes away . . . either way he was due for retirement and his days were numbered. "So be it, have it your way."

Kore stood straighter and motioned for Hoffman to get up and follow. Simms pushed away from his desk and stood a foot taller, looking down at her frail frame. "I need not remind you what impact this information would have on our society if it were to be leaked to the public."

"What I want with this information is none of your business. What I do with it is another matter which is not up for discussion."

Simms said, shrugging his shoulders, "Your government, and your rules, so from this point on I am merely a tour director. Your pet will have to stay behind . . . security measure.

She spoke gently to her beloved Nikko. "You have to stay here; I will be back shortly." Nikko understood and curled up on Simms's big cushy chair.

Simms rolled his eyes. "I hope he's house broken."

They departed as Simms slammed his office door behind them. "Follow me—just so we are clear on your demands I'm going to do this by the book to make sure I've got my ass covered when the shit hits the fan."

Kore sneered at Simms with an air of arrogance. "Whatever you say Simms, your future is none of my concern."

As they approached the high security area to the top-secret sublevel, they halted at the control center that documented everyone accessing the rapid descent platform to the bowels of the facility. Simms entered his key card and punched his pin into the control panel as the heavy steel door hissed open. Simms said with a sweeping exaggerated motion of his arm, "After you."

Kore entered with Hoffman on her heels. Simms rarely had the need to go into *the pit* as it was known and wished he could fast forward his days to retirement. "The security protocol is not much different from what you experienced upon your arrival, just now you will have to override the system by putting in your personal ID number along with your government ID number and wait for it to accept."

Kore was not amused. "I cannot stand wasteful redundancy!"

Simms chuckled to himself. "You must be accustomed to it as it's much like the government you work for." Kore glared back at him unamused as the green rings enveloped them in its grip. An electronic voice announced their arrival as it disengaged. "Welcome Prime Minister Athanatos and Doctor Allen Hoffman please enter your personal ID number followed by your government status number. She approached the keypad that was on a tall pedestal at the side of the entrance to the shaft. She entered her information. "Thank you, Prime Minister," the feminine voice said. Hoffman followed suit. "Thank you, Doctor Allen Hoffman." Simms grudgingly entered his information. "Thank you, Captain Eric Simms. Please enter the override sequence." Captain Simms entered a long series of codes he had memorized over the years. After a few moments the automated voice approvingly said, "You may proceed."

The huge cylindrical door slowly opened with a cold rush of air from its climate controlled interior, sending a chill up the back of Hoffman's collar. There was no control panel or keypad, just six seats in a circle with shoulder harnesses. Kore stopped in her tracks, having second thoughts, but took a seat, firmly adjusting her harness with Hoffman following suit and saying, "I don't like the looks of this."

Simms smiled. "Hope you enjoy the ride." The door slowly closed and locked as a timer ticked down five seconds and a red light strobed inside. At zero the small space dropped with a muffled scream coming from Hoffman while Kore sat motionless, her eyes squinted shut. Simms just smiled at seeing their discomfort. After what seemed to be far too many seconds of free falling, the capsule came to a slow descent and stopped.

Doctor Hoffman stood, knees shaking, asked, "How far down are we?"

Simms laughed. Far enough . . . trust me you don't really want to know."

Kore saw her breath as she spoke, "Can you please tell me why there is such a need for such dramatics! Such an unnecessary waste of resources to have such a place to store ancient and in my opinion somewhat insignificant artifacts."

Simms chuckled. "Lady we didn't put this here, it was already here

from the ancients that came to settle, apparently they like deep underground edifices to hide all their secrets."

Kore looked at him sideways. "You mean to tell me this facility has
been here the whole time and you have kept it as a secret base to continue to store these so-called ancient artifacts?"

Simms nodded, "That's exactly what I'm saying."

She shook her head in disgust. "Ridiculous!"

Simms agreed. "Our tax dollars at work."

Simms finally unstrapped himself and stood, apparently bored with
the task at hand. The internal motion sensors activated the door and it
slid open, exposing a massive chamber carved out of solid rock. Hoffman
with a long whistle was obviously impressed, their voices echoing in the
vast cavern as they spoke. "Now that is a sight to behold!"

Kore stood staring, stunned by what she saw before her. "Oh, my holy
hell, I don't believe my eyes!"

Coolie and Patsup landed Jobar's ship in a clearing behind his home, just
beyond the trees. Patsup was already whining about the distance they
would have to walk to get to the house. Coolie slapped him hard up the
back side of his head. "If it wasn't for your stupidity none of this would
be happening!"

Patsup scowled. "Well you don't have to get violent!"

"Violent! I'll show you violence!" Coolie kicked him out the hatch and
growled in a whisper, "Now hurry, we need to get in and out before anyone knows we returned and comes looking for us."

Coolie ran through the trees with only the starlight to guild them,
with Patsup struggling to keep up. Coolie stopped suddenly at the edge
of the forest, hearing the approach of one of the swamp lizards. He did a

quick assessment of the field behind Jobar's home making sure the coast was clear. "Come on and be fast on your feet because you don't want to be a lizard's dinner!"

Patsup gulped and ran as fast as his short squat legs could take him, staying close to Coolie's heels. Patsup heard the snapping of sharp teeth and screamed as he passed Coolie in a flat-out sprint. Once to the back fence he leapt up into the air but only managed to face plant against the hard wooden surface. Coolie with a firm shove from beneath managed to heave him over and taking a few strides back, ran forward and with one coordinated move was up and over the fence with jaws snapping at his legs.

They were both crouched down in the tall grass as they saw lights approaching. Coolie whispered, "I'm not sure but they might be watching our homes for our return—who knows what our Prime Minister may have done looking for her answers to the puzzle."

Patsup stood up and almost yelled what puzzle? Coolie yanked hard on his arm. "Shut up you dim wit!"

He stood crouched and grabbed Patsup by the elbow. "Come on and be quiet." They approached the back patio and stopped at the large glass door. Coolie knew his oldest friend's key code to his home and punched in the number, knowing in doing so they would not have much time before the keypad registered someone was entering the residence. The NWO governed by monitoring everyone's coming and goings even in their own homes, and if there was an alert attached to the code the authorities would no doubt be there shortly. They made their way through the darkened rooms to Jobar's office where he kept all their collective information they had gathered over the years. Every little tidbit was there that concerned their traveler friends, the lost city, information concerning the original New Western Ordinance, maps, images, ancient theories, even ancient gadgets they found along the way. All in hopes of someday finding the Otherlings and the Portal to the Other Side.

Coolie with a small glow stick held between his teeth grabbed Jobar's antigrav unit from the back of the room and started to load the crates and boxes onto it as he instructed Patsup to take everything out of the safe box, whispering the code to him and throwing him an empty box. "Put it all in there."

After what seemed to be an eternity, everything was loaded. Coolie did a mental note, not wanting to leave anything incriminating behind. They strapped everything down and effortlessly pushed it out the back door. Patsup swung his head around. "Oh no they are coming for us!" Lights were blazing and approaching fast. Coolie shook his head in disgust, "Damn the NWO and their constant policing!" He instructed Patsup to climb aboard the antigrav and hold on. He pushed the cart as fast as he could across the yard and as they approached the fence he pushed a button and the cart flew straight up into the air with Coolie hanging on, kicking his feet over the top of the fence as it came down the other side. Coolie then ran as fast as he could with sharp toothed giant lizards trying to get a hold of him. He took control of the accelerator hand grip, lurching himself onto the foot holds as the cart moved across the clearing at lightning speed. As they neared the tree line Coolie jumped off to slow them down to avoid crashing into a tree. He quickly maneuvered through the trees getting them to the ship. Looking back there were men in black surrounding the home in hopes of questioning them.

Patsup was gripping the straps that held the boxes with his legs straddling either side and with a squeal said, "Oh my we are fugitives now . . . what have you two been up to all these years that would cause such a stir?!"

Coolie was not amused and not in the mood; he grabbed Patsup by the scruff and dragged him off the cart as he opened the hatch. "Help me push this thing up the ramp and would you please shut up!"

Once inside Coolie jumped into the pilot seat, his muscles aching, and silently took off without guidance lights, knowing it wouldn't matter as they were on to them. They swiftly gained altitude and whizzed back to their friends. Coolie muttered to himself and Patsup, "We dare not try for my home . . . no need really as Jobar kept most of all of it anyway."

Patsup cried, "What of our sister and her family?"

Coolie growled back, "She knows nothing of what we have been up to . . . Jobar made sure of that for her own safety."

CHAPTER 44

Brenda had helped Dorathy onto an examining table in the med lab. She was hyperventilating and was losing consciousness. "Dora . . . girlfriend! Look at me, you're safe, calm down!" Dorathy was sobbing from fright and shaking uncontrollably. She was stammering, "That creature . . . was horrible . . . he was going to rape me . . . what if I hadn't gotten away . . . what if they didn't find me!"

Brenda took a vial from a cabinet and prepared a sedative. "Here baby, this will make you feel better." It only took a few seconds and Dorathy felt warm and safe as she fell into a deep sleep. Brenda checked her for other wounds and treated her bloodied feet, when she noticed the tips of her fingers were glowing from within. Then she squinted her eyes looking more closely as the skin on her entire body seemed to be glowing. Brenda didn't know what to make of it and continued to clean her wounds.

Henry entered the med lab with a horrible look of concern on his face. "How she doing?"

Brenda shook her head. "I had to sedate her; she went into shock. Come here." She instructed Henry to look at her hand as she lifted it in order for him to get a closer look. "What do you make of this?"

Henry stooped over. "Hmm, I don't know, but when we found her, she was standing at a dead end against a solid rock wall and was claiming she had stepped through it into a room where she found some kind of a message carved into the wall. When she tried to reenter it she couldn't . . . shit I don't know Brenda . . . I don't know what to make of it . . . any of it . . . get a sample of her DNA to see if anything has changed, maybe Dimitri can make a connection."

Brenda sighed, "Okay, well she's sleeping now . . . hope she's calmer when she wakes up . . . that really scared the hell out of her."

Henry ran his hand through his hair as he did when things were getting rough. "Jobar seemed to know what she was going on about—maybe he can shed some light on it."

Brenda asked, "Any word from Coolie?"

"Yup, Magnus just got word they are on their way, and with no time to spare; the bastards were already hot on their trail."

Brenda voiced her concern, "Hope they don't lead them back here to us."

"Nope, no chance of that, Jobar's got that ship pretty rigged up . . . he's a stealthy little bastard when he needs to be."

Brenda smiled with agreement as she yawned. "Damn I'm tired."

Henry knew how she felt, yawning himself. Brenda rummaged through her supplies. "I'll run some tests on Dora and get a sample of her illuminated DNA." Henry smiled at the off-color joke.

Jobar sat at the table crying, "Oh my, I hope Dora is going to be okay, it's all my fault . . . I forgot it was mating season and her head wrap was the color of availability! I will never forgive myself!"

Dimitri rolled his eyes as Magnus sighed, "Well that's one for the books."

"Ah!" Dimitri confessed. "She is a strong woman!"

Magnus disagreed. "She might be that, but she is human; even more so and something we often times seem to forget, one can only take so much before one snaps."

The ship shuddered as it did when Jobar's ship aligned itself for docking. Dimitri stood, being closest to the hatch and opened it as Coolie was wheeling the antigrav cart piled high with boxes and bags. Coolie slumped over it as he entered with Patsup bringing up the rear. "We got away in just the nick of time, they were on to us."

Jobar put his arm around his best friend while glaring at his pathetic brother. "Thank the heavens you are alright, I trust you were able to retrieve everything," he said as he looked over the pile of boxes.

Coolie asked, "Well hopefully you had less trouble than us?"

Jobar's eyes lowered. "We had an incident with our supply mission—Dora was captured but we were able to retrieve her before any great harm came to her."

Coolie dropped his head and shook it in regret, noticing the dirt-stained scarlet scarf on the floor. Furrowing his brows, he said, "What in heavens . . . did you lose your mind while I was gone . . . it's their mating season . . . don't tell me she had that thing wrapped around her!" He pointed down at the frayed fabric.

Jobar suddenly burst into tears again. "I am a brainless slug!"

Henry was happy to see Coolie and Patsup had made it back unscathed and assured Jobar, "Look it was an innocent oversight." He patted him on the back. Henry grabbed a chair and swung it around in front of Coolie, straddling it. "Look Dora got away, but just before we got to her, she found something."

"Yes!" Jobar perked up, wiping his nose on his baggy shirt sleeve. "I think she found one of the hidden encryptions left by the Otherlings!"

Coolie sat down, mouth open. "Oh my, that is astonishing—what did it say?"

Henry shook his head. "She said something about the thirteen planets, but we had to get the hell out of there . . . she's sedated now and resting."

Coolie and Patsup sat at the table as Magnus got them something to drink. Pointing to the pile of boxes Jobar said, "Over the years we have collected data such as old scrolls, and documents and in almost everything that we have been able to decipher there are references made to puzzle segments, but we have never been able to account for their significance."

Coolie added, "We have in many cases been made aware of messages hidden away, but only the righteous may gain access . . . and only if you were so lucky in finding them in the first place. These messages, legend says, hold the answers, but they have been hidden in the most obscure of places."

Magnus asked, "What do you mean only the righteous may enter?"

"Yes!" Dimitri recalled what Dorathy had said. "Dora was saying she had walked through a rock wall into a small cavern."

Henry sat with his chin firmly planted on his forearms over the back of the chair. "Look while Brenda was tending to Dora, she noticed she had an internal . . . glow . . . for lack of a better word . . . it seemed to be emanating from her whole body."

Jobar and Coolie exchanged knowing glances and said in unison, "She is glowing an internal light?" The group of them quickly exchanged looks of acknowledgment.

Dimitri spoke. "The Illuminati have always maintained they were the purest form of the alien DNA that seeded our planet . . . perhaps including all of the planets.

Magnus piped in, "Her DNA has granted us access where no other had been able to obtain, and therefore simple deduction tells us she carries the purest form."

Jobar and Coolie eyes were wide. Jobar softly spoke as he suddenly realized, "Dorathy is transcending, she is becoming . . . an . . . Otherling."

Patsup chocked at the implication.

Kore and Hoffman slowly shifted their gaze upwards at the most incredible vessel they had ever seen, its glassy darkened hull looming over their heads like a giant predator, wings spread in an elegant curve towards the back where twin shafts protruded in elongated funnels. And with a tubular ring affixed to its middle section, making it appear as it was flying through it. They stared at the craft, mystified. Kore said softly, "In all my years I never fully accepted the ancient tales but here it is in all its glory . . . unbelievable! Tell me Simms, how long has this been hidden here? When was it found?"

Simms shook his head. "It was found right here exactly as you see it, immobile and completely inaccessible. Carbon dating of the outer hull puts it as old as the universe itself."

"I knew it!" Hoffman shouted confirmation. "I knew this ship existed!"

Simms said as he was announcing something no one ever could imagine but always knew it to be true, "This ship brought our kind here roughly fifteen thousand years ago from a planet on the other side of our known universe, our dark space; might I add not far from our mysterious thirteen planets."

After many moments of silence, in awe of the implications, Kore asked a barrage of questions, "Why have you not been able to gain access to the interior? How are you familiar with its approximate origin?"

Simms held his hand up in protest. "Its origin has been carefully mapped in their documentation, but we cannot confirm its existence as it seems it resides in our dark space—gravitational forces suggest its existence, but that is all."

Hoffman said, nudging forward, "Which means have you exhausted your attempts to gain access?"

Simms smiled broadly. "It seems to be quite . . . aware." As he continued, he strode closer to the out-stretched forward section, its long arching neck with its aerodynamic-nosed cockpit at the front of the vessel. "At every attempt we have been denied and whatever the means being used had failed miserably. What secrets she holds within are hers alone; she will only share when the time comes."

Kore snorted, "Spare me the romantics, and please tell me you have tried more aggressive techniques."

Simms looked back over his shoulder. "Of course we have . . . whatever we try on her she returns the courtesy a hundred-fold! Many men have died trying to finesse the secrets from her."

Hoffman interrupted, "I have read countless articles alluding to this ship's existence. What our Prime Minister has in her possession shows a team of scientists in an unknown location with a smaller, yet still impressive, near replica of this ship you have here. I know you have more artifacts than the ship before us . . . remember I cataloged those items years ago!"

"Yes, yes Hoffman," Simms said reluctantly, "follow me."

Captain Simms marched them to a small vaulted room and entered his key code. The door opened with a heavy clank that echoed through the massive chamber. Inside were countless books of images and artifacts kept in this airtight, temperature-controlled space. Simms pulled out one of the massive slide-out drawers and said, "I think this is what you are looking for."

As he activated the book, he scrolled through images of unknown people from so many thousands of years ago, stopping at one in particular. It was a female wearing a blue uniform with auburn locks standing next to a contraption of sorts, with what looked to be a partially intact human specimen in a liquid-filled container. Kore's eyes widened as she could never mistake who the person was in the image . . . it was her . . . evolutionary differences, but unmistakably her.

Both Simms and Hoffman tried to read her expression, but shock seemed to sum it up accurately. She drew closer to the image. "Uncanny," was all she could say. She whispered back, "What else have you found?"

Simms shrugged. "It's all here . . . a smaller vessel and assuming, its occupants, the origins of their . . . our . . . species."

Hoffman demanded, "What is the nature of our species?"

Simms casually informed them, "We are a product of them but that goes without saying . . . we—and I am generalizing—are the product of a far older species, an interdimensional species that no doubt traveled the universe seeding life as they saw fit. Our separate evolution guiding our slight differences in appearance of course. But what is very curious here is their documents from the time showed an extraordinary concentration of the uncoded DNA to carry a sequence of sorts."

"Yes, Doctor Hoffman concurred, "One of the artifacts I was fortunate enough to examine showed twelve different blood lines, all of which had a remarkable quality to them; some of the same qualities that make up the hull of this ship."

"Precisely," Simms said, "Twelve bloodlines of the purest form of the original creatures that seeded the planets over billions of years in the making. These beings are thought to have transcended to a much higher dimension . . . some like to call them the Otherlings."

Kore, never wanting to buy into the fable, was hard-pressed to deny the implications. She pulled over her head her crystal capstone and found it to be changing in color and could hear a harmonic sound vibrating from within. "That's odd," she said as she handed it to Doctor Hoffman. "What do you make of this?"

Hoffman shook his head, "I don't have a clue."

Simms took a closer look. "Yes, this brings us to the talisman." He snatched it from Hoffman. "This particular artifact has a larger implication attached to it. How you were able to obtain it is even a larger mystery."

Kore grabbed it back and stuffed it in her bag, slinging it over her shoulder. "How I obtained it is none of your business, but you must know what it is used for."

Simms glared back at her. "Let's just say it has something to do with our thirteen planets. Our ancestors knew something we don't and demanded no one was to ever approach those planets . . . not that it would make a damn bit of difference considering their distance. So that little crystal pyramid of yours has about as much functionality as a paper weight!"

Kore gritted her teeth as she knew Simms was holding back valuable information.

Hoffman looked from one to the other and knew when to keep silent. Finally, Captain Simms said, "Are we done here?" He looked down at his timepiece. Kore reluctantly agreed, "Yes, get me the hell out of here."

Patsup could barely comprehend what he was hearing. "You cannot tell me you believe this nonsense!"

Jobar shot back, his eyes blazing, "What do you know of any of this . . . I will tell you . . . NOTHING! You have spent your entire life willing to live with your head in the clouds or buried in the dirt, while Coolie and I, and many more like us, have been searching for the truth! My dear brother you need to see the New Western Ordinance for exactly who they are!"

Patsup recoiled. "They are the ones that brought us out of the darkest years, and we have prospered from their involvement!"

"Involvement. Is that what you are calling it? *Control* seems to be a far more accurate term!"

Brenda walked in. "Enough with the shouting and bickering, you could wake the dead with it!" She leaned into Dimitri. I ran some tests on Dora—you're right, and by the looks of it her uncoded DNA is restructuring itself. Dim you might want to look at the data."

Dimitri stood stretching his back, "I will put it up here so we can all get a look at it." Dimitri strode to the console and pulled up a holographic image. Magnus raised an eyebrow as the image came into focus. Dimitri shook his head in astonishment. "Unbelievable. Her genetic code is re-aligning itself with her un-coded DNA.

"The question is," Magnus said, thinking out loud, "what does it all mean?"

Jobar sat with his hands on top of his head, eyes glazed over. "What this means, is that Dora can get us to the other side . . . given the fact that we are able to find the answer to the puzzle, and according to legend find this crystal capstone she saw depicted on the wall of the cave."

Patsup slowly registered what his older brother had just said and moments later, when the fog lifted from his mind, he suddenly stood up, knocking his chair to the floor. His eyes wide, his brain trying to recall the image of Prime Minister Athanatos on the flight field that day. "Yes!" Yes of course, he shouted. "yes, it all makes sense!"

Jobar said, with a more than usual annoyed look on his face, "Now what are you carrying on about, can't you see we are discussing something very important!"

"For once!" Patsup yelled, spitting his words, "Why won't you regard me as you regard him!" He pointed to Coolie.

"Because he isn't a self-righteous narcissistic fool!"

"So now your true feelings come out!" Patsup kicked his brother in the knee as Jobar buckled in pain. Jobar, holding his leg gritting his teeth in anger said, "It was your big illusions of grandeur that got us in this predicament!"

"Whoa. You two need to corral that shit . . . this isn't the time or the place." Henry said as he helped Jobar into a chair. "And you go sit over there." Henry pointed to Patsup.

"You can't tell me what to do!"

Henry rolled his eyes and stood leering down at Patsup, standing a good meter shorter than him. "Sit . . . down . . . now."

Brenda shook her head and had to laugh, as the rest of the group were holding back tears. "Now, now, children . . . we need to play nice." Brenda spoke in her usual soothing voice that was always reserved for when she wanted to get her way. "Now Patsup, please tell us what you were about to say . . . something pertaining to the crystal capstone."

Patsup looked into Brenda's eyes as if it were the first time, a flash of recognition appearing that had been hidden away beneath a veil of uncertainty. My God, he thought, the resemblance is uncanny. He sat in his chair scowling like a pouting child who had been sent to the corner. "As I was saying . . . before being rudely interrupted, our Prime Minister wore such a thing as you describe on a heavy chain around her neck. It flung itself out of her uniform as she un-buttoned her collar, yelling something about the heat. I remember it because the substance inside glows as this ship does."

All eyes were on Patsup now, who was feeling vindicated with his chin held high, arms crossed tightly over his chest.

Henry sat back for once in the normal sitting position. "Well that certainly puts a new twist on things."

Dimitri grabbed a chair and propped his feet up on the console. "How do you say . . . the shit is hitting the fan?"

"Precisely the words I was thinking, my Russian friend," Manus said, rubbing the stubble on his chin.

Henry stated the obvious, "The one person we were trying to avoid, has now become the person we aim to seek. How and why the hell would she have such an item?"

Coolie recalled from memory all the seemingly useless information.

"I believe she is in fact one of the direct descendants from your New World Order and if that is the case, she has a great interest in all of us as well . . . now that she has seen your ship, she has no doubt started to connect the dots."

"Yes . . . I'm sure she has, Henry said. "Time for us to devise a plan . . . considering the facts surrounding the evidence are accurate."

Patsup scowled back. "I'm sure of it!"

Dorathy slowly padded into the room. Henry rushed over to her. "How you doing kiddo?

"Drugged . . . I feel . . . I don't know . . . exhausted . . . and hungry. Brenda immediately got her something to eat and Dimitri gave her a shot of what was left of Coolie's moonshine.

Jobar could barely contain himself. "Please Dora, tell us of the message you found on the planet! Can you describe it to us, because it is very important to know precisely what it said?"

Henry loomed over her. "Give her some space, guys."

Dorathy rubbed her eyes trying to focus. "I'm fine," as she waved him off. She took the plate Brenda handed her and said with a mouthful, "Give me something to draw with."

Magnus punched a series of keys on the console and handed her a blank pad. "Here you go Dora."

She immediately started to draw the pictogram from memory, paying close attention to every detail. With every stroke a large image filled the room with ever-growing detail. Dorathy smiled and said, as she could feel the tension building, "Good thing I got my mother's talent for painting."

When she was done Patsup gasped, Jobar and Coolie exchanged knowing glances, and the rest of the crew knew what needed to be done. So, what's the verdict, because from your expressions, I may have missed something while I was snoozing?"

"Yeah, you did," Henry said reluctantly.

"Dora, hold up your hand and look at your fingers."

She did as she was asked with a puzzled look on her face. She didn't see it at first but slowly she noticed. "I'm . . . glowing?" Dorathy became faint and steadied herself. "Please someone tell me what's going on!"

Dimitri brought up the image of her DNA. "Dora, you seem to be *evolving* at a high rate."

She buried her face in her hands reeling from the past events. "What else . . . the looks on your faces tells me there's more."

Jobar cleared his throat and with a heavy sigh said, "We need to find our Prime Minister, she has the crystal amulet that she wears around her neck, and it is the capstone that has the power to open the portal."

Dorothy leaned back in her seat feeling queasy. "When is this going to end, can someone please tell me *when* this is going to be over?"

The silence that filled the room was deafening. "Dora, look at me," Henry said, kneeling in front of her. "We have to get this from her. Once she realizes its power and how to wield it, the dynamics will change. She will stop at nothing to find us . . . to find you. I that happens there will be a breakdown in their civilization knowing they can travel back and forth between here and the other side."

Dorothy sobbed, "Who are we to say who should have the power and who shouldn't'?" Henry held her glowing hand. "Dora you have the power and you need to protect it, and

I believe that was the sole purpose of you being here."

She looked back at Henry with weary eyes knowing he was right. "I'm exhausted Henry."

Henry kissed her capable hands. "I know . . . trust me I know."

Jobar bravely approached. "I owe you an apology Dora, if not for my absentmindedness you would not have been abducted and for that I'm truly sorry.

Dorothy didn't have a clue what he was talking about but simply looked at him and shone a weary smile. She neither had the words nor the strength.

CHAPTER 45

K ore sat in the dark staring at her amulet scattering a rainbow of colors, as it twirled from its chain in the glow of the firelight. It filled her small room with millions of pinpoints shining like the vastness of space. She sat contemplating her next move, knowing the power she had fitting in the palm of her hand, but not knowing its purpose. She rolled over in her mind what the missing piece might be. The planets, the ship, what was Simms not telling her.

Kore knew what she needed to do as she drifted off to sleep tightly clutching her crystal pyramid. Whispering to the darkness, *I need to find that ship.*

The next morning she arranged for Silas to take her to the planet she dreaded the most, with its hot swamps and annoying inhabitants. She stood in the cold airfield waiting for him to arrive, the wind whipping her cloak around her ankles. Breathing deeply, she could see his approach over the jagged mountain peaks, causing a flurry of snow as the ship sped past. In the distance she could hear the roll of thunder with an advancing storm.

Silas, showing off his expertise, slowed her ship to a hover with landing struts extended, gracefully swinging the tail section around and hitting the ground softly. Kore climbed up the ramp, moving with a purpose. "I trust my assistant has sent you the logs."

"Yes ma'am." Silas was not eager to make yet another trip back to the hot swamps of Alger but was growing impatient and wanted answers.

Hours seemed to pass like days in the presence of Kore and Silas was happy to comply with her demands and stay on the ship; this would give him plenty of time to do his own investigative work. She hissed as she left, "I will return shortly . . . be on stand-by for imme- diate departure."

Silas nodded and lowered the ramp, feeling the hot steamy air filling the cabin. Kore's joints froze immediately from the humidity and the increased gravity. Her escort from the local office of Space and Flight Administration was waiting for her on the busy space port as arranged. Entering the vehicle she scowled, "Lower the temperature at once before I melt!" He dutifully did as instructed, punching the air control hard with his fist.

Officer Gred was a squat, ill-mannered individual with very little pa- tience for redundancy. "So Prime Minister Athanatos, what's so damned important that I get called out for checking some poor shmuck for a minor infraction of not logging all flights; you know everyone does it around these parts. They're all a bunch of hard-working miners who are too damned tired to be constantly logging in and out every time they have to take a crap!"

She glared at him with eyes of steel. "*Why* I am actually here is none of your concern . . ."

Gred cut her off sharply. "It is my concern if I'm forced to cart you around on my time, lady!"

"You would be wise to re-evaluate the situation, or you will be left with nothing but time," she said, giving him a knowing glance that she was not in the mood for his insubordinate behavior.

Gred just rolled his eyes, knowing when to quit as they rode in silence through the marsh lands that resembled a place where time forgot, with its boiling mud pits and steamy water vapor so thick you could cut it with a knife.

They came to an abrupt stop in front of Jobar's home, saying, "Out of the homes searched of the three family members of this clan, this was the one that had been entered and by the looks of it ransacked in a hurry.

The officers on duty said, they went out the back and took off before they could apprehend them for questioning."

Kore knew all the details as she put the alert on Patsup and his family members after he escaped her questioning. Digging through his files was when she realized the ship in question was no other than his own brother's. Once authorities questioned their sister Mares, she had unwittingly contributed the information of Jobar's interest in Portal Seeking and his occasional mention of transient friends. Seeing that bit of information Kore immediately made the connection.

Kore entered the home knowing she would be the only one who could find the relevance of what may have been left behind. She peered into the office with Gred on her heels. He showed her a few random papers that had been collected that had been dropped along the way. "You coming here was a waste of *our* time," he said as he handed her the small pile.

She snatched the papers from him, staring him down her long nose. "I will be the judge of that"! She shuffled through the papers that included a drawing and knew immediately she was on the right track. "I want all information about Mr. Jobar and his ship sent directly to my office." She looked around the room to see if anything had been missed but she knew she had found what she was looking for. "Take me back to my ship," she demanded. Gred shrugged his shoulders and was only too happy to comply.

After a long day she sat in her large chair in the dark as she had for so many years. She rolled around all the questions in her head but was never able to find the answers she was looking for. The one thing she knew for certain was that they needed the one thing that only she possessed. She knew they would be coming for her as she looked around her small fortress. "I will be the bait and you will step right into my web."

Henry said as he stood, "Okay guys we know what we need to do, now we just need to figure out how we're going to do it." Everyone sat and looked at each other as they thought.

Magnus said abruptly, "If we plan on taking the amulet from her, we need to find the path of the least resistance: I think that would be where she resides."

Jobar turning a paler green. "How are we going to find that information, we can't just ask someone for directions!"

Magnus smiled. "No, but we can *take* that information, all we have to do is *extract* it."

"From where?" Jobar asked afraid he already knew the answer.

Henry knew he was right. "Sounds like that's right up your alley. We just need to figure out how we can get into the building."

Jobar shook his head trembling, "You can't be serious, and we can't break into the NWO headquarters, that's insane! It's suicide!"

Magnus thought back at all the places he had managed to escape from and all the mainframes he had hacked into, for the many diabolical fiends whom he called *clients*. "Piece of cake," Magnus said confidently.

Jobar looked at Coolie for help and all he got from his friend was a shrug. "But what if we get caught," he cried.

Henry strode over and slapped him hard on the back. "We won't."

"We won't? Really, that's all you have to say, that's not very reassuring you know."

Henry was already devising the plan as he sat at the console pulling up all the information they had acquired over the years about the Capitol City and its grand palatial centerpiece. "Okay let's do this."

After a few hours they had their plan. Henry said with a new-found enthusiasm in his voice, "We all have our assignments, now let's get some rest and then we head out." Jobar still had his doubts of them succeeding and let his opinion be known. Henry laughed. "Hey, I hear they serve good meals in prison."

Jobar did not find him amusing. "Not the way I want to spend my retirement years," was all Jobar could say.

Hours later in the blackness of night they approached the Capitol City in silence, running low and fast, the starlight reflecting off the ship's hull like a mirror, making them almost completely invisible. The air was cold and dry, still with barely a leaf fluttering as the ship came to hover over the top of the building that soared hundreds of feet into the air. Its middle column was the tallest with its winged head on the top level. At either side, two shorter buildings with a base on each in the shape of clawed feet made the structure look like a majestic bird with its long slender neck in the sitting position, surveying its territory and ready to attack.

Their ship, understanding the importance of a stealthy approach, had almost made itself completely undetectable by the naked eye or any other device that might be looking. It hovered silently inches away from the building as Magnus and Dimitri strode over onto the rooftop, clearing the abyss that faded off into darkness below. Henry, peering out the cockpit, watched them disappear as he maneuvered the ship slowly down the building's reflective walls to the courtyard below. Henry glanced at Dorathy sitting beside him, her tense posture reflecting what the rest of the group was experiencing with the mission at hand.

Over the years they had accumulated data about the security measures that were in place. Hoping nothing had changed, Magnus and Dimitri removed a panel that opened to the service elevator shaft. Once inside, they maneuvered into position below the compartment. They knew they only needed to use their personal antigrav packs down the center of the shaft to ground level. The supercomputer that kept tabs on every individual, on every planet, in all sectors that the NWO controlled, was kept in a highly secure facility in the sub-basements of this immense structure.

After squeezing themselves between the outer wall and the compartment, they peered down the shaft with head lamps but were only able to illuminate several meters down into the darkness. Magnus nodded to Dimitri as he jumped into the shaft, free-falling into the depths. A moment later Dimitri reluctantly followed suit. He looked at his readout and could see the glow of Magnus's head light below him and fired up his pack. Only a moment later they slowed as the bottom was rushing towards them.

After a slow descent the ship came to land in front of the grand staircase. The gothic- looking courtyard was built around a huge fountain that reflected an ever-changing rainbow of colors as it sent cascading water dozens of meters into the air with a loud thunderous roar.

Henry unstrapped himself, and turned to look at his nervous crew, and said, "Come on guys get your weapons ready and make sure they are set on stun; the night guards will be back around shortly."

Dorathy, Jobar, Coolie, and Henry exited, weapons aimed high, leaving Brenda and Patsup to guard the ship. Dorathy and Jobar flanked left while Coolie and Henry went right. There were four guards patrolling the grand entrance: two to the west and two to the east. One was above each staircase and one below, patrolling from front to back.

They timed it just as the guards were crossing each other to each side of the structure. Dorathy, being far more agile, climbed the staircase three steps at a time while Jobar continued over the greenery to approach his target from below, with Henry and Coolie following suit.

Dimitri came to a stop just beside Magnus, head lamps glowing in the cold musty shaft. Dimitri took a tool out of his pack and pried the doors open into housekeeping and food service areas. Getting their bearings and turning off their lights, they were off down a long hallway that ended at a door leading to the main gallery. Even with the lights brought down to a soft glow, this area was quite impressive to anyone who might be visiting, with its huge domed ceiling that twinkled a starry sky above and the globes of all the planets they controlled floating above their heads. After a short moment of gazing upward they moved quickly to the back where they knew there would be a lone guard at the security desk. Magnus shot a bolt of electric shock into the side of the guard's head and he slumped backwards in his chair.

Outside Dorathy found her target and fired her silent weapon and before the guard knew what hit him, he was face down into the pavement. A moment later Jobar, fumbling with his weapon, missed his target—the guard was about to fire back as he had a clear shot, his finger on the trigger. A split second longer and Jobar would have been dead if not for Dorothy's quick reaction time. She fired one shot from above, and the guard went down. Jobar looked up at her, his face pale as a ghost as he waved her on to proceed to the back of the building, where hopefully they would meet with Henry and Coolie.

Dimitri stayed to tackle the outside security feeds, while Magnus was running down the hall where he met his first obstacle. Magnus ripped into the security mechanism that controlled the elevator to the sublevels.

This was his art, his passion, his purpose in life. He had managed to break into some of the world's most secure locations, from online hacking to on-sight infiltration. There was nothing that lay in his path that he was not able to overcome. Ever. Until now.

Dorothy met Jobar as they approached the back side of the massive structure, Jobar struggling to breathe the cold thin air as he climbed the steep grassy embankment toward the back. Trying to speak between deep breaths he said, "Thought I was dead there, you came from above like an angel to save me, thank the maker!"

Dorothy patted him on the arm. "We need to go, and I hope our friends were as successful."

Coolie and Henry managed to take down the guards with very little effort. As they turned the corner towards the back, they unexpectedly came face to face with a guard that had been assigned to cover the back wall of the capitol building. By pure instinct from a career serving in the military, Henry punched the stunned guard directly in the throat then shot him as he gasped for air, rendering him limp on the cold damp grass. Just then Henry could make out the black shadowy figures of Dorothy and Jobar, with only the starlight to illuminate their approach.

Out of breath and cold, they made their way back to the front entrance of the building, knowing their time was limited. They waited patiently in the shadows of the immense clawed feet adorning the base of this giant bird of prey standing watch over the controlled masses.

Inside things were not going quite as planned. Magnus tried desperately to get around the firewalls of the security system while Dimitri stood guard at the security desk, already having the visual monitors from outside security cameras running old feedback in a repeated cycle.

Dimitri sat at the chair mostly hidden by the huge desk; he had dawned the cap of the fallen guard who lay limp on the floor, now beneath the desk, occasionally turning his gaze back to see if Magnus had succeeded.

Magnus, with sweat on his brow, finally managed to break the seal and the door hissed open. Dimitri rushed to his side and they entered the elevator with only one setting: down. As the doors closed, Dimitri voiced his stress, "Fuck, you British prick, what took you so goddamned long!"

Magnus looked up at Dimitri. "Take that stupid cap off your head, you look like a fucking wanker!"

The elevator came to a stop and the heavy metal doors slid open to a small area that was lit with an eerie red glow, revealing a glass door with its own security safeguards. Just beyond was a small room which was filled with the most advanced quantum bits Magnus had ever seen, filling the room from floor to ceiling with the most advanced computing systems ever known to mankind, from any dimension.

Magnus blew a long low whistle as he tossed his bag onto the floor announcing, "This is going to be a real bitch but with a little finessing she will eventually unlock and give up all her little secrets to me." Dimitri thought, *he really needs to get laid.*

Magnus immediately got to work, his nimble fingers attempting to coax the lock open, his small portable computer being hard-wired into the locking device, his fingers flying over the flat console. Minutes seemed to pass like hours—suddenly the door slid open with a rush of super cold air, sending a chill up their spines. Magnus whispered, "Ah, climax!"

Dimitri rolled his eyes. "Just get in there and find that location so we can get the hell out of here!"

"Patience my fat Russian friend, one cannot rush these things."

They slowly pushed past and up the aisle when Magnus spotted the correct area for a hard-wire penetration into the appropriate mainframe. He plugged in and let his console scroll the millions of files until it chimed—they had successfully downloaded the information they sought.

Magnus winked up at Dimitri. "Piece of cake." Then he added, "While we are here, we really should download everything pertaining to the origins of this New World Order."

Dimitri knew they were running out of time and possibly luck but also knew he never wanted to come here again. "Then find it quickly!" They both set out looking and found one console that seemed to be estranged from the rest. "Here it is." Magnus whispered, already plugging into it.

Moments later the red lights started to strobe. "Oh fuck," Dimitri groaned, "that cannot be a good sign!"

Magnus softly announced, "Almost there . . . just a few more seconds and . . ."

Dimitri yanked the cord out and shouted, "We are getting the hell out of here now!"

Magus gathered his equipment and hastily put it in his bag as they both sprinted towards the now-closing glass door of the elevator. They slipped through, Dimitri getting hung up by his robust frame tripped and slide into the back of the elevator as the door rapidly slid shut and shot them to the main gallery.

They immediately bolted out, running past the security desk, Dimitri shouting, "What about getting out of the main lobby, we never tripped the door locks!"

Magnus knew it was pointless now to having a stealthy departure, so he grabbed a heavy metal chair and smashed it into the glass doors that led to the outside and the grand staircase, sending shards in every direction. Now alarms were blaring, deafening all other sounds of fast-approaching air and ground support. The group waiting outside were stunned at the sights that seemed to be coming from everywhere. As they waited in the shadows they saw their partners in crime sprint past them and down the stairs. They followed and made a bee line to the ship that was already poised for takeoff. Brenda was shouting, "Jesus Christ, what the hell!"

Henry zipped past her up to the forward cockpit, throwing himself into his seat and making the connection to their ever-faithful ship. It hovered momentarily as Jobar was the last to enter. Brenda slapped the interior and the hatch shut as shots hit the almost invisible hull, ricocheting in every direction.

Ships of all sizes descended quickly onto the group as they flew sharply from side to side deflecting weapons being fired at them from all angles. Dorathy was chanting to herself, her hand pressed against the inner hull of the ship for support—*please help us . . . please get us out of here.*

Suddenly the ship sent out a massive electromagnetic pulse and every ship that had been pursuing them fell from the sky like poorly designed paper airplanes, sent crashing to the surface. One particular ship tumpled out of control and went careening into the capitol building itself, exploding on impact.

CHAPTER 46

Kore was not accustomed to being awakened in the middle of the night and groggily answered an urgent sounding call. "Slow down at once, you are making no sense whatsoever!" She tried desperately to understand the babblings over the loud sounds of static from a very poor connection. The person tried hard to make himself clear on the other end, shouting into the receiver.

Slowly as the fog lifted from her mind, the only words she could hear sent her into a contorted posture of dismay. Her voice steady in an angry sea, her eyes glowing red from the reflection of the glowing embers, the only words she could utter were, "Tell me the ship has been captured!" The answer she got was not the answer she wanted. Kore ended the call by throwing her communicator into the fire pit. She sat and stared as it hissed and sparked, as its components melted from the heat.

Dorathy finally opened her eyes after Henry gasped, "We're outta the woods!"

As the planet's atmosphere faded away to the clarity of an expanding universe, Brenda in her usual manner scoffed, "Can someone please tell me what the hell that was all about, because I sure as hell don't have a clue why we are all still here!"

Henry shook his head. "My readings tell me, *that* was an impressive EMP our faithful ship emitted."

Jobar was still shaken by the events, stammering, "Your ship saved us . . . how is that possible?" Patsup had a blank look on his face as if the current events had shocked him to the core.

Dimitri smiled at Magnus. "I think we all need a drink after that." He lumbered to the aft cabin.

Henry shot back, "Pour one for me too!"

Patsup sat quietly, as he had never seen such a display of utter disrespect for his precious NWO.

"How can you be so jovial and obtuse to what we have done here tonight?"

Jobar and Coolie rubbed the sweat from their eyes and started to laugh uncontrollably, the stress getting the better of them. Jobar playfully shoved his younger brother. "Relax! All this will be forgotten as people go on about their dull daily routines!"

Patsup snapped back, eyes glaring, "You are a bunch of terrorists."

Jobar shot back, "You are living in a very small box; it is time you grasp the bigger picture my dear ignorant brother."

Patsup crossed his arms tightly around his chest, staring in the opposite direction and fighting off the tears.

Dorathy winced as the air around her became too hostile for her to bear and stumbled to the aft cabin, her knees giving out from under her as she clutched a chair and fell into it. Brenda on her heels, seeing the look of a stress that had become more than Dorathy could bear poured her dear friend a drink and placed it in her hand. "Here baby, drink this, it will help."

Dorathy looked up at Brenda. "When can we get off this roller coaster?"

Brenda took a seat. "Look . . . What I have learned over the last few years is life is a journey, and so far, it has been a hell of a ride."

Dorathy bit her lip; her head was spinning, her emotions raw, and she could only muster, "Yeah . . . I guess so, but I'm exhausted. I just don't know how much more I can take."

Brenda wore a sympathetic smile. "There are not too many people who can say they experienced what we have managed to accomplish. But hey, now it gets really interesting . . . we go and get that crystal amulet."

Dorathy's thoughts of yet another invasion forced her to throw back the rest of Jobar and Coolie's moonshine, wincing from the burn as it hit the back of her throat.

The light of dawn was slowly creeping into Kore's darkened room, casting long hazy shadows and sending a beam of sunlight into her tired eyes. She had sat the entire night trying to reflect on the night's events. She stared into the charred remains of her communicator, a contorted blob of melted plastics and metal covered by blackened ashes. She tried desperately to compose a plan to finally capture her fugitives but knowing her commitments to her office would take all her energy, she struggled with her priorities. Her New Western Ordinance lay in ruins from the massive electromagnetic pulse and she feared chaos would return to the region if they . . . if she . . . didn't act quickly to re-establish power over the masses. She grew weary at the thought of the insurmountable amount of work that lay ahead of her, knowing she must put all her efforts towards rebuilding before things got too much out of control. She blew out a long breath and slowly stood. *I will get you my pretties . . . in time . . . but not today.*

The group sat around the table as Magnus decrypted page upon page of data that they had managed to download before their untimely departure. "Whew, when applying a search to this information it is truly unbelievable what the NWO has accomplished over the millennia. Their treachery runs deep; they have been desperately trying to hide something . . . but I just can't seem to get a handle on it."

Henry peered sideways at the screen. "Looks like we have enough to go over to last a long while, but I think for now we need to concentrate on the task at hand. We need to find the Prime Minister and relieve her of her crystal amulet."

Magnus understood. "It shouldn't take me very long to cross reference the main headquarters directory to her private residence."

Hours passed and Dorathy was lying beside Henry, trying to feel safe in his capable arms, but she could not shake the vision of Alex. She had befriended Henry, accepting his caring gestures, trying to come to grips with the loss of her life as she knew it. She looked at Henry now as he slept beside her. He was a kind man, a strong man, but he seemed to have a hole right through the middle of him that she dared not try to fill. She wanted desperately to embrace this new adventurous life she had been given but felt trapped knowing that only death or the success of this mission would eventually bring her to the *other side* . . . to Alex. She wept silently in the soft glow of Henry's room, feeling the coldness of space creeping into her bones.

Dimitri and Magnus sat in the main lab going over the information they had managed to extract. Dimitri, in his usual manner with feet propped up, head back with eyes closed, was staring at the back of his eye lids and was starting to doze off when Magnus shouted, "Eureka, I found her! Got the bitch!"

Dimitri almost tipped backwards. "What . . . where?"

Magus threw back the rest of his drink. "Look at this small fortress of a home." He brought the holographic image up of her stone castle at nearly the top of the steepest mountains on the planet. Her home was literally built into the side of an outcropping with a sheer cliff that dropped hundreds of meters to the valley below. Dimitri looked, frowning at the prospect of having to go mountain climbing, not seeing any other way to access the home that looked much like a fortress, its natural protection being its placement, teetering on the edge of a deathly abyss.

Dimitri moaned. "Of all the places to live she chooses this."

CHAPTER 47

K ore was dead on her feet; her nightmare was just beginning to unfold. The capitol lay in ruins, the uprising a tsunami, building power from its epicenter and spreading destruction. The masses threatened to rise against authority to embrace freedom, removing control from the clutches of the New Western Ordinance. The pain in her head was only matched by the seething desire to catch those who were responsible for this devastation. Hours seemed like days as she worked hard to regain control. She was exhausted, her hierarchy spread too thin and she was losing hope that her world would ever be the same—so she went home and waited.

The group sat around the main lab, ready to infiltrate Kore's home. After hearing reports of the mayhem they had caused, they felt confident that control was slipping through the fingers of the NWO as they tried to tighten their grip.

After a quick trip for supplies to a popular destination, they knew everything was changing at a rapid pace—the people were taking control back after thousands of years of repression. Jobar and Coolie knew business as usual was a whole different kind of normal as they managed to collect the needed items from a merchant. The inhabitants were running around hoarding supplies for what was going to prove to be the long haul.

Thoughts went to his sister and her children. What kind of world would they grow up in? He desperately wanted to fetch her but knew she would be fine for the time being, as she had always kept herself prepared with a hidden stash of food and weapons in her sublevel bunker. She had always kept it under lock and key, never mentioning to anyone of its existence. Mares was always full of surprises; Jobar smiled at the thought of his obstinate sister. He stood wearing a climbing harness, bundled up with heavy clothes to protect from the bitter cold outside, the ship perched precariously on the edge of the frozen jagged landscape. The gale force wind cut through them right to the bone.

Henry had wished Dorathy could stay behind on the ship, but he knew only too well that only she had the power they would need and whatever the circumstances were, he knew she had to face her demons. Dorathy's voice, carried away by the howling wind, shouted, "Henry I have to go down there, she has in her possession the one item that might be able to tell me why I'm here!"

Henry wouldn't persuade her otherwise and he knew she was right. He said prudently, "Stay close to me." He knew that Dorathy was far from needing his protection but felt obligated to offer it nonetheless. Coolie and Patsup anchored the ropes into the frozen rock, their faces being blasted by the freezing wind whipping the ropes as they fought to tighten them up. Jobar went over the edge first, gripping the rope in his gloved hands, allowing the slack to gradually take him to the bottom—which was some one hundred meters below where Kore's stone fortress sat built into the side of the mountain, with very little level surface area.

Once at the bottom, hidden by the shadows of the oncoming of night, Jobar secured the rope and waited as one by one, his friends repelled down to join him.

Brenda wrapped her face, covering tightly around her nose and mouth and feeling the bite of frost on her face. Magnus pulled out his equipment, ready to spring the lock to Kore's home but shockingly found it to be unlocked. Considering the structure's surroundings he now knew having a locked front door seemed a bit redundant. He slowly pushed opened the door; it creaked loudly over the howling wind as they entered the darkness, a musty scent filling their frozen nostrils.

Kore saw the flicker of her candle and felt the draft of air as she sat peering into her fire as she had done countless times over the years. Tonight, was no different except for her awaited guests arriving at her door. Nikko's fur raised at the back of his neck as he started to snarl a low foreboding growl. She gently stroked him, tugging on his leash and harness forcing him to heel.

Dorothy pushed her way to the front past Henry. She illuminated her way with a small head lamp and her hand tightly gripping her weapon. They slowly and cautiously entered into the small foyer while the rest of them entered single file behind her. Jobar took up the rear, slowly closing the door behind them. Dorothy had a bad feeling about this line of attack but knew there was only one way in, and one way out; they pressed forward into the main living area.

At the far end of the room burned a large fire with a high-back chair blocking its light. To the side they could see a beast's glowing eyes staring back at them, crouched and ready to attack—its ears pinned straight back, its wings twitching. He snarled and exposed large fanged teeth.

Kore spoke from behind the chair reigning in her anger. "I knew you would eventually end up on my doorstep."

Dimitri sat crouched next to the ship breathing in the frozen air; his eyes were closed and he drifted to another time and place where the scent of snow took him back to his time spent in his underground laboratory, in a cold musty bunker, exiled to the bitter cold of Siberia. His discovery brought him to this place and this time. He longed for home, for a life of normal. His mind churned over the unimaginable things he had done, places of wonder and sights of horror. One thing he knew for certain was that at this point of his life he knew that not much else could be thrown at him that he could not handle with ease, or so he believed.

Over the howling wind he thought he heard a roar, so he strained to look past the ship—but the conditions had turned from bad to worse with nothing but a blurred blanket of blowing snow in all directions. He stayed close to the hull as he felt his way past the tail of the ship, daring not to wander too far as it was a long way down to the bottom and the ground had become a slick frozen sheet of ice beneath him.

Coolie was with Patsup, who was asleep snoring in the captain's chair beside him in the cockpit. Coolie strained to see out the forward transparent dome. A dark shadow amongst the frosted white had caught his eye, so he climbed to his feet and leaned in close, rubbing his eyes, forcing them to adjust to the fading light of night. He had a bad feeling growing in the pit of his gut and as much as he knew the cold would strike him hard the minute he opened the hatch, he felt compelled to check on Dimitri standing guard outside.

Coolie wrapped his cloak around his body and pulled the hood down over his face and cinched it tight, leaving just enough room for his goggles. He paused and took a deep breath as the hatch slid open, blasting him with snow and frigid air. Coolie stepped out and the hatch quickly closed behind him as he groped for the hull to steady himself on his feet. He tried yelling for Dimitri but knew it would be in vain as he struggled to hear his own shrieking voice above the ever-growing howl of the relentless wind.

From behind came a blow that knocked Coolie to the ground; as he struggled, gasping for air he could make out something that looked like big black claws in front of his face. He hazily decided it was a pair of boots and with another blow to the back of his head he was assured it was indeed boots; his goggles twisted to the side, and his face was lying on the cold stiff leather; his vision narrowed to black.

Kore rose from the comfort of her worn chair facing her guests—her back to the fire cast a red halo around her withered shape and shadowed the features of her aging face. She held Nikko firmly by her side as she slowly approached. She searched and presented the crystal amulet, glowing and pulsating, hanging from the heavy chain around her neck. "I seem to have something that you seek to possess, and it seems to have been awakened by your presence." She stared into the darkened room illuminated only by a small head lamp; the shadowy figures moved in closer as Dorathy's lamp brought light onto Kore's pale face.

She winced at the light, but it was at that moment Brenda felt as if she were staring at the ghostly image of her mother, long past. Brenda moved in close removing her head wrap, "My God, who are you?"

"Who am I?" Kore asked in a whisper as she stared back at Brenda, recognizing the curve of her face and the color of her auburn hair and the glow of her bright blue eyes. "Now, that is a very good question, maybe you can answer that for me."

From behind a new booming voice startled and made them jump and grasp for their weapons. "Who she is has been kept a secret . . . but I have been waiting for you a very long time, my dear Dorathy."

Dorathy dropped her weapon to her side, the voice taking her back to another life and she almost forgot where and when she was. "Simon? Is that really you?" She turned and gazed at the face lit by her fading light. She struggled with the past rushing up to remind her of the implications. His bald head and the firm handsome features remained ageless, and she peered into the ancient eyes of her father's oldest friend, a dizzy feeling came over her. "How is this possible?"

Kore clamored to get to the meaning of it all. "Silas, what are you talking about, why are you here? I demand answers at once, and who in

Hell's name . . . is Simon?" Silas ignored Kore's requests for the first time in years and he felt free to disclose the truth . . . finally.

Dorathy was shaken as the reality started to seep into her cells. "I was told you killed my father!"

"Ah yes, I did indeed kill your father, and you died ever so tragically my dear girl, at the hands of Lucca Venturini . . . or actually his nephew Carlo who you so willingly took under your wing. They were trying to protect you and your ungodly bloodline. They thought if they killed you and had you sent here, they would get you out of harm's way and get you to the future to fulfill their mission. Unfortunately Simon killed, or shall I say, *I* killed your father before I had a chance to realize John Rosen had in his possession a very interesting artifact . . . its glow dimmed as life left your father in his final breath."

Dorathy started to shake as the information reeled in her head—a ghastly scene from a horror she had tried so hard to forget. "Why my father? My father helped mankind progress to a better future . . . Dorathy's voice trailed off as she remembered visions of her father's involvement with attempts to depopulate the planet.

"Yes Dorathy . . . search your feelings."

Dorathy started to cry. "My father knew as many did that our planet and its nearly ten billion inhabitants could not continue to be sustained." Her voice trembling, she said, "Something had to be done!"

"Yes, and something was done . . . by your blasphemous Illuminati. They abandoned nearly ten billion people to suffer and no doubt extinguish themselves! My dear, I killed your father because he was not human . . . I wanted you dead for the same reason."

Dorathy struggled with his words and was forced to recall every event in the last few months. The ship protecting her as if she were from the same species, the lost city, the message in the cave. She tried desperately to recall her father's journals, and it all started to make sense to her. Simon could see her wheels turning over the events of her new life, not knowing exactly what she had been through or experienced; but he knew her real identity was starting to sink in by the expression on her face.

"Yes Dorathy, you and the other twelve bloodlines of the Illuminati are of the purist alien DNA. The only way I could see this through was to wait for you to arrive to this time, a time when I would have the technology to explore your origins and destroy it."

Dorathy's head swam in the implications, knowing that whoever seeded the universe did so approximately fourteen Billion years ago from another dimension; everyone was merely a byproduct of their efforts to populate the universe from God knows where. An alien race far more advanced, evolved to a higher level of being. If there ever was a God, the beings were no doubt a part of the master plan. For the first time in her life she felt she was meant for something greater than what she had grown to know. It empowered her at a level she could not begin to comprehend.

Dorathy had had just about enough of Simon or Silas or whatever the hell his name was, and shouted, "You listen to me you small narrow-minded prick, it's you against the entire universe and I for one have had enough of your bullshit!"

Suddenly Kore started in and pushed her way forward to face Silas, Nikko snarling at her guests. She held the Amulet high above her head, the chain dangling down the length of her arm. "Someone tells me now what the meaning of all this is or I swear I will smash the crystal against the stone!"

Silas shook his head. "Patience was never one of your virtues. Kore, search your feelings, you do have them, don't you? You have been presented with a woman here—Silas rushed forward and with a quick movement grabbed Brenda and shoved her so close she could almost taste Kore's foul breath.

Henry had had enough, and in one sudden attempt to disarm Silas he and Magnus were met with fierce opposition. They exchanged expertly crafted blows, with Nikko growling and fighting against his leash. Kore reached around with her free hand still clinging to the chain, the amulet bouncing around and growing ever brighter and brought a dagger to Brenda's throat. "Stop now or I will finish her off!" Henry struggled to get to Brenda but was knocked hard to the cold stone floor, hitting his head and now lying dazed and on the brink of passing out. Magnus shifted his stance, disarming Silas and holding him by the scruff, ready to finish him off.

"Now Kore," Silas said, laughing an evil sound, "you wouldn't kill your only living relative, now would you?" Kore turned, dropping the knife and it clanked across the floor. Brenda moved away slowly, unscathed.

Facing Silas, Kore demanded, "We need some answers here, and clearly you are here for some as well."

Silas shook free from Magnus's grip and straightened the collar of his thick woolen coat. "Dorathy," Silas goaded her, "tell us about your amulet."

Dorathy spit at him, "I won't tell you a damned thing!"

Silas threw his head back in laughter. "You haven't a clue! Okay, I will go first. The reason Kore has the amulet is because I gave it to her very great grandmother, and she in turn gave it to our daughter."

Brenda's thoughts were rushing to her like a tidal wave of emotion slamming her to the ocean floor tossing and turning as she struggled to breathe. She gasped, "Oh God, you're my father!" Her thoughts and words drifted off to silence.

"Yes, your mother was helpful and very accommodating thanks to you. Your emotional note had struck a chord with her and she came with me to investigate but I assure you she never forgave you for abandoning her and together we left you. Time marched on as I watched over the Amulet through the centuries, watched it get past from mother to daughter." Silas turned his back on Brenda, leaving her reeling at the thought of her mothers' betrayal. Her thoughts churned on the idea that she had inherited his convoluted DNA.

Facing Dorathy, taunting her, Silas said, "You are its rightful owner and only you and your bloodline carry the power to activate it. So now I think you and I are going to go on a little trip in your magnificent ship."

Dorathy screamed so loud the walls shook up to the rafters sending dust particles floating down from above. "Never!" She turned to reach for the amulet as it grew hot in Kore's hand and lurched from her grasp, burning her in the process—then it shot across the short distance landing in Dorathy's out-stretched hand.

Kore shouted in pain as she held her scolded hand. "Give that back to me!"

Silas's eyes grew wide as the scene unfolded, and he found himself chasing them out into the bitter night. He shouted after them, "I know I will be seeing you again shortly because I have something you will no doubt want back, and they are long gone now!"

Kore screamed, "Silas, stop them at once, that is an order!"

Silas turned to face her. "I have waited a lifetime to do this!" He approached her with a look of a feral animal, a rage that had been building up inside of him for centuries and struck her hard across the face, sending her backwards to the hard floor, Nikko trying hard to sink his sharp teeth into his master's attacker. "Silence!" he yelled.

She was struggling, forcing her old bones up from the floor still having a firm grip on Nikko's leash. She tried to calm him as she now knew Silas was no longer the person he had been all the years of loyal servitude. He was indeed a stranger to her, this man by the name of Simon who had now taken the place of her devoted pilot.

Silas said, "I have my own agenda and you are no longer a necessity." He bent down and picked up her discarded dagger from the stone floor and with a precise throw, it struck Nikko in the chest and he winced and whined in pain, yelping for comfort. Kore screamed and cried, tears flowing freely now as she quickly drew the dagger from her beloved pet and ripped a portion from her cloak and tended to his wound. Anger welled in her like a dormant volcano coming to life; she held the dagger firmly in her hands and attacked Simon from behind. The cumulative effects of the stresses of her life and the events of the last few weeks had given her an unnatural strength that could never be matched. With a force of ages, she came down hard into Simon's back with her dagger, instantly severing his spinal cord and sending him lifeless to the floor. She withdrew the dagger and straddling him, brought it down hard into the base of his head, the dagger stopping as its tip broke against the stone floor. The blood flowing freely and gurgled as Simon took his last breath. Kore screamed a scream that could be heard over the centuries, time ever flowing but just a mere echo.

Henry was the last one to the top, out of breath, his throbbing head only matched by the pain of frostbite setting into his extremities. He clamored over the icy jagged rock with the help of Dorathy pulling at his coat collar. The others fought against the gale force winds threatening to blow them all over the edge. They slowed to a crawl, groping their way in the darkness, their eyes sealed shut by the freeze, finally managing to find their way to the outer hatch of the ship patiently waiting for them.

The hatch slid open, welcoming them into the warmth. The commotion startled Patsup; he stretched and yawned lazily as his senses came back to him and he ran to welcome them back. Patsup winced at the sight of them, Magnus and Henry both bruised and bloodied and covered in frost. The women were unscathed but traumatized by the ordeal with anguish written on their red frozen faces.

Patsup was helping Jobar with his coat as Henry moved past them towards the cockpit, shouting over his shoulder, "Get Dimitri up here—we need to vacate ASAP!"

Patsup now had a very confused look on his face and shouted after Henry, "Aren't Dimitri and Coolie with you?"

Jobar knew that look only too well as he grabbed Patsup by the collar, slamming him hard against the inner hull. "What do you mean Patsup! Where are they?" he screamed, his voice cracking as it thawed.

Patsup shrugged, "I don't know! I . . . I . . . was asleep, and when I woke they were gone, and I assumed you called them down."

Henry stopped short of the cockpit, remembering what Simon had said and turned back on his heels. "He has them. We can find them with the personal locator Dimitri has." Henry ran past them to the main lab bringing up the information, "If he's close by, we'll find him." His hands, stiff and sore, sailed over the console. "Damn it, nothing!"

Dorathy leaned against the hull shivering, clutching her crystal pyramid, her amulet that was her magical talisman, sobbing, her legs giving way as she slid to the floor. Hot tears were streaming down her face. "All of this is because of me, it's all my fault, the reason your lives have been stolen from you is because of me, because of my capabilities." She sobbed uncontrollably, "There is no place like home . . . I just want to go home now . . . please . . . we just need to go home."

Suddenly the ship lurched alive with a sole purpose. Everyone was thrown flat to the floor as it ascended at such an accelerated speed, that no one could begin to comprehend. Henry was trying hard to crawl to the cockpit in order to take command back, but it was a futile effort. The ship rose into space within seconds and was hurtling at an inconceivable speed. The innards seemed to warp and stretch as a rubber band would, stretching its limits into infinity. It grew so long and deformed; it was as if everyone had been separated by miles between them.

With a snap and a boom, time seemed to stop, frozen in the fabric of space. There were words being spoken, but it all sounded like a recording at the slowest speed, distorted and unrecognizable. With a flash of golden light brightly shining through the cockpit, immersing everything in its warm glow, they slingshot forward, and it was over just as suddenly as it started. Henry was the first to his feet, stumbling to the cockpit holding his aching head, Magnus on his heels. Jobar sat up like a pop-up cartoon character while Patsup rolled onto his side using Dorathy and Brenda as crutches to stand. Brenda, disgusted with him, pushed him back to the floor as she stood and helped Dorathy up.

Henry sat in his captain's chair, stunned and utterly shocked as tears formed at the beautiful sight that lay before him. "You need to look at this people, it is the most wonderful thing I have ever seen."

Dorathy came in behind him, tears staining her face. "Oh my holy God."

CHAPTER 48

The group all stood staring out into the darkness as the sun was just coming up over the horizon, glistening off the upper atmosphere of Earth. Dorathy held her hand to her mouth. How is this possible?" Her comment was met by silence as everyone was trying to absorb what had just happened. So many years of longing, so many years of danger and the unknown, so many years of being trapped and alone, facing overwhelming odds, all came to down to a few moments in time that had separated them from ages long gone.

Henry sat in his seat and took readings, as he had not yet fully comprehended the image slowly rotating beneath them. He knew in his gut something was not quite right. They were on the dark side of their long-lost home and it seemed so still, so vacant, so very wrong.

Magnus took the seat beside him. His tired eyes took in the calm darkness and he shook his head as the realization seeped into his soul. Everything that they had left behind was long gone. The look of acknowledgment settled into the fine lines of his face with a hint of recognition, as the shadowy figures of familiar land masses below turning into the darkness. Magnus with a look of despair said, "Our world mate . . . there are no lights. "

Brenda took a seat behind them and turned to look at Dorathy—the reality was a harsh thing that managed to creep in. "You know what I'm about to say."

With a blank stare Dorathy said, "Yes . . . yes I do."

It was apparent to everyone now. The question had always been where, where are we? Now the only question remaining was when. Brenda asked the question everyone was thinking, "How far forward in time are we?"

Dorathy softly asked, "Henry, take readings of the atmosphere and that should give us a hint."

"Already on it."

After a few seconds the reading came back. Henry looked over his shoulder, and said, "Hmmm . . . pristine . . . a paradise. No traces that man has ever scarred the planet."

The wheels were turning in Dorathy's mind. "Can you pull up the current location of Polaris?"

Henry did as he was asked, not knowing exactly what she was getting at but knowing enough about celestial navigation to know that Polaris was the North Star. Henry looked at the result and shut his eyes with a heavy sigh. "Polaris is off by several degrees. Jesus Christ, he whispered to the darkness below. Henry adjusted a few readings. "Vega is due north."

Dorathy's head spun as she fell back into the seat beside Brenda. Jobar was puzzled by everyone's reaction in the cockpit, trying to crane his neck from side to side on his tip toes. "Please tell me, what is it, what's wrong?"

Magnus got up disgusted and overwhelmed and pushed his way out of the copilot's seat. "Well, bloody hell, I've fuckin' seen enough!"

Henry turned to look at Dorathy for an answer; she starred back at him and blurted the answer he was afraid to get. "Due to the Earth's procession on its axis, we're about in the year fourteen thousand AD . . . give or take."

Brenda repeated what Dorathy had just said in an attempt to wrap her head around it. "We are fourteen thousand years in the future?" Brenda searched Dorathy's eyes for help, for a truth she wanted to hear, not the craziness that was being spoken; she only found in her eyes the realization of their predicament.

They sat in silence once again, absorbing the situation. Dorathy moved beside Henry. "I know after what we have been through you are not going to want to hear this request, but take us down . . . down to the

Antarctic." Henry peered at her through squinted weary eyes and glanced down, where in her lap she clutched the pyramid-shaped amulet glowing brightly in her hands.

"No . . . not until you tell us what you know of your . . . trinket."

"Fair enough, I think it best we take a break from . . . all this." Slowly they filed back to the main lab, allowing Jobar and Patsup to finally see out onto Earth, now a dark quiet place, a sanctuary . . . an oasis, or a mirage . . . the verdict was still out.

They all joined Magnus at the table; he was already throwing back his second drink. Henry sat craning and rubbing his aching neck, his head still throbbing from the down and dirty fight with Simon. A time that had seemed only minutes ago, now seemed as if a lifetime had passed.

Everyone's attention was on Dorathy as she closed her eyes, remembering her father's journal and the trip they had taken together so many years ago to Tibet. The air had been crisp and thin with the strong sweet smell of burning incense. The monks were chanting in unison a strumming sound that had vibrated off the temple walls. A sea of red silk, a calmness she had never experienced before with a feeling of oneness with all life that surrounded them. She remembered taking her father's hand and felt safe and loved—a feeling she would not have again for quite some time, until the time she first took Alex's hand in hers.

Afterwards they met with one of the elders. He had told them a tale that had been passed on over the centuries, a tale of man's beginnings and the chosen few whose bloodlines were kept intact. Dorathy recounted what he had said all those years ago.

Only those who are of the purest blood, may enter the temples for they hold the power within them. They came from the heavens, an attainable place and set upon the Earth their kind that we could someday join them. The temple you seek is buried beneath within the only land that has been untouched by man's hand. They hold the looking glass into our future.

After telling them this Dorathy continued, "my father wrote of finding the temple buried deep under the Antarctic ice. He also had his suspicions of Simon having been swayed from their common interests.

Henry knew there was more. "Dora what did he find down there?"

Dorathy held up the amulet glowing a blackish red. "This was in a pyramid buried and untouched by man, still in its original form with its ... occupant ... that lay in stasis ... ," her voice trailing off. "Waiting for one of us to awaken him. My father wrote as he entered the pyramid that there was a state of knowing and recognition, an overwhelming bond of pure love between him and the being. He was offered the amulet and when he accepted, the entity was released from his commitment and soared into the heavens."

Magnus set his empty glass down and took to his unstable feet, approaching the console bringing up the thirteen planets. They now hovered, taunting them to explore their mysteries.

"Brenda gathered her thoughts. "Look Dora you were sent to us, into the future to help mankind achieve its loftiest of goals ... to find the answers that have eluded man from the very beginning ... where do we come from? The question is all encompassing, the answer is simple and yet abstract. We come from there, somewhere within Orion and the thirteen rogue planets, thirteen blood lines, and one crystal talisman. You have the power to get us there, I no doubt believe you also have the power to uncover what mysteries lie ahead of us in these thirteen planets."

Henry added, "There is a connection, we just need to follow what we know so far."

Dorathy nodded; she understood she was the only one who could open a doorway to the other side. "I need to go down there and see for myself what my father saw—if there is anything I'm missing we will surely find it." Dorathy looked at the image floating over their heads. "Orion through the centuries had always been linked to so many tales. Pyramids all over the planet had been discovered, most of which were aligned to the stars of Orion."

Jobar softly added, "A message hidden in plain sight." Jobar asked, "But what of *our* existence?"

Dorathy answered, "we are all made up of the same stuff, and it would be no surprise if your species and other species carry the same blood lines."

"Okay then," Henry announced. "We go down after we get some rest and have some time to digest what has transpired; at least it's summer in the southern hemisphere."

Brenda sat still in her thoughts, looking over to Jobar and seeing the pain in his eyes—both fearing the worst for Dimitri and Coolie. The time was ticking away.

Dimitri woke in what looked to be a cargo hold of a small drone ship; next to him gagged and bound was Coolie, still slumped over, with blood caked onto his face from a massive wound to the side of his head. Dimitri struggled with his bound hands, kicking and squirming to stand in the small cramped space. Sweat pouring from his forehead blurred his vision as he managed to wipe his face with his shoulder. He turned to his side and lay horizontal, straining to see into the cockpit. As he suspected the ship was unmanned and was driven by remote on a preset coordinates. His head throbbing, he grunted past his gagged mouth and awkwardly kicked Coolie to wake him.

After a few kicks Coolie moaned and peeled one eye open, the other being pasted shut by frozen blood, his scaly skin peeling from the arid mountain air of Kore's home planet. He tried to speak but found he had been gagged as well. Panic set into him as he started to pitch and struggle, screaming something through his gagged mouth.

Moments seemed like days as they both struggled to free themselves. All the while the drone ship sped to an unknown destination. Dimitri managed to move his large frame in the tiny space, moving far enough forward to get a good look around to the control panel. He squinted hard to make out the readings and stopped with a rapid intake of air through his ever- growing congested nostrils. Through his faltering gag he said the words that Coolie knew only too well, and Coolie shuttered at the thought of what lay in their uncertain future: "We are headed to the military prison of the NWO."

Tears started to well up in Coolie's frantic eyes as he searched Dimitri's for comfort, but he was just as frightened and showed no hint of having an answer. Coolie sat lonely and prayed for a miracle.

The drone ship came in slow for a landing on a deadly wasteland; there was no escaping this nightmare. Dimitri and Coolie sat helpless, still bound tightly, and they could only imagine what horrors waited for them as they felt the deceleration, heard the slowing hum of the propulsion, and felt the drone lurch as it touched down . . . but where, where indeed. There was no need for windows on a drone, so imaginations were running wild. Coolie managed to grunt something; Dimitri knew what he was trying to say from the look in his eyes. "Yes, try to stay together, I have a tracking device that has been implanted, it will be our only hope of being rescued." Coolie nodded, fear permeating into every pore and he began to shake uncontrollably.

With a heavy clank, the ship was moving again but this time it felt as they were rapidly descending as Dimitri's ears popped. Dread was all-consuming, it weighed them down as they sunk deeper into the unknown abyss. Finally, they came to a stop and the drone ship felt as they were now on a conveyer belt moving forward. From behind a panel, a loud hissing sound was followed by a gas that quickly filled the small space. The two frightened occupants started to gag and cough, their heads tingling, eyes and throat burning as they gasped for air, their vision narrowing, and with one final breath they were gone. Death would be an easier journey.

Dorathy sat in her little room going over the milestones of her life as she thumbed through the photo book that had been placed in her cryotube so many centuries ago. She longed for the life she once had. An image appeared of her precious daughter Athena— thoughts of her lingered in her mind's eye. What a lovely day they had making sand angels on her little bit of paradise. Tears welled as she thought of all the things she had missed in her daughter's life: her wedding, grandchildren . . . that life she once had was long gone now, Athena longtime dead, having lived an entire life without her mother in it.

She missed her father—all the things she never discussed with him, all the things she wish she has known but she had pushed him aside because of his sketchy involvement with the Illuminati. She wanted to scream at him and hold him tight all at the same time. She started to sob uncontrollably thinking of all the heartache; there had been her small bit of happiness she found for herself, the one thin shred she so briefly had with Alex, only to have him stripped away, her happiness stripped away, her life taken, and every trace of it extinct. A pang of sudden anger welled in her gut, for only immense loneliness had now taken its place in this new life which had been handed to her.

She was racked by guilt for the people she now called her family. The sacrifices made by them so she could be brought forward to another place in time. Yet here they were, where they had started, everyone gone. Everyone had either transcended to another dimension or simply perished from the face of the planet, now haunting her from below.

The thought of distance and time had always been such a mystery to most—throw in a little dark matter, a dash of multiple dimensions, and a pinch of quantum entanglement, mix it all together and you got man's inability to comprehend. Was it distance and time or was it all separated by a thin veil occupying the same woven fabric. All being a spooky action at a distance.

Dorothy's eyes grew heavy as she still clutched the amulet tightly to her chest; sleep was something that seemed to elude her. The thought that she somehow had gotten just a tiny bit closer to the answers they sought only now that she had faced her demons, she had drifted off to sleep.

Morning brought with it a type of disconnect as the planet they left behind nearly fourteen thousand years ago had changed so much, its topography distorted, the polar shift changing the landscape. It was a serene and quiet place with only the sounds of nature, the sound of isolation that gave way to an immense feeling of loneliness.

Approaching Antarctica, all they could see was a desolate cold rocky dessert landscape that stretched out for miles. The ship who had turned out to be their most trusted friend had automatically zeroed in on their destination. As they sped over the wasteland a shining figure was coming up over the horizon, glistening brightly as the sun reflected off the white limestone structure.

Dorathy knew right away it was the place her father had written about in his journal so many years ago. The ship hovered above, almost as if it was making a connection to the past, relaying its thoughts to the creature that once inhabited its dark cold interior.

Dorathy tried not to state the obvious. "My God this was once buried by a mile of ice."

Henry went over his readouts and added, "By the looks of it, I would say it then spent some time under the ocean as water levels rose with the ice melt, then receded, exposing the Antarctic land mass as we see it now."

The air was dry and cold, the wind blowing over the dark greyish-black scenery, giving it an other-worldly appearance. As they came down to the barren land they started to see the evidence of it having been submerged for many centuries. Fossilized crustaceans that had been bleached by the sun had formed on the outer structure and over time were being eroded away, leaving the smooth white stone peeking out, the splendor of its original opulence being preserved.

As they disembarked Dorathy had a knot in her gut that grew to a panic that seeped to the depths of her existence. She looked over her shoulder back to the ship nervously hoping it would not leave them stranded on this desolate forgotten land mass. They walked across the land that over time had shifted and filled with sediment, blurring the onetime frozen water entrance. An image of a Russian submarine breaking the water as it emerged from the depths of the icy Southern Ocean was merely a ghost that came to haunt them now with the wind howling over the sharp edges of the pyramid.

Dorathy reached out with her bare hand and gently touched the surface of the pyramid closing the gap of time, knowing her father had done the exact same thing so many centuries before her.

With a grinding thud the door slid open and they cautiously passed through it with Dorathy in the lead.

Henry whispered; afraid he might wake up a sleeping beast within. "You said your father wrote he had awakened an entity of light that gave him the amulet."

"Yes, once he had taken it the being disappeared up through the baffled ceiling and out through the southern shaft."

They slowly entered and climbed up the ascending staircase to the grand chamber. Its narrow passage was a portal to the past. Magnus and Brenda ducked their heads and came in behind Henry and, peering up where there was a carving that seemed to be very familiar to them. Brenda craned her neck and pointed "Look, the Orion constellation."

Dorathy and Henry could see as Jobar and Patsup struggled to look up past their friends. Dorathy noticed the emphasis on the stars that made up the sword slung from the belt. "The Orion Nebula, Dorathy said quietly, "I bet this pyramid lines up to the middle star." Henry nodded his acknowledgment.

Dorathy's wheels were turning in her mind. "I think the carvings in the lost city have similar meaning, all lining up to points of our thirteen rogue planets, one carving for each planet giving a type of coordinates to find a pyramid . . . God, who knows."

Henry agreed. "I bet you you're right Dora. A type of map to a location on each planet . . . it would make sense."

Dorathy ran her hands through her now-shoulder length hair, a few greys glistening in the dim light coming from above. In front of them was a coffer structure which had been carved from a solid block of rose granite. They gathered round it as they peered into the now-empty shell, trying to imagine a being of light lying within since the beginning of time. The genetic engineer from another time, from another dimension, lying in stasis waiting for confirmation that his work was done.

Dorathy placed her hand on the stone, feeling a slight vibration, its frequency matching hers. She looked at Henry. "Can you feel that?"

Henry placed his hand next to hers and shook his head. "No . . . I don't feel anything."

The next thing they knew Dorathy was climbing inside and lying down within the cold stone. There was a warmth building within her. Off in the distance she heard Henry saying her name, *Dorathy don't . . .*"

Dorathy found herself lying in the cool grass—the scent was so familiar to her. She opened her eyes looking up to the hazy blue sky, a planet hovering over her head that took up most of the surrounding space, its beautiful rings glowing brightly around it. She sat up looking around, as she hoped her father or Athena would appear.

In the distance there was a whistle and a small dog barking. She turned towards the sound and saw her father approaching with her dog Zwicky leaping and bounding over the tall grass in front of him. She got up and faced him, Zwicky leaping into her open arms. "Dad . . . how am I doing?"

There was his familiar laugh. "You are doing just fine. I knew you could find your way. I also knew you could get back what was rightfully yours."

Dorathy opened her palm and the amulet's light sparkled and shone in all directions. "Dad what is all of this, why am I here, what is all of this even about?"

John Rosen's words floated by on a breeze, "Ah Dorathy look at your circumstances that brought you here . . . we were chosen . . . you, have been chosen."

"Chosen for what?"

"It is simple Dorathy, if you just open your eyes."

Dorathy searched herself for the answers. John nodded his head as he could see his daughter's eyes light up with realization and said, "They came and started life so that they could live on within us."

She pondered a moment, repeating her fathers' words, "So they could live on . . . they were a dying species?"

"No, they weren't dying, Dora . . . they were transcending. They had found a way to move from their physical form and wanted to leave evidence of their existence through us, so that we could somehow bridge the gap between the physical world and the spiritual world . . . their world . . . a world that they had evolved to. They left us a gate, a type of portal—we just needed to evolve in order to see it *through*."

Dorathy felt as if she could fall right into her father's gleaming eyes. "Dad, I don't get it, why just a few of us are able to . . . progress. We all have the code engineered into our DNA, so why just us?"

John spoke calmly. "Look honey, through the centuries most of our engineering simply degraded that's all, maybe it gives a new meaning to the term survival of the fittest. No controversy, just a simple fact of nature. No one's perfect Dora, which is why they left the gate for us- you just needed to find the key."

Dorathy asked, almost whining like a child, "Dad, why me?"

"Why? Because you can, that's why."

Dorathy sighed a big sigh, putting her little dog on the grass. "Why can't I just die like most people."

Her father laughed hard, throwing his head back. "You are not like most people, now go and open that gate, I have faith in you." John clasped his hands over hers, still holding the amulet, the vibration resetting her frequency.

Dorathy opened her eyes with a chill as she looked up at the pale faces of her friends.

"Jesus Christ!" Henry shouted, "What the hell happened to you?"

Brenda's eyes were fixated. "You were fading . . . you were transparent . . . I can't even explain it."

Dorathy smiled, "I'm fine . . . really . . . I know now why I'm here."

"Oh great, Brenda said sounding a bit condescending. "So tell us, why are WE here?"

"They . . . the Otherlings . . . they did leave us a gate or portal with hopes we would come to use it. That only the few can proceed through it to the higher level of existence. You see, if we have evolved enough to have the capabilities to venture so far from our planet that we have earned the right to proceed through the gate, to the other side. We are the ones who have managed to exceed our original engineering."

Magnus shook his head. "You, yes—I know that to be a fact . . . us— well that my dear is another story."

"No," Dorathy snapped back. "You were created from them, from their DNA, I was created by them *with* their DNA. The only difference is that my programming, my engineering holds the key . . . maybe they just didn't anticipate that we would find a way of replicating it with you."

Henry looked down at Jobar and Patsup, his mind wandering around in the shadows. "What about them Dora, they have the code . . . every being we have run into carries the same code."

"Yes," she answered, "I know. We have to believe with each race there is one person that has my capabilities—a few which have their code fully intact."

Henry leaned against the wall of the chamber, never feeling so old. "You were sent to us, and not only for the protection of your DNA, but so that we would finally finish the job of bridging the gap between realities. Who would be the righteous ones to pass through it, Dora?"

Dorathy's eyes shone in the fading light. "I don't know, I don't have the answer. Perhaps it's what we hold in our hearts?"

Henry looked from one to the other; all had the look of weariness written in sudden lines on their faces. "We have been through a lot, not to mention we are short two crew members. I for one have never felt so goddamned tired. We need to take a break here, but we can't stay . . . and Dorathy you can't come with us, we have to go and rescue Dimitri and Coolie, and it's not safe for you, so you're staying here!"

Dorathy went to object but knew he was right. If she were to be captured the mission could never be completed, or somehow the gate would be destroyed—the horrible possibilities were endless.

Brenda continued, "Let us not forget we were not designed to live in this dimension, we are slowly dying here." The group looked at each other, knowing what the others felt.

Jobar whispered to no one in particular, "No wonder I feel like shit."

Magnus answered, "Precisely my little friend, we have not been designed for the rigors of this reality."

Henry took Dorathy by the shoulders. "Where do you want to live, Dora . . . literally, the world is yours for the choosing."

There was only one place Dorathy could imagine staying for any length of time. "I want to go to my island . . . my home on the beach . . . well what's left of it, Dorathy smiled, a spark in her eye. "Maybe I'll finally get my treehouse."

CHAPTER 49

As soon as the crew boarded their ship, they started to gain the energy back that had been lost to them while on the land of Earth. Brenda looked in the mirror; the deep lines that had developed on her face were fading before her eyes, transforming her back to her youthful, genetically engineered *synthetic* self. "My God," she softly said to herself turning her face from side to side . . . "If only I could have bottled this I could have made a fortune."

They were speeding over the calm crystal clear aqua waters of the South Pacific. New Zealand was fast appearing over the horizon. Dorathy sat next to Henry in the cockpit thinking back at how many times she had flown over this part of paradise. She peered out in front of her as the islands rapidly came into focus. They appeared the same at first glance, but the land masses had shifted somewhat. The majority had shrunk in size or had simply disappeared below the depths. Others which had land mass and were not merely atolls had gained frontage with the shifting currents. They had never seen such a paradise so completely untouched . . . sterile of man.

Henry looked at the coordinates, announcing, "Next stop heaven."

Magnus smiled behind her. "I think I would not mind spending some time here . . . even if it kills me."

Brenda teared up with thoughts of Dimitri being tortured or worse. "Dim would have loved this.

Magnus added. "Then the two of you would have finally one thing you could agree on."

Brenda knew, saying, "He wouldn't leave this place . . . none of us would."

Jobar had a look of anguish not knowing what to say and blurted out in a desperate voice, "We have to leave . . . we have to get Coolie and Dimitri!" Henry and Dorathy exchanged looks, knowing he was stating the obvious.

Dorathy pointed to the direction of where she sensed her home used to be. The beach had shifted, the jungle peaks had eroded, the surrounding area had flattened out a bit, the lagoon was shallower and narrow, but the beach with its perfectly crescent bay still had a breathtaking waterfall that cascaded down to form a running stream of fresh rain water that flowed into the lagoon. Dorathy closed her eyes. "I'm home, I am finally home."

The ship came to land along the shoreline on the soft white sand, spraying water as it did. Birds ruffled their feathers and squawked loudly in the trees, by the strange sight of such an unusual creature.

"Alright people," Henry said as he was only slightly managing to control his emotions. "As much as we would all like to stay and simply enjoy what time we might have left, IF we were staying . . . We are not staying, we owe that to Dim and Coolie. "If the shit hits the fan, we just come back, but either way, we are coming back . . . one way or another." Henry continued, "If you start to feel like crap then get back to the ship, we all saw how we were able to rejuvenate once back on board. Don't risk it though, 'cause we just don't know how far is too far gone. Got it?" As they were already out the hatch, Henry whispered to himself, "Got it."

Magnus, fully clothed, dove into the shallow warm water and came up floating on his back, looking up at the blue sky with willowy clouds floating by way of the gentle trade winds.

Brenda tossed her shoes aside and sunk her toes into the flour-like sand, coming to the realization that they were finally home, while Jobar and Patsup walked along the beach, never having seen a place quite like this.

Henry came up behind Dorathy and put his arm around her waist, his eyes squinted by the bright sun and a warm breeze touching his skin. "I wish we had met in another life; I could have gotten use to this."

Dorathy shook her head. "All the years I could have just taken it easy . . . I didn't have to work that hard . . . I could have been here."

Henry smiled, "You are here now, whether you like it or not . . . and probably for a long while, by yourself, are you going to be okay with that?"

Dorathy responded, "I was thinking about that. I think with Brenda's help I can rig my cryotube for hyper sleep. I think that might be the best way. We put it somewhere secure, and when I'm ready I simply go to sleep for a while. Dorathy smiled up at Henry and saw the lines around his eyes growing deeper.

He looked into her dark eyes and was stricken by the feeling of loss. The thought of leaving her behind was tearing him apart at the seams. His somber voice would surly betray him by revealing his fear as he said with apprehension, "Sure, that sounds like a good idea."

CHAPTER 50

T he crew worked in shifts building a functional and very sturdy tree-house equipped with a dumbwaiter, a crow's nest, and plenty of living space. An aqueduct was formed from the fresh water stream and solar panels and windmills were put in place at various sites on the island, giving Dorathy the power she needed to run the equipment that would be left with her, and most important food storage, cooking and the desalination unit for the dry season.

Typhoons were not the norm for this part of the world, and all satellites if any, were either junk or damaged beyond repair and had failed or came crashing to Earth long ago. So Magnus took on the task of building a weather satellite and took it up, launching it from the cargo bay of the ship. To be on the safe side a cave had been found and fashioned into a bunker for a base of operations and was also perfect to be used for dry storage. This was also where her cryotube was placed and reconfigured to house her and her new little companion Zwicky for hibernation sleep. Brenda managed to finish the task of cloning Dorathy's beloved little poodle. The crew loved playing with him while they worked on Dorathy's new home.

Sadly, the time had come for the crew to depart. They all said their good-byes and waited for Henry in the ship. Henry started, "Okay Dora we have checked, double-checked and triple-checked everything down

here and up in orbit, are you sure there is nothing else you can think of
that you might need?"

Dora laughed, "Let's see, I have a fish farm, a garden with a variety of
things growing and a greenhouse with more of the same. I have a bunker
safe enough to protect me from nuclear fallout, I have a home built with
steel, titanium, aluminum- you have stripped the ship to the bare bones.
On top of that if it all goes to shit Zwicky and I will just take a long nap
and wait for you to come wake us up. I think we're good. Honest we'll be
fine."

Henry sighed, a worry written on his face that showed more than just
the effects of Earth destroying his cells at a molecular level; he showed
a deep sadness for he was going to miss her, and his heart was breaking.
He embraced her and kissed her, whispering in her ear, "Wait for me
Dorathy Rosen, because I love you.

Dorathy looked into his eyes. "I love you Henry; you are a good man.
Be safe my friend and try not to be gone too long. She wanted to bite
back her last words because she knew they could be absent for a lifetime.
With that he boarded the ship.

Dorathy put her hand to the hull sending it her instructions . . . her
feelings of love and admiration, her understanding for time and space
and instructions to protect and help its occupants. When her message
had been received, they slowly rose into the air and in a flash they were
gone, the ship slingshot back to where and when they had been, with a
golden flash and a sonic boom that sent the island's wildlife scurrying for
cover. Dorathy was finally home.

Dimitri woke shivering and nude, strapped down to a sterile cold steel
chair in a glaring cubicle, the light blinding him so badly he could barely

see his surroundings. His arms and legs were bound so tightly he could no longer feel them; the circulation was being cut off and the bindings were cutting into his skin. He screamed, "Hey, let me out of here, what do you want to know . . . I'll tell you!" He knew anything he said would never affect the crew, wherever they might be. A horrible thought passed through his mind . . . what if they had also been captured. He didn't even want to acknowledge that bit of information as the trauma would certainly kill him in such a hell.

Coolie, being in the same situation, heard a muffled scream but he could not tell from what direction it came as the sound echoed off the steel walls. Weeping and shivering, he was desperate for his friends, hoping, praying the others would come to rescue them.

A door suddenly opened without warning and standing before him was a dark shadow. He strained to focus; his eyes squinted shut from the glaring light. The voice of an old woman he did not recognize said, "You will tell me where your friends have gone."

Coolie's eyes watered, a fear building, sending a panic that washed over him, stammering, his teeth chattering and shaking as he choked on his words, "I don't know where they are . . . they are from an unknown universe to ours . . . they come from our dark space . . . I don't know any more than that . . . I swear to you I don't know."

The woman stooped down so Coolie could see the face of his captor; her eyes seemed to glow red with anger. She held and tilted his frail chin with her dry withered hand towards her. The resemblance to Brenda was striking and she saw the look of recognition in his terrified eyes. He grimaced at the pain as she slammed his head hard against the back of the steel chair. "I am not your friend and you will tell me what you know of the crystal amulet that was stolen from me."

Coolie was relieved to know they had achieved their goal of obtaining the amulet, but his fear was growing that he knew more than he cared to know about its purpose. He cowered down, sinking in his seat, his head and shoulders slumped forward and painfully straining against his bonds. He bravely said, "My friends are gone and with them the amulet. You don't have the technology to go where they are headed so even if I told you where, even if I knew where, you would never be able to go where they are headed to because you don't have their ship. So be that what it may, whatever I know won't help you in the least."

There was something lurking behind Kore's eyes that told Coolie he had said something important, that he had said too much, something that had meaning to only her—and a dread fell over him that sent a panic coursing through his veins. Kore crossed her arms and smiled an evil smile. "Ah yes their ship, unique it is, but obsolete. Now you and your friend will tell me what I need to know; we can do this the easy way, or we can do this the hard way . . . the choice is up to you."

CHAPTER 51

With a blinding flash of golden yellow the ship arrived back to where their adventure had started so many years ago. Henry rubbed his oh-so-tired eyes. He leaned back in his captain's seat staring out into the blackness of space. Time, he knew was marching by for Dorathy, every second warped, time ticking away rapidly. His love for her would continue far into the next reality. Dorathy had given him his soul that he thought he had lost, and his heart was aching with the thought of her spending her life alone. He had to find his way back to her; somehow, he knew he would, but he needed to complete this mission and concentrate on what they must do. They had been thrown together so many years ago and together was the only way they were going to accomplish the unthinkable.

It was going to be another overwhelming game against the odds. He thought of who now would dare to stand in their way. Henry looked beside him to Magnus then to Brenda and finally his eyes turned to Jobar and his young brother Patsup. Patsup's eyes shone bright with the knowledge of the way things were aligned so long ago, as if a veil of deception had been lifted.

Jobar was wiser than his age; his eyes were weary from the lifetime of searching for the truth. His gaze rested on Brenda—her unwittingly connection to an old woman from her past— so many years into the future, and her unlikely connection to a man she had grown to hate. And Dimitri the man she had grown to love. She needed to rescue him, as he was the man who was brave enough to have rescued her so long ago. And Magnus—his intelligence ran deep; his willingness to show it was only apparent when it was needed. Everyone knew he was capable of great things, except for him. His loneliness consumed him and his life to him had such little meaning. But now his journey was clear; his mind had sifted out the clutter of straw and he had a purpose and he was up for the challenges they certainly had in store.

They sat in silence, struggling to make their next move. All the pieces were falling into place and Kore was surely waiting for them—somewhere she would be lurking in the dark shadows planning her attack. They would have to stay one move ahead of her if they were to succeed in their mission. The task at hand was overwhelming for Henry, his command they respected, his resolve was teetering on the brink of collapse, wondering how the five of them could rescue their friends—but try they must.

The silence was interrupted by a faint ping on the control panel. Henry turned his gaze as the ping was interrupting his thoughts and punched a few keys. "Hmm, that's unusual."

Magnus looked and a spark of recognition washed over his face, as he would never question himself again. He said, "The signal has the same configuration as that of Dora's cryotube."

Brenda moved forward to see the data that was coming through on the panel. "My God, you're right. Now what could that possibly mean?"

Henry had grown so accustomed to changes and surprises over the years, that dealing with this new bit of information was just another irritant. "Shit, well, let's go check out whatever it is."

The cargo hold of the ship was instantly re-pressurized. They now stood above it as Brenda moved over the familiar controls. "Well guys whoever is in here has been cryogenically frozen. It has the exact same components as Dora's cryotube."

Henry felt a pang of fear in the pit of his gut, *leave it alone, I don't like the looks of it. Whoever it is in there, they can wait.*

Brenda stood to face Henry hoping she could read what was going on in his mind. His face was a perfect blank; his emotions had been buried deep, too deep for even her. Brenda stopped him before he could turn to leave. "We can't Henry, you know we can't wait, we have to revive whoever is in there now. The liquid nitrogen has boiled off . . . ," her voice trailed off.

Henry turned to leave, not wanting to hear the reality. "We have a far greater task at hand and I say we get a move on it because our friends are relying on us and we are short on supplies and the means of getting them replenished."

Brenda gently insisted, using a voice of reason. "Whoever is in there was clearly sent to us. We need to do this."

Henry stopped and turned to face her and with a heavy sigh he reluctantly agreed. "Fine, help me open it up."

Brenda and Henry worked together to remove the heavy panel of the outer casing to get to the dewar inside the cryocapsule. Removing it completely, they opened it only to find it empty. Whoever was in there had been removed likely years before.

Henry straightened his stance and twisted his neck to relieve the tension building. "Well I'd say things just got a bit more complicated. We were gone for quite some time so who the hell knows what has transpired in our absence. This ship of ours has taken us back in time then forward to leave us here, but the question now is, as it seems it is always the same damn question, when?"

Magnus's brain was churning with the thought of time travel and with a heavy sigh he said, "Yes very true, in our absence time here has ticked away; we can only assume we have arrived sometime in the future. Magnus nodding towards the empty dewar. "Furthermore whoever was in there was important enough to be sent to us. That person may have had something further to add to our ever-growing predicament."

Brenda searched around in her mind, her thoughts coming to a likely conclusion. "Perhaps our adversary in our absence found an important clue leading to this moment—quite possibly finding this person and apprehending whoever was in there."

Magnus chimed in, "Bait . . . , Kore could quite possibly use this person as bait to lure us into a trap. We need to keep our wits about us and never let our guard down."

Henry blew out a heavy tired sigh, slumping his shoulders. "Okay, we keep this possible scenario in the back of our minds. We must get started with our mission of getting this ship restocked and the greater mission of rescuing Dimitri and Coolie. That much we know for sure."

Jobar chimed in as his attempt to agree with Henry. "Yes we need to restock this ship first if we are to attempt a rescue for our friends that have been captured and taken from us, and we need to find where."

Patsup looked at Jobar, giving him a knowing glance and announcing, "I have reason to believe they have been taken to the NWO prison moon of Starlock."

Jobar nodded his head. "I agree . . . unfortunately I agree with my brother for once. There is no doubt in my mind that they have been taken to the maximum-security prison facility. The good news is I know a pair of ruthless individuals who can get us in . . . for a price."

Henry ran his hand through his hair as he always did when faced with a difficult decision. "How do you know these guys?"

Jobar held his breath and blew it out slowly. "Coolie and I have had *business* dealings with them over the years."

Henry's eyes narrowed, along with Patsup's, whose mouth now hung open in anticipation of the knowledge he was about to gain to the mystery of how his brother had acquired his wealth over the years of being a simple deep space miner.

Jobar sat his weary bones on an empty cargo crate. "It's the poppies . . . we sold them poppies you had gathered for us over the years. The ones from the forbidden planet got the most credits . . . It was our early retirement fund."

Patsup drew in a sharp breath. "You are a drug dealer! I knew it!"

Jobar shook his head as he was too exhausted to control his brother's over-reaction. He merely managed to say, "Ah, put a sock in it already!" He continued despite the irritation of his brother, "These guys would buy our poppies and then sell them within the prison. Most of its occupants and caretakers are addicts."

Henry let the information wash over him like a wave of water, then threw his head back in a stressed laughter. "Okay, that's great . . . just great. So how reliable are these characters?"

Brenda said, with the voice of reason, "Jesus Christ Henry, you can't be serious!"

Magnus held her elbow. "It might be our only chance at getting them out."

Brenda shook her head. "Oh, for God's sake, you're suggesting we join forces with a couple of criminals?"

Henry weighed the odds. "Who better to get us in and out of a prison than a couple of criminals?"

Brenda eyes were incensed. "You're serious, you really are serious."

Magnus asked the obvious. "Okay Jobar, what is our first line of attack?"

Jobar looked up with a twisted smile. "More poppies . . . lots of poppies."

Magnus leaned against the hull. "Well, shite I was afraid you were going to say that."

Henry knew it was the only way. "Look everyone we have depleted our supplies and have stripped the ship—we need to get more than just the poppies at this point."

Brenda added, "With the government upheaval we have caused, chances are we shouldn't be getting the usual attention, but I suggest we still stay away from heavily populated systems."

Magnus added, "We still have a good amount of credits, but with the upheaval might come a certain amount of price gouging."

Jobar added, "I think we will have enough with what Coolie and I had saved over the years. He walked across the cargo bay to a huge securely tethered crate they had retrieved from his home and kicked it. There are enough credits in here to resupply, and get us some decent weapons . . . we are going to need them for more than picking poppies."

CHAPTER 52

The very moment Dorathy had touched the sarcophagus in the pyramid that was built so many lifetimes ago. The structure hidden for thousands of years buried under a mile of ice; exposed now to the cold desolate place it had become. It sat alone waiting for her, as everyone else had perished. Her frequency had traveled through dark matter, bending the fabric of space and time; it moved across the vast distances and across the ages. Her signal had set in motion the beginning of the master plan, the foundation of what had been laid down since the beginning of time. All of mankind's achievements, all that had been and ever would be, all of the sacrifices made, came down to one single act: a simple touch of the cold granite surface, by the only person who was left to join the others. They had waited for her to complete her mission.

At that very moment when Dorathy touched the stone coffer, deep within the catacombs of the Lost City, the lights flickered alive, the energy source powered up. The forgotten tomb filled with a cloud of cold vapor, hissing as it was emitted from the chambers holding the essence of life, life that had been planted across the universe so long ago. The glass and metal casings vibrated, shaking a cloud of dust collected over the millennia. Slowly, one by one, each of the twelve cryotubes opened with a hiss, exposing the chosen ones within.

The crystal amulet holds the key to the gates of heaven and the gate keepers have been waiting patiently for their Key Master to return. Together they will find the path to the portal and finally continue their journey to join The Otherlings . . .

The adventure continues!

EPILOGUE

Personal Journal:

I sit in my treehouse overlooking the clear warm waters of the South Pacific, the sun sinking below the horizon casting its reds and pinks, color washing the clouds. As long as I live, I will never grow tired of the fragrant air brought by the gentle trade winds. The sound of the calm water lapping against the shore, the breeze ruffling the palm fronds, has been my lullaby for many years.

I feel my mind fading as I desperately try to hold together the last remnants of my sanity; my life seems to drift on as the currents shift with the changing tides of my life. I hold onto the thoughts of how things could have been different if not for my predicament but know the path I am on is the path that had been chosen for me for a greater purpose. I have been stripped of my existence and my life, such as it is, has shredded me to the core.

I have been left alone on this world, this distant planet a mere speck, an insignificant piece of space dust floating in the empty cold darkness. I often wonder about the people that once inhabited this world as they departed for the unknown. I think about all that they left behind and the corruption that led to this deserted beach, this deserted paradise. They left on mankind's greatest adventure into an unknown future. To explore what might be. Only to recreate what had already been.

I think back to the time of the first explorers that set out charting a course to their great unknown, enduring great hardships aboard their trusted ships—the lands they discovered along the way, the people that befriended them or fought against them. The cultures they encountered, expanding their views or leaving them to question their own beliefs—at the end of the day, it was and always will be a redundant act.

I think back to my life, my journey, and I can't help but compare myself to those first explorers. What would Magellan, Drake, or Columbus have to say about my adventure to the unknown? Would they applaud our efforts or condemn us for the blasphemous idea of approaching the gates of heaven as a conceivable place: a physical place, rather than the place that only the worthy may pass through?

Throughout mankind's existence we have looked to the stars for the answers to the most basic of questions, what is our true origin? We have always hoped that we were somehow a part of something bigger than ourselves. Somehow knowing, would make us feel just a wee bit better about our lives, giving us a purpose so that we might achieve greatness in knowing the truth. Our need to know, and our ability to evolve, had been left in the core of our very existence and to ignore it I think is unforgivable.

So here I am having gone to depths so unfamiliar and so unknown, so far from my home and my life, to be left completely alone on this beautiful speck of space dust. I go up to my deck above the trees and lie under the starry night sky with my eyes fixed upon the tiny twinkle of the middle star of Orion's sword. I cry up to him as he taunts me, and I think that one day I will find my answers as I pass through the gate to the place, we all call paradise. Is paradise a place where there is no pain or suffering, or is it merely a different way of living? I think to the wars we had fought, the lives taken in vain all in the name of religion, I pray that one day we shall have the answers that have haunted man back to the time when some long-forgotten antecedent in the path of our evolution, tilted his or her head back and looked upon the stars wondering what lay behind the twinkling points of light, with his or her curiosity building from somewhere within their very being. Is it a place of myth or a place of reality, and is that reality something tangible or is it just a place for spirits to congregate? I would venture to say from my short time visiting, it is a place not so different from my little strip of sand.

My precious Zwicky is now sleeping comfortably in his bed. He has been my constant companion and is growing to be an old man now with the white of his whiskers only matched by the grey in my hair.

Every day I have sat here reflecting on my life, my accomplishments and my failures, my love and love lost. My life has been quite a journey filled with an adventure like no other. But I grow weary and I feel it is time to rest now; my equipment has been taxed by the salt air, my hibernation unit, such as it is, I believe to still be functioning properly as I have devoted so many of my resources to keep it protected from the elements. I can't help but think about how much more time will pass before they are able to come back for me—will it be tomorrow or the next day or will it be many more years from now? I will never know what the tide might bring in. I suppose if I were to die waiting, I would have ventured off to the place I seek . . . so either way I will pass through the gates to heaven or whatever one might want to call it.

I wonder sometimes what is beyond the gate, beyond the Otherlings. Is it someplace that we might come to explore someday? Who knows what great adventures still lie ahead? It's that old song that keeps turning in my mind

Somewhere over the rainbow way up high there's a place that I heard of once in a lullaby . . . Someday I wish upon a star and wake up where the clouds are far behind me . . .

Depths Unknown
Written by Trevor Bystrom

I suck the juices from the sweet little weeds
I tell the stories I don't even complete
I carry on . . . no time to delay
The Earth feels like its movin' and I begin to stumble
I try to speak but every word turns to mumble
I am gone my mind starts to fade
I have gone, to depths unknown
So far from home, to be all alone
I feel the wheels turnin' but I can't go no where
I reached the pulpit but there's no one even there
I carry on . . . no time to delay
I climb the trees till I reach the starry sky
Look in the jungle give out my darkest cry
I am gone, my mind has faded.

BOOK TWO

Coming soon

THE OTHERLINGS AND THE LOST CITY

ACKNOWLEDGMENTS

First and for most this book never would have happened without the great talent and inspiration of Deirdre Van Collie. She is responsible for taking my jumbled-up mess of dyslexic thoughts and with patience and care ironed out something extraordinary. The knowledge I gained from her will follow me through to the rest of my writing career. There are no words to thank her for the help she offered. I also thank my friend Bob Beck for giving me the much-needed push to start the writing process with his gift of the book by Stephen King "On Writing". I thank Dr. Nick Szegedi for his praise and support of my aspiration to better my knowledge of science and physics and guiding me down the right path of research. I thank Carol Mason for her constant support and for whipping me when I came close to giving up, offering little gifts to force me to continue along the way and Martha D'eramo for dreaming big for me. I thank W. Scott Renner Captain, US Navy, Retired for his description of cold war era Navy submarines. I thank my niece Laura for her help and support and a big thank you to my very special physicist friend in Houston. I thank George Newell for sharing with me his time spent at McMurrdo Station in Antarctica. I thank Austin Nichol for his incredible cover art and Trevor Bystrom for allowing me to use the lyrics of his song 'Depths Unknown' which offered much inspiration. A big thank you to Stuart Thaman and Sarah Ferguson for taking me under their wing and getting it done. I thank the subreddits of Reddit to Daniel Chivvis of Harvard and all the Scientist, Physicists (even the smartass ones, you know who you are), Geneticist, Egyptologists, CERN, Self- publishing and the list goes on. What an incredible resource.

Finally, a huge thank you to my husband, family, friends and clients. You all know who you are and how you helped me. There is not enough paper in the world to write about how much you all mean to me. Whether near or far you were always there for me and always believed in me. Thank you for lifting me up when I was down and telling me repeatedly, "you got this girl!" I would be NOWHERE without your love and continuous support.

And I thank my beloved little dog Wicky for keeping me company at my desk all those countless hours and for my cat Lucy for her continuous help on the keyboard of my laptop, without her help I would have finished sooner. Mama loves you both.

ABOUT THE AUTHOR

S.V. Hurn, that's me. Born on March 16th, 1964. I grew up on the central coast of California and always looked to the stars dreaming of far off adventures. Having the greatest desire to learn about the physical world that surrounds us, I grabbed as many science books as possible. A tall task back in the days before the internet. My dream was to be an Astrophysicist but my inability to grasp even the simplest math equations was my one true obstacle.

I remember watching Sar Trek with my mother. I announced I was in love with Spok and not the Captain, this mystified my mother. Of course, when I grew up, I was going to marry Carl Sagan. He unfortunately married someone else.

My love for science fiction and having the greatest desire for action and adventure I used my life experiences to write this fantastical story. My motto has been, "Never give up and never surrender."

I pray this collection of words allows for my retirement from my day job or at least aids me in my desire for travel.

I currently live on the gulf coast of Florida and dream of living in a treehouse on a deserted island somewhere in the South Pacific with my constant companions Wicky and Lucy.

I hope you enjoyed The Otherlings and the Crystal Amulet. Reviews are very important but please remember what your mother taught you, "If you have nothing nice to say then say nothing at all."

I am currently writing the second book, The Otherlings and the Lost City. There will be a third book and the title is will be The Otherlings and the Forbidden Planets. Visit www.theotherlings.com for updates!

www.ingramcontent.com/pod-product-compliance
Lightning Source LLC
Chambersburg PA
CBHW030543020726
47494CB00005B/1466